# WARLORD OF AYODHYA

## REBELLION

What sets Shatrujeet Nath apart from his cohort of neo-mythologists is how well he writes. His words are easy, his images are strong, and given the fact that his books are action packed, his language is practically lyrical. The situations are believable, the characters he creates feel authentic, each with a complex psychological profile, each true to themselves. And this time, the addition of magic to Nath's own armoury of skills electrifies a fast-paced narrative that is a thriller to the end.

—Arshia Sattar, author & translator of
the *Valmiki Ramayana*

# WARLORD OF AYODHYA

## REBELLION

SHATRUJEET NATH

JAICO PUBLISHING HOUSE

Ahmedabad Bangalore Bhopal Chennai
Delhi Hyderabad Kolkata Lucknow Mumbai

Published by Jaico Publishing House
A-2 Jash Chambers, 7-A Sir Phirozshah Mehta Road
Fort, Mumbai - 400 001
jaicopub@jaicobooks.com
www.jaicobooks.com



WARLORD OF AYODHYA:
REBELLION
ISBN 978-93-91019-79-2

First Jaico Impression: 2022



Page design and layout by Inosoft Systems, Delhi

Printed by
Nutech Photolithographers, New Delhi

KOSALA
madhupura
Sarayu
VIDEHA
ayodhya
Yamuna
KOSALA
CHEDI
chitrakuta
KASI
ANGA
tamralipti

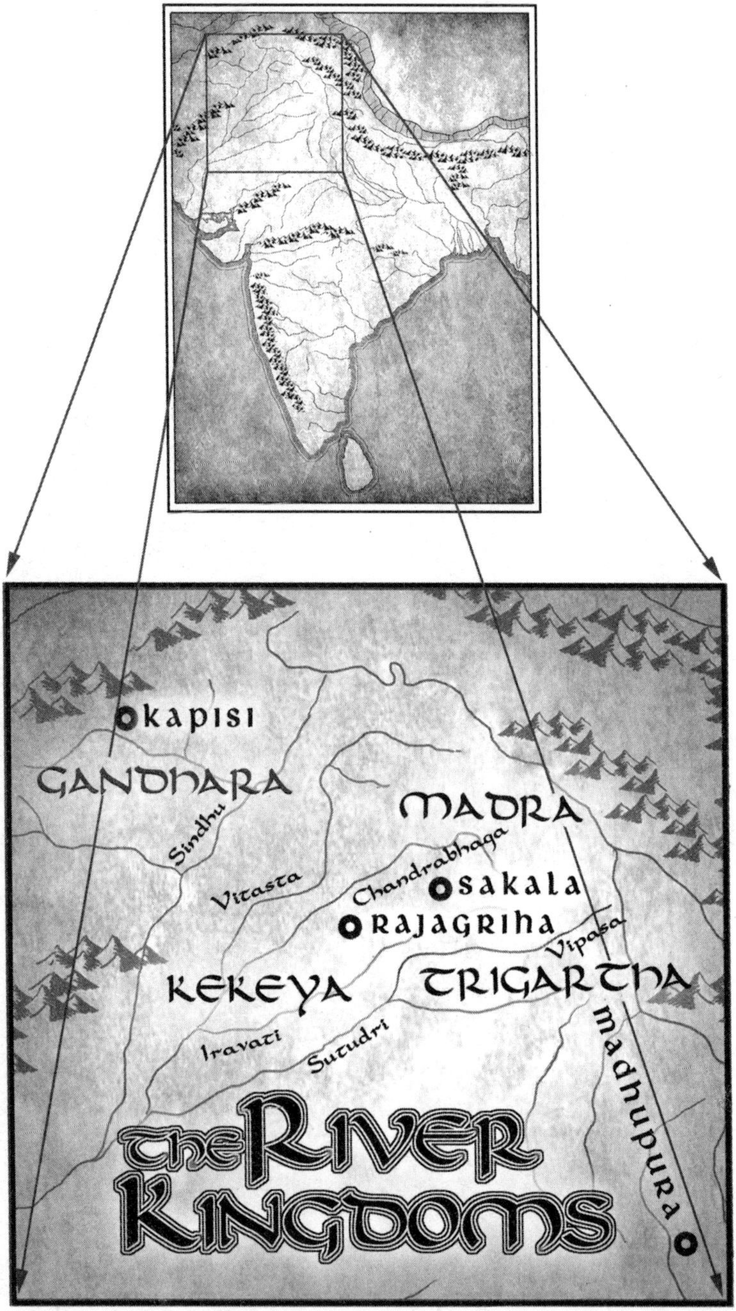
kapisi
GANDHARA
Sindhu
MADRA
Chandrabhaga
Vitasta
sakala
Rajagriha
Vipasa
KEKEYA
TRIGARTHA
madhupura
Iravati
Sutudri
The River Kingdoms

To

Ethan, Isabella, June & Mateus.

May you be blessed.

# Glossary

| | |
|---|---|
| adhipati | : lord, ruler |
| aghori | : a sadhu; a member of a sect of ascetics |
| ajameghya | : the acacia tree |
| amalakam | : Indian gooseberry |
| angavastram | : a stole or light shawl to cover the torso |
| ashoka | : a rain-forest tree |
| ashram | : hermitage |
| bheri | : a large drum |
| chausar | : an ancient Indian board game; precursor to Ludo |
| chhatra | : a caravanserai |
| dakshina | : an offering to charity |
| dandapala | : a palace investigator |
| dhoti | : traditional men's garment |
| draksha | : berry, grape |
| ghat | : steps leading down to a body of water, such as a holy river |
| ghee | : clarified butter |
| goni | : gunny, burlap |
| homa | : Vedic fire ritual |
| homagriha | : fire sanctum |
| kalash | : a pot |
| karapala | : a light sword |
| karshapana | : an ancient Indian coin |
| kashayam | : a brewed Ayurvedic medicine |
| khadga | : a heavy sword |

| | | |
|---|---|---|
| kshatri | : | chamberlain |
| kshurika | : | a small dagger |
| kumara | : | young man, prince; also a form of address |
| kunta | : | javelin |
| mahamuni | : | lit. great sage; also a form of address |
| mahanayaka | : | a commander |
| mahayoddha | : | lit. great warrior; champion |
| mama | : | uncle; also a form of address |
| manchika | : | a low seat or stool |
| munivar | : | a form of addressing a sage |
| nagarapala | : | a member of the city militia |
| nana | : | grandfather; also a form of address |
| nayaka | : | a captain |
| nishigandha | : | tuberose |
| paduka | : | an ancient Indian form of footwear |
| patthshala | : | school |
| peepal | : | the sacred fig tree |
| pippali | : | Indian long pepper |
| pranaam | : | salutation |
| raja | : | king |
| rajan | : | king; also a form of address |
| rani | : | queen; also a form of address |
| raya | : | another form of 'raja' or king |
| rishi | : | sage |
| roti | : | Indian bread |
| rudraksha | : | prayer bead |
| rupa | : | an ancient Indian coin |
| sala | : | the shorea robusta tree |
| sambrani | : | a balsamic resin used as incense |
| sandhija | : | rose mallow |
| sayyasana | : | a couch |
| shloka | : | a verse or hymn |
| shraaddha | : | a ceremony performed in honour of a dead person |
| shul | : | a heavy spear |
| stupa | : | the raised roof of a place of worship |

| | | |
|---|---|---|
| tambulam | : | paan; a betel leaf and areca nut preparation |
| upanayaka | : | a captain's deputy |
| uttariya | : | a scarf-like garment draped on the upper body |
| vaidya | : | physician |
| vajramushti | : | an ancient Indian knuckleduster |
| vajranaga | : | belladonna |
| vatika | : | garden |
| vrischika | : | scorpion |
| yajmaan | : | a respectful form of address |
| yuvaraja | : | prince; also a form of address |

# author's note

IT WAS A SUMMER AFTERNOON SIX YEARS AGO. MY FRIEND and I were discussing the Ramayana when a thought suddenly crossed my mind: What happened in Ayodhya during Rama's 14-year exile? What challenges did Bharat have to confront to keep the throne safe for his brother?

By the end of that day, I was convinced there was a story concealed behind those two questions.

It took me a week to outline Bharat's story, but since at that time I was still writing the second Vikramaditya Veergatha book, I put the idea on hold, telling myself I would return to it when time permitted. But on finishing the Vikramaditya series, I wanted to take a break from writing mytho-fiction, so I set out to write a psychological thriller instead. That story, however, needed me to step out and meet people as part of my research, which wasn't possible during the height of the pandemic. Thus, destiny guided me back to the tale of Bharat and the people of Ayodhya.

One of the biggest challenges while writing this series lay in making Bharat's narrative distinct from Vikramaditya's. Another was to curb the tendency to repeat things that had worked well in the Vikramaditya books. I was certain I didn't want you to shut this book with the lingering feeling that you'd read all of this before.

With this in mind, I have crafted a largely character-driven story for Bharat, whereas Vikramaditya Veergatha is almost entirely powered by plot. The other major departure is that this tale has no superheroes. Of course, you will find great warriors and epic battles in the pages ahead, but *no superheroes, no superpowers.*

Instead, what you will get here is *magic.*

I won't spoil it for you by going into details, but magic is at the heart of Ayodhya, at the heart of this story.

Magic lies at the heart of every story. That the story gets written is magic. That it gets published and read and loved is magic. I have seen this magic from close quarters, and I can vouch for it being real. And as always, there are the magicians who have helped this story get written and published.

My thanks to Arshia Sattar, who explained the concept of *rta* to me and helped me understand why rakshasas are on this perennial mission to obstruct *homa* rituals. The purist in Arshia will probably disapprove of the licence I have taken in marrying *rta* with magic, but it is my belief that the storyteller in her will appreciate what I'm striving to achieve here. Whichever it is, she has my gratitude.

Thanks also to filmmaker Ram Madhvani, in whose company, along with Arshia's, I spent countless afternoons and evenings discussing the Ramayana. Thank you for the love and the learning, Ram.

This book needed beta readers who could critique my first draft and come back with meaningful feedback. I found admirable support in my friends Ravi Balakrishnan and Debdatta Dasgupta, in my darling sister-in-law Ritu Madan, and in friend-cum-champion Sidharth Jain of The Story Ink. Your feedback made this story stronger, sharper.

Thanks, as always, to my publisher Akash Shah, who jumped at the story when I first gave him a two-line pitch six years ago. Your faith in me is astonishing. Thanks also to the team at Jaico, without whom none of my books would have been half as successful: Pheji Phalghunan, Radhika Raje, Nita Satikuwar and everyone else who works so hard on behalf of us authors.

Gratitude to Pragya Madan, whose involvement in my books starts on the day I eagerly tell her what my next story will be, plot holes and all. You listen to my ramblings with the patience of a Buddha and edit my manuscripts with the love and devotion of a gardener.

Thanks also to my agent Kanishka Gupta, and to my friends Paul Thomas and Shekhar Shimpi. Paul designed the stunning cover and titling, while Shekhar volunteered to make the two maps.

And finally, thanks to you, dear Reader, for placing your time, your money and your faith in my storytelling skills. Your trust is pure magic.

# *one*

THE FIRST OF THE TRADE BARGES NOSED OUT OF THE CLEFT in the hills as the sun rose on Manglapuri, bathing the quiet river market in the gilded radiance of a fresh spring morning. To the town's north, where the hills rose sharply on one another, the Vitasta was still in shadow, pale mist rising from its rippled surface, and the bargemen huddled in their shawls to ward off the chill as they eyed the settlement they were approaching.

Wooden docks abutting warehouses and merchants' chambers. A tumble of maybe fifty houses petering out halfway up a small rise. A dozen barges, tethered to bollards, bobbing by the pier. Three fishing boats in the river, the fishermen braced against the current and casting their nets. And at the centre of everything, set like a crownpiece and drawing the eye with its high, domed roof, the hall housing the town's trade guild.

Above the dome, flapping in the breeze blowing across the Vitasta, was the yellow standard of Gandhara, its blood-red flaming-torch ensign distinguishable from the convoy of barges.

It hadn't been a fortnight since that flag had been planted atop that dome by Gandhara's soldiers, after they had seized control of Manglapuri's guild, its market and its river barges.

As the four barges eased past the hills and slipped into the sunlight, the bargemen shrugged out of their shawls and took up long poles to guide the crafts to their berths, calling out instructions and warnings. Meanwhile, porters on the barges began preparations to offload the piles of *goni* sacks that were being ferried in.

"You're late," a voice rasped impatiently. "You were scheduled to dock last evening."

The lead bargeman turned to glance at the men standing on the pier. All three were clad in the dust-brown uniform of Gandhara, leather vests covering their torsos, doubling as armour. The one in the centre had his hands on his hips, and it looked as if he was in command and wanted an explanation. Knotting a rope around a mooring post, the bargeman nodded.

"We were caught in a thundershower," he said, stepping onto the pier and thumbing northward. "Had we not stopped for shelter, rainwater would've got to the sacks and dissolved the salt."

"Thundershower?" Squinting against the sun's glare, the commander looked towards the hills from where the Vitasta flowed. His tone was dubious. The sky was clean and blue all the way.

"Unseasonal," the bargeman shrugged. "Further up the valley." Though short in stature, he had muscular shoulders and arms. He sported a short, pointed beard that was prematurely grizzled, so he looked older than the thirty-odd summers he had soaked the sun's warmth. He considered the commander with bored, heavy-lidded eyes. "Can we unload now?"

The commander took in the six porters looking at him expectantly, sacks slumped at their feet. He waved his hand, urging speed. "Go on, hurry up," he said. "Make sure each sack is counted. No hanky-panky." He turned and left without waiting for an assurance from the bargeman, his men close at his heels. Despite the warning, he evidently didn't expect any hanky-panky from this lot.

The lead bargeman watched the soldiers depart before turning back to the porters. The other three bargemen joined him on the pier, and all four set off towards the town's centre as the porters began heaving the sacks of rock salt off the boats. The bargemen made their way to a tavern, where they ordered mugs of the local brew and huddled into a corner to wait. None of the regulars in the tavern—there were a few, even this early—appeared to recognize them or pay them any heed, which was just as well; for the sight of Yuddhajeet, yuvaraja of Kekeya, patronizing a pokey watering hole such as this one with his guards, that too in a backwater like Manglapuri—that too disguised as a common bargeman—was bound to raise eyebrows and set tongues wagging.

The doors shut with a resounding clatter, blotting the bright sunlight, and heavy bolts slammed and rattled into place.

As the footsteps of the porters, the warehouse overseer and the town's guild master receded in the echoing silence, he counted all the way to one hundred in the dark, then to another hundred for good measure. Once he was convinced he was alone and no one was coming back, he eased a *kshurika* out of his waistband and stabbed at the *goni* webbing that encased him. Sharp steel tore through coarse jute fabric, and in a matter of seconds, the sack opened like a cocoon and out he spilled, covered in sweat, jute hair and fine wood shavings.

Rolling free of the sack, he sat upright and blinked in the gloom, mopping his face with a forearm. The warehouse was dark and humid, the three narrow, slatted windows set close to the ceiling barely allowing light or ventilation. But it felt good to breathe in the open, without the sack to constrict him. Filling his lungs with air, he sheathed the *kshurika* and hobbled to his feet, easing muscles and joints that had locked stiff from being in the same position ever since the barges had drawn up to the docks and he'd heard an annoyed voice announce that they were behind schedule.

They were behind schedule because that was the plan.

There was no way they could have arrived here at sundown and achieved what they aspired to achieve in the fumbling dark, in a town they weren't familiar with. So, they had waited the night out and delayed their arrival to coincide with daybreak.

Wincing at a sudden rush of pins and needles, he inspected his surroundings, but it was hard to see properly in the feeble light. He muttered a mantra under his breath and snapped his fingers.

A sliver of flame—an *outline* of a flame—materialized over his index finger, translucent and half-formed, its light sinking on itself, as if intimidated by the dark. In an instant, it went out.

He grimaced and snapped his fingers again, with greater force. This time, the flame caught and wavered, its silvery glow illuminating his face for the first time. He was young, in his twenties, and dark-skinned, not many shades lighter than the black beard that covered his jowls. A lavish, curling moustache complemented the beard, and his striking black eyes held fire in them, though they seemed quick to humour as well. His brow was furrowed in concentration, two deep lines creating a cleft where the eyebrows met.

The flame sputtered and died.

Uttering a curse, he shook his head in disbelief. He had guessed that the magic in Manglapuri's atmosphere would be poor. This was, after all, a provincial town without a perpetual *homa* fire burning in it, and he doubted if the place had a rishi's ashram to monitor the air for magic. Still, he hadn't thought the magic here would be so tenuous, so scant…

Which was worrisome, for he was banking on magic—lots of it—for the work that lay ahead.

Be careful with magic, he could almost hear mahamuni Vashishtha's severe voice in his head, drilling the lesson into them when they had been children. When you draw on magic, you drain energy. The less the magic in the atmosphere, the more energy you lose drawing it. When there is little magic in the air, don't try tapping it. Instead, conserve your energy—

He dismissed the voice with a shake of his head. He needed illumination to see, so he shut his eyes and focused his senses hard on the words he whispered. With a flick of his wrist, he then tossed a pearly ball of light into the air. The ball flew up and hung over his head, turning slowly on its axis, rainbow streaks of opalescence skimming along its surface. Its light shone outwards, pushing back the shadows to reveal sacks stacked nearly halfway up the walls of the warehouse, the ones that the porters had just carted in—one with him inside—to his right. He ran a hand over a few sacks, checking randomly, and wasn't surprised to feel the hard, angular planes and edges of rock salt in each of them. Manglapuri was a minor river market on the Vitasta, but it was also the one closest to the salt mines that nestled in the ranges to the north, reached after a three-day journey by boat and mule trail. Manglapuri had made its modest fortunes in salt, and salt was what it stocked in its warehouses.

Salt didn't burn well though, which was a problem.

Thankfully, there were plenty of discarded sacks lying around the warehouse, and the building was made of wood. Old wood that would readily catch fire, he hoped.

He extinguished the light, the ball imploding like a bubble and vanishing. He had seen enough. And he *did* need to conserve his energy for later.

Once his eyes were accustomed to the dark, he began gathering the empty sacks and piling them against the shuttered door so he could set them on fire.

Fire to draw the enemy out into the open.

News of the taking of Manglapuri had reached the palace at Rajagriha ten days ago, disrupting the morning calm. A force of roughly fifty Gandharan soldiers had stormed the town and forced its way into the guild, divesting the guild master of the treasury keys. Manglapuri's civil militia had tried putting up a resistance, but the attackers had responded with professional ruthlessness. Three of the townsfolk had been killed and thrown into the Vitasta, and with that, all resistance had evaporated.

Raja Ashwapati had convened a council in Rajagriha, and once everyone had expressed shock and outrage, they got around to deciding what Kekeya's appropriate response ought to be. Though Manglapuri was loosely administered by Kekeya on behalf of the River Kingdoms, the town wasn't inside Kekeya's domain. Like a few other river markets that dotted the upper reaches of the Vitasta and the Chandrabhaga, Manglapuri paid taxes to the River Kingdoms in lieu of civic and administrative services. But for the most part, the town was independent, its guild master doubling as its *adhipati* or lord. In taking Manglapuri, Gandhara hadn't infringed upon Kekeya's territorial integrity, but it was a provocation, meant to test Kekeya's willingness to guard its interests. And as Yuddhajeet had argued, it wasn't just an instance of rogue riders from Gandhara extracting tributes from faraway markets in exchange of protection; this time, Gandharan troops had seized a guild and set up their base in town. They were flying Gandhara's banner over Manglapuri, claiming the market as theirs. This demanded punishment with war, was the consensus that the council arrived at.

An army of two hundred men was readying to march north and liberate Manglapuri when, the very next day, it came to light that during the town's capture, a couple of revenue officials from Rajagriha had been taken hostage. Kekeya's officers had been visiting Manglapuri to make fresh tax assessments on behalf of the River Kingdoms.

The presence of the two imprisoned officers forced a rethink. As long as they had hostages at their mercy, the Gandharans could keep Kekeya from attacking them—and if the need arose, even use the hostages to negotiate a safe getaway. Unwilling to give the attackers the luxury of bargaining for freedom and determined to keep the revenue officers from coming to any harm, Yuddhajeet had devised a plan to infiltrate Manglapuri by stealth and free the town and the revenue officers. And teach Gandhara to keep its filthy feet off Kekeya's backyard.

Throwing the last of the empty sacks onto the pile that reached a third of the way up the door, he stopped to study his handiwork. The door was the only means of exiting the warehouse, and once he'd set the sacks and the door on fire, he was entirely at the mercy of whatever magic he could muster to force his way out. If the magic proved inadequate—

—I'll have to bust those windows to get out, he thought, grinning and throwing wood shavings over the pile. Drawing a deep breath, he spoke a mantra with fervour as he snapped his fingers. This time, the flame flared with a shower of sparks before subsiding, burning white and steady an inch above his fingers. Still mouthing the mantra, he touched the flame to the wood shavings, setting the kindling on fire.

It was the rush of feet on the street outside, closely followed by the sound of distant shouting, that alerted Yuddhajeet and his men. But they waited until the others in the tavern had roused themselves and lurched into the open before they rose from their corner.

"Fire," one of the drunks relayed, wagging a finger at the spiral of smoke by the dockside.

"It's probably the guild."

"Or the warehouse," slurred a third. "Let's take a look."

The drunks took off, slipping into a stream of people heading for the guild, everyone chattering and calling to each other in excitement. The fire had broken the day's tedium, and the townsfolk were loath to miss the spectacle of the edifice burning to the ground, especially when it offered the added satisfaction of seeing the Gandharans lose the roof over their heads.

Yuddhajeet and his men hung back, the prince's eyes drifting casually to a squat building across the street, under a spreading *ajameghya*. Two soldiers darted out of the building, one hurriedly slipping on his leather vest as he elbowed into the crowds, and three more followed in their wake. Watching the Gandharans make a panicked beeline for the guild, Yuddhajeet ambled onto the road, his men four steps behind him. The race to get to the guild was understandable; that was where the bulk of Gandhara's troops had taken up accommodation. The building under the *ajameghya* tree, on the other hand, was a carpenter's workshop that now served as barracks for the rest of the invading force.

According to the information gleaned from traders, the workshop was also where the revenue officers were being held captive.

Praying that the information was accurate, Yuddhajeet sauntered towards the workshop, taking in the nine soldiers who stood by the door, staring at the rising column of smoke. Two of them left to investigate the fire, but the other seven huddled by the building's entrance to satisfy their curiosity from a distance.

Seven men blocking their path. There could be more inside, but the prince doubted it. Seven to four. And the seven were distracted, not anticipating an ambush in the midst of a fire. He could, of course, wait to see if some more of them departed and the odds evened a bit more, but at the back of his head, Yuddhajeet was conscious that his nephew was inside the burning warehouse, waiting for a signal from him. The more he delayed, the greater the risk to the boy—

The yuvaraja shot his guards a sidelong glance and gave a brief nod.

The warriors from Kekeya exploded on Gandhara's soldiers. Concealed *kshurikas* flashed in the open, arcing in the sunlight, every expertly directed stab and cut biting deep into enemy flesh. Yuddhajeet muttered a short mantra, his hand closing around a *shul* that formed out of nowhere, and the next moment, he was swiping at one exposed midriff, slicing it open, before twirling the weapon around to ram its head into the base of another soldier's throat. Gasps and grunts of surprise escaped from the Gandharans' lips, their dazed vision seeking out the men who fell upon them like spectres from a nightmare, slaughtering them before they had the chance to react.

In a matter of moments, it was over. Seven men writhing to their deaths in the dust of a land far away from home, their passing going unnoticed as a fire consumed a warehouse and everyone's attention.

Stopping just long enough to wipe the blood on his spear on one dead man's tunic, Yuddhajeet crossed into the building in search of more resistance. There was none, though. The workshop was empty. He swept through the rooms until he came to a door with a rusty padlock. He pointed his *shul* at the padlock and whispered a mantra. A dull shimmer coated the spearhead, but otherwise nothing happened.

There was practically no magic here, the prince realized, his thoughts going to the boy in the burning warehouse, struggling to channel magic against the advancing flames—

Yuddhajeet slammed a foot into the door with a snarl of impatience. The lock gave under the impact, wood shattering and splintering. Shouldering the ruined door aside, the prince barged in to find the officials from Kekeya cringing against the wall. The fear in their eyes turned to wonder and relief as both men recognized the intruder.

"Yuvaraja," the more senior of the two gasped in disbelief. "You came for us."

Yuddhajeet inclined his head. "Are you alright?"

Seeing the men nod and start to rise, he turned to his guards. "You two," he addressed two of them, "will escort these gentlemen to safety. Be quick, but be careful."

The yuvaraja turned and made his way out. Pointing to the bodies sprawled by the door, he spoke to the guard trailing him, "You and I can kill some more of these pigs." As the guard grinned at the prospect, Yuddhajeet extended one hand, palm facing the sky. Hoping he could summon some magic, the prince said a mantra.

Nothing.

Anxiety gripped Yuddhajeet hard. What if he failed to send the signal? Would the boy— *No.* He wouldn't let anything happen to the boy.

He drew his breath to repeat the mantra when the smooth, curved outline of a conch slowly took shape on his palm, weighing it down.

Gripping the conch, Yuddhajeet raised it to his lips and blew it with all his strength.

Straining his ears over the roar of the fire and the commotion outside, he listened for the signal, suddenly afraid that he'd already missed it.

"If the Gandharans sense that the fire is a distraction, they will be on their guard. Springing our officers from captivity will become almost impossible then," Yuddhajeet had said, going through the strategy for the third time. "So, you will have to stay inside the burning building until we pull off the rescue." His uncle's eyes had bored into his, as though trying to fathom his soul. "Are you absolutely certain you can do this?"

"Sure," he had replied with a relaxed shrug of the shoulders. "I'll handle it. Don't worry."

Now, watching the flames spread to smother the front of the building, he didn't feel so cocky about his capabilities. The fire was lapping at the warehouse's ceiling, the smoke made it hard to see the windows from below, and the heat was getting unbearable as the flames crept along the walls, seeking him out as he hunkered at the back. At this rate, he'd have to conjure up a cloak to shield himself, which would mean tapping into Manglapuri's measly reserves of magic. That would drain him, though, leaving him low on energy when it was time to break out of here, when he really needed both energy and magic—

*What if Yuddhajeet had already given the signal*, he wondered in rising panic. What if the time to break out had passed?

He was already feeling the fatigue, tatters and holes appearing at the edges of his consciousness. It must be because of the smoke, he told himself. Because of the shortage of breathable air. He also knew that wasn't true. He had been reckless, drawing on shreds of magic to fashion that unnecessary ball of light. He hadn't needed so much illumination, not when he knew there was so little magic to draw from anyway. He could have found his way in the dark, but no. So now, there was fatigue, and there were the black splotches that danced in his peripheral vision.

Voices erupted outside, shouting in alarm. The guild next door should have caught fire by now, he guessed, backing away from the encroaching heat and smoke. He had set fire to the door for a reason; as long as the door was burning, entering the warehouse was impossible. And if the warehouse couldn't be accessed, the fire couldn't be tended to, and it would spread...

Maybe it was a shift in the wind's direction. Or maybe the fire touched a particularly dry beam or rafter. Whichever it was, the blaze spurted in his direction, bearing a blast of heat that singed his nostrils and turned the hairs on his arms crisp.

He backed into the sacks of salt stacked against the rear of the warehouse, the rocks poking his back, making him recoil. There was no more space to retreat, he realized with a shudder. If the flames came any closer—and why wouldn't they?—he would have to cast a cloak to protect—

That was when he heard the shrill blast of the conch reverberate over the tumult of voices and the sound of the rampaging fire. Yuddhajeet's signal, informing him that the rescue had been accomplished.

Feeling the relief flow into his limbs like lifeblood, he rose to his feet, drawing his focus to the core of his body, centring his energies and summoning every available thread of magic to him so he could get out—

He stopped in mid-act, listening. He was sure he had heard something.

A tiny whimper.

He dropped to a crouch and looked around him, shielding his face against the heat. *There*, in a sheltered corner between two piles of salt, *a movement*. Crawling closer on all fours, he noticed two shadowy shapes wriggling about in the dark. Then, with another whimper, one of them sat up and surveyed him with sad eyes.

Even as his mind registered what they were, both shapes waddled over on stubby, shaky legs. Two pups, three weeks old on the outside, quivering with fright, but the tails still wagging in timid anticipation. One brown, the other black as the night.

The furnace heat coming from the left was intense, and he could feel his cheek and arm turning hot, his eyes smarting and beginning to water. Any moment now, he would smell his hair burning, he thought, as he threw a quick glance at the space around. There was no sign of the mother, who was likely out foraging. But why were the pups here, he thought frantically. Why hadn't someone moved them elsewhere… somewhere safe…

*You should be out of here*, his mind screamed at him.

Not without the pups, he screamed right back, eyes darting everywhere, looking for a way out. He wouldn't let the poor creatures perish in the fire—which *he* had started—if he could help it.

His eyes fell on the crumpled sack lying in one corner. The fire was all around now. Tears were streaming down his cheeks. Everything was hot, everything hurt. He grabbed the piece of *goni* as he slipped the *kshurika* from its sheath. With two swift slashes, he ripped the sack apart, laying it open on the floor. It was getting impossible to draw breath.

He scooped up the shivering animals and placed them in the centre of the stripped-down sack.

The pups whined but sat obediently, looking at him as though they knew they were in safe and capable hands.

Grabbing the sack by both ends so it formed a crude hammock, he hoicked it over his head and across one shoulder, slinging it behind him like a bag. He knotted the ends tight in front of him so that the pups nestled securely against his back.

The fire was two hands away, coming swiftly at him. He felt dizzy, and there was no air in his lungs. He sensed his skin turning red with heat and beginning to peel. He staggered to his feet.

Pulling all his faculties inwards into himself, blocking all sensory perceptions, he rattled off a mantra that left his lips like a small explosion, forcing the flames back, as though they'd been propelled by a sudden gust of wind. Still mouthing incantations, he broke into a run, cleaving a path through the fire, which gave way respectfully—or perhaps out of fear—to let him and the pups pass.

When he reached the warehouse's flaming door, he braked to a halt long enough to steady himself. With feet planted firmly on the floor, his hands open and away from the body on both sides, he put his head down to dredge up every last ounce of energy left inside him and convert it into the thing that was boiling in his ribcage… boiling and swelling and bursting outwards…

Part bark, part roar, a feral sound leapt from his mouth as power pulsed out of his body, electric blue and radiating outwards, blasting towards the burning door with great force.

With such tremendous force that the front of the warehouse blew apart, spewing masonry and splinters of charred and burning wood into the morning air and spilling smoke and fire at the ring of Gandharan soldiers who had been standing outside the building. Soldiers and onlookers scattered, ducking to avoid flaming projectiles, but a few were caught and thrown to the ground by the resulting shockwave.

Gandhara's fighters regained their feet to witness the dust and smoke part from the warehouse's gaping doorway, revealing a lean, dark figure standing in the shadows. Stepping over the burning threshold, the figure crossed into the sunlight. The Gandharans saw a soot-stained young man, a *goni* sack tied across his chest, glowering at them with bloodshot eyes.

The Gandharans knew trouble when they saw it.

"Get him," a commander shrieked wildly.

The voice seemed to come to him from a great distance, but its frenzied pitch—and the words—left little scope for ambiguity. Watching the Gandharan soldiers launch themselves in his direction, he raised both arms to shoulder level and pointed them forward, palms facing down. As he clenched his fists, grooves appeared on the armbands he wore, and short arrows slid out of concealment and locked into position, their heads glowing with magic. In a matter of seconds, the *vajramushtis* were primed and ready to shoot.

Without wasting a moment, he triggered the *vajramushtis*. Sizzling-hot arrows slammed into the men who were in front, lifting and hurling them backwards as they screamed at the sun and burst into flames. In quick succession, he fired arrows into the advancing line of soldiers, and one after the other, they all went down.

"Archers, fetch the archers," the Gandharan commander screamed. "Bring him down."

Feeling the pups squirm and snuggle into more comfortable positions against his back, he lined one arm up and fired at the commander. The blazing bolt struck the Gandharan in the neck with such violence that his head bobbled grotesquely, threatening to come unhinged from his torso. The scream building in the man's throat withered on the tip of the bolt, and he sank like a sack full of stones.

The darkness came down on him like a curtain when he turned to shoot the next soldier in line. He had discharged his energy reserves to break out of the warehouse and had channeled all available residual energy into the *vajramushtis*. He had run dry, and there was nothing left to draw from. So, the darkness came, and all he could do was drop his arms, shut his eyes… and wait for the Gandharan soldiers to close in and cut him to ribbons.

But that is not what happened. It was the Gandharans who were brought down, felled by a hail of arrows shot by the six porters who had come in the barges—six of the finest archers in the service of Kekeya.

He did not know this though, because he had nearly lost consciousness, falling in the mud by the yawning hole that had been the warehouse's front. He lay splayed on his stomach, cheek in the dust, hollow from the inside, and he imagined his uncle running up to him, kneeling by his side and cradling his head in his lap, calling his name…

"Bharat… *wake up*… Bharat. Are you alright? Quick, somebody call a *vaidya*. Bharat…"

The battle was over before the backup force from Kekeya arrived in Manglapuri an hour later, after it had got confirmation that the revenue officers had been extracted safely. The Kekeyans rode into a jubilant town, its citizens whipping and parading the captured Gandharans on the backs of mules and dancing around the burning guild—which, in a span of a fortnight, had bizarrely come to represent the detestable authority of Gandhara.

Once the Kekeyan army reestablished order in the riotous town and took stock of the situation, it transpired that seventeen Gandharan soldiers had died in the fighting and eight were wounded, two of them grievously. Sixteen men had laid down their weapons in surrender, while another seven remained unaccounted for, having slipped into the hills or fled west, taking the long road back home.

Kekeya had suffered one casualty. One of the archers, killed by a Gandharan arrow.

Then there was Bharat, who slid in and out of consciousness for the better part of the day before finally surfacing and stabilizing around sundown. This was, of course, extremely fortuitous for the captured Gandharans, as an anxious and vengeful Yuddhajeet had been planning to have the lot of them put to death at nightfall. With Bharat showing recovery, Yuddhajeet's anger abated, and he decided to spare the Gandharans' lives and take them to Rajagriha as prisoners instead.

But then Raja Ashwapati paid Manglapuri an unexpected visit the following afternoon, and he granted the Gandharans his pardon. "They have seen our rage," the old king said to his son when Yuddhajeet protested. "Now, it is time to show them a measure of our magnanimity." Of course, it wasn't magnanimity. Prisoners had to be fed and sheltered, they had to be watched night and day. Prisoners were a drain on resources, and in this case, they simply were not worth the effort.

It wasn't magnanimity. There was a quid pro quo, freedom granted in exchange of information.

"Gandhara is in turmoil," Ashwapati said as they observed the two dozen Gandharan soldiers leave Manglapuri under the vigilant eyes of Kekeya's troops. "Ukshma is on his deathbed, and his sons and nephews are jockeying for power." The raja ran his fingers through his long white beard thoughtfully. "Each one of them is doing everything he can to prove he is a worthy successor, but it's we who have to pay the price of those ambitions."

Day had just dawned, their shadows stretching down the hill from where they stood surveying the men trudge away in a straggling line, one borne on a stretcher. In four days, the weather had veered towards summer, the sun already hot in the sky, the coolness of spring just a memory. Bharat had regained most of his strength, though he still felt the weakness from his overexertion wash against him from time to time, a physical echo, gradually ebbing and receding. He studied his grandfather standing to his left, short and wizened, but packed with vigour that could put a younger man to shame.

"I don't understand, nana," he said.

"This attack on Manglapuri was someone's idea of gaining political mileage in Gandhara."

The boy puzzled over this for a moment before giving up.

The old man turned to Bharat, shrewd eyes above sharp cheekbones. "When you aspire for the throne, your challenge is to impress those whom you wish to rule, demonstrating that you are the perfect choice to lead them into a glorious future. One way of achieving this is by sharing your dream of growing your kingdom's size and influence—people adore kings who promise to expand territory, even if it is only the kings who benefit from this and hardly ever the people themselves."

"The attack was motivated by one of the contenders for Gandhara's throne," Bharat caught on.

"Nagnajit. One of Ukshma's many nephews." The raja pointed towards the departing soldiers with his chin. "Their master. An ambitious chap who understands the importance of being popular among his people. I was told he would fight every one of his brothers and cousins for the throne."

They watched the Gandharans in silence. Insects buzzed in the morning air.

"This is so absurd," Bharat said, frowning. "I could never dream of competing with *my* brothers for my people's support and affection."

"You wouldn't have a choice if you were competing for the throne," Yuddhajeet drawled.

"Then it's just perfect that I won't be competing with them for the throne either."

A fraction of a pause, and the boy added, "I don't want to be king."

Ashwapati and Yuddhajeet exchanged sharp glances before the prince looked away. The king turned to study Bharat, but the intensity of his gaze dissolved to kindness as his eyes rested on his grandson's artless face. He opened his mouth, then changed his mind about saying anything.

"Will they return?"

The question came from Manglapuri's guild master, a short, soft man who understood nothing of statecraft or warfare.

"They might," Yuddhajeet shrugged, and the guild master immediately looked worried.

"Which is why you will build a stockade around the town and have gates installed," Ashwapati said. "Also, watchtowers. And while I will leave a hundred of my men behind to guard the town for now, you must quickly hire men to defend Manglapuri. I will need my men back in Kekeya, and you need more than your civil militia here."

"I don't know where to find—"

"Hire two dozen Bahlika mercenaries," said Yuddhajeet, interrupting the guild master. "They are fierce fighters."

"They will cost us money. *All* of this will cost us money." The guild master shifted from foot to foot. "If… umm… if we didn't have to shell out such high taxes to the River Kingdoms, we could probably afford…"

A small bark, full of outrage and indignation, diverted Bharat's attention from the conversation. He turned to see a black ball of fur bounding through the tall grass on short legs, heading for a couple of crows that had alighted on the other edge of the clearing. The pup slowed as it neared the birds, keeping its eyes on the targets, a low growl in its throat. The crows were larger, not easily intimidated, and a minor face-off ensued. Then, one of the birds hopped closer in this test of wills, but the move backfired as the pup lunged forward, yipping in anger, unwilling to back down. Unnerved by this dogged display of resistance, the birds took to the air. The pup watched their flight with its head held high in pride. Then, forgetting all about the confrontation, it began rooting through the grass.

Bharat whistled, a smile on his lips. The pup dashed over, tail wagging wildly. It danced around Bharat's feet, overjoyed, licking his toes with its small pink tongue. The boy laughed and bent to gather the pup in his arms, and the little bundle of energy stretched its neck to reach his face, tongue going lap, lap, lap.

"Are you serious about taking it with you?"

Still grinning, Bharat looked at his uncle, who was staring at him and the dog with an amused smile. "Yes, of course." He scratched the pup behind its ear. "I have always wanted a dog. And this one chose me."

Which was true. Someone had cut the pups loose from the sack when Bharat had fainted to the ground, and the pups had disappeared. That should have been the end of it, but the next evening, the black pup was found sitting outside the door to the *vaidya's* house, where Bharat was under observation. Bharat had the pup brought in, fed, and sheltered for the night, and the following day, they had tried to unite the pup with its mother and sibling.

Except that no one could find the mother or the sibling. It was as if both had vanished, leaving the pup in Bharat's care.

"You can't take it with you to Ayodhya," Yuddhajeet said. "Remember, they don't let you keep dogs in the palace there."

"No worry, I won't keep him in the palace," Bharat grinned back cheekily. "I will leave him in Siripala's care. The palace has no rules against dogs being in stables, and no rules against my visiting the stables whenever I want." He rubbed his nose on the pup's head and spoke into its ear. "Of course, we are going to Ayodhya."

Yuddhajeet looked over to Ashwapati and the guild master, who were retracing their steps into town, still deep in conversation. "Come," he motioned to his nephew.

Halfway down the track, walking behind the older men, the yuvaraja asked, "Does it have a name, or are you simply calling it the dog?"

The boy gave this some thought. "He was found in a fire. He is black as charcoal." He chuckled at the image of the pup chasing the crows. "And there's fire in his heart. He is like an ember, so I will call him Angara."

"Angara," Yuddhajeet rolled the word in his mouth and nodded in appreciation. "Nice."

Bharat's face lit up with a smile. "What about you?" he asked the pup. "Do *you* like the name?"

The dog wagged its tail in response and nuzzled against the boy's chest, looking up at him with doting eyes.

On getting back to the guild master's house, they found a message from Rajagriha awaiting Ashwapati. Unfortunately, given the pathetic levels of magic in Manglapuri's atmosphere, the listening bells were able to receive only part of the message, while the rest was lost to the winds. Still, from the truncated message, they gathered that riders from Ayodhya had arrived in Rajagriha to take Bharat back with them to Ayodhya.

"It has to be about Mandavi," Bharat grinned, taking Ashwapati by the shoulders. "You are no longer just a nana, nana. You are a *great-grandfather*."

"The message didn't say that," the raja cautioned, though he couldn't help smiling at the prospect.

"Why else would they want me to come back? Shatrughna must have sent the news from Rajviraj." Bharat spun in circles, delirious with excitement. "I can't wait to hold my son in my arms. Let's go, let's go."

"Easy," Ashwapati admonished gently. "You haven't recovered fully—"

"Nana, *please*," Bharat pleaded. "Let's go. I must reach Ayodhya before Mandavi so that I can welcome her and my son into the palace. Come, come, come…"

"We will go if you promise to take—"

"I promise, I promise, I promise. *There*. Come, let's leave *now*."

"You don't even listen properly. You *never* listen," Ashwapati tutted in faux annoyance, letting Bharat lead him indoors by his hand. "First, you are rash and negligent with the magic, ignoring mahamuni Vashishtha's warnings. As a result, you fall unconscious, but you are careless about resting and recuperating. You are father to a child now, Bharat. You must be more responsible. Your father won't forgive me if something were to happen to you here—"

"But nothing has happened to me, nana," the boy interjected. "Relax. Father will be perfectly pleased with you when I tell him what a fantastic nana you've been. Now let us please hurry, can we?"

Despite Bharat doing his best to speed things up, it wasn't until a little past noon that they were ready to leave Manglapuri. The Kekeyan force had to be divided into those who went and those who stayed back; Ashwapati had to wrangle the guild master into setting money aside to fortify the town against any future attacks; the horses had to be fed and watered for the long ride back; and everything took time.

Bharat sat on his horse a furlong outside Manglapuri, frowning at the men milling around, waiting for their king to issue orders to march. "Come on," he scowled. "What's taking nana so long?"

"Let us start riding," Yuddhajeet offered, judging his nephew's impatience. "They'll catch up."

They rode together in silence, leaving the bustle of the market behind them so that soon all they could hear was the river flowing softly over smooth stones and the muted thud of their horses' hooves on mud. The day was hot, but the path ran under a canopy of trees, and the air was fresh and scented so that, in total, a calm settled over Bharat. He began whistling tunelessly and the prince joined in, giving shape and direction to the tune. Angara, who was riding in a cloth bag tied to Bharat's saddle, lifted his head and listened to the men before tucking his head back in and going to sleep. Yuddhajeet and Bharat exchanged smiles and moved to the next tune.

Half an hour later, scaling a hill, they reined in their mounts and turned back to see the Kekeyan force on its way, its tail free of Manglapuri's limits. The purple banner of Kekeya, emblazoned with the twin prancing horses in gold, fluttered at the head of the column, where Ashwapati was presumably riding.

"Finally," Bharat exhaled in relief.

"Yes," Yuddhajeet nodded. "But really, what is the hurry?" He smiled to rob the words of sharp edges. "A day's delay wouldn't make a difference, would it?"

"I want to be in Ayodhya to greet my wife and my son when they arrive."

"Okay." The yuvaraja thought about this for a moment. "And what happens if you are not there? Does it mean you love them less?"

"No."

"So?"

"So, nothing," Bharat threw his hands up. "It's just *being there*, something you do for those you love."

When Yuddhajeet didn't respond, Bharat rounded on his uncle.

"You really should get married," he said. "Then you'd understand."

"I don't see myself getting married," Yuddhajeet waved the idea off with one hand.

"Why not? I am sure there are plenty of women who would be happy to have you as a husband."

"Maybe, but I'm yet to meet a woman with whom I have wanted to spend more than one night," the yuvaraja countered. "The thought of spending my whole life with one of them is too dreadful to consider."

"What do you have against women?" Bharat blinked in bewilderment.

"Nothing. I just think they're too much trouble."

With a resigned shake of his head, the boy looked away. "Wait till you meet someone you fall in love with. You'll discover that the trouble is totally worth it."

"Hah," Yuddhajeet snorted, grinning to himself. He turned his horse to face south, and the men resumed their journey.

Hardly had a minute lapsed before the yuvaraja suddenly looked at his nephew. "What makes you certain it is a boy?" he asked.

"What?"

"You keep saying your son..."

"Oh," Bharat nodded. "I just know."

"What if it's not?"

The boy smiled. "I will still make sure she turns into one hell of a rider."

The sun had long since set and the star-studded night had seized control of the sky by the time the lights of Rajagriha came into view. Dinner was being served in most households when Ashwapati, Yuddhajeet and Bharat crossed the threshold of the palace and were ushered into a hall where the emissary from Ayodhya was awaiting them.

"Vijaya," Bharat recognized the tall, thin man who rose from his seat on hearing them enter.

"Yajmaan," the man bowed and offered a *pranaam* in greetings.

"Our greetings and our apologies," Ashwapati said. "We weren't here to welcome you because we were taken to Manglapuri on urgent business. We had no intention of keeping you waiting." He paused, then added, "I hope you have been fed and well looked after."

"We have been given no opportunity to complain, rajan," the courtier replied.

"I understand that my grandson has been summoned to Ayodhya," the raja of Kekeya looked expectantly at the emissary.

"What news do you bring?" Bharat asked, unable to keep a check on his excitement.

"You... didn't you get the message that was sent?" Vijaya stared at them in confusion.

"It didn't get delivered fully," said Ashwapati. "All we understood was that you were here for Bharat…" He stopped, then took a hesitant step forward. "Why… what's the matter?"

"*What's happened?*"

The words came out of Bharat's lips in a fearful whisper as he studied the emissary's face. The man's eyes were sad and tired, but his expression was shuttered, as if he was holding something in, afraid of showing it. Bharat noticed how everything about Vijaya drooped. His lips, his trim moustache, his turbaned head, his shoulders… "Is everything alright, Vijaya?"

The man's eyes locked with the boy's and he shook his head softly.

"Why don't you say something?" Bharat's voice rang with anxiety and exasperation.

"Raja Dashratha is dead."

"Father," Bharat let the word out with a sigh, the sound loud in the quietness of the hall.

"And yuvaraja Rama has been exiled from Ayodhya under the king's orders."

Ashwapati, Yuddhajeet and Bharat drew their breaths in sharply, recoiling in disbelief.

"Rama? Exiled? *By Dashratha*?" Ashwapati scrutinized the emissary's face, shaking his head as if willing the other to admit he'd made a mistake and alter his statement.

"For fourteen years, rajan," the courtier confirmed miserably.

"Impossible," the old raja's gaze was blank with incredulity. "Dashratha loved Rama dearly."

"Why did father do it, Vijaya…" Bharat pleaded with the courtier. "*Why?*"

Vijaya's eyes flitted from the raja of Kekeya to his son before settling on the boy.

"Raja Dashratha was acting on Rani Kaikeyi's wishes."

The stillness that followed was deep, as though all of Rajagriha was holding its breath.

Bharat's world began to spin out of control as his knees went weak. "*Mother asked for Rama's exile?*" he whispered in shock. "Why?"

Clearing his throat and sidestepping Bharat's question, the courtier spoke in a rehearsed voice. "Mahamuni Vashishtha has instructed me to escort you to Ayodhya, yuvaraja Bharat. You are to be crowned the new king of Kosala."

# *two*

THE SIGHT OF BHARAT STANDING UP TO HIS WAIST IN THE Sarayu, the fine drizzle creating dimples in the water around him as he offered his prayers while the priests chanted hymns on the river's bank, filled Shatrughna with a deep sense of unreality.

This can't be happening, one part of his mind seemed to be saying.

Why not, the rational part argued back. Father is dead, remember?

Father had been dead for a whole year, in fact, to the day.

He remembered receiving the news in Rajviraj right after lunch, as he had been sitting on the swing, Shrutakirti by his side, and Mandavi, heavy with child, reclining on a couch, surrounded by cushions. They were laughing at some joke he had cracked when the message from Ayodhya had arrived, the shock of the news sending Mandavi into labour…

He glanced over his shoulder in the direction of Shrutakirti and Mandavi, standing halfway up the steps of the bathing *ghat*. Mandavi had a baby in the crook of her arm, who was examining its mother's face, a clump of Mandavi's hair clutched in its small fist.

Father was dead, the message had said. Rama had been exiled from the palace. And Lakshmana and Sita had opted to accompany Rama in his exile.

It had all felt unreal that afternoon in Raja Kushadhwaja's country estate, as Shrutakirti and the maids had helped Mandavi indoors, the swing swinging on its momentum, the breeze from the mountains suddenly chill, giving him goosebumps. And it felt unreal now, watching Bharat wade out of the river in a slowly intensifying rain, mahamuni Vashishtha relaying instructions from the water's edge…

He caught Bharat's eye and Bharat nodded, beckoning him close.

"Why is she here?" Bharat muttered when Shatrughna drew up to his brother's side. "Who invited her?" Bharat spoke in a low undertone that was barely audible, but the anger and urgency were plain.

Following Bharat's gaze, Shatrughna caught sight of the woman standing on the topmost step, removed from the rest of the crowd. Draped in the white cotton vestments of a widow, the edge of her sari drawn over her head against the drizzle, she was of regal bearing nevertheless, the face statuesque and self-assured behind the curtain of black hair that fell to one shoulder.

"I have no idea," Shatrughna shrugged.

"She shouldn't be here," Bharat hissed. Before turning away to attend to the rituals, he added, "Ask her to leave."

His heart sinking, Shatrughna nodded and began climbing the steps. He didn't like the woman, but he liked the task that he'd been entrusted with even less. No one spoke to the woman nowadays and he didn't want to draw attention to himself by speaking to her, but she was already looking in his direction... *at him* now... her gaze steady, not wavering, as if challenging him...

"Erm... I..." he hesitated. "The king has asked me to escort you from here."

Instead of replying, the woman just stared at him, as if expecting a detailed explanation.

"You must leave—" Shatrughna began again, speaking more forcefully, but a voice interrupted him from behind.

"Stop."

He turned to find a woman standing two steps down, a hand on her hip. Short and plain-looking, she nonetheless exuded authority as she looked at Shatrughna. "She has every right to be here," she said, nodding at the other woman.

"Mother..." Shatrughna hedged. He could sense eyes turning this way, curious and inquisitive. "I... was doing as brother instructed—"

"It's alright, Sumitra," the woman at the top of the steps spoke into the folds of her sari. "I shall leave if the—"

"No. You should stay, Kaikeyi," the older woman cut in. "As one of Dashratha's three widows, you have as much right to be here as Kausalya or I." She paused, her expression cold as she gauged the other woman. Her next words jabbed like knives. "You should stay as this is all *your* doing... the outcome of *your* heart's desire, dear Kaikeyi. Watch and weep if you can summon the tears."

Sumitra exchanged a long, hard glance with Shatrughna before turning and heading back down the steps. Shooting Kaikeyi a look, Shatrughna walked away, feeling annoyed and foolish about the whole episode. This was what happened when you were the youngest in the family. Everyone expected you to do as you had been told, everyone ordered you around, everyone thought it was alright to disregard what *you* had to say… Scowling to himself, he crossed his arms and stood by the entrance to the *ghat*, watching Bharat roll sweetened rice into small balls to be fed to the crows. At least when Lakshmana had been around, the grownups had one more kid to push around, but as he was the only one left now… Not that Lakshmana let anyone lord over him, Shatrughna remembered with a smile; Lakshmana's temper is that of a *vrischika* and his sting twice as bad, mahamuni Vashishtha always used to say.

Shatrughna's eyes went to Kosala's head mage and royal tutor, lean and towering by Bharat's side, presiding over the ritual on the *ghat's* steps, his long white hair knotted into a high bun at the top of his head so he appeared even taller than he was. Two steps above and behind the mahamuni and Bharat was a row of Kosala's ministers and administrators, and Shatrughna paused to inspect the three who were the most eminent in court. Sudhanva, *adhipati* of Sankasya, and Sheshagupta, the revenue minister, were near the centre, rubbing shoulders; Sheelabhadra, the *adhipati* of Kusinagara province, stood to one side, maintaining his distance from the other two. The two *adhipatis* were sour-faced and kept their eyes averted from each other, their backs stiff and hunched in the rain. Once good friends, Sheelabhadra and Sudhanva were now rumoured to have fallen out in a tussle for the position of *kshatri* or chamberlain to Bharat. If talk was to be believed, it was only their fear and respect for the mahamuni that made the two noblemen keep the court's decorum. Shatrughna had broached the topic with Bharat, eager to know if there was substance to any of this, but

Bharat had brushed him away, urging him not to fall prey to palace gossip.

"You forget that both *adhipatis* were father's friends and advisors for years. Such people don't become rivals overnight." With a pause, Bharat had added, "There will be those who are always looking to sow conflict and create factions in court for their own gain. Stay clear of such people, brother."

Remembering Bharat's brusque tone, Shatrughna shrugged mentally and let his gaze drift along the *ghat's* steps, down to the riverbank, where people had massed in the thousands to attend the *shraaddha*. It wasn't just Ayodhya's citizenry; mourning subjects from all over Kosala had converged to pay homage to their departed king. Such was this kingdom's love for Dashratha.

Shatrughna's vision swept to the spot where he had left Kaikeyi standing; he noticed the place was vacant and Kaikeyi was nowhere to be seen. He craned his neck to look, wondering if she had left…

"How are you, young man?"

The voice came from somewhere near Shatrughna's shoulder, and he turned to see a short man with a grizzled beard and drooping eyes standing beside him, observing Dashratha's *shraaddha* ceremony.

"Mama," Shatrughna grinned. Yuddhajeet was Bharat's uncle, not Shatrughna's, but from their childhood, they had both addressed him as mama. "This is a surprise. When did you arrive?"

"Just now." The older man lifted his gaze to meet Shatrughna's eye. "So, how's everyone?"

"Everyone's fine." Shatrughna was gripped with a sudden apprehension that Yuddhajeet might have witnessed the exchange he and his mother had had with Kaikeyi. He had no sympathy for Kaikcyi, not after what she had done, but he had always been a little in awe of Yuddhajeet, and Yuddhajeet and Kaikeyi were siblings. It embarrassed him to think that Yuddhajeet might have seen him being disrespectful towards his sister. It was Bharat's fault, *he* wanted her out of here, his mind jabbered in defence. I was only following instructions—

"Nice moustache," Yuddhajeet remarked. "Pretty impressive."

Shatrughna blinked. "Oh," he replied, one hand going to the growth on his upper lip. He hadn't realized it had been so long since he and Yuddhajeet had met. "I've had it for nearly two years."

"Suits you."

It did. Everybody said so. It made his face look less boyish, and it went well with the mop of hair on his head, and his brawny arms and torso that had been sculpted in the various wrestling pits of Ayodhya and Rajagriha.

The younger man smiled and meant to say thanks, but something else had caught Yuddhajeet's attention. Eyes shining, he took a step forward. "That must be Bharat's son," he said, pointing to Mandavi.

He ambled over to where Mandavi and Shrutakirti stood, and Shatrughna followed. Seeing the prince approach, the sisters exchanged quick glances before giving him small awkward smiles. People were already noticing the visitor from Kekeya, and Shatrughna saw heads turn and word spread in an expanding ripple. Unfazed by the stir he had created, Yuddhajeet bent over the baby, who stared back solemnly for a full moment before offering a big grin that caused a dimple to appear on its chubby cheek.

"Ah, the fellow recognizes his big mama," Yuddhajeet said, taking the boy into his arms. Then, making his eyes big and round, he cooed into the smiling face. "Taksha will play with mama?" The baby chortled in delight. Yuddhajeet looked at Mandavi. "I want to think this fellow looks like my nephew, but the only way he could have got his beauty is from you."

This time, the pleasure in Mandavi's smile was genuine, and as Yuddhajeet handed Taksha back to her, Shatrughna couldn't help marvel at the ease with which the prince had delivered a double compliment. Just then, the sound of clapping came from near the water's edge, and they all turned to see Bharat bring his hands together to summon the crows. Almost at once, two of the birds swooped down from a nearby tree and hopped across the lower steps, making their way to the banana leaves held down by the balls of sweet rice.

The rain came down heavily, forcing everyone not directly involved in the *shraaddha* rituals to seek shelter where they could. The morning wound its way into the afternoon, and as Bharat was busy serving the priests food and *dakshina*, Yuddhajeet spent the time paying his respects to Kausalya and Sumitra. The meetings were formal and the conversation was stilted, everyone carefully avoiding any mention of Dashratha's death or Rama's exile, even though reminders of what had happened—and who was responsible for it—stood around them like spectres in mourning. Yuddhajeet expressed no desire to meet his sister and instead waited for Bharat to complete his obligations as the son of the deceased king. The day was near its end when Yuddhajeet was finally ushered into his nephew's presence. But even now, Bharat wasn't alone; accompanying him were Vashishtha, the courtier Sudhanva, and Sudhanva's son and successor, Yadudeva.

"Mahamuni, accept my greetings," Yuddhajeet joined his palms and offered a *pranaam* to the mage. He turned and bowed to the *adhipati* and his son. "My greetings to both of you as well."

"It is kind of you to have come all the way," Vashishtha appraised Yuddhajeet, his stentorian voice a rumble in the depths of his throat. The stern, angular face remained in shadow. "How is Raja Ashwapati?"

"He is well and sends Ayodhya his salutations," the yuvaraja replied, glancing around to include the nobleman and his son in the conversation.

Tall and well-built, even at his advanced age, Sudhanva had the natural physique of a warrior, with piercing eyes, a straight nose and a chiseled white beard that ended in a sharp point below his chin. Yadudeva, in contrast, was fleshy and bug-eyed and sported a moustache that drooped untidily around his lips. A fat mole called attention to itself on his right cheek. Let alone being father and son, it was impossible to guess that the two were even related by blood.

"It is a long time since we saw him," Sudhanva flashed a perfect set of teeth in a shallow smile.

"He would have come had age permitted it."

"Of course." Another smile, another flash of teeth.

Yadudeva said nothing.

"Do give him our regards," said the mahamuni. As Yuddhajeet inclined his head, Vashishtha looked at the *adhipati*. "We should grant the king and his uncle the privacy to converse."

More *pranaams* were exchanged before the mage and the lords made their way out, Yadudeva bobbing his head and observing the visitor from Kekeya keenly as he trailed the others. Bharat waited for the room to empty before striding over to sweep Yuddhajeet into a joyous embrace.

"Mama, you came," he grinned against his uncle's shoulder. Releasing his hold, Bharat stepped back. "It's wonderful to see you."

"Likewise."

"Let us talk outside," Bharat pointed to the terrace. "It's a lovely sunset, and I could do with some fresh air."

"Your grandfather sends his blessings," Yuddhajeet said, planting his elbows on the parapet of the terrace that overlooked the Sarayu. To the west, the rain clouds had parted, allowing the sun to wash the landscape in an orange light. There was a hush over the palace, the day's activities having left everyone exhausted.

"How is he?" Bharat enquired.

"Hardy as ever."

The young man was silent for a bit. "All well otherwise?" Seeing his uncle nod, he asked. "No fresh nuisance from Gandhara?"

"None so far," Yuddhajeet replied. "Nagnajit is still consolidating his position after claiming the throne. We hear he hasn't had much opportunity to think beyond taming his opponents."

"Was his rise to power brutal?"

"You bet," the prince chuckled. "Most of the other claimants to the throne are either dead or have gone missing."

"Missing, as in they've fled Gandhara?"

"That," Yuddhajeet shrugged, "or they've been taken as hostages for future negotiations, when loyalties will be bought in exchange for lives."

Bharat considered what he had just heard. "Do you anticipate trouble for Kekeya?" he asked.

Yuddhajeet took a moment to answer. "It's hard to say. But I suspect Gandhara will eventually make a bid to grab new territory."

"How have the councils of Madra and Trigartha reacted to all of this?"

"They are worried. They don't want war." Yuddhajeet made a face. "Of course, in the event of an attack, they expect us to fight to the last man to protect them."

"So typical of them," Bharat snorted. "Unwilling to fight, but happy to outsource the dirty work to Kekeya."

"Don't be so harsh on them," the prince said mildly. "Madra and Trigartha have nothing besides their civilian militias, men untrained for serious warfare. It's too much to expect the militia to come out and fight like a professional army." After a pause, he added, "And don't forget that the original agreement between Trigartha, Madra and us states that defending the River Kingdoms is Kekeya's responsibility."

"Sure, but back then, the task was simple. Keeping the trade routes secure from roving bandits, not fighting off a potential Gandharan invasion. Madra and Trigartha are just taking advantage of nana's commitment to that agreement."

"Maybe," Yuddhajeet said, "but we've given our word, and we'll stick to it at any cost."

"I can spare Shatrughna and a few hundred men." Bharat glanced at his uncle. "He'll be happy to go with you and take a stand against Gandhara."

Yuddhajeet thought about the offer but declined it with a shake of his head. "I think we can deal with Nagnajit."

The men watched the boats on the Sarayu for a while. "How's it here?" the yuvaraja asked finally.

It was Bharat's turn to shrug. "Nobody here wants me as their king. No one thinks I am capable of ruling Kosala." He squinted at the horizon broodingly. "They just want Rama back."

"Really?" Yuddhajeet scrutinized his nephew with a raised eyebrow. When Bharat didn't reply, he continued, "Has anyone ever said that to you… that they don't want you as their king?"

"They don't have to. I can see it in their faces."

"See what?"

"The disdain, the dislike, the distrust." Bharat turned to face his uncle. "Everyone here believes the plot to make me king was hatched in Kekeya, and that mother did what she'd been told by nana. Many are convinced that even I had a hand in all of this." The setting sun highlighted the deep frown on Bharat's brow. "And she doesn't make it any easier by showing up everywhere uninvited."

"I showed up here uninvited," Yuddhajeet said quietly.

"That is not what I meant, mama."

"Still, my showing up like this *is* inconvenient." After a thoughtful pause, the prince appraised his nephew. "I know Rama asked you not to send her away, but I can take your mother back to Rajagriha if that's your wish…"

"No," Bharat shook his head. "This is her home. And anyway, she won't go. Had she wanted to return, she would've left by now, considering how little anyone here cares for her. No, she *wants* to stay here. She is *adamant* about staying here. Guess why?" Bharat's lips twitched with irony. "Because she doesn't think she did anything wrong by asking that I be made king instead of Rama. She believes what she did was right."

"Well, I was there when your father made a promise to your grandfather, assuring him that the son born to him and Kaikeyi would succeed him as king of Kosala," said Yuddhajeet. "I might have been only thirteen then, but I remember."

"That's all fine, but I didn't *want* to be king and never once dreamed of the throne," Bharat growled irritably. "How about that?"

"Well, you *are* a king now, whether you like it or not," the yuvaraja retorted. "Rama has refused to return till the term of his exile gets over, and you've given your brother your word to rule this land and its people in his place." Yuddhajeet's manner softened, and he placed a hand on his nephew's shoulder. "I know it is hard, but this is what destiny has in store for you. Stop fighting it and accept it as best as you can."

Bharat sighed in agreement, but his shoulders remained slumped in defeat.

"It will be easier if you gain the trust and support of the people of Ayodhya," Yuddhajeet said. With an ironic smile of his own, he added, "Remember, we were discussing Nagnajit's rise that other morning in Manglapuri, and you said you'd never compete with your brothers for your people's affection?"

Seeing Bharat nod at the memory, the prince said, "Looks like you don't have a choice."

Bharat stared into the distance, lost in thought.

Yuddhajeet swivelled to face his nephew squarely. "Sometimes, the only way to win respect is to come out on top, ahead of everyone else," he said. "The pack follows the wolf that leads them to food and protects them from danger. Remember, there is no sentimentality in nature, only an instinct to survive."

The passageway was long and poorly lit, the door at the far end barely visible in the gloom, but as Yuddhajeet risked a step forward, a small incandescent balloon of light appeared to his right, illuminating his path. The moment he'd walked past the light, it blinked out of existence, but a second one immediately formed just ahead, shedding its light. Then a third, then a fourth…

The prince whistled in admiration at the precision of magic on display here. Magic was meant to work like *this*. Not intermittently, like it did in Kekeya.

He still remembered his first visit to Ayodhya and being wowed by the magic in this place. He had been fifteen, and they'd all come from Kekeya to celebrate the birth of Bharat. The palace domes were lit in multicolour, and magic lights twinkled like fireflies and spiralled up the spires that reached to the heavens. The river itself seemed to shimmer with iridescence, and when he lobbed bubbles of water into the air, they burst into firecrackers, dazzling the eye with hypnotic patterns.

There was also magic in the mundane. Doors could be commanded to open; curtains could be drawn with a wave of the hand. There were the listening bells, of course, the first of their kind he'd ever seen. Made in pairs and constructed out of bamboo, copper and silver, the bells were mated by magic to transmit messages between each other, so two people with mated bells could communicate over a distance of a dozen miles. Then there were the bionic horses and oxen that worked the fields, beasts engineered and modified by magic to work harder and longer at tilling the land and reaping the crop. And lastly, there were the weapons that Dashratha had brought out to display to Ashwapati; weapons that materialized in the hand at an incantation and shot and cut and slaughtered better than standard weapons, for they were charged with a magic that gleamed silver-blue in the sinews of the reinforced metal.

It was all the product of mahamuni Vashishtha's powers, his father had told him. "The mahamuni is revered in Ayodhya because he and his rishis make every little bit of this magic happen. The mahamuni virtually protects Ayodhya with magic, ensuring the safety of its king and its people. Except possibly rishi Vishwamitra, there is no mage as talented and skillful as Vashishtha in all of Jambudvipa."

The memory of being awed by Vashishtha—impossibly tall, gaunt and stern-faced—was fresh in Yuddhajeet's mind; the mahamuni had handed him one of the reinforced *shuls*, encouraging him to test it. The prince recalled driving the weapon into the dummy in the training arena and feeling the blade skewer through layers of wood, plunging right through the dummy and exiting on the other side in a spray of splinters. A spear had never felt so good in his hands before.

That was the sort of magic they'd had in Ayodhya, and they'd had it *twenty years* ago. Whereas in Kekeya, they had refined their magic to make weapons do the same kinds of things—though still not nearly as well—only six years ago. Listening bells had been introduced only last year.

It wasn't that Kekeya was primitive; it was just that Ayodhya was outrageously, hard-to-catch-up-ably advanced in its magic.

Yuddhajeet remembered Dashratha taking him and Ashwapati to the Sanctum of the Fire across the Sarayu, where the sacred *homa* fire burned night and day, tended by scores of learned rishis. Guided by mahamuni Vashishtha, the rishis maintained the fire to sustain *rta*, the cosmic order, which, in turn, enriched the ether, making it conducive to magic. The rishis then infused magic into the ether with the use of arcane mantras. Strong *homa* fires and powerful rishis were critical to magic everywhere, and Ayodhya had been blessed with both.

Nowhere in Jambudvipa was magic as potent and effective, and Ayodhya had made clever use of its good fortune, wielding economic power to expand its influence across the breadth of the continent. Magic was widely acknowledged to have a hand in Kosala's rich yield of sugarcane and indigo, cane and leaves producing the sweetest sugar and the deepest dyes in Jambudvipa. Sugar and indigo dye were Kosala's primary exports, finding their way west through Gandhara and Kamboja, and east through the ancient port of Tamralipti. Year on year, the crops fetched a bounteous income, filling the kingdom's treasury and fuelling its economic growth, which in turn drew the most talented rishis, traders and skilled craftsmen to Ayodhya…

The door swung gently on its hinges as he drew near, and Yuddhajeet was about to ascribe this to magic as well when he sighted Kaikeyi's face in the light of the last balloon, looking out at him.

Pulling the door all the way back, she said, "I wasn't sure you'd come by."

"You knew I was here?" the yuvaraja asked, stepping over the threshold and taking his elder sister into a gentle embrace.

"News has a way of coming to this corner of the palace, even if nothing else does," she replied. Her tone was matter of fact and not engineered to draw his sympathy, Yuddhajeet noted.

Kaikeyi withdrew, and following her, the prince found himself in a small herbarium. Kaikeyi picked up a small trowel and began tending to a *pippali* plant. Yuddhajeet took the opportunity to study his sister, whom he was seeing after more than two years. Given all that had transpired in Ayodhya—and her life—between then and now, she hadn't changed much. There were more lines around her eyes and her mouth, but otherwise, she retained the regal air that came naturally to her.

Separated in age by no more than a few years, they had been close as children, especially after their mother had gone away before Yuddhajeet had even learned to read. The prince remembered Kaikeyi being protective towards him, making sure he was fed and cared for while their father and uncles were away keeping land and livestock safe from roving bandits. Kaikeyi had taught him to ride a horse and bake a roti, and in that herbarium, the memory of her thrashing the boys who had dared to bully him came out of nowhere… Kaikeyi in pursuit of the boys, brandishing a stalk of sugarcane snatched from a nearby field, screaming curses at them, the boys bolting in terror…

"What's so funny?" Kaikeyi asked, looking up.

"Just something I remembered." Yuddhajeet wiped the smile off his face and tucked the memory away. "Here," he said, holding out an earthenware jar. "Sweetened *amalakam*. He made me bring it."

"Father thinks I still love this thing," Kaikeyi took the jar with a fond shake of her head and a smile. "How is he?"

"Getting old. Otherwise, he's fine."

"And you?"

"Same as father."

They stepped onto a terrace that led to Kaikeyi's chamber. "Friendly kid, Taksha," Yuddhajeet remarked, making conversation.

"He is, isn't he?" Kaikeyi turned to him with a bright smile. "Has he started talking yet?"

Yuddhajeet glanced at his sister, startled. On catching his expression, her smile faded, replaced by a look of pained longing. "He doesn't allow the baby anywhere near me," she said. This time, there was hurt in her voice. With a bitter smile, she added, "He says I was responsible for taking two sons from their mothers, so I must stay bereft of my grandson's love." She wheeled around to face her brother. "But how is that fair? I can understand *him* not speaking to me as punishment for the suffering that Kausalya and Sumitra are dealing with. But barring me from seeing the baby is absurd. It's not as if Kausalya and Sumitra have grandchildren they cannot see and meet. So, why me?"

Kaikeyi turned away. Yuddhajeet contemplated the room. The wounds we inflict on those we love, he thought. "He thinks the people suspect him of having had a hand in Rama's exile," he said aloud. "In my opinion, he hates you most for making him a villain in the eyes of the people. That is why he dislikes the idea of being king so much. By accepting the office of the king, he fears he will confirm whatever doubts persist about his role in sending Rama away."

"Correct me if I'm wrong, but resisting the idea that he's king isn't helping him either," Kaikeyi said archly. "If he thinks the people will begin liking him because he's a nice guy who doesn't want to be king, he is being foolish. If he accepts what has happened, it will become easier for everyone. For him, *and* for the people. But no." With a sigh of resignation, she sank down on a nearby couch. "I gave him fourteen years to erase Dashratha and Rama's legacy from public memory, but my son has already squandered one whole year by living in denial. And to think that I did all this—bearing the brunt of everyone's hatred, living as an outcast in my own palace—for *his* sake."

Yuddhajeet sat down beside Kaikeyi and put his arm around her. He didn't know what to say, but the silence had to be filled with some reassurance, some words of hope. "There are thirteen years left for Rama to return," he said. "Thirteen years of obstacles and challenges. I am certain something is bound to compel your son to embrace his destiny as king of Ayodhya."

"You've really taken what I said about showing up uninvited to heart."

"No, Bharat, I have not," Yuddhajeet protested, sounding aghast.

Crossing his arms, Bharat appraised his uncle with dubious eyes. "Then why the rush to leave right now, at such an unearthly hour? You could wait until dawn at the very least."

Shatrughna's gaze switched between the men as he tried to read the nuances that he was missing. Mandavi stood a little apart, cradling Taksha in her arms and watching the men unhappily. She looked as if she had an opinion on the matter, but she was keeping it to herself.

"I haven't taken your words to heart, Bharat," Yuddhajeet insisted in a gentle but fervent tone. "Believe me. But I *get* your predicament. I get how hard this is for you, without the public being constantly reminded of how things have come to be the way they are. So, the fewer the people who see me in Ayodhya, the better it is for you. That's why I want to leave now, in the dark, before daybreak, before the people who'll be returning to their villages take to the road." After a pause, he added, "Already there are plenty who would have noticed me at the *ghat* this morning—"

"It doesn't matter," Bharat cut in with unexpected harshness. "You are my mama, and you can come here whenever it suits your fancy, and no one can do—"

"I am not just your mama. I am Kaikeyi's brother. There's a difference."

Shatrughna's face cleared as he finally got it. He thought about saying something, then changed his mind. He, Bharat, Yuddhajeet and Mandavi stared at each other in the silence of the terrace, an awkward tableau with the breeze stirring the thin curtains while a nocturnal bird trilled from the direction of the river.

"Those who talk will talk anyway," Bharat said sullenly, but his body language showed he had conceded defeat.

Yuddhajeet walked over and put a hand on his nephew's shoulder. "Always keep that in mind," he said with a small smile. "The elephant is never distracted by the barking of the dogs. So, whether you are discharging the duties of a king, a brother, a son or a husband, never let loose talk bother you or impair your perspective of right and wrong."

Looking into his uncle's kind eyes, Bharat nodded slowly.

Taksha took that moment to gurgle at something in delight, and Yuddhajeet turned towards the mother and child. Going to Mandavi's side and smiling down at Taksha, he pried off a heavy bronze bracelet from his wrist and offered it to the baby. Taksha grabbed the bracelet, looking up at Yuddhajeet with big, curious eyes.

"What is this, mama?" Mandavi objected. "You've already got him so many gifts—"

"Those were from his great-grandfather," Yuddhajeet waved her to silence. "This is *my* gift to the little fellow. This bracelet has kept me from harm for over twenty years. Now, it will protect him." He stroked the baby's head lovingly. "May the gods be with him always."

"Thank you for your blessings, mama." Mandavi assessed Yuddhajeet with large eyes that were accentuated by the sweep of kohl and the natural arch of her eyebrows. "Can you not stay with us for a few more days…"

"I must go," Yuddhajeet said quietly, putting an end to the matter. He glanced at Bharat again, who accepted the decision with a nod.

The king walked to where three brass bells hung at the end of a rope suspended from the ceiling. "Come to the garden terrace," Bharat said to the bells.

"I will escort you out of the city," Shatrughna volunteered, happy to have a chance to contribute.

"That won't be necessary," Yuddhajeet began. "I have fifteen men with me—"

"Mama," Shatrughna snapped impatiently, looking at the older man in mock annoyance. "That wasn't a suggestion. I *am* coming to see you off. It's settled."

"Look at the hour," Yuddhajeet protested. Then, seeing Shatrughna's mind was made up, he threw up his hands. "I submit to the wishes of Kosala's yuvaraja," he bowed, eyes twinkling impishly.

"Let me inform Shrutakirti," Shatrughna chirped, pushing himself off the parapet against which he was leaning. "I shall meet you by the main gate." He bounded out, bright and excited. Bharat observed his departure with an indulgent shake of his head.

"Give our love to nana," he said, embracing his uncle.

"Rajan," a polite voice spoke from the direction of the door. "You called for me?"

A tall man with a long face and gentle eyes stood before Bharat with his hands clasped. This was Chaitanya, the palace marshal, his trim beard flecked with an abundance of grey hairs that shone silvery in the glow of the silver globule illuminating the terrace.

"Prince Yuddhajeet wishes to depart. Assemble an escort for him and his contingent," Bharat instructed. "Yuvaraja Shatrughna will accompany the prince some of the way, but our guards are to stay with the prince and not turn back for Ayodhya until the new day breaks."

Chaitanya bowed and stepped to one side. Yuddhajeet exchanged one final glance with Bharat and Mandavi before leaving their presence. The marshal followed, silent on his feet.

Mandavi went to stand near the parapet, from where she could look down at a garden that sloped towards the river. To the right was the pathway that led to the front of the palace, and as Bharat joined her, Mandavi observed Yuddhajeet emerge onto the pathway, Chaitanya following him at a slight distance. Watching the figures melt into the darkness, she sighed.

"I wish mama had stayed longer," she said.

"Mmm-hmm," Bharat agreed, and his voice turned spiteful. "See what she has done, how much harm she has caused," he snarled. "People have to leave like fugitives in the middle of the night because of her. The shame and misery she has brought on all of us is incalculable."

"Shhh," Mandavi said, patting his arm. "You'll frighten the boy," she whispered.

Bharat glanced at Taksha. The baby was in his own world, turning and twisting Yuddhajeet's bracelet in his hands. Bharat's expression cleared and he leaned over the boy, smiling. Seeing his father's face hovering above his, Taksha let go of the bracelet and lunged at Bharat with a wide grin. Taking the infant from Mandavi, Bharat lifted him up, rubbing his nose on the baby's little belly and tickling it so Taksha chortled and whooped with joy.

"Careful, he's just been fed," Mandavi warned with a laugh.

Lowering the baby, Bharat hugged him against his chest, holding him secure. Taksha cooed and put a thumb in his mouth, and Bharat pulled Mandavi to him. Leaning against one another, feeling the breeze from the Sarayu ruffle their hair and lift the perfume of *nishigandha* from the garden below, the little family stood on the terrace, the cares and concerns of life temporarily forgotten.

But later, lying awake in bed while Mandavi and the baby slept by his side, Bharat felt his mind turn to Kaikeyi once again. Helpless, as if he were a magnet to her north pole, he recalled her standing in her chambers the night he had returned from Rajagriha in answer to the mahamuni's summons. He had confronted her, angry and in shock, and she had been quick to retort, telling him things he didn't want to hear.

"What must I apologize for?" she had demanded. "Must I apologize for observing the dharma of a mother who wants the best for her son? In which case, I want every mother to apologize for putting her child ahead of everything else, for wanting the best for her child. Will you get that apology for me?"

Bharat had his mouth open to answer her, but Kaikeyi ploughed right on. "Or do you want me to apologize on behalf of a man who forgot a promise he had made? A promise made more than twenty years ago to your grandfather, Raja Ashwapati—the promise to make his son born of *me* his successor to the throne of Kosala. Yes, Bharat, *that* was the promise your father gave your grandfather for my hand. And *that* contract, *that* deal was what your father was prepared to breach when he named Rama his successor. Should I apologize for the late king's willingness to go back on his word?"

Bharat had blinked at his mother, stunned by the ferocity of her words. "Should I apologize for your father's inability—or should I say unwillingness—to love all four of his sons equally, to not favour one over the other three? You speak of me being selfish in putting *my* son first. But I have only one son, whereas your father had *four*. Still, he put *one* ahead, every time. And you want me to apologize because I desired to correct that imbalance in your favour, Bharat?"

"Enough," he had shouted back. "Rama was the ideal son *even for you*. I know that, so stop shifting the blame onto father for the wrong you have done." He halted to quell the quaver of emotion that made it difficult for him to speak. Drawing a long breath, he had sneered at Kaikeyi, "You know what? You sent Rama into exile in the hope that *your* son would become king." He shook his head. "But your son won't have that. He will never be king. He will bring Rama back to be crowned Kosala's king."

Bharat had had the satisfaction of seeing Kaikeyi stare at him in stupefaction, shaking her head in horror. "You won't do that, Bharat," she had said, taking a step in his direction. "You *cannot* do that, not after all that I have done for you," she had literally screamed as he turned his back on her.

He had walked out on his mother that night and had barely spoken to her since. Later, he heard that she had been pleased when Rama had refused to return to Ayodhya with Bharat, insisting on honouring the terms of his exile. Then, she was furious when Bharat made it plain that he would not sit on the throne, that he would instead wait fourteen years for Rama to claim his rightful place. She had raved and ranted when he had refused to let her see baby Taksha, and she was having her revenge by appearing in public and embarrassing him by refusing to relent.

Tired of tossing and turning, unable to summon sleep, Bharat quietly got up from the bed.

*Your father had* four *sons. Still, he put* one *ahead, every time.*

Holding his *padukas* in one hand, Bharat crossed the room on bare feet so the sound of wooden sandals on the granite floor wouldn't disturb Mandavi and the child's sleep. Though it wasn't particularly late, the palace was in deep silence, the guards on patrol lulled into a drowsiness that fled when they encountered their king in the galleries. A crescent moon hung in the sky, shedding a yellow light that threw shadows everywhere.

*Your father had* four *sons. Still, he put* one *ahead, every time.*

He had been seven or eight. Someone, perhaps one of the courtiers or maybe one of the queens, had suggested an archery contest for the kids. The winter sun was out, bright and welcome, so everyone turned up to watch as the four brothers and the sons of some of the courtiers had lined up in a field to shoot arrows at a target. It had been fun until one by one, kids had got eliminated, and they were down to just three—himself, Rama and the son of a courtier.

The third boy was the first to have a go, hitting the clay bird swinging from a branch twice, but missing on the other three attempts. Rama had been next, drawing his bow with easy confidence to strike and shatter all five birds in succession.

His turn had come last, Bharat recalled, as he slipped out of the palace and took the path leading away to a cluster of low buildings set far to the back, almost concealed by a copse of trees.

He had stood with his feet planted firm on the ground, perfectly balanced, and shot four arrows at four birds, smashing each bird to smithereens. Nocking the fifth arrow into place, he had turned to look in the direction of his mother, seated with Dashratha and the other queens in a pavilion. Kaikeyi had looked at him once, then looked away. His eyes had gone to his father, who was leaning forward, hands on his thighs, watching him and the target intently.

The memory of turning back to focus on the red-painted bird was vivid.

He had drawn the bowstring back and loosed off the shot.

Maybe there was a sudden breeze that made the arrow veer in its flight. Maybe the bird pivoted on its axis, turning and reducing in size as the arrow drew close. Maybe the shot was carelessly aimed.

The point was that he had missed the target and failed to draw level with Rama.

As a cheer broke out among the spectators, he had looked towards the pavilion in search of his mother's face. She wasn't looking at him; she was smiling at Kausalya, commending her son's performance.

And next to the queens, Dashratha had risen from his seat, beaming with joy and pride.

But had there been a subtler, more fleeting emotion under that expression of joyous pride? Had he glimpsed a flash of *relief* on his father's face that afternoon, under the shade of the pavilion?

He had watched his father run out and scoop Rama up and seat him on his shoulders, grinning in delight. He had watched people mob Dashratha and Rama before someone—he didn't remember who—had lifted him onto their shoulders, and people had come to congratulate him for nearly causing an upset, and he was smiling…

*Your father had* four *sons. Still, he put* one *ahead, every time.*

His thoughts were interrupted by furious barking from the direction of the buildings. Instead of slowing down in caution, Bharat smiled and pressed forward, whistling softly under his breath.

The barking ceased, but the next instant, the silence was broken by a frantic thrumming of feet on dirt, and a black shape close to the ground hurtled out of the dark and threw itself at Bharat, twisting madly with excitement, bounding uncontrollably around his legs, tail whipping the air in a frenzy.

"Angara," Bharat grinned and dropped to his haunches, hands spread wide. "How are you, mad fellow?"

The dog sprang into his embrace, hopping on its hind legs, paws on his shoulders. It lunged at his face, licking it with such enthusiasm that Bharat was forced to pull away and stand to escape its affection.

"Okay, okay," he laughed softly, patting the animal's head to calm it down. "I missed you too."

A light appeared at the door of one of the outhouses, framing a tall figure in its glow.

"Who is there?" the figure called in a deep, gravelly voice that called to mind vast resources of wisdom. The pointed *shul* silhouetted in the man's hand spoke of a readiness for combat.

"It's alright," Bharat waved a hand. "It's just me, Siripala."

Ten dark shapes floating half-submerged in the Sarayu, still as crocodiles, the water sliding off their scaly backs.

Ten pairs of eyes just above water level, pupils dilated to see better in the dark.

The ten let the gentle current carry them along, and only occasionally did they switch their lazy reptilian tails to correct their course, their heavy snouts pointed towards the north bank of the river.

Pointed directly at the stretch of wall shielding the Sanctum of the Fire.

Earlier in the day, disguised as village folk, they had entered Ayodhya by joining the concourse of people arriving for the king's *shraaddha* and had escaped the notice of the city's *nagarapalas* by losing themselves in the crowds. Once night had settled over Ayodhya, they had headed for the river and lain in wait for the sign.

All ten pairs of eyes were still trained on that sign, a powerful heat spell cast with black magic that only their specially trained rakshasa eyes could detect. A blue-black glow that the humans were incapable of viewing, but which guided them, the rakshasas, to the spot from where they could get into the Sanctum of the Fire.

It had all been planned months in advance. The dead king's *shraaddha*, which would grant them access into Ayodhya. Their agent in the city, who would get them inside the Sanctum. A night of fatigued slumber in the wake of the *shraaddha* ceremony, which presented the perfect opportunity to carry out the mission.

Threshing their heavy legs, the ten closed in on the north bank. The crescent moon had slipped to the west, but there was starlight, so they kept low to the ground while easing out of the water, careful not to make a splash and draw attention. They needn't have bothered with the secrecy; no lookouts were posted on the bank or along the length of the wall. The Sanctum was wreathed in protective magic and attempts to scale the wall or force the doors would spring booby-traps within the building complex and trigger alarms, alerting not just the guards inside, but also the *nagarapalas* in the city across the Sarayu.

Not that the rakshasas had intentions of forcing their way in.

Once they were on land, the rakshasas slipped into the shadow of the wall that reared up against the starlit sky, the diffused light from torches within showing at the top. The Sanctum complex comprised the dwellings of the rishis, a cowshed, a granary and a storehouse or two, in addition to the *homagriha*—the inner sanctorum and Ayodhya's nerve centre—where the sacred fire burned. Their agent had procured a map of the Sanctum, and all ten of them had spent weeks familiarizing themselves with its layout. Each one knew what would be found where. Or rather, *who* would be found where.

The rakshasas crept along the base of the wall on powerful reptilian legs, making for the blue-black halo that lit the dark ahead of a bend in the wall. As they hurried along, their appearance underwent a change, their facial muscles and bone structure shifting to resemble human heads, skin replacing the scales that covered their arms and legs, their tails disappearing entirely. The metamorphosis was swift and fluid, and by the time the beacon they had followed appeared in sight, suspended at eye level and burning in the night air, the rakshasas were indistinguishable from the *nagarapalas* who patrolled Ayodhya's streets and neighbourhoods to keep it secure.

The ten drew up to the beacon; seen from up close, it resembled the ghostly imprint of a human palm.

And beyond it, illuminated by the cold wash of its light, was a wooden door, scarred and bitten by time and neglect.

Stepping up to the beacon, the leader put his palm against the imprint, fingers touching fingers, heel touching heel. Straightaway, the blue-black imprint oozed into the rakshasa's palm where it was absorbed, traces of its glow fading on the rakshasa's fingers before vanishing. Without uttering a word, the leader went to the door, wrapped his palm around the copper doorknob and turned it.

Levers eased aside with soft clicks, and the door swung open an inch.

Not one alarm split the still night air.

The palm imprint that their agent had left for them had done the trick. The magic that guarded the Sanctum had recognized the imprint as belonging to someone who could be trusted inside. It had let them in instead of identifying them as intruders. Magic was stupid that way. Bankable, but stupid.

The leader let his breath out and looked at his companions in relief. He then threw his weight against the door.

It resisted for a second before grinding on its hinges and giving way with a low groan of protest. It hadn't been opened in years, shut and forgotten ever since the new landing had been built on the building's east side for boats ferrying firewood and supplies to the Sanctum. Sentries were never posted by this unused door, which was why the agent had picked it to grant the rakshasas their surreptitious entry.

One after another, the rakshasas ducked into the darkness that the door opened into, the last of them unsheathing a scythed *khadga* that glinted once in the starlight. The next instant, rakshasa and *khadga* had disappeared into the doorway.

The rakshasas stole up a pitted, moss-covered ramp, its narrow confines lit by a faraway torch. The ramp ended at a rusted and disused gate with a massive bolt in place. Expecting resistance, the leader yanked the bolt hard, but to his surprise, it slid smoothly aside and the gates parted.

Tightening his grip on his *khadga*, the rakshasa set foot in the Sanctum's grounds, lit here and there by white torches. The grounds appeared empty, and a steep silence prevailed everywhere. After ascertaining that they hadn't been observed, the trespassers exchanged glances, and without a word, five of them turned and loped away to the right. The leader led the rest of the rakshasas into the shadows of the storehouse to the left, from where they scurried, haphazard, one cover to the next, until they came to a strip of space open on all sides.

Faced with no choice, the rakshasas stepped into the open. But they had barely walked ten steps when a voice hailed them from behind.

"What are you fellows doing outside?" The tone was amiable.

Stopping on the tips of their toes, the rakshasas pivoted to see a pair of guards considering them from the edge of the clearing.

"Eager to be seen working hard so you can earn quick promotions," the second guard remarked jovially.

The leader offered a friendly wave, glad for their disguise. These fools hadn't a clue...

"No, really... what *are* you guys up to?" The first guard started across the open area, his tone only curious, not suspicious. His mate hesitated a moment, then decided to follow suit. "I didn't know... *urk*—" he choked, the words snuffed to abrupt silence.

The other guard's eyes widened unnaturally, registering shock, then horror at the *kshurika* that had embedded neatly at the base of his throat. Two *kshurikas* buried almost to their hilts, blood seeping from identical wounds and staining the guards' tunics. One man attempted a scream to sound an alert, but all he managed was a guttural chortle before falling dead from the rakshasa magic imbued in the *kshurikas*.

The leader of the rakshasas went over to the guards and extracted the daggers from their throats. Wiping the blood on the men's tunics and sheathing the *kshurikas*, he activated the aura sensors in his consciousness. He didn't fancy being taken unawares by the humans again; he wanted to be alerted of their presence, especially when they were warriors who could pose a threat to him and his companions.

The rakshasas traversed the yard and began picking their path as if nothing of consequence had interfered with their advance into the Sanctum. They displayed no hesitation and said nothing to one another.

There was need for neither hesitation nor words. It had all been planned months in advance, in meticulous detail. Every rakshasa knew the drill; what had brought them here, what they were expected to achieve.

They were here to eliminate the rishis in the Sanctum… *to rid Kosala of every last one of them.*

"Is something the matter, rajan?"

Instead of replying, Bharat bent to scratch Angara behind its ear. The dog extended its neck in pleasure and gazed devotedly at its master.

"Can I get you something?" Siripala asked, approaching on soft feet, though there was evidence of a limp in his irregular gait.

"No," Bharat shook his head and straightened.

Siripala flicked his fingers to conjure up a small globe that shed an umbrella of pale light over him and Bharat. Angara glanced from one man to the other and wagged its tail.

"What brings you here at such a late hour, rajan?" Siripala enquired, contemplating Bharat with large, soulful eyes. His skin had the texture of hide, and his face was bronzed in the light of the globe. A crown of wiry hair covered his head, white except at the roots, where it was still black.

"I have been thinking about father all day."

The other man said nothing and waited for Bharat to force his thoughts into words. The silence stretched between them. The dog dropped down by Bharat's feet, put its snout on its front paws and heaved a sigh of contentment. The sound of a snort issued from one of the buildings to the right, closely followed by a light whinny and the stamp of a hoof on mud.

"You knew him well," the young king said finally.

"I did, kumara," the old man lapsed into an old, familiar form of address. He was probably the only person to still address Bharat by that term, though it had gone out of fashion ages ago.

"Well enough to know his mind."

Siripala looked down at his large, callused hands and nodded. It was true. If there was anyone who could claim to know Dashratha well, it was Siripala. After all, Siripala had been the king's bodyguard from way before, when Dashratha had been just a young prince in one of Kosala's southern principalities. Siripala had fought at Dashratha's side during Kosala's unification and consolidation under one banner, and later, had accompanied the king on various campaigns that saw Dashratha emerge as a preeminent ruler of Jambudvipa. Dashratha and Siripala had grown to be more than king and bodyguard, sharing a bond of trust and fellowship that had lasted until Siripala had taken an arrow in his knee during battle. The arrow had shattered the kneecap, and Siripala had been forced to retire from service, but as a mark of gratitude towards the soldier who had served him so well, Dashratha had retained him as caretaker of the royal stables. That was where Siripala had become acquainted with the king's sons, and over time, he had grown particularly fond of Bharat, the most proficient rider among the four princes. Siripala gradually assumed the duties of grooming and caring for Bharat's horses, and the prince had reciprocated with kindness and respect, their friendship starting to mirror the one that Dashratha and Siripala had once shared.

"So, you would know why father loved Rama so much more than the rest of us."

"You think the king loved prince Rama more," the old bodyguard studied Bharat. It wasn't a question. It was a statement.

"I don't think. *I know.*" Bharat held Siripala's gaze. "I want to know why. Maybe he told you."

The older man shook his head. Moths flitted and fluttered around the globe of light. "He would never talk to me about something like that. He would never tell *anyone.*" A moment's silence. "But I think it got increasingly obvious that he favoured yuvaraja Rama more." He looked at Bharat. "Perhaps it was because Rama was better at everything. Except at riding a horse."

Bharat smiled at the small concession granted to him but scratched his beard in bewilderment. "That's it? Just because Rama was better?"

"That's it." Siripala gave the king a look of surprise. "That is what a king wants from a son. A father is different. A father will settle for less. He will be prepared to make allowances; he will even overlook faults in a son. But a king wants the best qualities in a son because the son is also his heir."

"And if another son showed those same qualities?"

Siripala looked at Bharat evenly. "Then it would be trouble. Another contender for the crown. Violence might follow, blood might flow. No king wants that. No father wants that either."

Angara raised its head and stared into the dark in the direction of the river, ears perked, a growl rumbling in its throat.

"So much better if the other sons display less competence," Bharat muttered, almost to himself. "So much better not to encourage them, fan their talents, give wings to their ambitions…"

"Let it go, kumara," Siripala said. "What is in the past should be left undisturbed."

Angara had got to its feet and was peering intently, the growl now more menacing. Bharat tried to see what had got the dog's attention, but it was too dark to discern anything.

"Nothing's there, Angara," Bharat coaxed. "Sit."

The dog wagged its tail once in acknowledgement and sat, but its eyes were trained towards the river.

"Must be a jackal," Siripala surmised.

"What about you?" Bharat looked at the bodyguard. "Would you favour one son over another?"

"I don't have sons to favour," Siripala said with a dry chuckle.

"If you had, for argument's sake. And if you were king."

The old man shrugged. "I guess I would be partial to the one who showed the qualities that are dear to me." Shooting a meaningful glance at Bharat, he added, "Aren't we all partial that way, rajan?"

Bharat gave this a moment's thought. But before he could speak, the heavy, hollow, booming of a *bheri* drum disrupted the calm of the night. Angara leaped to its feet and began barking, the hackles standing on its back.

Exchanging startled glances, the men looked to pinpoint the origin of the noise.

The bodyguard pointed. "It's coming from across the river."

From the Sanctum, Bharat realized as he turned back to the ostler. His eyes were frenzied. "My horse, Siripala," he shouted over the echo of the drum and Angara's furious yapping. "Hurry."

Drums had long been used to alert the *nagarapalas* to danger, before magic evolved and rendered them obsolete. A *bheri* being beaten to raise an alarm could only mean that the magic had been compromised in some way, and something was frightfully wrong... wrong in the Sanctum where the *homa* fire that had powered and protected this city for over two generations burned under the watch of the rishis.

Bharat glanced down at his bare forearms and grimaced. His *vajramushtis* were in the palace, and there was no time to get them. The same with his longbow. He slapped a hand to his waist and felt his *karapala* in its sheath.

The sword would have to suffice, he thought, staring in the direction of the Sanctum, from where the *bheri's* ominous drumbeat rose into the night.

# three

TORCHES WITH SILVER-WHITE FLAMES BOBBED IN THE darkness as the horses swept down the riverbank and stampeded into the Sarayu, churning the muddy water and sending spray everywhere.

Bharat and Siripala led the charge, spurring their mounts into the river. In their wake came the *nagarapalas*, Ayodhya's elite militia, distinguishable in the torchlight by their feathered turbans and broad-bladed *kuntas*. They emerged from Ayodhya's lanes and alleyways by the dozens, on foot and on horseback, the riders plunging headlong into the chase while foot soldiers commandeered boats, urging disoriented boatmen to hasten across the river. The sound of the drum had roused the city's public, and concerned citizens had begun to flock the Sarayu's bank to stare at the sprawl of the Sanctum in curiosity.

The drum inside the Sanctum hadn't sounded once in all these years, was the thought on almost every mind. What had caused it to be beaten now, at this unearthly hour?

*And why the drum*, Bharat fretted, *and not the gongs and bells activated by magic*?

"How many men guarding the Sanctum?" he shouted the question at the *nagarapala* riding at his side. He realized he had never wondered about this before.

"Fifteen to twenty, rajan," the militiaman replied. He had the medallion of a *nayaka* around his neck, indicating a captain's rank.

"That's all?" Bharat turned a shocked expression on Siripala.

"It is thought to be enough," the old warrior shrugged. "Anyone trying to break in will have to deal with the booby-traps and firewalls first."

*Of course.* The magic had been designed to keep intruders out, spells placed to ensure the safety of those inside. But the magic had never been tested before. Bells and gongs had failed to ring, so who was to say if the booby-traps and firewalls would be up to *their* job...

The riverbed dropped suddenly from under the horses' hooves, and the water rose up to the beasts' shoulders, slowing them down and making them whicker in panic. Bharat, who was in the lead, instantly began uttering mantras to invoke magic, and at once his mount surged up in the water, as if buoyed from below. Ripples of silvery current coursed down the horse's body before being absorbed into its limbs, and the animal responded by pushing through the Sarayu with renewed vigour. Siripala and the militiamen followed the example of their king, and for a short moment, the water was illuminated by electric ripples of magic. The horses threw themselves forward, kicking water and eating the distance, residual magic sparking at the tips of their flying manes. The air filled with the noise of splashing water and the boom of the drum, and the river beneath was a boil of silver light, reflecting the *nagarapalas'* torches.

Crossing onto firm ground, Ayodhya's defenders thundered up a rise before funnelling into the open yard in front of the Sanctum's main entrance. Bharat reined his horse in and dismounted. Taking a torch from a *nagarapala*, he walked forward, sword in one hand, the torch raised high in the other to appraise the Sanctum. Siripala and the captain of the militia joined him on each side. At this distance, the drum was incredibly loud. The wall towering over them was smooth and sheer all the way to the top, nigh impossible to scale. The place appeared dark for the most part, the main door shut tight so not even a ray of light escaped into the night.

There was no sign of any intruder anywhere.

Turning and handing the torch to Siripala, Bharat raised his voice. "You," he pointed to a dozen militiamen who had dismounted, "are going in with me and the *nayaka*. The rest… spread out and surround the place. Whoever or whatever is inside shouldn't get away. And don't forget to block access to the river."

"What about me, rajan?" Siripala asked hopefully. "Yuvaraja Shatrughna isn't here to help you —"

"No, Siripala," Bharat was gentle but firm. "Stay here and oversee the men outside."

"Take my *shul* at least." Hiding his disappointment, the old bodyguard hobbled to hand Bharat his spear. "Better than that *karapala* of yours."

The king considered Siripala before sheathing his sword and accepting the *shul* with a nod of thanks. "Let's go," he roared at the *nagarapalas*.

Striding towards the entrance, Bharat and the militiamen invoked mantras as they formed fists with their left hands. Magic sizzled and spiralled around their fists, and moments later, they all bore shields that glimmered briefly with opalescence. At the entrance, locks clicked to Bharat's touch and the door yielded without protest, spraying noise and light on the small knot of men crouched at the threshold, peering over the rims of their shields into the vacant courtyard inside.

Vacant except for the body of a single guard lying on the pavement beneath a flight of stairs, his head at an angle, so the men at the door were pinned by his glassy glare.

"Careful," Bharat mouthed, raising an arm in warning as he scanned the space inside the door to the fullest extent of his vision. No firewalls were visible, he noticed, and none of the booby-traps had been deployed. Observing the captain look at him in mystification, Bharat shrugged and placed a foot inside the door. When nothing happened, he led the way in, skirting the dead guard and running up the steps before pulling up short at the top. As the militiamen converged around him, Bharat surveyed the bodies littered around the Sanctum's grounds with grim eyes.

He estimated there were no less than a dozen scattered about, and from their feathered turbans, he could tell they were all *nagarapalas*.

*Fifteen to twenty*, Bharat remembered the captain saying.

*It is thought to be enough*, Siripala had explained.

Sure, as long as the firewalls and booby-traps worked as expected. For some reason, they hadn't, not today. And these fifteen or twenty men had paid the price.

The militiamen swore and muttered under their breaths, unnerved by the sight of so many dead comrades. "What has happened here?" the captain's voice shook in outrage.

Bharat didn't reply, partly because he had no idea, partly because his eyes were drawn to a pair of bodies lying by the flour mill off to the left. The torchlight barely reached there, but the king instinctively knew those two were not *nagarapalas*.

They were rishis of the Sanctum, tasked with tending to the *homa* fire and weaving magic into the ether.

Bharat's gaze swung towards the abodes of the rishis. "Let us check on the mahamuni and the rishis," he said urgently, his skin crawling at the thought of what they might discover.

Shields up, *kuntas* and *shuls* primed to strike, they split into two groups and went from house to house, sidestepping fallen guards, throwing open doors and searching feverishly for the residents. All the houses were vacant though, and neither the rishis nor their families were anywhere in sight. Even the apprentice rishis were not to be found in their dormitories.

"Not a soul around, rajan," the *nayaka* announced. Bharat didn't know whether that made him feel better or worse.

The Sanctum had come under some sort of attack, he thought, trying to make sense of what was happening. For unknown reasons, alarms, traps and firewalls had failed to deploy, and the guards were all presumably dead, as were at least two rishis—although who or what had killed them was a mystery. Meanwhile, mahamuni Vashishtha and the rest of the rishis were missing, along with their families and their understudies.

Had the mahamuni and the rishis been abducted and taken hostage? Was *that* what this was about?

"Can anyone hear that?" one of the militiamen pointed vaguely, head cocked to one side.

Bharat did likewise, straining to listen over the echo of the drum. Nothing—

"It is coming from the direction of the *homagriha*," the *nayaka* shouted in alarm.

The *homagriha*. The inner sanctorum, where the *homa* fire burned.

"What is it?" Bharat yelled, fearing the worst, his stomach lurching. Then, he heard it.

"Someone screaming, rajan," the captain said. Swerving around, he broke into a run. Bharat and the other militiamen sprinted after him, their feet pounding on hard sandstone.

Behind them, six of the fallen *nagarapalas* stirred and got to their feet.

Grinning to themselves, the six drew their *khadgas* and *kshurikas* and took off in pursuit of the unsuspecting king and his warriors.

He had sensed Ayodhya's defenders coming.

Not that this was remarkable in itself. The drum was so loud—and so infernally *persistent*—he wouldn't have been wholly surprised to learn it had ruined his lord's sleep in faraway Lanka; that Ayodhya would rightly interpret the din as a sign of trouble and send troops to investigate was inevitable.

No, what was special was that he had picked up the aura of Ayodhya's defenders as they swept up from the river in a galloping surge to lay siege to the Sanctum. He had sensed a small band of these men enter the Sanctum's precincts, and he had no trouble telling they were fourteen in number.

He had also detected from their auras that one was a *mahayoddha*—which told him one thing. Kosala's new king or his youngest brother were here in person, the last two *mahayoddhas* left in Ayodhya following the death of Dashratha and the banishment and departure of the other two brothers.

The arrival of the king or his brother was irksome to say the least. *Mahayoddhas* were warriors of a higher calibre, which implied that not only were they better skilled at combat and more resilient, but they could also take recourse to superior magic. A *mahayoddha* could present stiffer opposition than fifteen of Ayodhya's best militiamen, so it was imperative to take the one who had just entered the Sanctum out of the equation early…

Almost everything about this mission had turned irksome, the leader of the rakshasas concluded, as he sent another probing blast of sorcery at the force field that was stonewalling the rakshasas and keeping them from getting at the rishis. Everything had upended and gone downhill from the moment the rishis had dug their heels in and put up a spirited defence under the guidance of the gaunt, white-haired Vashishtha, famous even in Lanka as a redoubtable mage.

The rakshasa cursed as his sorcery collided and shattered harmlessly against the force field, like a wave striking a rock and breaking into a million tiny atoms of nothingness… *Come on, come on*, he egged himself, *there has to be a way through, and we can find it…*

Their disguise being so credible, the rakshasas had disposed of the guards with embarrassing ease, and so had expected the rishis to capitulate in much the same fashion. But the rishis saw through them, and even though a couple went down early in the onslaught, Vashishtha had rallied the others to tap a level of magic that the rakshasas hadn't thought these rishis were capable of channelling. The rishis had cast spells that blocked the advance of the rakshasas by triggering illusions of nausea, seizures and blackouts, and as the rakshasas had fought these ill effects with remedial spells of their own, the rishis had withdrawn and barricaded themselves and their families inside the building at the centre of the Sanctum, where the *homa* fire burned. Being this close to the sacred fire had aided the rishis with their magic, helping them build a force field around the building, which had hitherto proved unbreachable.

But the neatest trick that Vashishtha and the rishis had pulled had not involved magic.

The rakshasas had taken care not to trip booby-traps and firewalls and alarm bells, but the rishis had somehow got hold of the old *bheri* drum to signal their distress, and now a *mahayoddha* was in the Sanctum to rescue the rishis who, instead of dying gracefully, were alive and secure behind their force field…

Frowning in frustration, the rakshasa leader tested the force field once again, looking for a flaw he could exploit. The force field was a physical thing, a translucence in the dark that possessed the optical properties of mist and smoke and moonlight, but was none of these. It thinned and waned deceptively, giving the rakshasas hope, so they stabbed and prodded with their *khadgas* and *kshurikas*, searching for a way in, while the four Sorrows they had summoned forth circled in silent anticipation, waiting for the field to disintegrate so they could get to the rishis. But the force field held, while the king or his brother drew closer…

*Not for long*, the rakshasa told himself as he raised his head and screamed at the night sky, making sure the sound carried to those who had come to the rishis' rescue. The pitch was modulated to mirror a human voice in terror and was designed to draw Ayodhya's defenders further into the Sanctum... into the trap the rakshasas had laid.

As the scream's echoes receded, the rakshasa centred his energies and fused them into a single thought, *into one raging, all-consuming purpose*—the breaking down of the force field. He clenched his hands and knitted his brows, sweat breaking and beading down his neck as he retreated into the core of his being, seeking the power he needed, harnessing it. In one forceful expulsion of energy, his body lit up, simmering with primal heat, and he hurled every ounce of all that he had forged inside him at the force field.

A burst of white-hot anger slammed into the force field.

Buffeted by rakshasa will and sorcery, the translucence wavered and weakened... but managed to hold together somehow. His anger projection sizzled like a film on the force field and slowly evaporated.

*It was futile*, the leader of the rakshasas sighed, his shoulders deflating. *He was failing his lord.*

Utterly miserable and wondering what to do next, he stopped on hearing voices raised in panic issuing from within the building. To his surprise, he observed that the sanctorum was teetering and listing precariously, twisting and rending at the seams. Feeling an upheaval underfoot, the rakshasa peered at the building's foundation to find that the ground beneath the structure had started caving in to form a sinkhole.

The rakshasa grinned in delight and wonderment. The force field had cocooned the sanctorum from all sides except below, so although his sorcery had failed to pierce the translucence, it had dug into the earth to tear the ground out from under the target of his rage.

"Direct your powers from under the ground," he hollered to his fellow rakshasas. "Let's put an end to this stupid resistance."

Before turning his attention back to demolishing the sanctorum, the rakshasa trained his sensors outwards in search of the *mahayoddha*. His sensory pulses traced the band of warriors running in the direction of the sanctorum, rising to the bait, approaching fast.

*Not fast enough*, the rakshasa smirked in pleasure, knowing it was a matter of moments before they were brought down by the six rakshasas coming after them; the six he had sent to trick the humans into thinking they were dead *nagarapalas*. The deception was bound to succeed as the soldiers of Kosala had no cause to suspect a fallen guard as being the enemy in disguise... and the deception *had* succeeded.

In the rush to fulfil the call of duty, Ayodhya's warriors had let themselves into a trap, leaving their backs exposed, and now they were about to be taken by surprise and felled from behind...

It was sixth sense that made Bharat drop his pace and look back over his shoulder.

It was sixth sense that saved Bharat that night inside the Sanctum of the Fire.

He turned and looked. The *kshurika* was a blur in the dark, almost impossible to detect, but the magic infused in its blade left a faint thermal wash in its wake that Bharat's honed senses were able to spot instantly. Meant to strike the back of his head, it flew straight at the king's right temple now, mean in appearance, murderous in intent.

The dagger was no more than a hand's distance from Bharat, speeding in to part him from those he held dear, when acting on reflex, he caused a mantle of protective energy to manifest around him. The *kshurika* came in contact with the mantle immediately, and strong magic encountered stronger magic, triggering patterns of electric charges. The dagger's tip pierced the mantle and pressed towards its target, but on entering the mantle's power field, it was overwhelmed by the purity of Ayodhya's magic.

Exploding in a flash of light, the *kshurika* vaporized inches from Bharat's head.

"Get down," he screamed in warning.

*Too late*. The king had dodged death in the nick of time, but his militiamen weren't as fortunate. *Kshurikas* smacked into five heads, cracking skulls open and burying in deep to deposit potent rakshasa magic into the men's bodies. Five *nagarapalas* dead on their feet, their legs carrying them forward, running with the rest until they lost momentum and went crashing to the ground in a jumble of limbs, their javelins clattering and spraying on the hard floor.

"Watch out," Bharat called again, whirling to face the source of threat, shield up, the *shul* ready. He sensed the *nagarapalas* slowing down, alerted by his shouts. He also heard shrieks of terror rise from the direction of the *homagriha*.

A fresh bout of apprehension seized him. That was probably the rishis or their—

His eyes caught movement and widened in relief at the sight of six *nagarapalas* emerging from the dark. He wondered where they had been all this while. Had they been fighting the attackers who—

That's when Bharat noticed the residue of the magic in the *nagarapalas'* hands—the thermal stains left by the *kshurikas* that had just been thrown at him and his men.

*Disguise*, the word skidded and bounced through his mind. *Or was it a betrayal...?*

Opening himself to superconsciousness, Bharat sought the identity of the attackers in the light of Ayodhya's magic. Their disguise immediately fell away in a shower of dust, and stripped of illusion, the six revealed their true forms to Bharat. His eyes widened at the sight of the magic tattooed across their bodies, glowing like neon stigmata, lighting up their dark blue faces, their hair and beards white as snow.

*Rakshasas*, he gasped in disbelief, his resolve wilting for a moment as the enormity of what was happening struck him with the force of a battle-hammer. Not once in Kosala's long history had rakshasas struck at Ayodhya. Not once had they attempted storming the Sanctum during the reigns of Dashratha and his forefathers, and though they had invaded Kosala from time to time, they had always been stopped and repelled well short of Ayodhya, first by Dashratha, and later by Rama and Lakshmana, who had famously fought and defeated the formidable Lankan general Tataka almost a decade ago.

Importantly, unlike Rama and Lakshmana, not once had he faced a rakshasa in battle, Bharat realized, as he ran his tongue over dry lips. This was proving to be a night of many firsts.

"They are rakshasas," he shouted, suppressing the panic stirring in his chest. Hearing footsteps slowing behind him, he called over his shoulder, "Keep going. I will handle them."

He fervently hoped the *nagarapalas* had heard him and would do as they had been told. Someone in the *homagriha* was in urgent need of help. "*Just keep going*," he repeated, dropping to a crouch to face the oncoming rakshasas, unsure of what to expect, not knowing how to react.

The rakshasas unloosed another volley of *kshurikas*, two aimed squarely at Bharat, but he was better prepared. Flinging his shield sideways to intercept the daggers meant for the militiamen, he said a mantra and cast another energy mantle, which expanded in a bubble around him; the *kshurikas* thrown at him struck the mantle and disintegrated on impact. His shield meanwhile knocked two of the other daggers from their paths, but the last two blades zinged past, and Bharat heard cries from behind him as both weapons found their mark.

"I said I'll handle this… *just go*," he bellowed, awake to the threat of losing all his *nagarapalas* right away. Listening to the militiamen's footsteps recede, he sighed inwardly in relief.

Faced with defiance, the rakshasas slowed their charge and began spreading out, the two in the middle assailing Bharat repeatedly with *kshurikas* while the others tried to flank him from the sides. Having dispensed with the need for a disguise, all six had reverted to their rakshasa identities.

Knowing he couldn't allow the rakshasas to circle past him, Bharat marked an arc on the ground in front of him with Siripala's *shul*. Sparks flew from the spear's tip as it grated on stone, and a shimmering curtain of energy sprang out of the arc between him and the rakshasas. Daggers dashed against this magic and were destroyed.

Balanced on the balls of his feet, Bharat drove the *shul's* point rapidly into the curtain, turning all the while in a tight semicircle. Every thrust of the spear generated a magical spearhead that steamed and hissed with energy as it sped from the curtain and struck the rakshasas. Spearheads scorched the space between the combatants, sending the rakshasas staggering back in surprise, but they regrouped in no time, spearheads ricocheting off their magic armour as they conjured wreaths of Sorrows that reared into the sky, large mouths wailing noiselessly in preparation to swoop down on Bharat.

Watching the attack materialize, the young king hesitated, trying to anticipate what was coming next. He had never heard of anything that matched the six soot-grey apparitions looming before him, shapeless and lacking all features other than a bulbous head and a rudimentary mouth that yawned pit-black, darker than the night all around, darker than anything he had sighted before. He raised the *shul* in defence, but he supposed the spear would be anything but effective against these amorphous forms. He even doubted if magic would serve any purpose…

He darted a glance at the rakshasas, who had started edging around him. In two minds whether to focus on the apparitions or stall the rakshasas, Bharat turned his spear to the energy curtain when the Sorrows lunged at him. Bharat instinctively cast the mantle over his head and ducked, praying the mantle would keep the entities out. To his immense relief, the smoky forms pulled to an abrupt halt a yard or two in the air above, hanging for an instant, as if in indecision… and then their mouths split wide to disgorge a blackness, a void, that poured and splashed over the energy mantle before seeping through to cascade over the king's head and shoulders. The same moment, a wail broke like a wave against Bharat's eardrums.

In a flash, he recognized the wailing voice as his own. It was coming not from his mouth but someplace deep… *deep inside his ribcage.*

And sorrow—heavy, bone-crushing, soul-crushing, spirit-sapping sorrow—engulfed Bharat in a flood, mopping all other thoughts, feelings and emotions from his consciousness. It scoured his mind clean, leaving nothing but an unbearable black pain in its wake. A pain impossible to explain, its source unknown. A pain, a sadness, that manifested from itself, existing in isolation, but feeding on all the collective pain and sadness that the young man had ever experienced in his life.

Heavy, soul-crushing sorrow that caused Bharat's knees to buckle as he drew breath in and sobbed in sheer grief, the *shul* loosening from his grasp and slipping from his fingers…

Weight. Ceaseless and pressing down from all sides, squeezing him breathless.

The weight of rakshasa magic. Magic that had renewed since the last few occasions the humans had met the rakshasas in conflict, mahamuni Vashishtha was forced to admit.

Improved magic, more vigorous, and debilitating in impact. Magic that was new to him.

With a wince and a grimace, Vashishtha detached his thoughts from the ache in his limbs and in his lungs to concentrate on his own magic, bracing himself against the sorcery of the rakshasas. It wasn't easy. Assailed by the rakshasas' spells, the ground beneath him grumbled and shifted, making the sanctorum rock unstably. Fissures had begun showing on the paved limestone floor, widening and spreading at an alarming rate, threatening the *homa* fire that had burned incessantly for eons as the firestones that supported it wobbled and dislodged under the strain. Loose red tiles showered from the roof, clattering to the floor and breaking into fragments.

Rishis sat around the great fire, sweating in its heat and in terror as they chanted mantras while their wives and children cowered in fright. The rishis' apprentices did what they could to calm the nerves and failed. Outside the *homa* hall, over the sound of the mantras and the shrieks and whimpers of the women and children, the *bheri* boomed, but over it was another noise that the mahamuni's refined hearing caught—the shallow gurgle of the rakshasas' incantations, a base and wet noise, like the bubbling of a miasmic lava pool, full of hatred and violence.

The attack had been shrewdly planned and executed, Vashishtha conceded, striving to retain his balance as the ground pitched under him. During past invasions, the rakshasas had marched large armies against Kosala and its neighbours, but each time, they had been undone by Kosala's superior magic and the prowess of its *mahayoddhas* Dashratha, Rama and Lakshmana. So, this time, the rakshasas had tried a different tack; no buildup of troops along the frontier, no warning, nothing to suggest this surprise attack on the

Sanctum, aimed at striking at the heart of Kosala's magic. If harm was to befall the fire or the rishis *or both*, Kosala's magic output would suffer and the kingdom would be vulnerable to attack, the rakshasas probably having gauged that Bharat was no Dashratha or Rama in capability and experience. It struck Vashishtha that Bharat and Shatrughna should have been exposed to rakshasa warfare when the chance had presented itself, but then Bharat had been in Kekeya most of his growing years and not *once* in Ayodhya when the rakshasas had attacked. And Shatrughna had been too young to send to war anyway… Rama and Lakshmana's prolonged absence from Kosala was a contingency no one had planned for, the mahamuni realized, a lacuna that the rakshasas were now exploiting to their maximum advantage.

With the sanctorum being destabilized from below, the rishis' faculties were being stretched to the limit. Not only did they have to defend themselves from a subterranean assault, but they also had to maintain the force field to keep the rakshasas as well as the four ghost entities out. A cursory examination of the entities' properties had told Vashishtha these were products of new rakshasa magic, each birthed from the sorrow and suffering of its parent rakshasa, manifestations of pain adept at crippling their victims with sadness. The rishis also had to ensure the *homa* fire didn't get extinguished, while propping the sanctorum up so it didn't collapse over everyone's heads. The mahamuni could sense that all of this was draining the rishis of their vital energy, and that something would give if relief didn't arrive soon from across the river. Mopping the sweat off his forehead, he shot a pulse of magic outwards, seeking reassurance that help was at hand.

The magic transmitted an image back instantly: Bharat standing almost doubled over inside the Sanctum, plagued by more of the ghost entities and reeling in anguish as half a dozen rakshasas charged at him with *khadgas*. And closer to the sanctorum, a knot of *nagarapalas* swamped by more rakshasas in a fight that the *nagarapalas* could never expect to win by themselves.

The mahamuni's heart sank to the pit of his stomach in trepidation.

*Why was Shatrughna nowhere to be seen? Not that he would make a big difference... If only Rama and Lakshmana were in Ayodhya...*

It took Vashishtha effort to clear these frantic thoughts. Bharat needed his help, needed more magic to boost his strength so he could fight better...

The ground lurched as fresh blasts of rakshasa magic burrowed into the sanctorum from below. The building jolted and shook in response, prompting even the sterner rishis to cry out in fear. Their focus went awry. The force field waned and went threadbare. Sorrows leaped at the tatters that appeared, pushing through, while the *homa* fire teetered on the edge of ruin...

Vashishtha closed his eyes and willed spells into the Sanctum's atmosphere, his body shivering with the effort, fighting the stress, countering the weight of rakshasa magic. His consciousness sought Bharat out in the dark, desperately hoping this last-ditch effort to save the Sanctum and the sacred fire would work.

If it didn't, *if he failed*, Ayodhya was lost.

Weight. Crushing him from outside and in, so it felt like his ribcage would implode and explode at the samc time with all the pent-up grief.

The weight of the void. Black and heavy and filled with nothingness. Calling him into its dense, velvety folds. Demanding his surrender. And he, giving in, *willingly*. Because he had no choice.

He thought he heard the beat of a drum and the slap of footsteps on stone, running, approaching fast, but he couldn't be certain with the wail of the void in his ears. Or was the wail in his throat now… or on his lips… tearing out of him as it dragged him deeper into the black. And he, going in, *willingly*…

Then, out of nowhere, he sensed an image forming against the oppressive darkness, golden and incandescent. A young face, staring at him with large, trusting eyes.

*Taksha.*

Surprised by the suddenness of its appearance, he gasped, reeling a bit as he felt the weight lift off his shoulders. He knew not how or why the image had manifested—*was it inside his mind or outside?*—but now that it was there, it spread warmth, filling him with happiness and hope. And the will to resist—*to not succumb to the void*—flowered inside him, fighting the sadness, swelling in size, pushing back…

Bharat forced his eyes open. He stared at the sandstone between his sandaled feet. He stared at the tip of the *shul* trailing on the sandstone. Hearing the sound of feet rushing towards him, he lifted his head and looked at the six rakshasas, now no more than twelve paces away and closing in fast. He raised his eyes and assessed the Sorrows, their distended mouths spilling black void onto him. He took in the energy curtain, sizzling between him and the advancing rakshasas.

Taksha. The light of his life. Taksha. Worth fighting for…

Uttering a mantra, Bharat focused his energies on the image of his son before touching the *shul* to his forehead. The weapon shone with the transference of magic, its head turning golden with heat.

Rising to his full height, Bharat whipped the burning spearhead horizontally across the middle of the energy curtain. Instead of severing in two, the curtain collapsed and fused into the tip of the *shul,* where it merged with the heat of magic to form a blazing belt of energy. The king spun the spear over his head to build momentum before lashing at the Sorrows, the belt sweeping up to snare the wretched forms, binding them to one another. In the same fluid motion, Bharat sent the belt skimming at the rakshasas, unleashing the Sorrows back on them, reuniting entities with parents so the rakshasas slammed to an abrupt halt, their *khadgas* falling from benumbed fingers as they were overcome with a sadness that was now suffused with Bharat's own misery.

Drowning in grief and drained of resolve, the rakshasas couldn't hold off the energy belt, which scythed through their magic armour. The neon-bright tattoos on the rakshasas' bodies dimmed and sputtered out, and everywhere the belt made contact, rakshasa skin blistered and burst and peeled, Ayodhya's magic melting the flesh and seeping to the marrow to sap the rakshasas of strength. All six sank in distress, striving to summon fresh spells and failing. Twirling the *shul*, Bharat flogged the rakshasas, not letting up, not giving them a chance to regain control, meting out justice… until fresh cries issued from the direction of the sanctorum, breaking through the red rage that had laid claim to Bharat. Laying the belt across the shoulders of the rakshasas one last time, Bharat wheeled and sprinted away, leaving the rakshasas moaning in anticipation of their deaths.

The scene at the sanctorum was one of chaos, where everything competed for Bharat's attention. A lesser warrior might have been overwhelmed into inaction, but Kosala's king took stock of everything in a single sweep of the eye: three rakshasas laying into the last three *nagarapalas*; the *homagriha* sinking into the ground as chunks of masonry broke and rained down around the rishis and their families fleeing from the crumbling edifice; the four Sorrows that ambushed the rishis, vomiting misery on them and paralyzing them; and the rakshasa who moved amidst the rishis, cleaving their heads and hacking their torsos open with his *khadga*.

A portion of the sanctorum gave way and crumbled in a cloud of dust. Bharat tightened his grip on his spear and charged at the rakshasas, screaming at the top of his lungs. One rakshasa spun around to face his challenge, *khadga* poised to parry the *shul*, but Bharat plunged the spear past the rakshasa's defence at lightning speed, burying its head into the massive chest and twisting hard. The rakshasa stared in shock and surprise as Ayodhya's magic got the better of him, the *khadga* falling from his grasp…

Yanking the *shul* free, Bharat caught the *khadga* with his free hand and eased past before the rakshasa struck the floor. The ground shook as another part of the *homagriha* came crashing to earth, and Bharat screamed an order to the militiamen at the top of his voice.

"Help the rishis… *Go…*"

Sensing danger, the second rakshasa turned and swiped at Bharat, but the king fended the blow with the *khadga* before skewering the rakshasa with his spear. The rakshasa doubled over, and Bharat brought the *khadga* down on his head, splitting the skull open in a sickening crunch of flesh and bone. Already beleaguered by the *nagarapalas*, the third rakshasa barely saw the *shul* as it pierced his side to let the life out of his beating heart.

"Get the rishis out," Bharat called again as he made a dash for the *homagriha*, his eyes tracking the rakshasa attacking the rishis. "I'll take the rakshasa." He saw there was just one ghost entity left over the sanctorum, spewing black void; he guessed the others had died or dissipated along with the three rakshasas he had dispatched.

The militiamen took off to do their king's bidding. Bharat invoked a mantra and swept the *shul* over his head so that energy looped and streamed from its tip. He cast the belt at the solitary Sorrow, snagging it in a flash before setting it upon the rakshasa, but the rakshasa proved himself alert to the threat. Dodging the belt, he straightened to lock eyes with Bharat, and the two appraised each other, bathed in sweat and blood, while tremors shook the ground and debris fell from the sanctorum and the rishis ran helter-skelter.

Then, crying out in frustration, the rakshasa sprang at the rishis, hacking them with bestial fury.

Blood sprayed in the torchlight, and screams of terror rose above the banging of the *bheri* and the rumble of the earth. Bharat charged, weaving past the panic-stricken rishis who blundered into his path, impeding him and slowing him down so that the rakshasa had even more time to inflict his cruelty…

Focused on dodging the rishis and bent on not losing sight of the rakshasa, Bharat nearly missed the Sorrow swooping down on him from above. He glimpsed the grey form at the last moment, and as it opened its mouth, the king pictured his son's doting smile as he cast an energy mantle over his head. Black void poured out of the Sorrow, but the mantle held, guarding Bharat from the outpouring of grief—

—and the earth chose that instant to give a mighty shrug and drop away in disappointment.

Thrown off balance, the king floundered to his knees. The mantle unravelled and vanished.

Tugged downwards, the *homagriha* buckled and sank to its foundations in a roar of brick and stone.

Slack-jawed and on all fours, Bharat stared at the devastation in disbelief. *The inner sanctorum with the sacred fire inside, reduced to rubble...*

The rakshasa came at him with a fierce swing of the *khadga*.

Bharat scrambled for his *shul* and *khadga*, raising the latter in time to block a blow that would have taken his head off his shoulders. The force of the blow sent the young king reeling to the ground, and rakshasa leaped forward to drive the point of his *khadga* into his adversary. Bharat cast the mantle between himself and the rakshasa, *but the mantle failed to materialize this time*. Twisting around, he frantically drove the *shul* into the rakshasa's torso while channeling magic, but the only magic he could muster was weak and unresponsive.

It had to do with the sanctorum and the sacred fire, Bharat thought to himself in desperation.

Meanwhile, the rakshasa wasn't to be stopped.

Unmindful of the spear gouging into him, knowing he was at death's door, the rakshasa pressed forward, *khadga* raised high to deliver the fatal blow to the human king.

The rakshasa's hands swung downwards and the *khadga's* tip arced towards Bharat's head with the aim of splitting it open, but Bharat thrust his *khadga* into rakshasa's stomach. At the same time, drawing from deep reservoirs of knowledge passed to him and his brothers by mahamuni Vashishtha, he called up cryptic mantras that allowed power to flow between *shul* and *khadga* through his body. Ayodhya's magic bonded with rakshasa magic in a virulent mix, redoubling in potency, and currents of arcane magic drilled through the rakshasa's body, burning his blood, singeing his flesh and hurling him backwards. He thudded to the ground, the *khadga* smacking the earth and bouncing away, his skin turning to the colour of charcoal as one by one the tattoos winked out until the only light that showed was the reflection of the torches in his dead, black eyes.

The banging of the *bheri* drum. The frenzied shouts and calls of the rishis and their loved ones. The stampede of confused feet. The slow settling of the earth in subterranean sighs and groans. All these sounds slowly re-registered in Bharat's ears, disjointed at first, as if coming from far, and then more clearly as he picked himself up from the ground and hobbled to his feet. Propped on his *shul*, he swayed giddily, sucking in large gulps of air and allowing spent energy to replenish. Finally, as the splotches in his vision cleared, he straightened, tossed the *khadga* aside, and jogged towards the fallen *homagriha*. Rishis milled around the slump of wood and masonry, and Bharat could see the *nagarapalas* clearing away the debris.

It was impossible for the sacred fire to have survived such a ravaging, he realized with a shiver.

Pushing the dreadful prospect to the back of his mind, the king elbowed his way to the front. "Anyone trapped inside?" he asked.

One of the rishis turned to him and nodded. "The mahamuni."

Bharat's eyes widened in horror.

*Mahamuni Vashishtha. Kosala's head mage, protector of Ayodhya.*

"Why was the mahamuni still inside?"

"He was guarding the sacred fire, rajan."

Giving the *shul* to the rishi for safekeeping, Bharat joined the militiamen in clearing a way into the broken-down structure. Dust got into eyes and nostrils, fingers grazed, and palms developed cuts and calluses as stone and wood were cast aside and the men tunnelled in. Someone had sent news to those outside the Sanctum, and more militiamen arrived to join the search for the head mage. The rescuers dug through the jumble outside only to discover that the roof over the great hall had fallen in, and another massive pile of masonry had to be cleared. Everyone got to work, but it was hard labour, and the sky had begun lightening to the east when someone finally called out—"Here… I can see the mahamuni."

Bharat rushed to where the men had gathered. A couple of them had already wormed their way to the mage, who lay huddled on his side, barely conscious, both hands pressed to his stomach. The men eased the mahamuni out from under the debris in small shifts and nudges, and Bharat assisted in lifting the mage free and bearing him into the open, where he was gently lowered to the ground.

"There's something in the mahamuni's hands," someone exclaimed, pointing to a pulse of light emanating from between Vashishtha's cupped palms.

An old rishi reached out and pried the mage's fingers open; inside was a small transparent ball of silver magic, within which a tiny lick of flame wavered, golden in colour.

"He saved the sacred fire from being annihilated," the old rishi breathed in relief and reverence, holding the ball up for everyone to see before handing it to an apprentice for safekeeping.

Bharat cast a light globule and directed its glow over the mahamuni's face. There was an intake of breath from all around at the smudge of blood on Vashishtha's scalp, right along the hairline. The blood had soaked into the mage's hair, dyeing it red. Fearing the worst, one rishi placed a finger under Vashishtha's nose.

"I can feel the mahamuni's breath," he announced to everyone's great relief. Vashishtha's eyes fluttered open at the same time.

Bharat's face lit up with joy and gratitude. "It is over, mahamuni," he said. "We defeated them."

Instead of replying, the mage stared at the ring of faces above him, his eyes moving in an erratic pattern. His lips stretched briefly, a gurgling croak sounded in his throat, but speech failed him. His fingers twitched once and went still.

Vashishtha's eyes turned cloudy and anxious.

"What is it, mahamuni?" Bharat asked, feeling an uneasiness creep in on him.

The mage made another attempt to say something, but what came out was a despairing, rattling moan. He looked up at Bharat, terror in his eyes.

Then, his eyeballs froze and went immobile.

# *four*

THE *NAGARAPALAS* WERE EVERYWHERE, ARMED AND ALERT, patrolling Ayodhya's streets, setting up pickets and manning the gates, inspecting the trade carts and caravans entering and leaving the city and conducting searches when their suspicions were aroused; they were on the Sarayu, keeping a close eye on river traffic; they were in the countryside, combing fields and farmsteads for suspicious activity. And they were out in numbers guarding the palace, where the mahamuni and the fire he had rescued from the *homagriha* were now sheltered. The militiamen's workload had increased twofold, so more citizens were being urgently drafted to ease the pressure, and there was a long queue of candidates at the recruitment camp adjacent to the palace grounds and the *nagarapalas'* headquarters.

"How is it going?" Dileepa enquired of a senior *upanayaka* who appeared to be overseeing the recruitment.

"Not bad," the militiaman replied, eyeing Dileepa's ceremonial black turban and sash, which marked him as a *dandapala*, an investigator of the royal court. "Mostly people from the interior, though... rural folk," he gave his head a disapproving shake. "They will need to be fully trained before they can be deployed as *nagarapalas*."

"Can't deploy anyone without full training, can we?" Dileepa observed with a small smile. Tall and pleasant to the eye, he had deep-set, considerate eyes, a sharp chin and a dandy moustache.

"True, but these people aren't even *familiar* with Ayodhya… its layout, what is where, how to get somewhere," the *upanayaka* glared unhappily. "How can one expect them to be the city's *nagarapalas*? We will have to handhold them every step of the way."

Dileepa thought of reminding the man that these people had at least responded to the palace's call, whereas Ayodhya's own residents hadn't stepped up to secure their city against future threats. But he chose to keep quiet, knowing the militiaman's frustration came from having to deal with inexperienced recruits when the *nagarapalas* were already overstretched, guarding a city that was gripped by fear. So, with a nod of understanding, he moved on.

Fear and uncertainty had settled over Ayodhya as soon as reports of what had happened in the Sanctum of the Fire started seeping into the city along with the early morning mist that rose off the Sarayu. First came the news that a dozen rishis and all the *nagarapalas* defending the Sanctum had died—*killed in cold blood by rakshasas*, the rumour said. Next, the report of the *homagriha* collapsing and mahamuni Vashishtha having been grievously wounded. Then the final confirmation that the attackers had indeed been rakshasas, based on the examination of their dead bodies.

That the rakshasas all appeared to have been killed in the counterstrike led by the king didn't seem to count in allaying the people's fears. The fact that rakshasas had surprised Ayodhya in the dead of night, demolished the *homagriha* and nearly destroyed the sacred fire, slayed over thirty-five *nagarapalas* and rishis, and caused serious harm to the mahamuni was enough to send everyone into a state of panic. It didn't help that someone had planted the notion of an unknown number of rakshasas having escaped the Sanctum and entered the city, where they could well be in hiding, waiting to strike again... The possibility could neither be ignored nor rubbished, especially after it came to light that the rakshasas might have had inside help; the prospect of someone in the city aiding rakshasas was prompting everyone to look at everyone else with suspicion.

Rumour and speculation abounded, leaving Ayodhya on edge, but the answers to the questions remained elusive, forcing the king to entrust the *dandapalas* with the investigation. Not that that had worked any wonders; the six investigators uncovered the same facts and ran into the same dead ends. The rakshasas had come in from the river, reptilian prints leading up from the water's edge before transforming into human footprints close to the Sanctum's old, unused door. Footsteps had trampled the ground outside the door, and the same feet had left muddy tracks inside the door. There was no evidence of the door having been forced, which explained why the alarm, the booby-traps and the firewalls had not been triggered.

This meant just one thing. Someone on the inside had let the rakshasas into the Sanctum.

But the big question was, who? It could have been any of the seventeen *nagarapalas* who had been posted on duty at the Sanctum that night, but there was no way of finding out as every one of them was now dead. Or it could have been any of the rishis, their apprentices or their family members. But eleven rishis had been killed that night while another twenty were badly maimed, so that line of enquiry had to be pursued delicately. The rishis were highly respected in Kosala, and the *dandapalas* were aware that any unsubstantiated slur on the reputation or character of any of the rishis would attract the public's displeasure. Lastly, there was always a possibility that the rakshasas had been aided by someone who had left the Sanctum before, during or after the attack…

While the *dandapalas* went around in circles, the city's anxiety grew and peaked when news went out from the palace that in the course of the rakshasa attack, mahamuni Vashishtha had suffered a severe paralytic stroke that had rendered him incapable of speech and movement. Every prominent *vaidya* in Ayodhya was consulted, but none of them were able to bring the slightest improvement to his condition. This had prompted lesser *vaidyas* from far and near to turn up at the palace and try their hand at treating the mage, knowing that rich rewards awaited the one who succeeded. Still, for three days, there had been no breakthrough for either the *vaidyas* or the *dandapalas*.

On the fourth morning, while examining the attendance roster that listed the *nagarapalas* who were assigned duties at the Sanctum, Dileepa came across an anomaly.

On the day of the attack, there had been *eighteen* militiamen posted on duty at the Sanctum.

Seventeen of them had been accounted for. But there was an eighteenth who had not been there—*dead or alive*. One *nagarapala* whom everyone had miraculously overlooked and forgotten about in the aftermath of the attack.

Dileepa had traced the militiaman to a picket on the road that led south to the kingdom of Kasi.

The man was an ageing *nagarapala* by the name of Samanta, who when confronted by Dileepa, admitted that he had been on duty at the Sanctum that day. But due to a severe bout of chronic acidity, he had been compelled to leave work and go back home, an act that had saved his life. Learning of his narrow escape, the *nagarapala* had been on the verge of telling everyone how lucky he had been when word that the rakshasas had had local help reached his ears. Being the lone survivor, Samanta had realized that the finger of suspicion would inevitably fall on him, so in a display of great stupidity, he had decided to keep silent, hoping that no one would remember him being at the Sanctum that day.

But for Dileepa and the attendance register, he might have even succeeded in his endeavour.

Skirting the palace ground, Dileepa entered the *nagarapala* headquarters, which was bustling with activity. No one spared him a second glance, the investigator's turban and sash giving him unrestricted access and setting him thinking about the ease with which anyone could get in here by sporting a *dandapala's* turban and sash. He made his way to the back of the building, where the *nagarapalas* held suspects in temporary custody, and approached four militiamen who stood before a cell, chatting amiably with its inmate. Seeing the investigator, the four men withdrew, their expressions wary and unwelcoming. It was natural for people to stand up for one of their kind, and Dileepa guessed these militiamen knew Samanta, believed his story, and were sympathetic to his predicament.

"Kindly open the cell," he said. Seeing the men exchange glances, he added, "Samanta is free to go."

The *nagarapala* emerged blinking in relief, his palms joined in gratitude. Dileepa bowed to the man in return before speaking.

"I have just met the *vaidya* with whom you consult," he said. "He confirms that you suffer frequently from severe acidity and that he has been treating you for years now. He also confirmed that you went to him on the evening before the attack and he administered a dose of medicine to ease your discomfort."

"I told you so, didn't I?" Samanta whined.

"Yes, but my job as *dandapala* is to ascertain whether what people tell me is the truth." Dileepa looked around for somewhere to sit, but there was nothing. "Come," he turned to leave. "There is something I want to know…"

The two men walked to a mammoth peepal that cast its shade over the courtyard outside. Sitting down on the stone platform that surrounded the tree's base, Dileepa looked at the *nagarapala*.

"Tell me something about that day… whatever you can remember."

Samanta frowned for a moment and shook his head. "It was just an ordinary day."

The *dandapala* let out a sad little sigh. "You know, there is only so much I can ask the rishis," he said in an appealing tone. "And anyway, they are so busy with their work they never notice anything. But you *nagarapalas* are different. You are trained for these kinds of things. And you are the only one who's still around. Help me. Tell me what you saw, who came, who went, and if there was *anything* out of the ordinary that happened…"

"I only got there after lunch, when my duty commenced," the militiaman said, thinking hard.

"That's fine. Anything you tell me could be useful."

"Nothing much happened. Some of us sat around playing *chausar* for a while. Then one of the apprentices dropped his washed dhoti into a well and one of us had to go and retrieve it, which was quite hilarious." Samanta smiled at the memory. "Then a few of us helped stack the firewood for the rishis' kitchens—"

"Do you do that often? Is it part of your job?"

"No, it's not our job, but we do it out of goodwill for the rishis' wives."

"Go on," Dileepa nodded.

"That's it. Nothing else happened. Like I said, it was an ordinary day."

"And when did you start feeling unwell?"

"Sometime around then, I guess," the *nagarapala* shrugged. "I was feeling okay when the man from the recordkeeper's office came—"

"Who is this man?" the investigator interrupted.

"He is a clerk at the records office. He comes to take stock of wood, provisions…"

"Often?"

"A few times a month."

"You know him?"

"Well, I have seen him around the Sanctum, and we greet each other if we meet."

"And he is a regular at the Sanctum?"

"For some years now," Samanta nodded, but his eyes looked troubled as a new thought occurred to him.

"What is it… *tell me*," Dileepa pounced on the man's expression.

"It's just that he always comes to tally the records in the mornings… before noon. But that day, he came much later, around sundown," the *nagarapala* scratched his chin. "That's unusual."

"And what did he do?"

"He went off towards the storehouses like he always does, and we let him. I didn't see him after that."

A clerk at the recordkeeper's office dispensing his duties at an odd hour—that too on the day of the old king's *shraaddha*… a *holiday*.

Dileepa perked up, his nose picking up the scent. "This records clerk… does he have a name?"

The militiaman had to reflect for a moment before replying.

"Bakula."

"This has never happened before," the old lady wailed, her voice shivering with grief and lifting into the atmosphere of the Sanctum. "We came to Ayodhya because we believed we would be safe from the rakshasas under the protection of the Ikshvaku kings, but… oh… my husband is gone…" She broke into sobs, clutching her chest in anguish and falling onto three other women who sat around her, consoling her. The verandah that gave into the bereaved woman's dwelling accommodated more women, all of them wives and daughters of the rishis, all overcome with sadness, all in mourning.

"Who could have thought the rakshasas would dare to come *here*?" another of the wives said in shock.

"First, dear Rama was exiled, then King Dashratha died," a third woman lamented. "Now *this*."

Bharat, standing at the tip of the verandah, felt his face begin to flush with the heat of censure. Painfully aware that they were making it sound as if it was his fault, and conscious of the many pairs of eyes that were on him—waiting for him to react, judging him—he swallowed hard and opened his mouth to speak, but—

"These are ill omens," a crone warned from the end of the verandah. "Worse is to come."

As if on cue, the women all burst into tears, weeping for present and future losses.

"The rakshasas won't come again, I assure you," Bharat spoke in a hurry, eager to dispel the fear, so the words came out garbled. "I would... we will protect each... all of you. Trust me, *please*."

"Nine of us have been widowed, and word is the mahamuni may not rise again," remarked one of the women, showing no sign of having heard the young king.

"These are just rumours," Bharat insisted. "Please don't believe in them."

"Please don't speak of rumours to our nine sisters who have lost their husbands, rajan," another rishi's wife stated pointedly.

"Sorry, I meant the mahamuni," Bharat shuffled uncomfortably, feeling stupid and defenceless.

"Sisters," spoke a deeper voice from the young king's side, and a figure stepped forward, regal in stature, his luxuriant white moustache and beard in contrast to his dark skin that appeared to have acquired its distinct shade from long hours in the sun.

"Sisters," he said again, to draw the attention of the women, "All of you were and *are* under the protection of the Ikshvaku kings, who have sworn to guard the sacred fire with their very lives and defend the rishis until their last breaths. If it was raja Dashratha and yuvaraja Rama yesterday, today and tomorrow, it will be Bharat and Shatrughna of the same bloodline. From what I understand, your king fought the attacking rakshasas and singlehandedly dispatched each one of them. It is my belief that had Bharat not come to the rescue in time, the losses suffered here would have been far greater." The man turned theatrically to the retinue of courtiers standing behind Bharat. "Am I right in my belief?" he asked.

The men all nodded in agreement. Satisfied, the man addressed the grieving women again.

"This is not meant to discount what you have gone through... are *still* going through," he said, looking at the women with sober, respectful eyes. "All I am asking of you is to keep your faith in the rulers of Ayodhya, the sons of Ikshvaku. These fine *mahayoddhas*," he pointed to Bharat and Shatrughna, "will do their utmost to keep you from harm. I say this not because I am related to them, not because they are husbands to my lovely nieces Mandavi and Shrutakirti. I say this as Seeradhwaja Janak, king of Videha, who would be happy to have one *mahayoddha* like any of Dashratha's four sons in his court. And you have *two* right here." Pausing to catch his breath, he added, "In all of Jambudvipa, there is no place safer than Ayodhya for you and your husbands."

Comforted by the esteemed king's words, the rishis' wives composed themselves, wiping their eyes and suppressing their sniffles. Taking his cue, Bharat spoke, this time with a greater degree of assurance.

"We shall indeed do everything to protect you and the sacred fire. Not just Shatrughna and I; every soldier of Kosala, every *nagarapala* is committed to doing what is necessary if the need arises. As you already know," he flung an arm out, pointing, "a garrison is being built right next door to house a regiment of Kosala's best warriors, who will guard the Sanctum night and day. The garrison will be under the direct supervision of *mahanayaka* Gajakarna." Bharat looked at a broad-chested man with bushy grey eyebrows and a matching moustache standing to his left. The veteran military commander of Kosala nodded in acknowledgement.

"Also, no efforts are being spared to hunt down those who colluded with the rakshasas," Bharat continued. "The traitors will be brought to justice and will pay for the lives that were taken that night."

The promise that revenge would be exacted had a soothing effect on the women, and the visitors from the court took their leave to continue their tour of the Sanctum of the Fire. In addition to Bharat, Shatrughna and Seeradhwaja Janak of Videha, the party comprised close to a dozen court officials including Sudhanva and his son Yadudeva, and a sharp-faced, clean-shaven man who bore a strong resemblance to Seeradhwaja. This was Seeradhwaja's brother Kushadhwaja, *adhipati* of Rajviraj and father-in-law of Bharat and Shatrughna. Upon hearing about the attack on the Sanctum, Seeradhwaja and Kushadhwaja had hastened to Ayodhya with a few hundred soldiers and three *vaidyas*, arriving just after daybreak. While the *vaidyas* had joined the efforts to tend to the mahamuni, Seeradhwaja and Kushadhwaja had opted to accompany Bharat in a survey of the Sanctum and the garrison coming up next to it.

The rebuilding of the *homagriha* had already commenced to reinstitute the sacred fire inside it. The flame that the mahamuni had rescued had been placed in a temporary *griha* within the Sanctum complex, where rishis were now tending to it. But a sacred fire had to be established in a proper *homagriha* for *rta*, the cosmic order, to function at the optimal level. Any corruption of *rta* would mean a drop in magic, and Ayodhya couldn't afford to have the magic over Kosala thinning out, leaving it weak and susceptible to fresh attacks. Building the new *homagriha* was expected to take a year, so the sooner the project got underway, the better for Kosala's security.

For a very short while, in the immediate aftermath of the attack, the idea of shifting the Sanctum across the Sarayu and locating it somewhere adjacent to Ayodhya had gained popularity in the belief that defending the Sanctum would be easier that way. But finding suitable land was hard, and the fact that the entire complex would have to be constructed from scratch at considerable cost outweighed the benefits of better accessibility. With walls and magic already in place and a garrison coming up for reinforcement, keeping the Sanctum where it was made simpler sense.

"Thank you for what you did there," Bharat said to Seeradhwaja as they picked a path through piles of sand, stone and rubble. Though work was on in full swing, at that moment, the grounds were empty of workmen, who were taking their midday meal in whatever shade the Sanctum's buildings offered. Palace hands bearing silk parasols had come with the party, but Seeradhwaja had politely turned down the offer of a parasol; so now, everyone walked in the raw heat of the sun, bareheaded or wearing turbans, sweat coursing down their foreheads and marking lines on their dusty faces.

"Make no mention of it," Seeradhwaja waved his hand in reply. Bharat and Shatrughna walked in front with the lords from Videha, while the rest of the courtiers followed a little way behind.

"Really, I had no idea what to say to them," Bharat continued. "For a moment, I thought nothing could console them..."

The old king nodded. Glancing at Bharat, he said, "Don't take whatever they said to heart. The ladies were speaking out of grief, and grief, like rage, doesn't know discretion."

"Of course," Bharat agreed. "And anyway, they weren't entirely wrong. It *is* the first time the rakshasas came into Ayodhya. Never before have they—"

"You must stop that right away," Seeradhwaja said sharply, his tone amplifying in the stillness of lunch hour.

"If only I had been there to help instead of being with Yuddhajeet mama—" Shatrughna began.

"And *you* must stop that," the king of Videha interrupted again. "Both of you must stop hitting yourselves for what has already happened. It's over, and your feeling bad about it is not going to change anything." Looking at Bharat, he said, "You fought well and did enough to save the rishis and the sacred fire."

"It is the mahamuni who saved the fire," Bharat specified.

"But *you* reached here in time to stop the rakshasas so everyone could look for the mahamuni," pointed out Seeradhwaja.

The young king inclined his head in agreement, and for some time, everyone walked in silence.

"I hope he recovers," Bharat exhaled. "Ayodhya will be crippled without the mahamuni."

"I can't remember a time when Ayodhya didn't have the mahamuni," Kushadhwaja spoke for the first time, his voice even deeper and more rough-edged than his brother's.

"You are right," nodded Seeradhwaja. He turned to Bharat with a thoughtful look. "You should think about appointing a *kshatri* to assist you."

"We haven't had a *kshatri* in the palace for ages," remarked Shatrughna.

"Father didn't need one because he had mahamuni Vashishtha," Bharat reminded him.

"Exactly my point," said Seeradhwaja. "There is no saying how long the mahamuni will remain in his present condition, so in his absence, it would do well to have a capable chamberlain."

"I am so relieved you thought of bringing this up, raja Janak," said Sudhanva, catching up from behind. "The rajan knows I have been asking him to consider this for a while now." He addressed Bharat, "You must appoint a *kshatri*, especially in light of all that has happened in the last few days."

Bharat inclined his head without making a commitment.

"It's a good idea," said Kushadhwaja. "Let us know if you need help listing down candidates."

Giving it a moment's thought, Bharat replied, "I shall."

It was nearly an hour before the party re-entered the palace and started dispersing. Seeradhwaja begged off lunch, citing the hearty meal they had been indulged with on arrival in the morning.

"I think I will drop in on Urmila," he announced. When Bharat offered to escort him, the king smiled and shook his head. "I can always find my daughters; they will either be in the herbarium or in the library." For a fleeting moment, the tired eyes were marred with grief at the memory of the other daughter living in exile, but in no time, the face cleared, and with a smile that left crow's feet at the corners of his eyes, the raja of Videha turned and left.

"I will ask Shrutakirti to get lunch ready," Shatrughna volunteered and went off on his mission.

Kushadhwaja and Bharat were watching Seeradhwaja go when a voice interjected from behind Bharat. "Rajan, if I may have a word..."

Bharat turned to see Sudhanva and Yadudeva, the former all decorous and flashing his teeth.

"Yes?"

"I couldn't help overhearing your conversation with raja Janak about the mahamuni and the saving of the sacred fire." The *adhipati* bowed. "All I wish to say is that you should never doubt that it was *you* who helped save the fire *and* the mahamuni."

The young king looked at the courtier in surprise. "It is kind of you to say that."

The brawny *adhipati* bowed. "If I may make a suggestion," he paused for Bharat's permission before continuing, "the garrison being built by the Sanctum should be named after you." Seeing the young man's eyebrows rise, the nobleman nodded eagerly. "Let the garrison serve as a reminder to the people that it was their king who saved the Sanctum and the city from the rakshasas."

Bharat looked tentatively from father to son and back. "I will consider the suggestion," he said at last. "Thank you."

"We are at your service," Sudhanva bowed again, including Yadudeva in the conversation. The son quickly bowed as well, and they both withdrew.

Kushadhwaja, who had been observing this exchange with a cocked eyebrow, waited for father and son to go out of earshot before speaking. "Looks like you've begun receiving applications for the *kshatri's* post," he said with a whimsical smile.

"They are good men," Bharat replied, to which his father-in-law gave a slow, deliberate nod.

"There's a bit of time for lunch," Bharat said after a brief pause. "Would you like to rest?"

"I'd like to see Taksha," Kushadhwaja's face lit up at the prospect.

Bharat and Kushadhwaja traversed the length of the palace to the inner chambers. But on arrival, they found that Mandavi and the baby were not in their rooms. Bharat called for them from room to room, until he came upon a maid who was tidying the floor of baby rattles, coloured balls and other playthings. Seeing the king, the maid teetered to her feet, a guilty look on her face.

"Where are the queen and the baby?"

"Mmm... They... I didn't see them, rajan," she lied badly.

"What are you hiding?" snapped Bharat.

Before the maid could answer, the king saw movement outside the window—Mandavi, with Taksha in the crook of her arm, on a terrace two flights below, returning from the direction of the western quarters.

"Where did the queen go?" he growled at the maid, eyes blazing.

"Rajan…" the woman quailed, "She is visiting Queen Mother Kaikeyi."

"What is the matter?" Kushadhwaja asked, entering the room.

"Nothing," Bharat whirled to go outside. "Please wait here… let me find Mandavi…"

The king slipped along a passage and headed down a stairway that brought him to a turn where two levels met. He stood with his back to the wall, listening to the tread of Mandavi's feet, anger bubbling inside him. Once Mandavi had made it to the top stair, Bharat stepped out and blocked her path, hands on his hips, eyes smouldering. Surprised, Mandavi let out a small cry… and then her hand flew to her mouth as she saw who it was.

"Why did you go there?" Bharat's voice rumbled in disapproval. "And why with *him*?"

Mandavi's lips and mouth were too dry to respond.

"You know I can't stand her shadow falling on his face. I have…" Bharat stopped as a thought came to him, and he narrowed his eyes. "How long has this been going on…?"

"Today is only the second time…"

"*Only?*" Bharat took one step forward, lips quivering in anger. "Why," he finally exploded, "when I have expressly forbidden it?"

"Because she called for him, and she is a Queen Mother of the palace, and I must obey her."

"She is no Queen Mother," Bharat scoffed. "She has lost that position. There is no need to obey her anymore."

"She is my mother-in-law," Mandavi said. "No matter what you say, that's a position she hasn't lost, and I cannot disobey my mother-in-law if she asks me to bring her grandson to her."

The figure sat on a reed mat, the legs crossed and head and shoulders hunched over a copper vessel brimming with boiling water. A broad square of cloth formed a tent over his head and the vessel, trapping the rising steam and stopping it from escaping into the room where three other figures stood in respectful silence. The sound of laboured breathing issued from under the cloth, disturbing the quiet stupor of the afternoon.

"I can't... I just *can't*..."

The figure cast the cloth off his head and surfaced for air, snorting noisily to clear a blocked nasal passage. Moisture mingled with sweat and poured down his face, which was oily and naturally puffy, the cheeks covered with a two-day stubble that was quickly going grey, much like his closely shorn crop of hair.

"Rajan, you must try," one of the men in the room protested. "Inhaling is good for your cold and—"

"Not you," the man on the mat scowled in annoyance, his tone nasal and grating. "I'm talking to them."

"Apologies, rajan," the first man, a *vaidya* by the looks of him, mumbled and stepped back.

"I simply *cannot* refuse her this time," Lavanyasurya repeated, addressing the other two men. Mopping his face, he rose and went over to a *manchika*, snapping his fingers at a palace hand who rushed over, waving a peacock fan. Lavanyasurya settled down and appraised the two men, one of whom was clearly a courtier of rank. The other was a clerk. "She has threatened to leave the palace if I don't meet her demand," he grunted dolefully. "These women are all taking inspiration from Kaikeyi."

"Building a *vatika* that large on the banks of the Yamuna is an expensive proposition, rajan," muttered the courtier, a thickset man with curly hair and eyes that bulged in their sockets. "The coffers will be badly strained."

"Your queen wants it, Amulya," Lavanyasurya reminded him. "You are Madhupura's guild master and revenue minister. Find a way."

"We could delay upgrading the city's sewage system," the courtier rubbed his nose doubtfully. "That would save us some money, though it means Madhupura will be flooded again when the monsoon arrives in three or four months. Even so, there won't be enough to fund a garden—"

"Raise taxes."

"We just did that a couple of months ago, rajan," Amulya coughed to clear his throat.

"So?" Lavanyasurya raised a fat finger. "As raja of Madhupura, I can levy taxes whenever it suits me."

"That is not advisable, rajan. There should be sufficient gaps between each raise so that the burden of taxes doesn't appear oppressive. People should forget one increase before the next is imposed."

"Hmm," the king sniffled and looked away, unhappy with the outcome, but wise enough to see merit in what was being suggested. "Raise trade tariffs then," he stated.

"We did that too," the guild master reminded him. "Recently."

"How recently?" Lavanyasurya cocked an eyebrow.

"About three months ago, rajan."

"So, quite some time has passed."

Amulya shuffled his feet. "The other kingdoms weren't too pleased with the last raise."

The king gave a snort. "Who wasn't pleased?"

"No one was. There was a general feeling that the tariffs were already high and a raise was not justified. Kosala's guild master even met me to express their dissatisfaction—"

"Who cares about Kosala's satisfaction?" Lavanyasurya cried in a shrill voice. "Can't they stop being pesky and interfering for once?"

"They are one of our largest trade partners, rajan," said the guild master. "The sugar and indigo that Kosala sells through Madhupura's markets contribute to a very sizeable share of our yearly revenue."

"That is my point," Lavanyasurya stressed. "Kosala and everyone else uses *our* markets to earn revenue. Without us, they'd be making nothing. I can't see why they're having such a problem paying us a higher percentage of their earnings."

"We need them as much as they need us, rajan."

"That is where you are wrong," the king said with a leer. "You've forgotten this is Madhupura, the commercial axis of Jambudvipa. From Tamralipti to Sakala, and Bhrigukaksha to the snowbound passes that lead to faraway Cina, every trade caravan traversing this vast continent has to cross Madhupura. Madhupura is where merchants and wayfarers from all over come to trade in goods and to rest and entertain themselves. This is the traveller's oasis, the trader's beacon. And as raja of Madhupura, I can levy trade tariffs as I wish on those who seek benefit from this bountiful city of ours." Lavanyasurya stuck his neck out at Amulya. "Do you see?"

"I do," Amulya nodded, assuring himself that he could. "I do, rajan."

"And those who find our tariffs too steep are free to take their trade elsewhere," the clerk chipped in with an obsequious giggle.

"See?" Lavanyasurya looked at the guild master while pointing to the clerk in approval. "And good luck with finding another Madhupura," the king laughed, highly amused, but then stopped halfway, nose crinkled, mouth open—"*Achhoo,*" he sneezed with violence once, then a second time.

"Okay, let us increase tariffs with immediate effect," he said, wiping his nose and rising. "Issue an order right away." He paused to look out of the window. "Naika will have her garden by the Yamuna."

"Yes, rajan," the guild master and the clerk bowed simultaneously and withdrew.

The *vaidya* stepped forward. "Rajan, the water has cooled. Shall I ask for another—"

"No," Lavanyasurya raised a hand to stop the physician. With a theatrical wave, he said, "Leave me alone."

Once the *vaidya* had left, the king waddled to the window on squat legs and looked out at the small palace garden where he had bruised his knees many a time as a child. Wild and unkempt, the garden looked pathetic in the glare of the afternoon sun. Yes, he would like a bigger garden by the Yamuna, he realized. One with vast, flowing landscapes and a statue of himself on a pedestal at its centre.

The excitement and enthusiasm that had gripped Dileepa when he had learned about the records clerk earlier that morning had deserted him, and now, as he picked his way through the twisting lanes of Ayodhya's old quarter as the evening settled around him, the *dandapala* was overcome with a weariness that arose from another promising lead slowly fizzling out.

Right after his meeting with the *nagarapala*, the investigator had gone to the records office to look for the man who had made an unusual and unscheduled visit to the Sanctum of the Fire on the day of the attack. However, Bakula was not in office. The *dandapala* was told the clerk was out on a routine visit to the city's neighbouring districts and was expected back only later in the afternoon. The man who provided this information being the chatty type, Dileepa decided to probe a little, asking him about Bakula. From what the investigator gathered, the clerk didn't fit the mould of a scheming villain.

Bakula, a native of Angadesh, had come to Ayodhya with his wife and a toddler nearly twenty years ago, looking for work. As he was found to be good with numbers, someone had stationed him at the records office, where he had served without complaint—or cause for complaint—ever since. The man was diligent and mild-mannered to a fault, Dileepa understood, and in the two decades of being at the records office, he had won the admiration of his colleagues and bosses. The *dandapala* was told that Bakula was a widower. His wife had died of pneumonia a few years earlier, her death making the poor man quite miserable, though he had improved in spirit under the care of the daughter she had left behind. The man added that Bakula had recently purchased a tract of land outside Ayodhya, where he hoped to cultivate a mango orchard. The clerk from Angadesh was clearly looking forward to his retirement.

Disheartened though he was by what seemed an impeccable account of an honest man, Dileepa had refused to let the matter slide and returned to the records office in the afternoon. Though Dileepa had waited for a couple of hours, the clerk hadn't shown up, and then it was time for the office to shut for the day. The *dandapala* had decided to come back the next morning, but as the pressure from the palace had increased and the investigation was expected to show results, he changed his mind and took down the clerk's address.

That address was what Dileepa was now following as he slipped deeper into a part of Ayodhya that he was not at all familiar with. Hailing from Kusinagara and relatively new to the city, the *dandapala* had spent much of his time in and around the palace during the rule of the old king, learning to be a royal investigator. This was his first real assignment, and he was eager to come out of it with full credits. This drove him to ask his way from shopkeepers and the urchins playing on the roads. The sun had yet to set, but darkness came early in these lanes hemmed in by tall houses. So, lamps already illuminated doorways and windows when Dileepa arrived at the plain wooden door to Bakula's house.

The investigator raised a hand to knock, but before fist could make contact with wood, the door opened inwards. Light washed into the darkened alley where Dileepa stood. Framed in that rectangle of radiance was a woman, her face in shadow, her hair flowing in soft lines and falling to her waist, her curves captured as if by an artist's hand, in silhouette. A string of red *sandhija* flowers trailed from one of her hands.

"Oh… I thought it was father."

At the sound of the words, the *dandapala* woke as if from a trance and blinked. "I'm sorry?"

"I heard footsteps and thought father was back," the woman's speech had the cadence of music.

"You are Bakula's daughter?" Dileepa remembered the man at the records office mention her.

"Yes." She paused, then asked, "And you are…?"

"I am a *dandapala*," Dileepa replied. He strained to make out her features, but the angle of the light was all wrong. "Isn't your father home yet?"

"No." She took a half-step forward, her voice inflecting with anxiety. "Is everything alright?"

"Yes."

"You said you were a *dandapala*…" She raised a hand to tuck a strand of hair behind her ear, and her bangles clinked and caught the light. Dileepa could tell she was growing alarmed and found that he didn't want her to.

"It's nothing," he said quickly, hoping to sound reassuring. "Just a routine enquiry."

"Oh," she sounded relieved.

"Mmm… Any idea when he is likely to be back?"

"Could be anytime now, could be late at night," the girl answered with a small shrug and a toss of her head. "I think he had work outside the city today, so it will more likely be later than sooner."

Dileepa nodded. "Alright, I'll meet him tomorrow then."

He started backing away from the doorway when the woman spoke. "I'll let him know about your visit."

"Sure."

"Can I give him your name?"

The investigator felt the flush of blood in his cheeks. "Dileepa." He hesitated, then asked, "May I know yours?"

"Nandana," came the playful reply, the face still hidden from the light.

With that, the door closed and she was gone, and the brightness went out around the *dandapala*.

"Oh…" Quick to hide her surprise, Kaikeyi's eyes narrowed, and her tone dripped with sarcasm as she continued, "…look who has come to pay me a visit." Sticking her head out of the door to look around the darkened herbarium outside, she asked in mock innocence, "Did you lose your way around the palace?"

Standing at the entrance to his mother's chambers, Bharat clenched his jaw in anger. "I am here to tell you to stop what you are doing."

"Oh," Kaikeyi said again, before turning nonchalantly and withdrawing from the door, leaving Bharat in the dark of the threshold.

The king stood for a moment, undecided. Then, left with no choice, he stepped into a tastefully decorated chamber filled with brightly painted clay pots of various sizes. Bharat had sat at the potter's wheel years ago, getting his hands icky with clay as Kaikeyi had tried teaching him the craft, but he was terrible at it. What he had enjoyed was swirling paint and applying it on dried pots in broad brushstrokes, and mother and son had spent many summer afternoons in each other's company, making pots that later sold in Ayodhya's markets on the novelty of being made by Kosala's youngest queen and her little son.

"Sit," Kaikeyi pointed to a *manchika* as she settled down on one herself. Bharat folded his arms across his chest and stood stubbornly facing his mother.

"So, what exactly am I doing that I shouldn't be doing?" Kaikeyi asked, arching her eyebrows.

Bharat drew a deep breath to get a hold on his temper. "Stop ordering Mandavi to bring Taksha here."

"I didn't order anyone. I just sent a request—"

"Then don't. I don't want Taksha to see you."

Kaikeyi's lips thinned in defiance. Leaning back in her seat, she crossed her legs and laced her fingers around one knee. "You can't stop me from seeing him," she said with a tilt of her head.

Taken aback, Bharat paused before placing a hand on his hip and rising to the challenge. "I can and I will," he scowled. "If need be, I will have you exiled from here. As king of Kosala, I can do that."

"Isn't it wonderful to see you finally accept your position as king of Kosala… even if it is only to separate a grandmother from her grandson," said Kaikeyi with an icy smile.

"Don't," Bharat warned in response. "Just don't tempt me."

He was about to turn around and leave when his mother spoke again. "You will not exile me."

Again, a challenge in her words, again that needling tone. Bharat looked to see Kaikeyi shaking her head at him pityingly. "You will not send me anywhere," she continued. "You might want to, perhaps even desperately, but you won't. I'll tell you why. Because Rama has told you not to, and *you* will not go against your brother's instructions, however much it hurts you. So no, you will not send me anywhere."

"What do you want?" Bharat shouted, throwing his hands up in exasperation.

"What do *I* want?" Kaikeyi repeated. Rising to her feet, she came and stood in front of her son. "I want you to sit on the throne of Kosala, and I want to see Taksha—"

"No!"

"No what?"

"No to both." Bharat turned away from his mother but swivelled right back. "Do you have any idea how much grief and misery you have caused… are causing *even now*?" he asked. His voice rising once again in anger, he continued, "It is because of you that mama had to slink out of Ayodhya in the dark of the night like some common thief." Bharat saw Kaikeyi open her mouth to say something, but he didn't give her a chance to speak. "Seeradhwaja Janak is in Ayodhya—"

"I heard…" Kaikeyi said.

"—and it broke my heart to see his anguish at Sita's absence—"

"It was Sita's wish to go with Rama—"

"—and Urmila shut in her room or in the library all day, all year round, living another version of an exile—"

"Again, it was Lakshmana's decision. I didn't ask for him to be exiled, so how am I responsible for Urmila's sorrow—"

"*How are you responsible?*" Bharat asked incredulously. "You are the only one responsible. It is your desire to see me as king that is responsible. It is your decision to demand Rama's exile that is responsible. You, you... *only you.*"

Bharat faced away from Kaikeyi in torment, and for a small moment, the room was quiet. Then, Kaikeyi spoke in calm, measured tones. "Your father gave your nana his word to name my son as his successor. He won my hand on the back of that assurance. Not once did I doubt that your father would keep that promise. But your father betrayed me and your nana by proclaiming Rama as his heir behind my back. *And I am the one being called bad here.* If I am responsible for anything, it is for following the dharma of a mother who wants what is her child's by right. Let me ask... had the situation been reversed, wouldn't Kausalya have wanted the same for her son? Would she have stood by and watched your father hand you a throne promised to Rama?"

The young king blinked and looked away, struggling for answers. Finally, with a sigh, he turned back to her. "I can understand a mother's desire to see her son become king. But what I fail to comprehend is your demand to have Rama sent into exile. Father made nana a promise to make your son king after him, so you insisted he honour his promise. Everyone tells me father agreed—"

"After lots of persuasion," Kaikeyi interrupted stonily.

"Still, he agreed, and you got what you wanted. Why the call for Rama's banishment then? What compelled you to be so thoughtless, *so* heartless?"

Stepping closer, Kaikeyi took her son by the shoulders. "Thoughtless?" she peered into Bharat's face. "You think I was thoughtless?" she laughed humourlessly. "You refuse to sit on the throne in Rama's absence. What are the chances you would have taken the throne had he *been* here?" After a pause, she continued, "Let us for a moment assume you had taken the throne. I have heard how you believe the people of Ayodhya dislike you because you became the king instead of their favourite Rama. If this is what it is like with Rama in exile, imagine what it would be like having him in Ayodhya when you are king. Ayodhya would be divided in its loyalty, and Kosala would have sunk into civil war in no time. By demanding Rama's exile, I saved Ayodhya and Kosala from being torn in a war of succession." She shook her head. "It wasn't thoughtless. I saved Ayodhya—for *you*."

"But why me?" Bharat threw his hands up as a bitter smile twisted his lips. "Why, when I wasn't even your favourite son?"

"What do you mean?" Kaikeyi narrowed her eyes in doubt and confusion.

"You know what I mean. When we were children, you used to heap praises on Rama for every little thing he achieved but ignored me no matter what I did. It was always 'Rama is so good at this, Rama is so great at that,' as if I was of no consequence to anyone. You were always putting Rama ahead, comparing me to him and finding that I didn't measure up. I was always less adequate, less talented. For as far back as my memory goes, I competed with Rama for every single thing—*including your love*. You made me compete, and Rama always won, and I always lost. Why didn't you just let me be then; why did you stop Rama from becoming king?

Did father's stupid promise to nana matter so much to you that you sent your favourite son into exile for the son who perpetually came second best?"

Astonishment blended with concern on Kaikeyi's face as she stared at her son. "Rama was never a favourite, Bharat," she spoke in a shaky voice. "And I never loved Rama more than I loved you. *Never*. You were everything to me."

"Then why those never-ending comparisons to Rama?"

Kaikeyi took a shallow breath. "That was *love*, Bharat," she said. "The idea behind praising Rama was to set him as an example so you'd push yourself harder to emulate your brother. I wanted you to strive towards the greatness that came so naturally to Rama. I didn't praise you because I didn't want you becoming complacent and settling for second best." Kaikeyi raised a hand to touch Bharat's cheek tenderly. "My praise for Rama didn't mean I loved him more. My praise for him was a mother's love at play—*my love for you*."

Bharat studied Kaikeyi in silence. A bird called somewhere, and sentries laughed. Pushing her hand away, Bharat stepped back. "This is insane. I don't get this love of yours, and if *this* is your idea of love…" he shook his head with vehemence, "I don't want Taksha to come under the influence of your love. *Ever*."

As he turned to leave, Bharat raised a finger in a final warning. "Stay away from my son."

A half-moon rode the western sky, bathing the palace and its grounds in its pale light as Bharat headed towards the royal stable. The night was still, and except for the muted swish of his dhoti against the long grass that bordered the narrow footpath, the silence was complete. Large bats swooped and skimmed occasionally over the king's head on broad, noiseless wings.

This time, Angara appeared suddenly, without a sound, out of the grass and straight in Bharat's way, twisting and wriggling with excitement, ears folded back in pleasure.

"Hey there!" Bharat dropped down in delight to pet the animal. "How are you, my friend?"

Angara leaped on his master with so much force that Bharat lost his balance and sat down with a bump. "Hey," he shouted in surprise. This only served to enthuse the dog, and it immediately clambered on top of him, paws on his shoulders, snuffling and panting heavily.

"*Shoo*... get off..." Siripala called, clapping his hands together as he limped out of his quarters.

"It's alright," Bharat laughed. Pushing Angara away, he got to his feet and dusted himself. "We were having fun."

The bodyguard approached. "I didn't expect you'd come, rajan. I mean... because of the guests in the palace."

"Oh, everyone's retired for the night," Bharat replied.

"You should too," Siripala said, knowing he was taking a liberty with the king. He gazed up at the night sky. "It's late."

"I couldn't sleep, so I thought I'd come and meet this fellow. It's been quite a few days since I last saw him." Bharat gave Angara's head a vigorous rub and the dog responded by nudging closer. "Has he been fed?" he asked.

"Yes. Like I said, I didn't think you'd come by..."

"It's fine." The king bent to stroke the dog, which stood with its tongue out, tail swishing idly as it enjoyed the affection being showered upon it.

"Five days."

Bharat looked at the bodyguard in confusion. "What?"

"It's five days since you saw him. It was the night of the attack."

Bharat nodded, remembering. Somewhere far away, a cricket chirruped.

"Hard to believe it was just five nights ago." He turned to look towards the river. Siripala lifted his eyes to take in the indistinct outline of the opposite bank, where the shadow of the Sanctum rose into the night.

"Everything was so peaceful," Bharat went on. "Then, suddenly, everything changed."

"We did well," said the old bodyguard. "A few lives were lost, but we did well."

"I am relieved we managed saving the sacred fire and most of the rishis." Bharat let out a sigh. "I only wish we had got to the mahamuni in time."

"No improvement there, I hear." Siripala paused to flick a globe of light into existence, but the king shook his head.

"There's plenty of moonlight," he pointed.

"Yes, rajan." Siripala snapped the light out. "What do the *vaidyas* say about the mahamuni?"

"They are as clueless." Bharat straightened, and Angara ambled off to investigate the grass. "I don't know what I will do without the mahamuni to guide me. He was such a pillar of strength."

"You still have the council," Siripala said. "Men whom your father trusted for support."

Bharat nodded and glanced again in the direction of the river. After a while, he turned to the bodyguard. "Can I ask you something?"

Siripala inclined his head.

"Sudhanva and Sheelabhadra… father obviously trusted both of them."

"Sheshagupta as well," the bodyguard added, speaking of the revenue minister.

"Right. But between Sudhanva and Sheelabhadra, whom did father trust more?"

Siripala shrugged, confessing ignorance. After a brief silence, he asked, "Does it even matter?"

It was Bharat's turn to be quiet. "If father had wanted a *kshatri*," he said at last, "which of them would he have picked for the post?"

This time, the silence stretched longer as the bodyguard pondered over the question. Finally, he looked at Bharat and said, "Did you know there were more eligible candidates than Gajakarna for the position of *mahanayaka* of Kosala's army? Braver men, better fighters?"

The king gave his head a puzzled shake, not knowing how Gajakarna came into the equation.

"Yet raja Dashratha made him the *mahanayaka*. Why?"

"Why?"

"It's funny how I asked your father the same question right here, in front of the stable, as he was preparing to ride somewhere," Siripala smiled. "His reason for picking Gajakarna was that unlike all the other candidates, Gajakarna never cared about being a *mahanayaka*."

The dog was back, nuzzling Bharat, demanding attention. "I don't get it," the king said, patting the animal's head.

"Your father was of the belief that when someone didn't care about a post or the privileges and authority it offered, they would discharge their duties without the fear of losing that post. They would choose a course of action that benefitted the greatest number of people, *and not one that ensured their own position remained secure.* Such people wouldn't care about staying in anyone's good books, and their actions wouldn't be dictated by self-interest."

"And Gajakarna was one such man," said Bharat slowly.

"He *is* one such man. He could be wrong, but he'd never be selfish. That is why he was made *mahanayaka*."

"And the reason father picked neither Sudhanva nor Sheelabhadra to be his *kshatri*," Bharat worked this out in his head, "was because he knew both wanted the post badly, and he didn't trust either of them to rise to the responsibility."

Siripala said nothing. The king looked away, deep in thought.

"Father was lucky to have had the mahamuni," he said at last with a sigh. "What am I supposed to do in the mahamuni's absence? Where am I to find someone who isn't interested in becoming a *kshatri*?"

Except for a few windows, the houses were all dark, and nothing disturbed the hush of slumber cocooning the old quarter. Even the dogs had gone off the streets, as though in deference to the lateness of the hour, and the only noise was the trudge of the night patrol's footsteps sounding in the main streets at regular intervals.

Behind one of the illuminated windows was Bakula's bedroom, where the records clerk sat on his bed cross-legged, watching the girl pour a measure of milk into a tumbler. The man seemed tired, shoulders slanted, bags under his eyes, age and gravity pulling his body downwards a little more every day.

"The *dandapala* didn't say why he was here," Bakula said thoughtfully, rubbing his knees with both palms to relieve the stiffness in the joints. "It could be anything..."

"It could," the girl replied, but her tone wasn't in agreement with her words.

"But you don't think so," said the man, catching on.

"In all these years, hardly has a single *dandapala* stepped into this street. Now, all of a sudden, one shows up at our door... Too much of a coincidence, don't you think?"

Bakula frowned and nodded. "They suspect something,"

"I'm not sure if *they* suspect something or *he* suspects something," the girl slipped a spoon into the milk and stirred it. "Had the *dandapalas* suspected something, they'd have come with a full force of militiamen to take you in for questioning." She shook her head. "I think *this* particular *dandapala* has a suspicion, but because he is unsure, he first wants to chat with you..."

"Maybe it is better I leave when I have the chance—"

"Don't be foolish. If you run now, it would be an admission of guilt and we'd all be finished."

"What do I do then?"

The girl came to the bed and handed the tumbler to the clerk. "Drink your milk and go to sleep," she said with a reassuring nod. "We will think of a way out in the morning."

Bakula took a sip and made a face. "Mrrph," he grunted. "How I hate this thing! Yes, I know..." he raised a hand to stop the girl, "... it is good for my health. I know..."

Lifting the glass to his lips, he downed its contents in one long pull before handing the tumbler back, hacking and clearing his throat to rid himself of the drink's aftertaste. Slowly, he stretched his legs and laid his fatigued body down on the bed.

"If the *dandapala* who called is the only one having a suspicion, maybe we should remove him from our path," the clerk mused aloud as he crossed his fingers over his stomach to gaze at the ceiling. "Did he say he would come again tomorrow? We could offer him something to drink..."

"He said he would meet you, but he didn't say where."

"Mmm-hmmm. Maybe I should first see what he wants, how much he knows... Like I said, he might want to meet about something else... something totally unconnected..."

The girl nodded, watching Bakula keenly.

"What...? What's the matter?" the clerk asked. "Why are you looking at me like tha—"

He stopped, suddenly conscious of the flutter in his chest. He felt light-headed, and sweat began beading his brow as his breathing became laboured and his vision swam.

"What is happening?" he gasped, grabbing at the sheets and kicking his legs in panic. He turned to the girl with wide, unfocused eyes. "What have you done to me?"

"You were right," she stated calmly. "It is better you leave than be caught by the *dandapala*."

"What did you do?" the words came out of Bakula in a strangulated scream. "*It was the milk.*"

"A pinch of *vajranaga*, that's all," the girl said. "It will soon be over."

"Why..." The old clerk's face contorted in anger and bitterness. "Vile creature... you evil..."

A fit of coughing overcame Bakula. Gagging and groaning, he rolled off the bed and fell to the floor, clawing his chest as pain shot through his torso, the poison taking effect. His eyes rolled back in their sockets and he flipped to one side, retching and huddling into himself in the final throes of death. The girl watched the whole thing with a blank expression, arms folded in front of her. The clerk drew a huge breath and his body heaved up once before it sank to the ground in ultimate surrender.

After waiting to ascertain that she had succeeded in her mission, the girl walked over to the small bookkeeper's desk that Bakula used. Seating herself on the mat, she opened the desk and drew out a few palm leaves and a wooden stylus. Slowly, without hurry, she composed a message on the leaves, unmindful of the clerk's body lying less than three yards away. Once she had put all her thoughts down, she set the stylus aside, uttered a mantra and blew on the leaves. The leaves caught fire and turned crisp. Crushing the blackened leaves in her fist, the girl rose and crossed to the window.

Opening her cupped palm, she blew the cinder out into the dark.

The black of the burned palm leaves met with the black of the night, and enabled by black magic, the girl's message took flight and carried from Ayodhya to the far, far south.

# *five*

FOR THE SECOND YEAR RUNNING, SUMMER CAME EARLY AND full of resentment.

Unbearable heat laid siege of Ayodhya from daybreak and beat down on the city all day, forcing people to remain indoors and punishing those who strayed out with sunstrokes. The Sarayu had depleted over the year, receding from its banks and leaving its bed exposed with cracks where frogs nestled and died. In the mornings and evenings, monkeys flocked to the river to quench their thirst and cavort in the damp mud, and herons stalked the shallows searching for fish. The heat lasted late into the night, not letting up until a few hours to dawn, so morning after morning, the city looked sleepless and irritable. Half the year had passed and the monsoon was due, but the sky stayed blue and rid of clouds, so canals were forever being dug to irrigate the fields and keep the crops from withering.

Bharat was up early as usual, and Taksha seemed to have taken after him in this respect, so that they were now on a balcony, observing one of the endless troops of monkeys making their way across the palace grounds. The adults all walked in sober, sedate lines along the roofs and ledges of the palace, but in contrast, the baby and adolescent monkeys leaped and scrambled and swung as it pleased them, exploring the world with curious eyes. Taksha studied the animals carefully, wriggling this way and that on Bharat's arm to follow the antics of the baby monkeys.

"There," he lisped, pointing and turning to face his father. He was going to be two soon, but he was slow in speech, though he could run and romp around with Angara tirelessly for hours.

"There," Bharat nodded and smiled.

The sun was up, illuminating a portion of the wall across the balcony bright orange and framing a mother monkey and her baby seated on a ledge. Taksha and Bharat watched the baby scamper along the ledge while the mother looked on with bored detachment. Losing interest, the mother monkey rose, and with a leap, gained the parapet running a couple of feet above the ledge. The baby looked at the mother, her back turned in indifference… and it became plain that the baby monkey was too small to make it to the parapet without support.

"Watch what it does," he whispered to Taksha, who was staring with big, round eyes anyway.

The baby monkey surveyed the parapet, assessing its situation. Then, grabbing its mother's tail hanging down the side of the parapet, it pulled itself up hand over hand and eased into its mother's lap.

"Did you see that?" Bharat laughed, surprised and amused by the baby's resourcefulness.

"That," Taksha repeated, kicking and grinning with mirth. "See?"

"Ah, here you both are!" Mandavi stepped onto the balcony. "What's all the excitement about?"

"Monkeys, what else?" replied Bharat. "This monkey likes them." He poked Taksha in the side, making the boy giggle and twist away.

"I think he likes all animals," said Mandavi, handing Bharat a small bowl filled with sugar and grated coconut. "The maid was saying that he likes to visit the cowshed to play with the calves. And anyway, he is best friends with that dog you brought from Rajagriha."

"From Manglapuri," Bharat corrected, setting Taksha down. He shook a scoop of the sugar and coconut into his palm and tossed it into his mouth. "And the dog has a name. Angara."

"Angara?" the kid asked, looking up at his father with hopeful eyes.

"Yes, but not now," Bharat smiled and ruffled the boy's hair. "The court is waiting for me. We will go in the evening."

"Go... evening..." Taksha said, showing he had understood.

"Here." Mandavi extended a length of finely spun cloth to her husband. Taking it and spreading it open, Bharat held the cloth by its corners and scrutinized it carefully. Made of quality cotton, it was a complicated weave, incorporating subtle geometric patterns that appeared to shift shape whenever the angle of the light changed.

"This was what you were weaving for me," he observed.

"Do you like it?"

"When have I ever not liked anything you have woven?" He looked away, distracted.

"That's not an answer to my question."

"Of course, I like it." Bharat draped the *angavastram* over his shoulders. "Makes me handsome, see?" He struck a dashing pose, hand on hip, chin up, the face in profile, before giving Mandavi a broad grin.

"I miss that smile these days," Mandavi said quietly.

The grin unravelled on Bharat's face. He checked to see if the kid was listening and leaned close to Mandavi. "There's been another disappearance," he murmured into her ear.

"One more?" Mandavi's eyes widened. She instinctively reached out for Taksha and drew him to her.

Bharat nodded. "I must go," he mumbled.

The chamber where Bharat conducted the affairs of the state was next to the Ayodhya's Throne Room. Once he had made his mind up against sitting on Kosala's throne, Bharat had, in a show of symbolic defiance, placed Rama's *padukas* on the footstool at the base of the throne. "There is place for only one pair of feet on that footstool," he had said to his mother that same evening two years ago, "and that place has been taken by Rama's *padukas*. They will remain there until the day brother returns from his exile to take the throne." The decision to use the annex instead of the Throne Room for administrative purposes was an extension of the same logic, a reminder to everyone that he was here only on behalf of the true king of Kosala.

That morning's court being a private affair, public petitions were not being entertained, and the chamber and its environs were relatively quiet and free of activity. No more than twenty people were in the room that could seat at least a hundred, and as Bharat walked in, the buzz of voices dropped away into silence. The king made his way to a *sayyasana* and sat, motioning to everyone else to take their places.

Bharat sought out the courtier Vijaya. "The latest disappearance," he paused. "The details…"

"A girl from the riverside, the daughter of a basketmaker." Vijaya's expression was grim. "No older than fifteen."

Bharat felt his heart sinking amid fresh murmurs of disquiet.

"It's the fourth disappearance within a month," someone muttered.

"When was this?" Bharat asked.

"She was last seen yesterday evening around sundown, rajan," Vijaya answered. "She had been sent to the well to fetch water, and it seems she spoke to a couple of her friends there, who then left her and went back to their own homes. When the girl didn't return, her parents went to look for her, but she was nowhere to be found."

"Did they look in the well?" a courtier asked ominously.

"They did. She wasn't in it."

"She could have run away," someone else suggested, though without much conviction.

Bharat frowned. While the possibility could not be overruled, he wasn't inclined to believe the girl was absconding. The disappearance followed the pattern of the previous three cases, people vanishing without a trace, leaving questions and grieving families behind. Worse, this time, the missing person was a young girl, which made it even more unsettling. Word would spread and panic was bound to take root. It was over a year since the rakshasas had come, but they had left a fear behind that seemed to roam the streets and alleyways of Ayodhya, preying on the public at will.

"Have the *dandapalas* been informed?" Bharat asked.

"They have, rajan," said Vijaya.

"Not much good will come of that," remarked an old, bent courtier. "They're perfectly useless."

The king made a note of the heads nodding in agreement. The skepticism was understandable. Even a year after the event, the *dandapalas* had discovered nothing of value about the rakshasa attack and its origins, and even though a month had passed, they'd made practically no progress in their investigations into the spate of disappearances. This wasn't a performance that inspired confidence.

"What exactly are the *dandapalas* doing?" he asked irritably. "Three people have been missing for close to a month now, and I'm yet to see any reports on the efforts taken to find them." He snapped his fingers and looked at Vijaya. "I want to meet the head of the *dandapalas* right after we're done here. Also, get *mahanayaka* Baladitya to increase the number of *nagarapala* patrols in the city. Those behind what's happening must be found and stopped."

Once Vijaya had left to carry out the instructions, Bharat turned his attention to the palm leaves stacked neatly by his side, relieved to have something other than the disappearances to occupy his mind. The leaves were etched with revenue records and rustled drily as he thumbed through them. Overhead, ropes creaked and magic occasionally hummed from the bamboo-pleated fans that swung from the ceiling.

The relief lasted all of one minute.

With a deepening frown, the king tapped the palm leaves. "This is worrying," he addressed the men seated before of him. "Net income has dropped for the third month in a row."

The men shifted in their seats. "There are many contributing factors, rajan," said Sheshagupta. A small, diffident man with a round face and a white beard, he had served as Kosala's revenue minister for well over three decades, winning

Dashratha's trust and respect for his meticulous approach to economic planning.

The year's revenue projections had already gone haywire due to the attack on the Sanctum, the rebuilding of the *homagriha* and the construction of the Sanctum garrison having driven expenses up. The recruitment of new *nagarapalas* had also had an adverse impact on revenue reserves, and as most of the inductees were from outside the city, a new garrison had to be built for them, further adding to the crunch on the coffers. If unexpected costs had spiralled on the one hand, a pathetic monsoon—the worst in living memory—had ensured income was negligible. Prices of most commodities were on the rise, and essential goods like grain and oilseed were in short supply.

"I understand the year has been bad," said Bharat, "but we must arrest the slide."

"There's only so much in our control," Sheshagupta shrugged. "The monsoon failing the way it did last year was totally unexpected."

"It's all because the sacred fire was nearly destroyed in the attack," one of the courtiers opined from the back.

"Then things should return to normal this year," another man replied, sounding hopeful while gazing out of the window with uncertain eyes. Already, whispers of the rain playing truant again were doing the rounds, and a spectre of drought hung over Kosala. "Once the fire has been reinstated in the *homagriha*, conditions are bound to improve," he insisted, not sounding convinced by his own words.

The doubts and fears were natural. Mahamuni Vashishtha still lay in the palace, paralyzed from head to toe and unable to utter the potent mantras that caused the sacred fire to burn bright and sustain *rta*—*rta* that not only made the ether fertile for magic, but also made the land bountiful and enabled the seasons to turn so that the rains could come on time. Sure, the rest of the rishis were tending to the *homa* fire, and the general belief was the fire would burn better and brighter once it was shifted to the new *homagriha* in about a month or so. But in the mahamuni's absence, no one knew how effective these efforts would be and whether they would all add up to keep Kosala safe from deprivation.

Not just the monsoons, there were signs of the magic beginning to wane as well. Nothing major or dramatic. Small things, like a globule failing to illuminate on the first try, a flour mill losing speed without reason or bionic horses not responding fast enough to mantras. Minor flaws that would have been overlooked elsewhere in Jambudvipa, but not in Ayodhya, because magic hadn't wavered in Kosala since the time the *homa* fire had come under the guardianship of mahamuni Vashishtha more than a generation ago.

Now that the monsoon was missing and the magic had begun stuttering, there was trepidation in people's hearts…

"Can't we raise taxes?" enquired a bald courtier, who was in charge of urban planning.

"That would be hard on the people, especially on the back of a bad monsoon," Bharat replied.

"I agree with the rajan," said Sheshagupta. The courtier settled back in his seat.

"The real problem is Madhupura," the revenue minister continued, combing his beard with his fingers. "Lavanyasurya has revised tariffs *three* times in the last year or so."

"Arbitrarily," Bharat emphasized.

"Oh, totally. His father would consult us, talk to your father and the others before raising tariffs. But the son… *nothing*. Forget consulting anyone, not once has he bothered to inform us or give us notice of any kind. One day we are paying such-and-such amount as tariffs. The next day, it's a new figure." Sheshagupta scowled. "Formal requests have been sent, twice, asking Madhupura to maintain a consistent tariff revision policy, but Lavanyasurya hasn't cared to reply at all."

A murmur of outrage swelled at such blatant disrespect by Madhupura as Bharat addressed the courtier seated to Sheshagupta's left. "What do *you* think?"

The man was dark and handsome, with a neat black moustache and signs of grey at the temples. He wore the sash of a guild master over one shoulder. This was Pushyanta of Sravasti, possibly the biggest merchant in Kosala. "Pardon me, rajan?" he blinked, looking preoccupied.

"Why is Lavanyasurya doing this?" Bharat clarified.

"Because he can," the guild master replied. "He knows he has a stranglehold on trade that goes through Madhupura… which is effectively *all* the trade in Jambudvipa."

"Perhaps you could have a word with the guild master of Madhupura?" Bharat suggested.

"I met Amulya when I was there last year, and I shared our concerns with him," said Pushyanta. "He insists he is powerless to intervene."

"I suspect he has no reason to either," said Sheshagupta. "They are raking in money, so where's the incentive to intervene?"

"But there has to be a limit," Bharat exclaimed.

"I shall send Madhupura another note," the revenue minister said, quickly adding, "*—on your behalf—*raising our concerns and explaining why we think these tariffs are steep and unfair. I shall urge Lavanyasurya to consider rolling back the tariffs a little."

"I doubt he will do that," Bharat said, setting the palm leaves aside. "But tell him to desist from increasing tariffs at such short intervals. If he goes on like this, we'll have no choice but to increase the prices of the goods we export."

"That will harm trade," the guild master objected. "We'd lose what competitive advantage we have."

"I thought our competitive advantage was quality, and not price," observed another courtier.

"Quality is a competitive advantage only when the price is right," Pushyanta countered.

"And anyway, there's evidence that demand can drop even when the price is consistent," a deep voice spoke from the far left. Heads turned to look at Sudhanva of Sankasya.

"How do you mean?" Bharat appraised the nobleman.

"As the respected guild master will vouch, revenue generated from the cultivation and export of indigo dropped last year… *though its market price remained the same*. What this means—"

"That is nonsense," another voice rose, harsh and agitated. This was Sheelabhadra, the *adhipati* of Kusinagara, and the largest cultivator and exporter of indigo in Kosala. "There has been no drop in revenue—"

"I am not making false claims, rajan," Sudhanva raised his hands in defence. "The guild master can verify the facts for us—"

"There has been *no* drop in revenue from indigo—" Sheelabhadra insisted, rising to his feet.

"Sirs... *respected* sirs..." Sheshagupta pleaded. "Please calm down."

Sheelabhadra sank to his seat and silence descended on the gathering. Bharat eyed Pushyanta. "Is it true that the revenue from indigo dropped last year?"

"Mmm... well," the guild master hesitated, "it is not like the revenue dropped—"

"There," Sheelabhadra cried out in exultation. "See?"

"—it is that the demand for indigo did not see an increase," Pushyanta concluded.

"See...? There's a difference there between revenue dropping and demand not increasing," the *adhipati* of Kusinagara called to Sudhanva in a challenging tone.

"When demand doesn't increase, revenue doesn't increase either," said Sudhanva with a smirk. "Whereas in the case of sugar, demand as well as revenue increased. Our revenue minister can easily confirm this for us."

All eyes went to Sheshagupta, who nodded. Even Sheelabhadra kept a grudging silence.

"So, if I may make a suggestion," Sudhanva went on, "we should increase our focus on sugarcane to boost the economy. More land must be opened for cane cultivation, and more resources should be allocated for the production and export of sugar. The demand for indigo is flattening, so let us divert resources to sugarcane—"

"You are saying this because you are in the sugar business," Sheelabhadra protested.

"I am saying this because the economy needs all the support it can get," Sudhanva countered, pointing to the palm records in Bharat's hands.

"Just because indigo didn't see an increase last year doesn't mean anything," Sheelabhadra rumbled

"If demand doesn't increase even when the price remains the same, it means people are tiring of the product; they are saturated," Sudhanva shrugged. "That's bad news."

"What… where are you getting your information from?" Sheelabhadra stuttered, going red in anger, the natural creases on his forehead deepening.

"I think the guild master can confirm that the lure for indigo is fading in the western markets," Sudhanva looked expectantly at Pushyanta.

"I… have heard it said…" Pushyanta started and stopped.

"Heard? From whom? *Where*?" Sheelabhadra exploded. "I am in the business of making dyes, and I have not heard this from *any* of my merchant friends." He gave the guild master a sarcastic smile. "You'd hear anything that is in the interest of your father-in-law there—" he pointed to Sudhanva.

"What do you mean by *my* interest?" Sudhanva demanded angrily. "The drop in demand for indigo is a fact that has nothing to do with the guild master being my son-in-law."

"Sure," Sheelabhadra snorted. "Thankfully, I keep independent track of my businesses, so I'm not at the mercy of the guild and all the misinformation being churned out of there."

"Maybe you should listen to the guild then," Yadudeva spoke with a leer. "You'd be wiser."

"What is that supposed to mean—"

"Enough… *enough.*" Bharat's voice cracked like a whip, bouncing around the vast and empty chamber. He looked from Yadudeva and Sudhanva to Sheelabhadra and back. "This is the court of Ayodhya, where you serve as esteemed courtiers. Let it not be said that this court has started displaying the characteristics of a market."

Bharat waited for all three men to subside into silence before continuing. "Kosala is at the mercy of another bad monsoon, and its people are suffering. There is something inexplicable out there that is taking people away, and we don't know why or where. The magic is dipping, and mahamuni Vashishtha can't help us. Kosala is faced with challenges as never before, so let us not fritter our energies on arguing the merits of sugar over indigo or vice versa. The indigo and sugar we grow, that *you* grow, have made Kosala what it is, and we can proudly say that the kingdoms of Jambudvipa and beyond envy us for our indigo and sugar. Yajmaan," he looked at Sudhanva and Sheelabhadra, "you make us proud."

The *adhipatis* joined their palms in a *pranaam*. Bharat addressed Sheelabhadra first. "One poor year is no indication of a trend, so we shall continue to invest in the production of indigo as we have always done." He turned to Sudhanva. "The court is delighted to see the demand for sugar is increasing. We will do our best to make sure cane cultivation does not suffer in any way and our output of sugar continues to keep pace with the growing demand."

Finally, Bharat looked at Pushyanta. "If the guild has an inkling that a product which we export is losing its appeal, the guild should make an informed study and give its report to the esteemed revenue minister and the court. It will not suffice to have rumours floating around, influencing policy. I hope that is clear."

Bharat's words still hung in the air, and the court had barely settled down when Vijaya appeared at the door. Seeing the courtier's expression, the king paused. "Yes?"

"Mitraka, the chief of the *dandapalas* is here," the courtier said. With a pause, he added, "Also, we may have another disappearance. The old palace jeweller. He was a favourite of all three queen mothers. His sons say he wasn't in his bed this morning, and he hasn't been seen since."

They had stalked the riders all morning, and they set up the ambush in a steep ravine where the path narrowed beside the mountain stream.

The riders were seven in number, and all wore swords and daggers in their belts. Besides their own mounts, they had between them four pack horses laden with *goni* sacks and crude wooden crates, and they were passing through a remote and inhospitable part of the hills that even the nomadic goatherds avoided—out of fear of wild animals and outlaws.

In fact, it was a family of goatherds that had alerted the Kekeyan patrol about the mysterious band of riders two days earlier; a band riding so far north of the established trade routes that it had immediately aroused the patrol's suspicion.

The riders were forced to ride single file through the ravine, the rushing stream to their right, a sheer wall to their left. They had no room to manoeuvre, all of them stringed out and vulnerable, and they were in the middle of the gorge when the captain of the Kekeyan patrol stepped onto the path at the head of the defile and hailed them.

"Rein in your horses and stay where you are!"

The riders instinctively went for their *karapalas*, the ones at the rear also trying to turn their steeds around, but the captain of the patrol stalled them. "You are surrounded by Kekeyan forces. Do not offer resistance or my archers will shoot."

On cue, three Kekeyan archers materialized from behind the trees at the opening of the gorge, their arrows nocked and pointed at the seven riders. The riders looked behind to see four more archers blocking the other exit, while two archers stood above their heads at the lip of the gorge. Five or six swordsmen also emerged from the tree line on top to join the captain and the archers.

"Which of you is the leader here?" the captain asked. The rider in front reluctantly put his hand up, and the captain motioned him to dismount. "Get down and come here. The rest of you, stay in your places." Seeing the riders hesitate and glance at one another, the captain drew his *karapala*. "Do as you are told or face the consequences."

The leader of the riders approached the captain on heavy feet. He was a tall man, but the captain was still taller and powerfully built. "Who are you?" the captain asked. He gestured at the pack horses. "And what do you have there?"

"We are Gandharan merchants, sir," the leader of the riders replied. "Returning home."

"Merchants?" the captain ran a skeptical eye over the rider's sheathed sword and dagger. "Why those?" he asked, pointing.

"To guard against outlaws, sir."

"Hmm. Where are you coming from?"

"Sakala, sir."

"You are way north of the road that traders usually take, you realize. Why the circuitous route?"

"We lost our way in the dark of night."

"You carry weapons to defend yourself against outlaws, but you aren't careful about sticking to the safety of the familiar road." The captain frowned. "I find that strange."

The other man said nothing. The riders in the gorge fidgeted on their horses.

"Okay, so you are merchants. Let us see your guild seals and trade receipts." The leader blinked in incomprehension, so the captain said pointedly, "Your guild seals? Given to you by the trade guild at Gandhara, which authorize you to trade? Your trade receipts? Proof that you have traded whatever you have on the backs of those animals, and without which you wouldn't have been cleared to leave Sakala?"

Seeing the man clear his throat nervously, the captain placed the tip of his *karapala* on the leader's chest. "Don't move, or I will lean on my sword." He raised his voice so the rest of the riders in the defile could hear him. "Drop your knives and swords and get off your horses. Easy, or every one of you will die."

"Please, there has been a mistake," the leader spoke quickly. "You have confused us for robbers—"

"By not producing the guild seals and trade receipts, you have *confirmed* that you are robbers. Shut up and drop your belt."

It took the Kekeyan patrol a few minutes to disarm the riders and herd them out of the ravine. As the riders were forced onto a grassy embankment and made to sit down, the captain spoke to one of his men. "Let's see what they have been stealing," he nodded towards the laden pack horses.

"Sir, we are not outlaws," the leader of the riders began. "This is a big mistake—"

"It is a big mistake, but you will have plenty of time to repent for it in our prisons," the captain cut him short. "Now, keep quiet."

"Sir, we are soldiers from Gandhara. We haven't stolen any of this. These are gifts from Madra—"

"*Gifts* from Madra?" The captain's eyebrows rose in mock surprise. "A moment ago, you were merchants. Now, you are *soldiers*. Next, you will be princes, I presume?"

"You must believe us—"

"I *must* believe you?" The captain grinned at his men. "I *must*, it seems." He turned back to the riders. "And what if I don't?"

"Captain..." the soldier who had gone to inspect the sacks on the pack horses called. "I think you should look at this."

"What is it?" the captain asked, scrutinizing the object in the soldier's hand. It was too far to see clearly though, that too in the shadow of the ravine. "Bring it here."

When the soldier drew near, it became clear that he bore a scroll made from cloth and wood. The captain took the scroll and unfurled it. The cloth was of white silk, and on it, painted in delicate letters, was a message.

An order, actually... *an extortion note*.

The Kekeyan captain read the message slowly, eyeing the official seal stamped at the bottom of the scroll. His eyes widened as he reached the end of the message.

He turned his head and looked at the leader of the riders, suddenly unsure of himself.

There was nothing to connect the five disappearances, Dileepa thought to himself, nothing that any of the five people had in common, other than the fact that they were all from Ayodhya.

The farmer had been the first to go, almost a month ago. As always, his wife had taken him his lunch where he was tilling the land. But when she got there, all she found was the oxen standing in the half-turned field in the baking heat, yoked to the plough. No one had been around to witness what had happened or where her husband had gone, and no one cared much when she made a noise about it. Husband and wife had been known to quarrel, and everyone assumed the farmer had had enough and had left his wife for good. Then, the utensil maker's apprentice vanished; he had gone to take delivery of a new set of implements, but he never reached the market, and he never came back. The man had no family in Ayodhya, and his master had no clue where he could have gone. The disappearance wouldn't have been reported had the apprentice not gone off with the thirty *karshapanas* meant for the purchase of the implements. "He left when he had the money and the opportunity," the utensil maker had told Dileepa with a scowl. "I should never have trusted that thankless dog."

The next to go had been the eldest son of a prominent moneylender, the first person of influence to vanish. The young man had gone to collect an outstanding sum of money from a debtor, and when he didn't return home at night, his father informed the *nagarapalas*, who launched a hunt but couldn't find him. Suspecting the debtor of foul play, the moneylender petitioned the raja's court to launch an investigation, and the *dandapalas* had stepped in. The debtor, a well-known cloth merchant, insisted he had handed the money over to the son, who had then left his house. The finger of doubt lay firmly on the merchant when a witness—a senior scribe in the palace—revealed that he had met the moneylender's son the afternoon he had disappeared. The scribe testified that the young man had told him he was on his way home after collecting money from a debtor, which confirmed that he had indeed been returning from the cloth merchant's house.

That was a week ago, and the *dandapalas* had no new information on the moneylender's son. And now, the basketmaker's daughter and the old jeweller had vanished, and the raja was furious and wanted results. Mitraka had been issued an ultimatum, and the chief had given Dileepa and the rest of the *dandapalas* an ultimatum.

Dileepa had nothing on which to go on, no lead that he could follow. He had already met the girl's family; the worried father, the inconsolable mother, and two kid sisters old enough to realize something was wrong without really understanding the gravity of the situation. The girl was obedient and well mannered, both parents swore, and would do nothing that brought disrepute to the family. Her friends seemed to share that opinion, adding that she was doted upon by her parents, which made the possibility of her having run away seem unlikely. There were no signs of any struggle near the well where she had gone to draw water, nor any along the route home. So, if she hadn't been abducted by force, and if she hadn't gone away on her own accord, *where was she?* And speaking of abduction, what was the point in abducting the girl and the utensil maker's helper? He saw why someone would abduct the moneylender's son or the jeweller, or even the farmer. But the basketmaker had no money to offer in exchange for his daughter, and the other fellow didn't even have a family to demand ransom from. The five people were so different that it was hard to find a pattern behind their disappearances...

There was *one* thing that the five disappearances had in common—there was no evidence of what had happened, no one had seen anything. Which was pretty strange, Dileepa considered, as he turned into the old quarter. The farmer had gone from the fields outside Ayodhya, but the others had disappeared from within the city; yet none of them had been seen by the *nagarapalas* at the gates, or by anyone else, for that matter. One moment, they were there, and the next... *poof*... It was almost as if they had been swallowed whole by the city.

Absorbed in his thoughts, Dileepa let his feet guide him down streets that he had become quite accustomed to walking over the past few months. A year ago, he had had to ask his way around the old quarter while hunting for the records clerk's house, but now he was familiar with most of the roads, particularly the ones that led to the crumbling mansion that lay almost at the centre of the quarter. In fact, it was towards this building that Dileepa was now headed in the hope of seeing the girl he had first laid eyes on the night he had knocked on the records clerk's door.

Nandana, the girl had told him her name from that enchantingly lit doorway.

The second time he saw the girl, she was a wreck, seated on the floor of her house and weeping over the death of her father. Dileepa had learned that the records clerk had passed away on the same night he had called, the *vaidya* in the locality attributing the cause of his death to a heart failure. The girl was alone and broken in spirit, and seeing the state she was in, Dileepa had decided to abandon his enquiry. He hadn't brought the records clerk to the notice of his superiors so far, and with the man now dead, the trail had run cold anyway, he figured. He also didn't have the heart to tell the poor girl that he had suspected her father was connected to the attack on the Sanctum. Later, when Nandana had asked him why he had wanted to see her father, the *dandapala* had lied, saying he was looking for lost records pertaining to old land deeds, and he'd hoped her father could have helped him find them.

With neither parent there to care for her, Nandana was being looked after by kindly neighbours, but it was obvious to Dileepa that she could not live off the generosity of others forever. The *dandapala* had been secretly formulating a plan to free Nandana from a debt of kindness when, one morning, dropping in to check on the girl, he was shocked to see a trade cart in front of the house, loaded with her belongings. The girl had told Dileepa that she was leaving for Angadesh to be with her maternal aunt, and the *dandapala* had quietly locked the door on his plans and cast the key away while bidding her a sad farewell.

That had been almost a year ago, and Dileepa had since got his life back on track when one evening six months later, while lounging along the city's waterfront, he observed a barge laden with weaving looms and furniture draw up to the dock. Two women stepped off the barge, both striking in looks. But the young *dandapala* had eyes for only one of them. The one he had never expected to see again in this lifetime.

Nandana had returned to Ayodhya.

Dileepa turned into the street at the end of which sat the mansion that Nandana's aunt had since acquired for herself and her niece, and which also housed the looms that they had brought with them from Angadesh. It transpired that the aunt was an inspired designer and an excellent weaver, who had earned quite a name for herself in Angadesh. Though Nandana had joined her, the girl's heart was clearly in the city where she had grown up, so aunt and niece had relocated to Ayodhya, where the aunt set about rebuilding her weaving practice. The enterprising woman had put her life's savings into the old, sprawling mansion and set up shop, hiring talent locally to work the looms. In just a few short months, the cloth produced inside the mansion had caught the attention of the city's bigger textile merchants, and Ma Parnalata's name was already being spoken with respect in the relevant circles.

Feeling the same sense of exhilaration that had coursed through him that evening on Ayodhya's pier, Dileepa turned into the mansion's open doorway, crossed the outer courtyard and climbed the ten steps that brought him to the building's inner courtyard. The scent of *sambrani* greeted him as he entered the courtyard, which was filled with fragrant smoke that caused the sunshine that came in from the high, sky-lit ceiling to fragment into beams. Large fans hung from poles, stirring the air and sending the smoke into lazy swirls, and seated under the fans in the pool of sunlight, draped in smoke, was Ma Parnalata, laughing heartily at a joke that one of the women sitting around her had cracked. Approaching her sixties, Ma Parnalata was chubby in a caring, maternal sort of way, with a round, jovial face that appeared to be on the constant lookout for an excuse to laugh. She had crinkly grey hair that showed a tendency to escape in all directions, refusing to stay in the bun she had made on top of her head. She wore a necklace of *rudraksha* beads with bracelets to match. Her eyes, which she had now turned upon the *dandapala*, were green in colour, and had an indistinct quality about them.

"Oh, look who has come visiting," she croaked in a hoarse voice that wasn't lacking in warmth, waving away the smoke that enveloped her. "Get up, girls," she shooed the women around her, "get a *manchika*. You… bring our guest a glass of fresh, sweetened lime water. Come… welcome to this hovel, *dandapala*. I apologize for this mess. We are working on new designs… come, sit. Girl, get the fans to move faster. It must have been hot in the sun…"

"It's okay, Ma," Dileepa smiled, patting down the air in front of him to get her to relax. "Please. I was just passing by, so I dropped in to give you my regards. I must take my leave now."

"So nice of you to come… But you can't go just like that. Sit down a minute. Have something to drink. Ayodhya will not come to a standstill if you take a moment's break." She laughed and the *dandapala* did likewise. "Sit, sit," she pointed to a *manchika* that Dileepa lowered himself onto. "How have you been?"

"I am well."

"And your mother and father and little brother?"

"They are well too, Ma." Nandana called her Ma, and when he had called her that, nobody had objected. So, he had stuck to Ma.

"You must bring them to the city sometime," Parnalata said, brushing threads of yarn from her lap. "We would love to meet all of them."

Dileepa felt himself blush, but he hoped the old woman hadn't noticed. If she had, he hoped she would ascribe it to the sun's heat. One of the women employed to work the looms handed him a tumbler of sweetened lime water. The *dandapala* took a sip and instantly felt refreshed. The mansion was strangely silent, so the clacking of the wooden looms on the floors above felt loud, as did the crackle of magic in the rings of current that powered the fans. The street noises that had accompanied him seemed to have stayed outside, and sitting here, it was hard to guess the mansion was in the midst of the busy old quarter.

"How is work?"

"Tough," shrugged Dileepa. "I am investigating the disappearance. You would have heard..."

"Yes. Some moneylender's son."

"A young girl disappeared yesterday. And a jeweller's been missing since this morning."

"Young girl?" Parnalata's hand flew to her mouth. "Where?"

"Near the river. She went to fetch water and didn't come back. We're looking everywhere."

"What is the world coming to?" the woman shook her head sadly. "Imagine had this happened to Nandana when she was alone here... I mean, I know you were here and all that. But still..."

Taking another sip of the drink, Dileepa glanced at the balconies that overlooked the courtyard. "Where is Nandana?" he asked, trying to sound casual. "Isn't she home?"

"She is," Parnalata smiled. "She's probably resting... I'll ask one of the girls to wake her—"

"No, no," Dileepa protested, "let her rest. I just asked out of curiosity—"

"No, it's alright. It is time for her to wake up anyway... Listen," she called to one of the women, "wake Nandana up. Tell her the *dandapala* is here."

"It's okay. You needn't have bothered," Dileepa said, muffling his protestations in the tumbler.

When Nandana descended the stairs and entered the courtyard a little while later, Dileepa felt his breath catch in his throat. The woman had had that effect on him from that first evening when she had met him in the doorway of her old house, but in the *dandapala's* eyes, she had grown even more beautiful with the passage of time.

"This is a surprise," she said, smiling when their eyes met.

"I was just passing by—" Dileepa began.

"He came in to pay his regards, and I made him sit down and drink something nice," Parnalata finished.

"Good of you, Ma." Nandana turned her black eyes on Dileepa. "And good of you to come."

"Now that you are here, why don't you show the *dandapala* the lotuses blooming in the well?"

"The lotuses have bloomed?" Dileepa asked in excitement. When aunt and niece had moved in, he had brought some lotus seeds to put in the big well that had been built to the rear of the house. "I'd like to see them."

"Come on, then."

The *dandapala* fell in step beside the girl, and they walked into the shadows beyond which was the stone well, filled with frogs and big, black fish. Dileepa was engrossed in listening to Nandana, mesmerized by the soft velvet of her voice, so he didn't look back at Ma Parnalata.

If he had, he might have wondered about the expression on the old woman's face—especially her smile, which went from indulgent to cunning in a matter of seconds.

Shrill squeals of delight rose into the still evening air as Taksha ran around in circles, his face flushed with excitement, Angara bounding after him, tail and ears up in the eagerness of play. The dog was larger than the boy, but it displayed a gentleness to the kid, making sure Taksha came to no harm as they romped in the tall grass that grew around the royal stables. The sky had turned purple for the most part though a red-orange stain still spread to the west, where the silhouettes of birds flew home to roost. The day's heat had subsided just a little, and an intermittent breeze blew in from the river.

"He likes animals," Siripala observed with a small smile on his lips. His hair had grown whiter, but otherwise, the year that had passed had done nothing to him.

"Funny how Mandavi was saying the exact same thing this morning," Bharat replied, following the dog and the boy with fond eyes.

"I think he will make a good rider, like his father."

"You think so?" Bharat turned to the old bodyguard. "Should we try putting him in the saddle?"

"In a bit, kumara. He is just two. Let's give him another six months."

"I started when I was two. That's what mama says."

"It was your Yuddhajeet mama who put you in the saddle." A fond smile lit Siripala's face. "That's one of the first things you told me the day we met."

"I remember," the king chuckled.

"He taught you well," said Siripala. "They also have such lovely horses in Kekeya."

"Yes," Bharat said, heaving a long, nostalgic sigh. "Everything about Kekeya is beautiful. The green, grassy plains, the mustard fields with their bright yellow flowers, the brown wheat fields with the Vitasta, the Chandrabhaga and the Iravati glittering in the distance… There are times I truly miss not being in Kekeya."

Siripala glanced at the king out of the corner of his eye but said nothing.

Taksha took that moment to come running to his father, arms flailing, a happy grin on his face. Bharat bent and scooped the kid up, lifting him clear of Angara, who immediately jumped on Bharat, putting its front paws on Bharat's arms and pushing its snout between father and son, seeking attention, demanding to be petted. Bharat stroked the dog's head, and Angara's tongue lolled as its tail wagged in pleasure.

"Shall we go back now?" Bharat asked Taksha.

The boy gave his head a furious shake, wriggled from his father's grasp and slid to the ground. He then wrapped his arms around the dog's neck, holding it close in an outpouring of love. The next instant, he let go and took off wildly, with Angara chasing after him.

"No day is long enough for a child to squeeze in all the play in his heart," smiled Siripala, and Bharat laughed in agreement.

The king and the ostler were still watching Taksha and Angara when they heard a small cough and turned. A solitary figure was approaching them from the direction of the palace, but in the gathering dusk, they couldn't tell who it was.

"Who is it?" Siripala asked. Acting on instinct and years of training, he stepped between Bharat and the figure, shoulders squared.

"It is I, Sheelabhadra," the figure replied. "I have come to have a word with the king."

"Come, yajmaan," Bharat called as Siripala drew back.

Reaching the king's side, the *adhipati* bowed and offered a *pranaam* that Bharat returned. The old bodyguard snapped his fingers and a ball of light formed over the king and the courtier's heads. Bharat looked at Sheelabhadra's rugged, weather-beaten face in surprise.

"What brings you here at this hour, yajmaan?" he asked.

"I wished to offer my thanks for what you did in court this morning," the *adhipati* replied. "For standing up for me."

"Oh," said Bharat.

Siripala cleared his throat. "I must tend to the horses, rajan," he said diplomatically with a bow.

"Please keep an eye on Taksha," Bharat called over his shoulder. Siripala bowed again in reply.

The king returned his attention to Sheelabhadra. "I accept your thanks, but I didn't really stand up for anyone in particular."

"You warned Pushyanta and Sudhanva against circulating rumours about the indigo trade."

Bharat had to agree he'd done that. "I did what anyone in my place would have done."

"Anyone who is *fair and just*," the courtier stressed.

"Okay," Bharat accepted with a nod.

"The truth is that Sudhanva has been doing everything in his capacity to undermine my indigo business. This morning's attempt was aimed at lowering my business and me in your eyes, rajan. I am not surprised he took his son-in-law's help for this, but I can't believe the guild master actually extended his support to the lie." Sheelabhadra took a step towards Bharat. "They are all out to get me, and they are all lying, rajan."

Bharat blinked. The morning's exchange in court had flummoxed him, and now Sheelabhadra's words were leaving him even more baffled. He was not sure how to respond to the courtier.

"Rajan, with the passing of your father, Ayodhya's court has degenerated into a pit of vipers," the *adhipati* went on, speaking with vehemence. "Do not trust anyone's counsel. They are self-serving snakes, every last one of them."

"Mmm… thank you," said Bharat, groping for words. "It is… I shall keep your words in mind."

Sheelabhadra bowed but showed no signs of taking his leave. He kept standing there in the deepening twilight, and the silence stretched between king and courtier. Taksha could be heard talking to Siripala in his lisping, broken lingo, protesting about something.

"There is one more thing, rajan…"

Bharat knew there was. He turned and inclined his head at the *adhipati*.

"Besides the poor monsoons and the disappearances, there is another crisis facing this kingdom, which you aren't perhaps aware of."

The king stiffened in apprehension.

"You know that the shortage of foodgrains and other essentials is pushing up prices," Sheelabhadra said. "But what you perhaps *don't* know is the reason for this shortage, rajan."

"Rainfall was scarce last year. That impacted the production of foodgrains." The condescension in Sheelabhadra's tone was beginning to irk the king.

"A poor monsoon isn't the only reason for the current shortage." The *adhipati* paused. "In fact, I would go so far as to say the shortage is nowhere as acute as it is being made out to be."

Bharat's jaw tightened as he turned to face the courtier. "Make yourself clear."

"Rajan, as you know, Pushyanta is the biggest merchant in Kosala, and he procures all the grain produced in the kingdom for sale and distribution." Sheelabhadra glanced around, making sure they couldn't be overheard, though this was more for effect than anything else. It was too dark now to tell whether anyone was indeed eavesdropping. "Pushyanta's granaries and storehouses are piled to the ceiling with grains and other food stock. There is enough in his storehouses to bridge the shortage and bring prices down… *if* the stock is released into the market. But instead, the guild master is hoarding it to drive prices even higher so that he can mint even more money out of the situation."

Bharat stared at the *adhipati* of Kusinagara in astonishment.

What Sheelabhadra had revealed amounted to profiteering, a severely punishable offence under Ayodhya's law. Not only was it a shock to Bharat that black marketeering was being practiced right under his nose, but the fact that it was being orchestrated by Pushyanta, who held the public office of guild master, left the king flabbergasted.

"If that is true, why didn't you bring this up in court?" he asked. "Why tell me in secret?"

"I have no desire to draw attention to myself or to my well-wishers who share such information with me," said the *adhipati*. "God knows I have enough enemies in court already."

Bharat scratched his beard. "Pushyanta is masterminding a hoarding racket?" he mumbled.

"You don't have to take my word for it, rajan," the courtier insisted. "Make your own enquiries. But you will discover that what I say is the truth." He bowed and offered another *pranaam*. "It was my responsibility to bring this to your knowledge. Let me take your leave now."

Watching the *adhipati* depart, Bharat was overcome with confusion. He did not know whether Sheelabhadra could be believed; the man had, after all, a reason to be spiteful towards Pushyanta. And he himself had warned Bharat against trusting anyone's counsel, calling them self-serving snakes. What if Kosala's primary indigo trader was the pick of the untrustworthy lot? But again, would anyone make such a wild allegation against a fellow courtier and businessman without basis or proof? And it was Sheelabhadra who had urged him to verify the facts to his satisfaction, which implied that the charges levelled at the guild master would stick.

*With the passing of your father, Ayodhya's court has degenerated into a pit of vipers*, the words rang in Bharat's ears.

A pit of vipers.

Who was Sheelabhadra pointing at? Sudhanva and Pushyanta, obviously, but what about the revenue minister, Sheshagupta? Would a revenue minister not know how much foodgrain had been produced in a kingdom in a year? And if he did, wouldn't he be able to tell when a shortfall had been created artificially to drive prices up and send profits soaring? Did that mean Sheshagupta was part of the racket being run by the guild master? Was it even possible that the rot in Ayodhya's court ran so wide and so deep?

Hearing Siripala and Taksha's banter as they approached, Bharat drew in his breath. Sheelabhadra was right about one thing, he realized. He had to make his own enquiries. He had to uncover the truth for himself.

The problem was he didn't know whom he could trust to do the job for him.

# *six*

THE BUILDING OF THE *VATIKA* HAD BEGUN ON A HILLOCK by the broad sweep of the Yamuna, planned such that it would be unmissable from the river. The statue of himself that Lavanyasurya had originally had in mind had undergone alterations, doubling in size and pomposity—and in cost estimates—till it now had him seated on a horse, surveying the river traffic. The plinth for the statue had already been laid, after the architects had guaranteed that the statue would be easily distinguishable from the opposite bank and would draw the eye of everyone arriving in or leaving from Madhupura. The garden itself had suffered cost overruns, necessitating more raises in tariffs. And now, someone had suggested that the statue ought to be carved out of white marble instead of being sculpted in bronze. This meant another increase in the *vatika's* budget, but as Lavanyasurya had reminded Amulya, no cost was to be spared in giving Rani Naika the garden she wanted.

The king and the revenue minister now walked up the rise leading to the spot where the statue was meant to be put up, both men labouring under the weight of their bodies and the afternoon sun reflecting brightly off the Yamuna's waters below. Torn and uprooted trees lay everywhere, withering in the heat, and wide stretches of the earth had been gouged out in accordance with the architects' ideas of landscaping the garden. The clink of chisel and hammer striking stone filled the air as masons carved figurines of dancing apsaras and mermaids that would eventually line the *vatika's* paths and adorn its central fountain.

"This messenger from Ayodhya…" Lavanyasurya panted, "…he's gone back, has he?"

"He waited a couple of days before leaving," Amulya replied. "I would have asked him to wait longer had I known when you'd be back from the hunt."

Lavanyasurya grunted and gazed in the direction of the plinth, on top of which his statue would be raised. He then looked inland, away from the river. "Are the architects certain the statue will be visible from the city?" he asked distractedly.

"They said it would be, rajan," the guild master confirmed.

"Mmm," Lavanyasurya said, neither looking nor sounding convinced. "Just to be certain, have them cut down those trees there," he pointed, "all the way down to the bottom. That will give the people an unobstructed view."

"Yes, rajan," Amulya agreed.

Satisfied, the king resumed walking, and the minister waddled along behind. "What audacity!" Lavanyasurya exclaimed with feeling. "Telling me what not to do. Who does this Bharat think he is? Not half his father's son and behaving as if he owns me."

Amulya tutted and shook his head.

"This is the third time they've written, if I am not mistaken." Lavanyasurya eyed the minister for confirmation. "Always on and on about dropping tariffs. What did this latest message say?" The king stopped as much to catch his breath as to hear the courtier's answer. "What were the exact words?"

"I don't remember all of it."

"The part about our tariffs being unfair," Lavanyasurya snapped.

"Mmm… something to the effect that these sudden and steep increases in tariffs are arbitrary and unfair—"

"Arbitrary and unfair," the king growled. "*Arbitrary* and *unfair*." His face was flushed, though it was hard to say whether this was on account of his rising temper or the heat and the exertion.

"The letter also requested you to roll back tariffs—"

"Like hell I will," Lavanyasurya scowled, resuming the climb.

"—and urged you to consult with all trade partners before raising tariffs in future."

"Why should I consult with anyone? *You* want to trade via Madhupura, *you* do the consulting and the calculating. Not me."

"There's no question of rolling back tariffs," Amulya concurred.

"There's no question of agreeing to anything Kosala wants," the king shot back. "In fact, I have half a mind of giving it right back to Bharat… that fool of a boy. All four of Dashratha's sons, actually. Spoilt and full of themselves, acting superior to everyone. And for some reason, father thought they were models of good behaviour… humph."

They had reached the peak of the rise, and Lavanyasurya scouted around for shade. He pointed to a couple of ashoka trees that had somehow escaped the axe. As they ducked under the spreading branches, the king shook his head.

"Consult with him, humph. What happened when Chedi and Kasi thought our tariffs were too high?" He paused for Amulya to answer but lost his patience almost immediately. "Raja Hemaganga and Raja Meghavanta came to us in person, requesting that we reconsider. *That* is humility, *that* is culture, *that* is respect for partners. And what does Kosala do? Sends letters via messengers. *Messengers*. And then they expect *me* to consult with them..."

Not knowing what to say, and fearful of contradicting his king, the guild master shook his head.

"Tell me something," Lavanyasurya turned to Amulya with a wicked gleam in his eyes. "Those trade concessions that father gave Kosala, are they still in place? Does Kosala still benefit from them?"

"Yes, rajan," the minister replied slowly. He had a sense of where this was going, and it alarmed him. "The new tariffs were structured for Kosala keeping those concessions in mind."

"So, they still pay far less than what Kasi and Chedi and Angadesh and everyone else do, right?" the smile on the king's face widened.

"Yes," Amulya licked his lips.

"How is that fair?" Lavanyasurya sprang upon the courtier's reply. "The concessions are unfair to Kasi, Chedi, Angadesh and everyone else, and in his letter, Bharat wants us *not to be unfair*. We should remedy this unfairness straightaway."

"Rajan... those concessions go back a long way..." said Amulya by way of a caution.

"Too long, in my opinion," the king said with adamancy. "It is time for a correction."

The concessions went back nearly thirty years, to the time when Madhupura was emerging as Jambudvipa's commercial epicentre. A big city drawing traders from everywhere had quickly caught the attention of bandits, who made their haunt in the nearby forest of Madhuvana and began raiding Madhupura, extorting merchants and looting caravans entering and leaving the city. Struggling to keep his city safe from the bandits, Lavanyasurya's father Madhavraj had sought aid from neighbouring Kosala, and Dashratha had come to Madhupura's assistance by launching a campaign against the bandits. Following months of fighting, Kosala's troops had flushed the bandits out of Madhuvana, killing over a hundred of them and taking three times as many captive. Kosala's army had then trained and equipped Madhupura's militia, making it capable of looking after the city. In addition, Dashratha had stationed a small unit of men in Madhupura to help the militia guard the city—a garrison that Dashratha never called back to Ayodhya as a gesture of goodwill between the two kingdoms. The garrison was still located within Madhupura, half a mile from its main market. In lieu of all that Kosala had done for him, Madhavraj had granted Kosala sizeable concessions in tariffs that had helped Kosala gain competitiveness in trade.

"Rajan, we will be upsetting thirty years of tradition by repealing those concessions," Amulya entreated.

"Everything changes in thirty years, and we must not be slavishly bound to tradition," the king said. "More so when father is dead, as is Dashratha. Why should a deal survive those who made it, especially when Madhupura can benefit from a break from the past?"

"I think we should give this proper thought—"

"You think my thought has not been proper, that I am—"

"That is not what I meant, rajan. All I ask for is a well-considered decision."

"Okay, consider this." Lavanyasurya looked the revenue minister square in the eye. "Consider the amount of money Madhupura can make by *not giving* Kosala the sops they currently enjoy. Consider how much more money you will have at your disposal for repairing the city's sewage system." A slight pause, and his next words came out soft and sinister. "Alternately, you could consider the possibility of not being the guild master and revenue minister of Madhupura."

Amulya went pale under the bright afternoon sun. "Would you like me to draft a reply that our messenger can take with him to Ayodhya, rajan?"

"I would indeed," said Lavanyasurya. "I would like to teach Dashratha's son a lesson for trying to tell me how to do things. He wanted rollbacks; he wanted consultations. I will put that upstart in his place by making Kosala pay tariffs that are on par with what everyone else is paying us."

The king stayed in the shade of the ashokas and watched his revenue minister go down the hill. *Rajan, we will be upsetting thirty years of tradition,* Amulya had said. Thirty years of tradition, Lavanyasurya snorted at the idea. Thirty years of slavish compliance to the demands and dictates of Kosala was more like it. If that was the tradition he was being asked to preserve, he was happy tearing it to the ground. Thirty years of being lorded over were coming to an end. It was payback time.

He was getting there, though he wasn't fully ready yet. He needed more time. Until then, Kosala could pay in other, *more literal* ways. Like shelling out higher tariffs…

Fear was everywhere.

It was fleetingly visible in the eyes of the palace guards and the *nagarapala* patrols before they concealed it behind their tough, soldierly exteriors. It could be glimpsed in the courtiers' faces as the day progressed and they waited to form groups so they didn't have to return home all by themselves. It was palpable in Ayodhya's streets as people shuffled along, furtive and watching their backs before ducking down doorways. It was apparent in Mandavi's reluctance to let little Taksha out of her sight. It was plain in the nervousness of the boatmen who ferried him to the Sanctum and in the manner of the rishis' wives observing his approach from the verandahs of their homes.

The people of Ayodhya were scared of the occurrences in the city.

Three more people had gone missing over the past five days. The middle-aged wife of a boatman, the younger brother of a spice merchant and a retired *nagarapala* from a village six miles east of the city. Like the others who had gone earlier, these three had also vanished without a trace, although there were rumours that the boatman's wife might have eloped with a trader from distant parts. The matter was being investigated, but the incidence of these disappearances was clearly escalating.

Bharat had been ushered into a small hall meant for receiving guests. The hall was not far from the upcoming *homagriha*, and the king could see the work in progress, men on scaffolding sculpting the base of the stupa. The sharp sound of stone being chipped and chiselled fell on his ears.

The rishi who entered the hall was short and on the heavy side. He wasn't exactly youthful, but in the Sanctum, where there were hardly any rishis with black hair left, he was an exception. Remarkably, for his age, he was mahamuni Vashishtha's chosen deputy, and in the mahamuni's absence had assumed the responsibilities and duties of his guru.

"Rishi Surochi," Bharat rose and offered his *pranaam*.

Returning the salutation, the rishi gestured to the king to take his seat. "What a surprise! What brings you here, rajan?" he asked, crossing his legs on the straw mat.

"I wished to see the progress," Bharat waved his hand in the direction of the *homagriha*.

The rishi looked puzzled. "I got the impression you had specifically asked to see me."

"I did," Bharat admitted.

"So, what can I do for you?"

"Munivar," the king composed his thoughts, "you must know that the people are suffering."

Surochi inclined his head. "One can't escape the reports of the disappearances," he agreed. "It is a stressful time to be in Ayodhya."

"I speak for all of Kosala, munivar, and it's not the disappearances alone, painful as they are. The rains are failing us for the second year, the magic is slowly but surely dwindling… the people are being affected in so many ways."

The rishi gave an understanding nod. "That the people's plight concerns you is a sign of a good king."

"What good is my concern if it cannot do something to ease their misery, alleviate their pain?"

Surochi silently considered Bharat for a moment. "The harshest lesson life teaches parents is that they can't always guarantee their children's happiness," he said. "The same way, a king cannot always bring his people comfort." The rishi's tone became kinder. "But this shall pass. Once the sacred fire is housed in the new *homagriha*, the rains shall return, and the magic will revive."

The king wasn't reassured. "The institution of the *homagriha* is easily a month away," he said. "Isn't there something that can be done sooner?"

"Nothing can be done before its time, rajan," Surochi shook his head. "Sometimes, the best we can do is anchor ourselves to patience."

Bharat looked away, staring out of the window. "It is hard to anchor myself to anything when the people are being washed away by the tides of circumstance."

"I wish I could help you," said the rishi. He gathered himself to rise. He had other things to do.

"I understand, munivar," the king nodded.

Displaying no signs of taking his leave, Bharat transferred his gaze to his palm. Studying it, he asked, "I once read about the *agnimanasa homa*." He looked up at Surochi. "Do you think that could help?"

The rishi's face was expressionless as he stared at the king. "*Creating* magic is not the same as *using* it," he said.

"That wasn't my question, munivar," Bharat persisted.

Abandoning the idea of getting up, Surochi sat heavily and crossed his hands over the bulge of his stomach.

"What do you know about the *agnimanasa*, rajan?" he asked.

"Not much," Bharat confessed, "but I gathered that the one doing the *agnimanasa* builds magic into the ether using his own energy. That is, he substitutes himself for the *homa* fire."

"That is correct," said Surochi slowly. "Soul-energy becomes the fire that creates the magic."

"So, it can be done," Bharat's eyes shone with hope. "I could do it."

"It can. But…" the rishi held up a cautionary finger, "the question you must ask yourself is: If it can be done, why isn't it done more often, why isn't it a lot more common?"

The king knitted his brows in vexation.

"Ask yourself, why do we rishis never suggest an *agnimanasa*, rajan?" Surochi finished.

"Why?" Bharat asked.

"Because there is a heavy price attached to the creation of magic. Nothing can be created out of nothing, and magic needs the strength of the *homa* fire to come into being. But during the *agnimanasa,* there is no *homa* fire. So, the magic draws strength from another source: a thing or a person that the one doing the *homa* holds close to his heart." The rishi paused to look the king in the eye.

"The loss is inevitable. It is a sacrifice that the magic demands and exacts, rajan."

"What could I lose—"

Surochi held up his hand again. When he spoke, his tone was firm. "Let it be, rajan. The price is not worth the effort." Again, his face softened. "Your desire to assist the people is admirable, but the best you can do is go back and wait for the sacred fire to be installed in the *homagriha*."

The room in the palace of Rajagriha was silent as the trade advisor-cum-envoy of Madra slowly read through the message painted on the scroll of white silk. Raja Ashwapati and Yuddhajeet had their arms crossed as they waited for the fat man to get to the end, their faces impassive, as though carved from stone. Outside, a faint drizzle fell from a dull sky, and thunder growled somewhere in the distance. Reaching the end of the note, the advisor, who had been summoned to the palace from his chamber in the city, looked at the king and prince nervously as he rolled the scroll up and knotted it back with deft fingers.

"This," Ashwapati pointed at the scroll, "fell into our hands when one of our patrols intercepted some Gandharan soldiers as they were heading west from Sakala with four pack horses loaded with what they termed 'gifts' from Madra." He paused, then asked sternly, "Do you know about this?"

The advisor hesitated. "I have… had heard about the demands from Gandhara, rajan."

"This is apparently the third such trip the Gandharans have made to and from Sakala in the past year." It was Yuddhajeet's turn to speak. "That is what the Gandharan soldiers we apprehended tell us."

The official from Madra said nothing.

"That makes *twelve* pack horses loaded with tributes to Gandhara," Ashwapati observed. "Why is Raja Sampada surreptitiously paying Gandhara tributes?"

"Rajan…" the advisor stopped, then gathered the courage to continue, "the note says it all."

"What does the note say?" The king demanded. The stroke he had suffered a few months earlier had left him weaker and he had taken to walking with a staff for support, but the steel still rang in Ashwapati's voice. "It says Gandhara will raid and sack Sakala if a tribute is not paid, right? That's just bullying. I would have expected Sampada to stand up to it."

"The note is from Gandhara," Madra's envoy said, as if that was explanation enough.

"What is the big deal about Gandhara?" Yuddhajeet threw his hands up in exasperation. "Have you forgotten how we kicked a much bigger force of Gandharans out of Manglapuri two years ago? Why do you think they have been sneaking in and out of the hills and forests to the distant north, carefully avoiding Kekeya all the while? And why have these demands been made of Madra but not us? Because they're scared of Kekeya. Gandhara doesn't want to tangle with us. It's that simple."

"Why didn't Sampada just come to us instead of yielding to Gandhara's demands?" Ashwapati asked. "That is the contract between the River Kingdoms, isn't it? That Kekeya will protect Trigartha and Madra? And haven't we done that, keeping you safe for so many years?"

"Pardon me for overstepping the bounds of my office, rajan," the trade advisor said, "but while there is no doubt that Kekeya has defended the River Kingdoms very well in the past, that was against thieves and highwaymen. This is different. Yes," he bowed to Yuddhajeet, "Kekeya did deal the Gandharan force a drubbing in Manglapuri, but that was two years ago, when Nagnajit was still not king. Nagnajit has maimed and butchered his way to the throne, and it is said that once he sets his heart on something, nothing can stop him from getting it. Gandhara under Nagnajit is a terrible foe to have, and my king Sampada acted such that unnecessary bloodshed could be avoided and we could all be left in peace to pursue trade and commerce."

"For someone who professes to have only *heard* about Gandhara's demands, you seem to know a lot about your raja's thoughts and compulsions." Ashwapati remarked, shifting in his seat.

"Peace," Yuddhajeet added caustically. "How much will you surrender for peace? For how long? *What* all will you surrender… your dignity, the fruits of your labour, those you love… what?"

The advisor kept quiet.

Father and son looked at each other. It was useless. Nothing was to be gained by arguing with someone who was merely a representative of Madra. Ashwapati extended his hand, asking the scroll to be returned.

"Have your men come over to collect the tributes that were bound for Gandhara," the old raja said. "We relieved the Gandharans of the four horses and their burdens before letting them go home."

"You set the Gandharan soldiers free?" The envoy considered father and son cautiously.

"With a warning to Nagnajit," said Yuddhajeet.

The advisor watched the prince in anticipation, and Yuddhajeet obliged.

"A warning that the next time we spy Gandhara's troops in the River Kingdoms, we will lose our patience and lock them away in our prisons for good."

Madra's representative paled. He opened his mouth to speak, then decided against it. With a bow, he left the room.

Bharat looked the *dandapala* up and down.

"Dileepa?" he asked, and the man nodded. "You look quite young to be a *dandapala*."

"Everyone says so, rajan."

"What are you working on?"

"We are..." he stopped and cleared his throat. "The disappearances."

Of course. All the *dandapalas* were involved in the investigation, yet they had so little to show for it. Not that they were entirely to blame; they had practically nothing on which to go on, Bharat knew.

The king rested his elbows on a window that offered a view of the Sarayu. The sun beat down without remorse, and the land on both sides of the river had turned brown. The Sarayu itself had shrunk even more in size, so the boats and trade barges could no longer dock at the pier and had to be tied to bollards that had been driven into the dry, exposed riverbed. A heat haze blanked the far horizon, making the trees in the distance shimmer and dance indistinctly.

"I gather you aren't from Ayodhya."

"No, rajan. I belong to Kusinagara," Dileepa licked his lips and stood straight as a rod. He was nervous as hell; he had no idea why the king had suddenly asked to see him, and he was fighting hard to remain calm. Maybe someone had found out that he had been investigating Bakula and that he hadn't followed the enquiry to its logical end, he thought furiously. And now he was being pulled up for his mistake, and the king was going to take him to task…

"Kusinagara?" The king raised his eyebrows at *dandapala*. "So, you know Sheelabhadra."

"I know him in the sense that he is the *adhipati* of the province," Dileepa said. "That's all."

"And how long have you been in Ayodhya?"

The *dandapala* did a quick bit of math. "Just under three years, rajan."

*Do not trust anyone's counsel. They are self-serving snakes.* Sheelabhadra's warning played in Bharat's mind as he studied the young investigator. But he had to trust *someone*. Someone who hadn't been corrupted by the system, who hadn't yet forged an alliance with one faction or the other. From the information he had gathered, this *dandapala* appeared to fit the bill. Three years was too short a time for an outsider like this *dandapala* to win the confidence of a clique and be accepted as one of their own…

"Can I trust you to keep a secret?"

Dileepa was plainly taken aback, but he nodded.

"I want you to investigate something for me. Topmost priority. Drop everything else that you're working on."

"Yes, rajan."

Beckoning the *dandapala* to follow him, Bharat went down a corridor that opened onto a broad, open terrace. It was sweltering outside and the sun burned the skin, but the king didn't appear to notice as he strode all the way to the far edge of the terrace. Dileepa blinked as the sunlight dazzled his eyes, sweat breaking out on his brow and instantly dampening his turban.

"Stand closer," the king ordered, "and listen carefully."

Dileepa stepped as close as protocol allowed. Bharat glanced around, making sure no one was within earshot. Then, dropping his voice, he spoke.

"I am sure you are familiar with the guild master Pushyanta of Sravasti..."

"You should have seen the beast. It was *massive. Huge.* A *brute* of a creature, crouching there on the outcrop, snarling down, big teeth bared in rage, ready to spring on us. I'll bet most of us were about to faint on the spot. But our raya... no, he just stood there, looking the thing in the eye. Stared right back at the monster, freezing the blood in its veins with his fierce gaze. Believe me, it was a sight, seeing the raya and the leopard face each other. And then, without warning, it jumped."

There was a collective drawing of shocked breaths, and in the short dramatic silence that ensued, the slap of everyone's footsteps on the cold stone floor of the corridor was suddenly very loud.

"Everyone just scattered," the man recounting the tale said, making a fearful face. Around him, his four listeners gaped with open mouths, eyes wide as they latched on to every word. "But no, not *everyone*... Not our raya," the narrator tilted his head at the man walking two steps in front, and the listeners all turned worshipping eyes on him. "Our raya didn't budge an inch. He stood there, all alone… Then, he began circling the beast."

But for the haughty smirk that danced on his lips now and then, the man in front made no show of listening to the narrative unfolding behind him. His stride self-assured, his shoulders squared and his head set at a cocky angle, he embodied confidence, and though he wasn't an inch taller than the men around him and probably not even as broad, it was evident that authority answered to him and him alone, at least in this corner of the earth.

"Round and round they went, and time appeared to stop on that mountainside… but then, I saw the leopard's muscles tighten as it readied to make its leap. My throat was parched, my mouth was dry, but I wished to warn the raya, so I parted my lips. Of course, I was being plain foolish, for don't we know nothing escapes the raya's eye? He had seen what I had seen, *only he had seen it sooner*."

"Of course, of course," the listeners murmured in approval.

"So, before a sound rose from my throat, his arm shot out."

Again, a suspenseful silence filled with the sound of footsteps.

"The spear whooshed like the wind and caught the beast as it reared up to spring. It struck the animal on its chest, burying deep… The image of red blood spurting and staining white fur is vividly imprinted in my memory."

Gasps of rapture issued from the listeners' mouths.

"The thing just fell there, never to rise," the narrator concluded with a note of triumph.

"Remarkable," one of the listeners reacted.

"One blow was all it took," observed another, looking at the faces around in approval.

"And all by himself," the narrator stressed. "Don't forget that!"

"Facing a leopard all by yourself... How do you summon the courage, raya?" wondered a third.

The man in front threw a glance behind him, kohl-lined eyes flashing in his handsome, bearded face. "It is not the beast outside that presents real danger. It is the one within: fear. Kill that one first and you're safe," he said with a casual shrug.

"Marvellous," the men teetered and fawned. "So simple."

"Wish we'd been there to witness it for ourselves," said one of them.

"But that's the point of where we're going," the narrator said. "So that you can all witness what happened in its full grandeur."

The men nodded enthusiastically, and the small concourse wound its way along echoing halls and corridors until they drew up to a door, which swung open to reveal a sprawling atrium with a balcony at its end, affording a panoramic view of a snow-capped mountain range. Closer at hand were clusters of pomegranate trees, interspersed with rows of grape vines that produced Gandhara's famed *kapisi madhu*, a dark and potent wine rapidly gaining popularity beyond the kingdom's borders.

Two men stood in the atrium, one on each side of a big table occupying the centre. They bowed, staying bent at the waist until the raya and his men drew to a halt before of one of them.

"Salutations, Raya Nagnajit," the man said, reverting to an erect posture.

"So... can I see it?"

"Indeed, raya," the man motioned towards the table, and the group moved forward, all eyes on the tabletop.

"Here is the artist, raya," the courtier pointed to the other man standing to one side. He was incredibly young, hardly more than twenty, a lean, bony young man with alabaster-white skin.

The men huddled around the table, over which was spread an expertly woven piece of tapestry, depicting a royal hunt. At the scene's centre was a handsome, bearded man wielding a spear, while across him crouched the snow leopard, slightly exaggerated in size but otherwise proportionate and realistic. Not a wrinkle of fear showed in the man's expression as he hauled his arm back to hurl the spear at the big cat. Away from the centre of action, spreading towards the sides and the upper edge of the tapestry, a group of seven or eight other hunters surrounded the leopard, their spears primed to help their raya bring the animal down. Near the bottom were a set of drummers and men holding flaming torches to keep the beast cowed and in check. The scene had been exquisitely rendered with multicoloured threads, conveying a sense of believable drama to the viewer's eye.

"Ooh," sighed one of the men who had accompanied Nagnajit.

"Look at the raya," whispered another in adoring tones. "Noble and fearless."

It took a few moments for the others to realize that Nagnajit hadn't yet uttered a word; the raya of Gandhara simply stood staring at the tapestry with his hands on his hips. As everyone slowly went quiet, eyeing their lord apprehensively, the raya frowned and raised his head to look at the artist. "Come here," he beckoned.

The boy was quailing, the blood draining from his already white face so he resembled a ghost. He wobbled around the table and the others drew back, presumably to make room for him—though it was equally possible they were only creating space for blood to fly and a body to fall.

"Come," Nagnajit put an arm around the young artist's shoulders and drew him close. "This is a lovely piece of work," he said. Looking into the boy's face, he added, "Really, it is."

The boy, who had literally stopped breathing in terror, exhaled and smiled, relief flooding back into his thin shoulders. "Thank you, raya," he mumbled.

"Really nice. But… can I suggest some improvements?" Nagnajit asked.

"Yes, raya," the artist nodded, licking his lips.

The raya drew the heavy *karapala* that hung at his waist. Everyone else immediately took another step back. The boy went white again and an involuntary moan came out of him.

"You are undoubtedly talented, but there is much to learn," Nagnajit said, holding the boy tight. "For instance, this," he waved the sword over the tapestry, "has too much going on, *too* many distractions. It needs to be a lot simpler."

Without warning, the raya drove the sword's point into the tapestry. The boy screamed out in reflex. "This needs editing," Nagnajit grunted, tearing a ragged line into one end of the fabric. "Just unnecessary information." Freeing the *karapala*, he slashed another corner of the cloth. "Learn to sharpen your focus." Another stab, another rip down one side. Over and over again, he attacked the tapestry, cutting it to shreds and tossing the rags aside until he finally ran out of breath and stopped.

"There," he panted, pointing again with the sword. "See that?"

Everyone craned their necks to look. The tapestry was in ruins, shorn down to half its original size. What was left showed the raya throwing his spear fearlessly at the leopard. That was it. No ring of hunters cornering the cat, no helpers beating drums or men with torches. All that had been torn to strips and discarded.

"That," Nagnajit pointed, "is a picture of the royal hunt. The raya taking down a wild beast. That is all that's important about a hunt; that is all that the people need to know and remember. Everything else is useless detail." He looked at the artist. "Can you remember that much?" Seeing the boy tender a weak nod, the raya sheathed the *karapala*. "You are young. You can have a long career as an artist of this court."

He turned and marched out of the atrium, the courtiers rushing after him. The artist waited until his lord had reached the door before sinking to the floor in a half-swoon, the tatters of his labour of love scattered all around him.

Exiting the atrium and stepping into the corridor, Nagnajit was about to head to the right when he sighted a soldier coming from the left and stopped. The man, a soldier of rank, was in a rush, and he began bowing and saluting even as he scurried to join his lord's side.

"Salutations, raya," he said, drawing to a halt. "I bring a report from the frontier."

"What is it?"

"While on their way from Sakala, our men were stopped by Kekeya's troops. The tributes were confiscated, raya, but our men were let go."

Nagnajit's face darkened. "Wait, wait… Tell me clearly, from the beginning."

The commander recounted the capture of the Gandharan soldiers and the seizure of the tribute from Madra. "Our men were taken to Rajagriha, but instead of being imprisoned, they were set free with a warning, telling us not to come back," he concluded.

"Where are these men? And how many are they?"

"There are seven of them, all still at the outpost at the frontier, all in good health. The Kekeyans treated them well and were kind enough to let them go, raya."

Nagnajit took a step forward, bridging the gap between himself and the commander. Placing one hand on the hilt of the sheathed *karapala*, he spoke into the man's ear in a chilling tone. "You don't want to be heard talking about the kindness of the Kekeyans again, do you?" He looked at the man, who nodded quickly to show he had understood. "Good," Nagnajit looked satisfied. "And I don't want those seven to come back and spread stories about Kekeyan kindness either. In fact, when those seven are brought through Kapisi, slung on the backs of their horses, their hands tied and their throats slit open from ear to ear, I want stories of the brutality and vileness of the Kekeyans to spread through this land. Am I clear?"

The commander stared at his raya for a moment, not believing he had heard right. Then, gulping hard, he nodded and bowed.

Once the man had departed, one of the courtiers spoke softly. "What happens now, raya?"

Nagnajit was silent for a moment. The Kekeyans were making a habit of interfering with his ambitions. This was the second time they had challenged him, and while it was possible to overlook something once, twice was going to be hard, especially when all these courtiers and nobles were watching him, waiting for him to make one false move, take one misstep. "We'll cross the mountains and go to war," he announced. "We will teach Kekeya what it means to provoke Gandhara into a retaliation."

"Is Gandhara equipped for a full-scale campaign against the River Kingdoms, raya?" asked another of the courtiers. "We will be up against the armies of Kekeya, Madra and Trigartha."

The raya smiled thinly. "That is what emboldens Kekeya. Because they are three against one, they think we won't risk moving against them. But we won't go alone either."

The men glanced at one another, some in confusion, others in anticipation.

"Send a message to Mahasa's grand tent, asking him to prepare for battle," Nagnajit ordered. "It is time for Kamboja's horsemen to prove their loyalty and usefulness to Gandhara."

# *seven*

IT HAD BEEN A FULL WEEK SINCE SHRUTAKIRTI HAD experienced her first fainting spell. The *vaidyas* were consulted and they drew their conclusions, but to be sure, the palace midwives were also called in; these women came back to happily report that Queen Sumitra's daughter-in-law was indeed with child. Since then, the palace had been running on excitement, and Ayodhya was in a state of buoyancy. Every night, for one week, lamps had been lit outside every door to ward off evil spirits, and in the city's temples, people offered prayers for the mother and the unborn child. Gifts and greetings poured in from all corners of the kingdom, and for the moment, the imminent drought was forgotten as the people immersed themselves in celebrating the coming of another descendant in the Ikshvaku line.

The day's heat was without mercy as Shrutakirti was escorted from her chambers to the central hall, where rishis sat chanting *shlokas* around a *homa* fire. Mandavi and Urmila accompanied Shrutakirti, all three smiling through the sadness of Sita's absence on such a joyous occasion. Rishis added ghee to the fire, and smoke filled the hall as the ceremony got underway. Kushadhwaja, who had arrived from Rajviraj the night before, stood by Shatrughna's side with Taksha in the crook of his arm, beaming at the prospect of becoming a grandfather for the second time. Shatrughna looked proud but self-conscious, while Kausalya and Sumitra sat chatting on *manchikas*, waiting to bless the mother and child after the ceremony. As the unborn child's only uncle to be around, Bharat attended to the needs of the rishis during the *homa*, his face drawn and solemn.

"May the gods watch over you," Kushadhwaja blessed Shrutakirti once the rishis had given their benedictions. "Your uncle sends his blessings too." Seeradhwaja Janak had not been able to accompany his brother as one of them had to stay back to oversee the tilling and sowing.

Kushadhwaja grinned at Taksha, who had been taking in everything with great curiosity. "Soon, you'll have a little brother to play with," he said.

"Or a little sister," said Mandavi.

"Little…" Taksha lisped.

Having received the blessings of Kausalya and Sumitra, Shrutakirti, her sisters and Bharat were preparing to feed the rishis when Kausalya spoke up. "What about Kaikeyi?"

The hall fell silent as everyone looked at Kausalya. She was a small woman, made even smaller by age, her face pinched around an upturned nose and a mouth that was once given to laughter. She wore her thick grey hair in a bun that rested at the back of her head.

"What about her, mother?" Bharat slowly ventured.

"Isn't Shrutakirti going to seek her blessings?" Kausalya asked.

Everyone exchanged uncertain glances. Bharat shook his head. "That's not necessary."

"Why not?" Kausalya looked at Bharat. "Since when has the blessing of an elder become unnecessary?" When no one answered, she added, "Kaikeyi is still a queen of this palace."

Shrutakirti stole a glance at her sisters. Mandavi shot a look back, but Urmila's expression was closed.

Sumitra considered what Kausalya had said and nodded. "Who will take her to Kaikeyi?" she asked.

Bharat avoided answering by looking away. Shatrughna fidgeted. Urmila laid banana leaves in a line before the mats meant for the rishis to sit on.

"I shall take her in the evening," Mandavi volunteered to everyone's relief.

Later in the afternoon, once lunch had been partaken, Kushadhwaja searched the palace for Bharat. He found his son-in-law on an east-facing terrace, painting a clay figurine of a farmer carrying a plough on his shoulder.

"Don't tell me you made that," said Kushadhwaja.

Bharat glanced up in surprise. "This?" He held up the figurine. "No, I got someone to buy it from the bazaar. All I can do is paint, and that too not very well."

"May I join you?" the *adhipati* of Rajviraj asked.

"Of course." Bharat motioned to the vacant space on the mat.

Kushadhwaja watched the younger man swirl blue dye on a salver and daub a spot of the paint on the figurine's turban. Not satisfied with the outcome, Bharat mixed more black dye into the blue.

"So, how are things here?" Kushadhwaja asked, assessing his son-in-law's grave expression.

Bharat gave a noncommittal shrug.

"You look tense," the *adhipati's* eyes were shrewd. "It's these disappearances, isn't it?"

Bharat gave his head a helpless shake. "Bizarre and impossible to explain. As of today, fourteen people have gone."

"And no leads on what might have happened to them?"

Another shake of the head. "The *dandapalas* are at it, and we have increased patrolling, particularly at night, but nothing. Fear has taken root and people want answers, but we have nothing to give them." Bharat looked at Kushadhwaja. "The relatives of those who have disappeared show up every second day to see me. They wait all day, refusing to leave until I have met them and listened to how deeply they suffer. And I offer hollow reassurance and make empty promises of finding their dear ones when no one has the faintest clue where they are. What kind of a king am I when I can't help the people? And the worst part is because we have no idea what's happening, we are completely powerless to prevent further disappearances."

"Don't be so hard on yourself," the older man sympathized. "You're doing your best, and the people know it. And you're bound to make a breakthrough soon."

Bharat's silence said he was neither hopeful nor particularly reassured.

Kushadhwaja let it be. A spot of silence, and he asked, "All well otherwise?"

The king paused. Putting brush and figurine aside, he wiped the paint off his fingers with a rag. "You know our guild master Pushyanta," he said.

"Not very well. Why?"

Bharat told Kushadhwaja about the differences that had arisen between the *adhipatis* and about Sheelabhadra's accusations against Pushyanta. "It all sounds so unbelievable. I've got a *dandapala* to get to the bottom of this, but I'm not even sure if he'll find anything concrete," Bharat concluded.

"Serious charges," Kushadhwaja observed. "What will you do if they are proved right?"

"Arrest Pushyanta… Definitely bar him from the guild."

Kushadhwaja looked up sharply. "Isn't that too light a punishment for such a serious crime?"

"I don't know. He was appointed to the guild by father. And he is Sudhanva's son-in-law."

"Neither is a good enough reason *not* to punish a wrongdoer."

"I know," Bharat nodded.

"And if you can't find evidence against Pushyanta, what about Sheelabhadra? He might have cooked everything up just to set you against Pushyanta, you know."

Bharat gave his head an unhappy shake. "I doubt it. He seemed very sure he'd be proved right."

They lapsed into silence. Bharat picked up the brush and the figurine to resume painting, but stopped. "And besides all of this, Madhupura has revoked all the trade concessions previously granted to Kosala," he sighed. "Lavanyasurya's notification arrived early this morning."

Kushadhwaja's eyebrows crept up in surprise. "Why all of a sudden?" he said. He understood why Bharat had looked so preoccupied at the ceremony. "This isn't good for Kosala."

"Not at all. We have been competitive in the market all these years because of the exemptions that Raja Madhavraj had granted us. Without them, we'd be compelled to raise prices, and we won't remain competitive any longer." Bharat rubbed his forearm against his forehead in a display of nerves.

"Any idea what prompted Lavanyasurya?"

Bharat scowled. "He has been raising tariffs steadily over the past year. I guess this is part of his newfound drive to squeeze all trade that enters and leaves his city."

"He does have everyone in a chokehold," Kushadhwaja agreed, "but a move to abolish long-standing concessions somehow feels personally motivated, like settling scores."

Bharat considered this, then shrugged. "I don't know, but something needs to be done about this. Otherwise, our treasury will be hit hard."

"What do you propose?"

"I must pay Lavanyasurya a visit and convince him to change his mind."

"Let Shatrughna go."

Bharat looked at his father-in-law in surprise. "No," he protested, "he is too young—"

Kushadhwaja was ready for that. "No, he isn't. He will be a father soon."

Bharat frowned. "Shatrughna wouldn't know how to deal with a jackal like Lavanyasurya."

"He will learn if you give him the opportunity. I can tell he's eager to help and be useful. You have to learn to trust him."

"It's not that I don't trust him," Bharat began. "It's just that—"

"If you trust him, let him go to Madhupura. Your trust has to go beyond mere words."

"I do trust him," the king insisted. "It's… I just fear for him. That something like this will make him hard, make him lose his innocence, make him weary and cynical and manipulative like the rest of us. You want me to give him an opportunity to learn. I fear that. Look at him. So young, so happy." Bharat looked at Kushadhwaja. "Do we have the right to take that away from him?"

"I see what you mean," Kushadhwaja leaned to place a hand on his son-in-law's shoulder. "But then, do you have the right to hold him back just because you fear for him?"

Bharat shot the older man a perceptive glance.

"He has to grow," Kushadhwaja continued. "Growth is inevitable. We can't stop it, but we can make the passage easier for him by selecting his responsibilities for him. As his brother, it's the best you can do."

Seeing Bharat brood over this, Kushadhwaja made one final, determined pitch. "The challenges in ruling a kingdom are plenty, and often, they come all at the same time. You can't do everything yourself. You must build a wall of trustworthy people around you, people who can help you deal with these challenges. Shatrughna is one such person. Place your faith on him and let him learn how to shoulder some of your responsibility."

Bharat studied the figurine, turning it this way and that in the light. Then he looked at his father-in-law and nodded.

"Shatrughna will go to Madhupura," he said, "to negotiate trade terms with Lavanyasurya."

The palanquin that squeezed through the winding streets of the old quarter was large. The men who bore the palanquin on their shoulders were large too, with large biceps and large bellies. And the woman who emerged from the palanquin in front of the door to the old mansion was also large, diamond nose-bud flashing in the sunlight, a jangle of bangles announcing her entry into the mansion's outer courtyard.

Standing in an upper-storey window, Ma Parnalata and Nandana watched the woman's arrival with satisfaction.

"The fish has been baited," the aunt said to the niece as they turned to go downstairs.

By the time they got to the courtyard, Parnalata's helpers had greeted and escorted the woman to a comfortable seat. The helpers, who all hailed from Ayodhya, clearly knew their guest by sight and reputation, and Parnalata noticed that they were all a bit in awe of her.

Seeing Parnalata come into the courtyard, one of the women hurried over. "That is Varnakavi," she whispered in excitement, "the daughter of Sudhanva of Sankasya."

Sudhanva's only daughter. Also, the sister of Yadudeva, and the wife of guild master Pushyanta. Three powerful men related to her by blood and marriage, men who exerted influence over the palace. Sudhanva had been advisor to the old king, and everyone seemed to agree he was set to play a crucial role in Bharat's reign as well.

Parnalata smiled. Varnakavi was to be their access to the three men, Sudhanva in particular. And through Sudhanva to Ayodhya's two young *mahayoddhas,* whom she had come this far to neutralize.

"Welcome," she said, going over to her guest. "It's kind of you to have graced this doorstep."

Varnakavi glanced at Parnalata before her gaze was drawn to Nandana, her eyebrows arching at the girl's lustrous beauty.

"My niece Nandana," the older woman said. "And I am Parnalata, at your service."

"Fine," said Varnakavi disinterestedly, brushing away the sugarcane juice that had been offered to her. She inspected the courtyard carefully before casting her eyes upwards, following the sound of the looms from the floors above.

"Would you like to see some of our wares?" asked Parnalata.

"I wouldn't have come so far if I hadn't wanted to," Varnakavi gave Parnalata a lingering look.

But for the expression of bored superiority stamped permanently on her face, she would be an attractive woman, thought Parnalata. "I would have come over if only you had sent word," she said in a mollifying tone. "It would have saved you a journey in this afternoon heat."

"It's alright as long as what you have here isn't a total disappointment," Varnakavi replied.

As her girls brought out stacks of colourful saris woven out of the best silk, Parnalata reflected on how their guest had fallen into the trap laid for her. It had all started with a well-chosen sari that Parnalata had gifted the wife of one of Ayodhya's most prominent cloth merchants; it had seemed like a calculated gesture of goodwill, a piece of marketing to win the merchant's favour and open the doors to business. But its real intent had been different. Nandana had learned that the merchant's wife was on excellent terms with Varnakavi and that they met regularly, so aunt and niece had decided that she would be their conduit to the guild master's wife. An exquisite sari was guaranteed to spark a conversation among women, and even incite desire and envy, and Parnalata had bet that Varnakavi would either drop by or send for them by the turn of the week. She was pleased to have been proved right.

"These are all patterns and weaves that I have seen before," the aristocrat complained wearily as she tossed saris aside. "I expected something truly unique."

"Do you have something specific in mind?" Parnalata enquired innocently.

"Something that stands out," Varnakavi said. "That makes people stop and look." She was too vain to admit she'd been impressed by something that a friend, a merchant's wife, had worn.

"I think I know what you mean," Parnalata said, rising to her feet. "Please wait."

When she returned, Parnalata held a bundle in her hands. "I had woven this with someone from the palace in mind," she confessed in a conspiratorial tone. "But seeing you are no less a queen, this is for you." She unfurled the sari with a flourish to sighs of rapture from all those present. Sunlight fell on rich, pearl-grey silk inlaid with fine magenta and gold threads, which showed up only when light struck the fabric at certain angles. Intricate silverwork marked the length of the fall, winking in the sunshine.

Seeing Varnakavi's eyes widen, Parnalata knew the woman was hooked. "Perfect for someone as discerning as you. See?" She bent to spread a section of the sari across the lady's bosom and shoulder. "So stunning."

"It's nice," the guild master's wife agreed, trying not to look too impressed. "Perhaps I'll take it."

Inwardly, though, she was sighing with pleasure at having found the perfect sari to wear to the consecration of the new *homagriha* two weeks away. Draped in it, she would outshine all the Ikshvaku queens present. She'd preen, she'd be the centre of everyone's attention…

Varnakavi ended up taking nearly a dozen more saris in addition to the pearl-grey one, the large palanquin and large bearers coming in handy after all.

"A footstep into the palace," Nandana said with satisfaction as she stood beside her aunt and watched the little party disappear down the street.

"At least until we find a way of reaching the queen mothers or the queens," Parnalata agreed. She turned to the girl. "Now for the rishis' wives. Our lord is eager we breach the Sanctum quickly."

"We will, soon."

Nandana turned to go inside, but Parnalata stopped her. "How is your *dandapala*? It has been a while since he dropped by."

"His work has taken him out of town."

The aunt nodded. "Win his confidence. Gain his trust. You never know when he'll be useful to us."

Winning confidence and gaining trust were going to be crucial if she was to succeed in her scheme—which involved corrupting Ayodhya's sacred fire and rendering it powerless. No sacred fire meant no magic in Ayodhya's atmosphere, and in the absence of magic, even the redoubtable *mahayoddhas* would be incapable of protecting their kingdom against a rakshasa attack. For decades, the lord of Lanka had been trying to take Kosala, but every time, he had been thwarted by the *mahayoddhas* and the magic.

She had been sent to Ayodhya as Nandana's kind and loving aunt, Ma Parnalata, to change that.

She was here to pave the way for a rakshasa invasion.

She, Simhika.

Mother of Shadows. Sorceress of Lanka.

A small crowd of onlookers—mainly palace hands, some stable boys, two men cutting grass by the edge of the palace ground and a passing *nagarapala*—lounged under a spreading neem and observed Bharat and Shatrughna with curious eyes. The brothers, who were on horseback, drew apart, riding to opposite ends of the ground, their backs straight and swords drawn. Those under the tree switched their gazes from the brothers to Siripala, who stood in the middle of the ground and waited for the riders to turn their horses around to face each other, both animals in perfect alignment.

When he was certain the brothers had his attention, the old ostler raised one arm high. He held something small that was indistinguishable from under the neem tree, but the brothers nodded almost in unison. Siripala bent and placed the object—it was a lemon—on the ground before clearing out of the path of the two horses. He limped a dozen steps, then lifted his hand straight up again. This time, he held a red rag that blew in the intermittent breeze.

Without warning, the bodyguard let the cloth drop from his fingers.

Those watching from under the tree instinctively took two steps forward, edging closer in anticipation of the promised action and excitement.

Dust and thunder exploded under hooves as both horses charged towards each other in a straight line. Bharat and Shatrughna leaned out of their saddles, swords pointed and rock steady in their hands, their eyes pinned on the tiny lemon that lay in the mud, waiting and vulnerable. The distance between the steeds shrunk rapidly, the brothers slung lower, aiming their swords at the lemon—

—now they were crossing each other, swords stabbing the ground—

—now they were riding into one another's dust clouds—

—and Bharat thrust his sword into the air in triumph, waving it above the dust cloud, the lemon planted on the weapon's tip, punctured and bleeding its juice down the shiny blade.

Reining his horse in, Shatrughna turned and cantered back to his brother. "I missed by an inch," he said ruefully.

"You missed by a mile," Bharat grinned, plucking the fruit from the sword and tossing it aside.

"Okay, two to you, one to me."

"Two to go," said Siripala, approaching. He clutched the rag and two fresh lemons in his hand.

The brothers returned to their places, and Shatrughna took the next round.

"Two each," Siripala announced, smiling. "Quite fitting. One is the better swordsman, the other a superior rider."

In the decider, both horses sped like the wind, both swords came down upon the hapless lemon like flashes of lightning, and the crowd moved from the tree's shelter in its eagerness to observe the result of the contest.

Both swords struck the lemon, but only one split the fruit's rind, wrenching it open as the steeds passed each other—and Shatrughna whooped in delight as he brandished the ragged lemon at the end of his sword. A murmur of admiration broke from the watchers as the outcome became clear.

"Three–two in your favour," smiled Bharat. He clapped his brother affectionately on the back.

"This was a test of swordsmanship," grinned Shatrughna. "I had to win."

"Absolutely," the king said, carefully avoiding the sharp looks he was drawing from Siripala.

Seeing the brothers dismount, the spectators started disassembling to go their ways. Bharat took his horse by the bridle and led it towards the stable.

"We gave them something to marvel at," Shatrughna said, indicating the men leaving the shade of the neem. He couldn't stop grinning as he fell in step with Bharat.

The king eyed the crowd. He had never understood why the sport had not caught on in Kosala; its appeal was plain, given the number of people who watched and cheered them on whenever they played.

"It's been a while since we did," Bharat agreed.

"It's been ages," Shatrughna said, looking pleased. "I wasn't sure I'd hit the target even once."

"They say you never forget what you learn in childhood," said Bharat.

"That makes sense," the younger brother replied. "We played almost every day in Kekeya. I remember mama teaching us how to lean out of the saddle." His eyes had a faraway look now. "Later, we'd go to the spot where travellers threw coins into the Vitasta for good luck, and we'd dive underwater and compete to collect *rupa*s and *karshapana*s. Remember? And you wouldn't let me go deep because you were afraid I'd win." Shatrughna smiled to show he held no grudges.

Bharat shook his head. Two boys, both motherless in

Kekeya, left to their devices with no one to look out for them. Shatrughna had been so much smaller back then, scrawny, bones jutting out everywhere, not the brawny wrestler he had recently turned into. "I didn't let you dive deep because I was scared something would happen to you."

"Funny, because I'm the better swimmer. I remember racing you across the Vitasta and beating you every time." Shatrughna grinned. "Such fond memories. I'm happy you sent for me. I haven't had as much fun in such a long time."

They were tethering the horses when Bharat glanced at Shatrughna. "I actually asked you to come for a very different reason," he said. Choosing his words carefully, he went on, "Apart from denying you those dives for a handful of *karshapanas*, there is one other thing I have knowingly kept you away from, brother."

"And that is…?"

"An active role in the administration of Kosala."

Shatrughna looked at his brother, mildly puzzled.

"I didn't want to burden you with responsibilities, so I kept you away from the court even when you showed an interest in helping out. But I see that I might have made a mistake, as I did with the diving. Maybe we'll discover you're good at this too." Bharat chuckled and scooped some hay, which he dumped in front of his horse. "There's only one way of finding out."

Shatrughna's expression changed to one of anticipation. "You mean you will involve me in the running of Kosala's affairs?"

"Yes, it is time—"

"I would love to help," Shatrughna reached out to grab his brother's arm. "I will—"

"Listen to me," Bharat said patiently. "I know you are eager to assist me, and I don't doubt you will fulfil your responsibilities well. But it will not be easy. You will be called to make tough, unpopular choices. You might have to decide people's fates, determine who lives and who dies. Wisdom and compassion will vie with the need to deliver justice, peace and security. Fairness might not be enough to keep people happy. There will be times when there are no right answers. This is the life I am asking you to step into from tomorrow."

"I understand," Shatrughna said, his boyish face serious for the first time.

Bharat squeezed his brother's hand. "Help me run this kingdom and honour the promise I made to brother to keep Kosala safe and its people happy until he returns from exile."

"I will do what I can, to the best of my abilities," Shatrughna said firmly. "Let me know what you want done."

Bharat looked at the young man's solemn face and smiled. "I want you to leave for Madhupura on an urgent mission to meet Raja Lavanyasurya..."

It was dark by the time Mandavi and Shrutakirti knocked on the door of Kaikeyi's chamber. The outcast queen peered suspiciously out of the crack in the door before the visitors' identities registered in her mind.

"This is indeed a surprise," Kaikeyi exclaimed, pulling the door open. "Come in..."

Shrutakirti followed Mandavi in, her head bowed, her eyes darting furtively from the queen to Mandavi, watching her elder sister for cues on what to do and say next. Mandavi bent to touch her mother-in-law's feet, but as Shrutakirti stepped forward to do likewise, Kaikeyi caught her by the shoulders, stopping her.

"That is alright, child," she said, looking into Shrutakirti's wide, wonderstruck eyes. Letting go of the girl, she switched her gaze to Mandavi and said, "Take a seat while I get you some cool buttermilk."

Kaikeyi was turning away when Mandavi said, "Mother, don't bother. We should get back soon; it is nearing time for dinner. I just brought Kirti here to seek your blessings."

The queen paused and turned, her face losing brightness. Her eyes went to Shrutakirti.

"She is..." Mandavi began, but Kaikeyi was already nodding.

"I heard," she said. A quiver of emotion rippled through her voice. "I didn't expect you to come to seek blessings from me."

"Mother Kausalya insisted," said Mandavi.

If she was surprised, Kaikeyi didn't show it. When Shrutakirti bent before her, the queen placed a hand gently on her head. Once the girl had straightened, Kaikeyi gripped her by the shoulders again and looked at her with kind eyes. "May the child you bear be your source of strength and joy, and may the child make you proud. Bless you, my child."

"Thank you, mother," Shrutakirti murmured.

"Thank you, mother," Mandavi added. The sisters exchanged sidelong glances, silently telling each other that the purpose of their visit had been achieved, and it was now time to leave. "We must go," said Mandavi, taking a step back.

Shrutakirti was almost at the door in the rush to be out of there, when Kaikeyi addressed her.

"I would like a word with your sister. Can she stay?"

"Mother, it is dark outside and Kirti is alone—" Mandavi began, but Shrutakirti broke in.

"No, it's okay. I can find my way." She nodded at Kaikeyi. "She can stay."

The queen waited until Shrutakirti's footsteps had dwindled into silence before she asked, "How is he?"

"Who? Bharat?"

"No." An impatient frown wrinkled Kaikeyi's brow. "*Taksha.*"

"Oh, he is doing well. He simply loves running around outdoors with Angara."

"That's the dog Bharat brought back," Kaikeyi nodded. "You could have brought him along."

This time, Mandavi rightly interpreted that the queen meant Taksha, and not Bharat or the dog. She shook her head. "I cannot disobey my husband's orders."

Kaikeyi took a step towards her daughter-in-law. "Does Bharat realize his responsibility to Taksha?" she asked with concern in her voice.

"I don't know what you mean, mother."

The queen let out a short sigh. "Bharat will not listen to me, but with you, it's different. Talk to him. Ask him what he is doing to ensure that his son's future is secure."

"I don't understand," Mandavi blinked.

"He refuses to become king, but has he considered how his decision will impact Taksha? What legacy is he planning to leave for his son? What will his son do when he grows up; where will he rule? Or will he end up as a royal without a kingdom of his own? Is Bharat even thinking about this?"

"I don't know, mother."

"That is why I wanted to talk to you. Bharat must realize that as a father, he has a huge responsibility. He must learn from his father's mistakes. Dashratha was so blinded by his love for Rama that he forgot he had three other sons. He thought only about Rama, never about the other three. He assumed they would serve their elder brother, but why would one assume that? It's the same with Bharat. Why should he assume Taksha will want to serve Rama's sons? Taksha might want to be king one day, and it is on Bharat to make the boy's dream come true. And he cannot do that by refusing to sit on Kosala's throne."

"But... Rama's brothers are happy to serve him," said Mandavi.

"Really?" Kaikeyi arched her eyebrows to show she disagreed. "Perhaps you are right. But the truth is that we will never know for certain. Maybe if they had lands to rule, they would have shown the ambition and the inclination to be kings. But thanks to their father's shortsightedness, they have none, and so they are left to serve their eldest brother." Seeing the confusion on Mandavi's face, the queen proffered a harsh smile. "A sensible father would have made sure there was enough territory for all of his sons to rule over. If Dashratha had wanted one son to sit on Kosala's throne, he could have taken Kasi, Chedi and Madhupura for his other three sons. He was a powerful king; he could have done that. Four sons, each with a kingdom to rule. Everyone would have been happy. But no, that's not what he did. Dashratha failed as a father because he did nothing to provide for the ambitions and the future of three of his sons."

"He chose friendship with Chedi, Kasi and Madhupura over war," Mandavi said in a soft voice, scarcely believing what she had just heard.

"He did. And what did he get in return? Some trade concessions, nothing else. And, remember my words, Chedi, Kasi and Madhupura will stab Kosala in the back the moment it suits their interests. I have said this to my father as well; there are no everlasting friendships in politics."

Mandavi studied her fingernails, her mind spinning with everything that her mother-in-law had said. Could this even be true? That Bharat, Lakshmana and Shatrughna secretly nursed ambitions of becoming kings, but could not because Dashratha had not had the foresight to expand his kingdom…

"Taksha may not develop ambitions of becoming king," she said.

Kaikeyi gave her daughter-in-law a smile that was one part pity, one part scorn. "Certainly not, if his father is his role model."

Mandavi said nothing for a moment. Then, "I should go."

Kaikeyi nodded once, then motioned for her to wait. She looked about the room, and her eyes alighted on a clay stylus holder resting on a table. Selecting an ivory stylus yellowing with age, Kaikeyi took the younger woman's hand and placed the stylus on her palm.

"This was gifted to me by Taksha's great-grandfather," she said. "It was his. It is now the boy's. I am told he has started learning the alphabet."

"Thank you," Mandavi closed her fingers around the stylus, surprised and touched by the older woman's gesture.

"Teach him well. Teach him that his destiny is to be king," said Kaikeyi. "Be a better mother to Taksha than I was to Bharat. Go now. It is indeed dark."

Deep in thought, Mandavi turned the stylus in her hands before taking leave of her mother-in-law. She had her back to Kaikeyi when she stopped and turned.

"There's something that has bothered Bharat that I meant to ask you," she said.

"What is that?"

"You might have wanted Bharat to be king, but couldn't you see that Dashratha always wanted to name Rama as his successor?"

"It never crossed my mind that he did," Kaikeyi replied. "Not until the moment he said Rama would be the next king of Kosala."

Mandavi stared in bewilderment. "But he loved Rama more, *adored* him. Even *you* knew it."

"Of course, he did, and of course, I knew. It was obvious."

"Then what made you believe he would make Bharat the heir to the throne?"

The queen's eyes narrowed at the memory of Dashratha's promise to Ashwapati all those years ago. "The notion that for an Ikshvaku king, his word would carry far more weight than his love for someone."

An icy smile flitted across Kaikeyi's lips. "Apparently, I was naïve in expecting adherence to such lofty ideals."

Kushadhwaja nudged the door open and peered in to find Bharat pacing the width of the chamber, his head bent, his eyes on his feet as they measured the floor.

"You wanted to see me," said Kushadhwaja, easing into the room.

Bharat stopped and looked at his father-in-law. "I didn't call... I didn't mean to ask you to come," he said. "I sent the attendant over to see if you were still awake so I could come—"

"Ah, it's nothing," Kushadhwaja waved his hand. "I figured you wished to see me. Your coming there or my coming here... it's all the same." He paused as he drew near his son-in-law. "What is it? Why do you look so troubled?"

Bharat pulled a face and drew his breath. "I just got confirmation of Pushyanta's activities."

"What Sheelabhadra told you is true?"

"All of it."

Kushadhwaja drew a breath of his own and blew out his cheeks as he let the news settle. "What did your *dandapala* discover?"

Motioning to his father-in-law to follow him, Bharat walked to a side table on which lay a square of folded linen. The king flipped the folds back, and in the light of the globe that hung over the table, Kushadhwaja saw a crude but legible map of Kosala drawn on the cloth.

"The *dandapala*... his name is Dileepa," said Bharat, "spent a whole week watching every one of Pushyanta's storehouses in the city. He discovered that four of those storehouses have a disproportionate number of guards deployed, and the guards are watchful and suspicious of anyone loitering in the vicinity. Dileepa did manage getting inside one of these buildings by posing as a labourer, however."

"What did he find?"

"The place was stacked with *gonis* of rice and lentils."

"It is reasonable to assume it'd be no different in the other three storehouses," Kushadhwaja remarked.

Bharat nodded. "Interestingly, Dileepa discovered two more well-guarded granaries here and here," he pointed to two spots marked on the map.

"Outside Ayodhya," the older man raised his eyebrows.

"And he overheard workers mentioning a granary in the town of Banasi," Bharat pointed at the map again. "He followed that lead to a freshly turned wheat field right at the foothills of the Himalayas. There, under the field, deep in the earth, is another hidden storeroom where every imaginable foodstuff is being hoarded."

"Remote and well concealed. Probably the base of the operation," Kushadhwaja surmised.

"Well concealed and well guarded."

"The *dandapala* gained his entry by pretending to be a labourer again?"

Bharat shook his head with a smile. "He told the guards he worked for Pushyanta, and that he was there to assess if they were up to the mark and were doing their jobs well. People tend to be accommodating towards those who are evaluating their performance, and Dileepa got the guards to show him everything he wished to see."

Kushadhwaja clicked his tongue, impressed by the investigator's ingenuity. After a moment, he asked, "Is there proof to link the storehouses and granaries to Pushyanta?"

"There is."

"What if Pushyanta claims the foodstuff is meant for the market and that the guards are there only to stop attempts at robbery and pilferage?" Kushadhwaja asked. "It's a plausible defence."

"It is," agreed the king, "except that if they were intended for the market, as part of his duty as guild master, Pushyanta would have informed Sheshagupta about the arrival of fresh stocks in the city. The revenue minister shared the latest tally of grains and other materials with me just this afternoon… and there was no mention of fresh supplies of food in his report. Why?"

"An oversight?" Kushadhwaja suggested, playing the devil's advocate.

"Not in a time of looming drought and spiralling food prices," smiled Bharat mirthlessly. "Also, the *dandapala* has further learned that none of these granaries or storehouses is listed in official records. Why is Kosala's guild master storing commodities in unofficial godowns instead of stocking them in designated storehouses, *where guarding them against pilferage is the responsibility of the palace and the city's administration*?"

"The *dandapala* has found a lot of incriminating evidence against Pushyanta," Kushadhwaja acknowledged. "Is he the one waiting outside? I saw a tall, nice-looking fellow as I came in… young for a *dandapala*."

Bharat nodded. "I asked him to wait for my instructions."

"Hmm," said Kushadhwaja, but before he could say any more, the light dimmed and shadows came down like curtains as the globe sputtered and waned over the open map.

Both men stared until the globe caught and burned anew, as though nothing at all had happened.

"It's occurring more often?" the older man gestured towards the light with a raised eyebrow.

"The magic..." Bharat muttered, blinking and staring away from the globe's glare.

Kushadhwaja nodded. "Right, so there is enough evidence to have Pushyanta arrested."

"Yes, but..." Bharat ran his fingers through his hair in a display of indecision, "shouldn't I let *adhipati* Sudhanva know beforehand?" he asked.

"Why?" the older man probed.

"The guild master is the *adhipati's* son-in-law."

"So?"

The young king shucked his shoulders. "Father and the *adhipati* were old friends; they enjoyed one another's trust. So, just out of respect for Sudhanva..." He paused. "If father had been faced with this choice, I believe he would have informed Sudhanva."

"Okay, so your father informs Sudhanva. Now, what if Sudhanva asked your father not to arrest and charge Pushyanta?"

Bharat stared at his father-in-law, caught off guard. "Why would the *adhipati*...?"

"Pushyanta's arrest will tarnish Sudhanva's reputation, that's why. Nothing riles nobility more than a bad name, and it will go to great lengths to protect its image."

Bharat pondered this in silence.

"Given the scale of corruption Pushyanta has indulged in, do you think your father would agree to let the guild master go free on his friend's request?"

"No. Father would convince the *adhipati*."

"Now, what if Sudhanva asks *you* not to arrest and charge Pushyanta?" Kushadhwaja prodded. "Would you let Pushyanta go unpunished out of respect for Sudhanva?" With a pause, he asked, "Will you be able to convince the *adhipati* that Pushyanta must be arrested? What if he insists his son-in-law should be let off?"

Overwhelmed, Bharat shook his head.

"It is unfair to model all your actions on your father's because your realities are different," said the lord of Rajviraj. "You have to act on the basis of *your* reality."

The king nodded slowly but didn't reply. The silence of the night pressed in around the two men.

"You should act," said Kushadhwaja. "You keep saying that public morale has been low ever since the rakshasa attack. Then the drought, people going missing, rising prices. You finally have an opportunity to act decisively and show the people you are unwilling to tolerate anyone taking them for a ride. Give people something to be pleased about. Show them you are firmly on their side."

The king mulled this over.

"There's one other thing," he said finally, turning to his father-in-law. "What if Pushyanta isn't alone in this? What if there are others involved in this racket? Big names from the court..."

Kushadhwaja watched Bharat. "Whom are you thinking about?"

Bharat shrugged. "I don't know. Sheelabhadra termed the court a pit of vipers while urging me not to trust anyone. Considering he was right about Pushyanta, he's probably right about other things as well."

"Let us assume there are others," Kushadhwaja egged the king on. "What's your concern?"

"Once I act against Pushyanta, everyone else will be alerted. They would have enough time to cover their tracks. But if I wait and strike *after* I've got evidence against everyone, no one will escape punishment. Everyone goes down together."

"There is merit in your thinking," Kushadhwaja conceded. "But if you don't act now, how will you free the foodgrains lying in Pushyanta's undisclosed granaries? How will you bring relief to the people who are suffering because of food shortages and rising prices? That is your first responsibility."

Bharat nodded. "I hadn't thought about that."

"Moreover," said the older man, "if you don't act quickly, you might even give Pushyanta the chance to clean up after himself."

"How is that?"

"Banasi is but a day's journey from here. Someone there can easily bring Dileepa's visit to Pushyanta's notice. Just a casual mention is enough. Pushyanta wouldn't know what to make of it, but he'd know for certain *he* hadn't sent anyone to inspect the security at the granary. That's it. He'd figure out someone was prying into his dodgy dealings, and he would immediately set about destroying all the evidence linking him to his crimes."

Bharat smacked his forehead in exasperation. "I'm not thinking straight." Striding over to a set of listening bells, he literally bellowed, "Chaitanya."

"Your *dandapala's* zest for truth and justice is quite admirable," Kushadhwaja remarked drily, "but his resourcefulness might already have alerted the guild master. Hopefully, it's not too late to nab the man."

Chaitanya appeared at the door.

"Fetch Baladitya," Bharat ordered. "Tell him to assemble a hundred *nagarapalas* double-quick. And on your way out, ask the *dandapala* to come in."

The palace marshal left, and a moment later, Dileepa stepped into the chamber.

"You will go with Baladitya," the king said, speaking of the *mahanayaka* of the *nagarapalas*.

"Yes, rajan," Dileepa replied. He knew more instructions were to follow and what they'd be.

"As the *dandapala* running this investigation," Bharat continued, "you will lead the raids on Pushyanta's storehouses and arrest the guild master for committing treason against the good people of Kosala."

# *eight*

SUDHANVA WAS SEETHING WITH ANGER AS HE STALKED out of the palace and turned into the path leading to the royal stable.

Angry at whoever had tipped the palace off about Pushyanta's misdemeanours.

Angry at Pushyanta for having been stupid enough to leave a trail behind.

Angry at his contacts within the palace, who had failed to pick up the scent of trouble brewing against his son-in-law.

Angry at the palace for having ordered Pushyanta's arrest without first informing him—*him, a loyal and veteran councilor of Kosala*—about the arrest.

But angriest at having had to cancel his trip into the cool mountains of Sankasya for a hunt with his friends, a trip that he had been looking forward to for many weeks now.

Painfully conscious of the stares of palace hands and officials—the news of Pushyanta's arrest had spread rapidly—Sudhanva slowed to a statelier tread, more in line with the persona of a powerful *adhipati* of the provinces. His jaw remained clenched though, and his breathing was strained as the stable came into view at the other end of the palace ground, partly concealed by the trees.

He had been in the middle of a dream—a very pleasant one, that's all he remembered—when he was shaken awake by a wailing Varnakavi and a worried Yadudeva, informing him that the *nagarapalas* had taken Pushyanta into custody in the wee hours. Even as the shock of this had settled in, reports of Pushyanta's storehouses in Ayodhya being seized and sealed arrived. Irate and inconsolable, Varnakavi had harangued and hectored him into meeting the king to demand the immediate release of her husband.

The sun had lifted itself free of the horizon, and in its golden-yellow light, Sudhanva could see the old bodyguard Siripala leading a horse out of the stable as Taksha ran around the front yard with the dog that Bharat seemed very attached to. There was no sign of the king himself though, the *adhipati* thought irritably as his gaze swept the ground. They'd told him in the palace that Bharat would be here…

Noticing him, Siripala let go of the horse and limped out to meet him. "Greetings," the bodyguard said, joining his hands in a *pranaam*.

Sudhanva joined his hands in a cursory manner, his eyes roving in search of Bharat. "Isn't the rajan around?" he enquired.

"He has taken his horse for a gallop, yajmaan," Siripala replied.

*Taken his horse for a gallop*, Sudhanva stifled the urge to shout out in frustration. Here, his son-in-law was under arrest and his daughter was throwing one hell of a fit about it, and all the king was concerned about was riding out with his horse. "Any idea where he has gone or when he'll be back?" he asked as politely as possible.

"It's getting time for the kumara's breakfast, so he should be back soo—ah, there he is!"

The nobleman followed Siripala's finger to see Bharat and his mount come into view. The king rode with an ease that came from being put in the saddle at an early age, and Sudhanva realized that part of it was also the result of growing up in Kekeya, where horsemanship was taught and mastered before the alphabet was learned. Bharat slowed the galloping beast to a canter before reining it in next to the stable. The ride had vitalized horse and rider, and Bharat was positively glowing with pleasure as he dismounted and looked in Sudhanva's direction.

"Greetings," the young king said. He obviously knew what had brought Sudhanva to the palace this early in the day—he must have even *expected* this visit, Sudhanva guessed—but it didn't show in his face.

"Greetings, rajan," the *adhipati* said tersely.

"How are you?"

"I am well, rajan."

"Good." Bharat looked at Taksha, who was drawing in the mud with a stick. The dog had gone to sniff at the horses, who seemed quite unperturbed by the attention they were getting. "Come, it's time to go," Bharat called out to the kid. The kid pretended not to hear.

Sudhanva ground his teeth together and tried to put on a pleasant face. "I'd like to have a word."

"Yes?" said Bharat.

The nobleman didn't speak immediately but motioned with his head for more privacy. Bharat walked half-a-dozen paces to put some distance between them and Siripala.

"Yes," he said again, coming to a stop.

"May I ask why Pushyanta has been arrested like a common criminal?"

"Because he has behaved like one," the king said.

Sudhanva was taken aback by Bharat's choice of words. He had expected the boy to make conciliatory noises and offer reassurances—maybe even an *apology*.

"What has he done?"

"Hoarding, profiteering… serious crimes against the people of Kosala."

"It can't be. Someone is trying to frame him."

"His storehouses and granaries were under surveillance for more than a week. We found what was inside. Not just here in Ayodhya. There's evidence of hoarding even in Banasi." Bharat looked the *adhipati* in the eye. "There is a granary there… *hidden under a field*."

"It…" Sudhanva cast around for ideas, "maybe it's the managers and overseers who're doing this. Pushyanta has no clue."

"Since he is the owner of those granaries and storehouses, it is his responsibility to keep tabs on his property and the people he employs," Bharat shrugged. "Anyway, he will have the opportunity to defend himself when he is presented in court."

"Presented in—you'll *do* that? Why?" the nobleman sputtered in outrage. "It's not necessary. This is *all* so unnecessary. Think about the scandal. The people are all going to talk badly about the aristocracy. Spare a thought for our reputation, Bharat." He paused to draw breath. "For God's sake, if you had to have him arrested, you could have put him under house arrest instead of hauling him away to the cells in chains." He shook his head. "Your father would *never* have approved of this."

Bharat froze for a moment, his face clouding with sudden doubt. But then, his features hardened, and the eyes he turned on the *adhipati* were narrow and cold.

"What father would never have approved of is this filthy scam that Pushyanta has dared to pull on Kosala," he hissed. "Pushyanta was using the office given to him by father to scheme against the kingdom for personal gain. He didn't miss a beat in breaching father's trust once father was gone… *so don't bring father into this to tell me I was wrong.*"

The vehemence of those last words startled Sudhanva, and Bharat took advantage of the silence to drive his point in. "And if the aristocracy is so bothered about its reputation, perhaps it should behave in a manner that doesn't give people the opportunity to talk badly of it." The king turned to his son. "Taksha, we must go now."

Maybe it was something in Bharat's tone, or maybe the child was just bored. Either way, Taksha rose, threw the stick away and toddled over to take his father's finger. Seeing his friend depart, Angara came bounding along, tail wagging. Sudhanva eyed the dog with suspicion. He disliked dogs following him. It reminded him of the time he'd been chased and bitten by one as a child.

"Why didn't you bring this to my notice the moment you got to know?" Sudhanva asked, falling in step beside the king while keeping his distance from Angara.

"How would that have changed anything?"

"We could have investigated the matter discreetly, got to the root of things and caught the real culprit."

"That is assuming we haven't caught the real culprit."

Behind them, Siripala whistled sharply to call the dog back.

"Pushyanta is innocent and has been framed," Sudhanva's tone hardened again.

"If he is, he will be set free and the guilty will be caught."

"That won't help. It will be too late," the *adhipati* complained bitterly. "Our names would have been dragged through the mud."

Bharat didn't reply. They walked side by side, Taksha trotting between them. Angara had gone back to the stable.

"I don't know whose advice you took, but you've acted rashly, Bharat," Sudhanva spoke again. "You should have taken me into confidence. You really do need a *kshatri* to advise you better."

"It was a carefully thought through decision," the young king insisted.

"Really?" the nobleman sneered. "He is my son-in-law. You didn't spare a moment to consider our standing in the community."

"Your son-in-law didn't spare a moment to consider the suffering of the people," the king shot back, realizing how right Kushadhwaja had been about the nobility's pride.

They had reached a fork in the path. Sudhanva slowed to a stop. "I must see him," he said.

"You will, when he is presented tomorrow in court."

"I can't wait," the *adhipati* snapped.

"He is in the custody of the state and can't see anyone."

"He is my son-in-law," Sudhanva said, now positively angry.

Bharat studied the older man. "I would have shown greater leniency if Pushyanta had been just a greedy merchant," he said finally. "But he is also Kosala's guild master, and as guild master, he has breached the public's trust. That is unpardonable. So, even though he is your son-in-law, Pushyanta must and will answer to the court and the people of this kingdom."

The small boy had to stand on his toes to peer into the depths of the well, from whence the pail emerged at the end of a rope, brimming and sloshing with water. Up and up it came, hauled by strong hands until it cleared the well's lip, where the man standing next to the boy grabbed it.

"Nari, step back," the man scolded in a voice ringing with concern. "I have told you to keep your distance from the well. One slip of the foot…" he left the rest unsaid as the boy quickly pulled back. He was about seven, slightly small for his age, with floppy hair and mischievous eyes. Though they were father and son, the two shared little resemblance. In his late thirties, the man was on his way to flabbiness, his belly becoming his most prominent feature aside of his kind, jovial face with its thick moustache and friendly eyes. "Just be careful," he added in a soft tone of conciliation. "Okay?"

The boy nodded and gave a timid smile, glad to have escaped more severe censure. The man grinned and altered his grip on the bucket. "Here, take this." He chucked the pail's contents at the boy, who anticipated the move, but only pretended to dodge it. Cold water soused with fractions of sunlight sped across the intervening space to hit the boy, who squealed and whooped in delight as the father gave a hearty laugh.

"Aren't you two done with bathing yet?" a voice called.

The man turned to look at the woman who had appeared at the backdoor of the house abutting the small yard with the well.

"Almost done," he called back.

"Hurry up or you'll both be late," the woman said before retreating inside.

The man eyed the boy and pulled a funny face. "Hurry up or you'll both be late," he mimicked the woman good-naturedly, and the boy burst out laughing, bending over in mirth.

Later, when the man and the boy sat on the floor as the woman laid banana leaves before them, the boy gave his father a sidelong glance and grinned slyly. "Mother," he addressed the woman. "Father was making fun of you."

"Really?" the woman asked, only half-listening as she ladled vegetable gravy onto the leaves.

"I did not," the man stared at the boy in mock outrage.

"He did. He was pretending to speak like you do."

"Nonsense," the man growled.

"Well, if your father can at least pretend to *think* the way I think, it'd be a huge improvement," the woman chuckled with a sweet smile. She was short and plump and wore a silver nose ring that had impossibly tiny silver bells in its hoop.

"Oh," the man retorted, looking at his wife.

"See?" the woman pointed. "*Oh*... that's the best he can muster when faced with facts."

The boy laughed, thoroughly enjoying the exchange that he had set in motion.

"What are you laughing about?" the man asked. Pointing to the leaf, he ordered. "Eat."

Turning back to his wife, he asked, "Where is Asmita?"

"She is getting ready."

"You ask us to hurry up and—"

"She's already had breakfast."

"Oh," the man muttered and tucked into his food as mother and son exchanged impish smiles.

Asmita appeared from an inside room, dressed fastidiously, her hair in two proper plaits. She was five years older than her brother, and she had the same smile. The man's face lit up with pride and pleasure at the sight of his daughter.

"Ready?" he asked. "Give us both a moment."

"I'm done," said Nari, folding the banana leaf back and rising.

"I think she should start paying attention to the household," the wife said. "She hasn't learned to cook yet and she is—"

"Mother," Asmita protested, then looked to her father in appeal.

"Vedika…" the husband began.

"All I am saying is she is growing up and reaching marriageable age," said the mother.

"Vedika, she is just *twelve*," the man insisted. Rising from his place, he went to wash his hands. "Let her study. She has plenty of time to learn cooking and everything else—"

"When I was her age, I knew how to run a house."

"When you were her age, you didn't know how to read or write," the man pointed out patiently as he wiped his hands dry on his wife's *uttariya*.

"Even *now* she doesn't know how to read or write," Asmita glared at her mother in petulance. "She needs Nari or me to total the household expenses."

The woman's face fell, and her shoulders sagged.

"Not fair, Asmi," the man turned solemn eyes on the girl. "Your mother is making an effort to learn and you know it." In response, the girl dropped her gaze and slipped out of the room. The man took his wife's hands into his. "Let her study. We know she is good at it. When the time comes, she will learn how to run a home, okay?"

"You love her a lot, so you let her do whatever she wants."

"I love *all* of you, so I let *all* of you do whatever you want—including saying things like I am in need of improvement." He smiled to show that he understood she had spoken in jest, and he held no grudges.

"You, Swagata of Kosala, are in no need of improvement," Vedika looked at her husband with doting eyes. "You are perfect the way you are."

"Aren't we getting late?" Asmita called from the door. Nari stood next to her, satchel in hand.

"Yes, let's go." Swagata hurried to join the kids, gathering up his *upanayaka's* staff as he went.

"Take your lunch," Vedika called in exasperation. "You're getting so forgetful nowadays..."

It was another fifteen minutes before Swagata dropped the children off at Madhupura's main *patthshala* and picked the route leading to Kosala's garrison in the middle of the city. Passing along the side streets where shops were just opening for business, Swagata greeted friends and acquaintances, stopping on occasion to exchange pleasantries in the shade of makeshift awnings put up to guard against the heat and glare of the sun. These were familiar faces seen along familiar roads, and everyone in the city met him like he was one of their own and not a native of Kosala.

It was nearly two decades since he had been sent to Madhupura as a replacement for a soldier who was taking his retirement. The garrison had been around from the time of the bandit raids on Madhupura, but it had reduced in strategic importance and now served more as a symbol of goodwill and bonhomie between Kosala and Madhupura. Designed to house two hundred men, the garrison now had a strength of less than twenty, and this included cooks and stable boys. A posting to Madhupura generally meant an easy life, though the chances of advancement were also limited. Not that this mattered to Swagata. He was already an *upanayaka* and happy where he was; with some luck, the garrison's *nayaka* would retire in a couple of years, and Swagata would take his place. Command over twenty men—more like a dozen, discounting the cook and the stable boys and cleaners—meant nothing in terms of real authority, but a *nayaka* was a *nayaka* and there was prestige attached to the post. And anyway, Swagata didn't want much more than he already had in life.

When he had first come to the city, he had been friendless and full of ambition. He had cursed the moment that had brought him to Madhupura, and he couldn't wait to get back to Kosala so he could have a real shot at rising up the ranks. But the years passed, and he wasn't called back. Then, one afternoon, he encountered an ageing boat repairman sprawled in a backstreet. The man had suffered a heatstroke, and Swagata had helped him to his house, fetched a *vaidya* and saved the man's life. He had also met his only daughter, Vedika. A year later, they were married, and after two months, the old repairman died, leaving his house to his daughter and son-in-law.

Five years had passed since Swagata's last visit home when his mother had passed away, and the *upanayaka* no longer missed Kosala. Madhupura was now home. It was where his wife hailed from, it was where his children had been born and raised. It was where he belonged. Kosala was but a fading memory, the garrison and its men the last link to a past life that seemed to belong to a different lifetime.

Of course, Swagata was not thinking about any of this as he turned at the periphery of the city market and went down the lane that ran past the garrison's back entrance. Whistling to himself, he thought about the money he had carefully set aside to purchase a plot of land on the outskirts of Madhupura, where he and Vedika planned to grow mangoes. The house they lived in would go to Asmita and Nari, while he and Vedika moved out to live in the lap of nature, surrounded by mango—

Swagata's pleasant little reverie was interrupted by the sound of raised voices and the creak of a gate opening. Looking up, he saw a pair of the garrison's soldiers jog past the end of the lane; they seemed armed with swords…

Gripping his ceremonial staff, Swagata broke into a run. Ten strides brought him to the end of the lane, where he stopped to see the two soldiers disappear around a corner. Turning right, he entered the garrison's headquarters through the small open gate that was set into a larger closed one. He crossed the small rear courtyard and walked in through the door to see three men come rushing down a flight of stairs. They were his colleagues, and they were bearing javelins.

It was with some surprise that Swagata noticed the soldier in the lead was the *nayaka*.

"Good you're finally here," the *nayaka* shouted as their eyes met. "Get a *kunta* and join us."

"What's going on?" Swagata asked. He couldn't remember a time when they had all been ordered to arm themselves and step out of the garrison.

"Trouble," the *nayaka* shouted as the three men brushed past.

"What sort of trouble?"

The *nayaka* slowed to looked at Swagata. "They're stopping Kosala's trade carts from entering Madhupura."

"Who is stopping the carts?"

"The city's guards. Just get your javelin and come."

A subdued murmur rose and fell around the medium-sized hall, heaving and rolling like a tide from end to end and back. Heads huddled and secretive glances were shot in every direction as courtiers conferred among themselves, each one trading fact and fiction in equal measure. Eyes scanned the room for a glimpse of Sudhanva or Yadudeva, but father and son were conspicuous by their absence, fuelling more rounds of debate and speculation, with someone even hazarding the suggestion that the *adhipati* had also been taken into custody with his errant son-in-law.

"He was here in the morning," whispered one knowledgeable soul. "To beg the king's pardon."

"I heard he was willing to buy Pushyanta's freedom," offered another courtier. "A big donation to the kingdom's coffers."

"Nonsense," differed a third. "Sudhanva is not the kind to grovel."

"And definitely not the kind to part easily with his wealth," came one derisive snort.

"My sources tell me he has fled to Sankasya. My guess is the king threatened to put him away."

"It's possible. He's not here," the first speaker pointed out.

"Why would he demean himself by coming here anyway?" someone else asked.

"You're right. It's so humiliating."

"Maybe he was told to stay away."

"I am telling you, there's no way Sudhanva did not—"

The speaker stopped in mid-sentence as a hush fell over the room. Looking up self-consciously, he saw Bharat walking in, followed closely by Sheshagupta, Sheelabhadra and Kushadhwaja. Everyone turned to face the king, eyes flitting from the king to the three men in his company, everyone wondering what kind of fate lay in store for Pushyanta and what the outcome of all this would be.

"Today isn't court day," Bharat began when he was sure he had everyone's attention. "But you have all been summoned here for reasons you already know something about. To put rumours to rest, guild master Pushyanta has been arrested on charges of hoarding food with the intention of selling it at a higher profit. The arrest comes in the wake of an investigation conducted by a *dandapala* appointed by the palace, and plenty of evidence has been gathered to press charges. The guild master is in custody, and a case is being made against him as we speak. He has been stripped of his responsibilities as guild master, and his properties, including his storehouses and granaries, have been sealed and confiscated until the case reaches its conclusion. He will be presented in court tomorrow to stand trial for wilfully working against the welfare and interests of the people of Kosala." He paused to look around. "Does anyone have any questions?"

Whispers broke out in pockets around the hall. One courtier raised a hand. "This investigation," he said, "did it look into anyone other than the guild master? I mean, are there others still under investigation—"

"No, the guild master was the target of the investigation." Bharat eyed the speaker. "But if you have a reason to believe that the scope of the investigation needs to be widened, the palace will be happy to hear your thoughts."

With a shake of his head, the courtier lowered his hand, suddenly aware of a lot of eyes on him.

"Anything else?" asked Bharat. The question was met with silence.

"As we are in need of a guild master until the case against Pushyanta is decided," he continued, "I hereby appoint yajmaan Sheelabhadra as provisional guild master of Kosala." The king looked at the veteran minister. "Please accept the responsibility of heading our trade guild and giving us the benefit of your knowledge and experience."

Sheelabhadra put his hands together and bowed quietly.

Bharat turned back to the crowd. "I have one more thing to share with all of you." He paused, collecting his thoughts. "As you know, Kosala hasn't had a *kshatri* in years. I have often been advised to appoint one," he smiled ironically. "In fact, as recently as this morning, I was told I needed a *kshatri* who could give me proper advice and guidance. I realized there was merit in those words, so I have decided to submit to them and appoint a *kshatri* for the palace. Let me introduce you to the new *kshatri* of Kosala…"

The king swept his hand towards the men by his side. "… Raja Kushadhwaja."

Gasps of surprise rose from the assembly and words were whispered as Kushadhwaja stared at his son-in-law, his mouth half-open.

"Our best wishes to the raja," said Sheshagupta, breaking the spell. The courtiers all broke into cheers, words of congratulations washing over Kushadhwaja, who blinked and smiled in return.

An hour passed before Kushadhwaja finally found himself alone with Bharat. "What was that?" he asked. "You could have at least warned me…"

"So you could say no," said Bharat with a grin.

"I can still say no."

"To me, yes. But not to the courtiers, not now. You have accepted their congratulations, remember?" The king laughed. "It is too late to back down."

"You conned me," said Kushadhwaja. He didn't look very upset about it though.

"I need you," said Bharat in a conciliatory tone. "Please."

"I am an *adhipati* of my own province… I have responsibilities there…"

"I am not asking you to turn your back on those responsibilities," Bharat argued. "All I want from you is support in the form of your presence and your advice whenever they're needed."

The older man heaved a sigh. "Why me? You could have picked Sheshagupta—"

"He is already burdened with the state's revenue."

"Or your new friend, Sheelabhadra—"

"Remember what you told me just yesterday?" Seeing his father-in-law frown, Bharat added, "When you urged me to send Shatrughna to Madhupura?"

"What are you referring to?"

"You said I must build a wall of trustworthy people around me to help deal with challenges. You reminded me that Shatrughna is one such person."

"I remember."

"Well, you are another. I trust you to help me in times of crisis and not let me down. Will you not be a part of the wall I am building for myself?"

Kushadhwaja was silent as they wound their way through the palace. "I had planned on leaving for Rajviraj with Shrutakirti in a day or two," he said.

"I know. Mandavi mentioned it. She wants to go with the two of you."

"I won't be able to take up the duties of the *kshatri* until after I am back."

"You had planned to be back in time for the consecration of the new *homagriha*. You can take the *kshatri's* oath the same day."

"The consecration is still two weeks away," Kushadhwaja eyed his son-in-law. "How are you going to keep your impatience in check for that long?"

Bharat laughed. "I have waited two years for a *kshatri*. I am sure I can wait another two weeks."

"Why aren't you granting our trade carts entry into the city?" the *nayaka* of Kosala's garrison demanded. "What is the problem?"

"Your merchants are refusing to pay the revised tariffs," the head of the guards at Madhupura's east gate scowled back. "*That* is the problem."

"We aren't *refusing* to pay anything, sir..." insisted the merchant who had become the de facto spokesperson for Kosala's detained traders. "We just don't have that much money with us. We didn't know that the tariffs had been revised... *again*."

"We have been told that your king has been informed about the revisions in trade concessions," the guard eyed the merchant with suspicion.

"We know nothing of this," the tubby little man pleaded his helplessness. "Nobody told us."

"I have my orders," the head of the guards stuck to the script pigheadedly. "Make your payment and I'll let you in. Otherwise, there's nothing I can do."

The sun beat down on the east road, which was filled with carts rolling in from Angadesh, Kasi, Chedi and countless smaller, independent principalities existing on the peripheries of the larger kingdoms. Madhupura's guards checked, cleared and waved these carts into the city, the traders all staring inquisitively at the seven carts from Kosala parked to one side and the men standing arguing around them. Guards from Madhupura were everywhere, outnumbering the men from Kosala's garrison by a very sizeable margin.

"Let us refer this to our trade advisor in Madhupura," Swagata spoke into the *nayaka's* ear. "It is his job to come over and mediate in such matters."

"He's not here." Seeing Swagata frown, the *nayaka* added, "I'm told he is in Ayodhya attending some wedding."

"Great," the *upanayaka* murmured under his breath.

"Look," the *nayaka* returned his attention to the head of the guards. "These men and these carts cannot stay here until our trade advisor returns to sort everything out. Let them in so they—"

"I can't, I can't—" the guard shook his head firmly.

"—so that they can have a place to stay until the trade advisor is back—"

"Don't you hear me?" the head of the guards shouted. "Don't you understand what I am saying?"

"Don't shout—" the *nayaka's* own voice rose in anger, but Swagata hurriedly pushed himself to the front.

"Sir, please listen to me," he addressed the head of the guards, cutting the *nayaka* off. "We are not asking you to clear their entry or grant them permits to engage in any trade-related activity. All we are asking is that you let them in so they can await the return of our trade advisor. That is all."

The guard considered this as he twirled his rich grey moustache. "Okay, assume I let them in," he said. "Where will they stay; where will they eat? They can't rent quarters in any of the city's *chhatras* or inns as they don't have the permit to be in the city."

"Then grant them those permits," snapped Kosala's *nayaka*.

The guard turned a sour face to the *nayaka* while pointing to Swagata, "He just said don't clear their entry. You say give them permits. Can you two first make up your minds about what you want?"

"Okay, okay…" Swagata butted in again. "How about this… You let them in without permits, and they eat and stay at the Kosala garrison till the trade advisor returns. No *chhatras*, no inns, no permits, nothing. Is that fine with you?"

The head guard mulled this over as a caravan of camel-carts rumbled out of the gates. "In theory, yes, but am not authorized to allow anyone in without—"

"Please consider this—" Swagata began.

"Come on," the *nayaka* exclaimed. "The garrison is Kosala's. You can't stop us from providing shelter to our own people."

"The garrison might be Kosala's, but it is *in* Madhupura's territory," the guard reminded hotly. "Gifted to Kosala by *our* king for your use."

"So that *we* could protect you during the bandit raids and train you to become capable fighters," the *nayaka* retorted with a smirk.

"Yeah right, *you* taught us to fight," the guard grinned derisively.

"Yes, we did. None of you fellows could even tell the difference between the tips and tails of your *shuls*—"

"Listen…" Swagata tried interrupting as more guards began swarming around them, drawn by the altercation. "This is not helping—"

"You watch your mouth, or I'll shove one of those *shuls* into you," the guard snarled, taking a step forward.

"I'll cut you open before you can even touch your *shul*," the *nayaka* roared.

"Come on, then," the head guard shouted, rising to the challenge. "Let us see how fast you are." He thrust an arm out to push the *nayaka* hard on the chest, sending the man staggering back three steps. At the same time, he snatched a spear from the hands of one of his men and braced himself for a fight.

The *nayaka* recovered his balance and stared at the head guard, his teeth bared, his eyes wide with rage. "Okay, you fool," he bellowed, pointing his javelin at the guard. "You die now."

"*Wait—*" Swagata screamed, not believing the speed with which this situation had descended into madness. He wanted to step in front of the *nayaka* in the hope of stopping him, but it felt like a heavy hand rested on his shoulder, holding him back. Time slowed and grew viscous before his eyes as he watched the *nayaka* hurl himself at the head of the guards. The javelin streaked towards its target, but with a combination of skill and good luck the guard succeeded in parrying the blow. All around them, Madhupura's guards were levelling their weapons, as were the soldiers in Kosala's small contingent. The air was rippling with anger, steel zinging loudly in the sudden silence that precedes hot, bloody, explosive violence.

*Wait—*

The *nayaka* and the head of the guards jabbed and thrust at each other, *shul* rattling against *kunta* until the press of the fighting pushed them close. Constrained, they kicked and wrestled for leverage, feet scuffing the earth for purchase, their free hands reaching out to grab, punch, claw and throttle. The guard took a blow on his cheek that left a livid bruise, but he gave back as good as he got, landing a cracking punch that split the *nayaka's* lips, leaving it bloodied and pulpy. Swords and spears arced in the harsh light as men on both sides let their instincts take over, and the air rang with the clang of metal and the grunts and snarls of men who had let their inner beasts out of their cages.

*Wait—*

Swagata flailed his arms, desperate to restore sense when someone slammed into him from the side. He reeled, ground and sky spinning and going lopsided as he lost his balance, and before he knew it, he had crashed to the ground. He lay there, his cheek in the mud, watching the sandalled feet of the men brawling around him, waiting for a foot to stomp his face…

"Stop…" a voice called out. "I said *stop*!"

There was a rush of feet, and as Swagata struggled to sit upright, he saw soldiers of Madhupura massing all around.

"Drop your weapons," someone ordered. "Drop them."

Swagata attempted to get to his feet, and he was grateful when hands grabbed him by both arms and assisted him to stand. He glanced to his right and left with the intention of offering thanks, but found he was flanked by hard-faced soldiers of Madhupura who refused to relax their hold, their fingers digging into the soft flesh of neglect that characterized his biceps and triceps.

"Last warning… drop your weapon!"

The *upanayaka* turned to see the *nayaka* let go of his *kunta*; it landed at his feet with a supple bounce. Immediately, a couple of guards grabbed the *nayaka*, pinning his arms while a third guard locked him in a chokehold from behind. Swagata noticed they were surrounded by the guards of Madhupura.

"What a disgrace," Swagata heard a voice say and realized it belonged to the person who had ordered the fight to a halt. Twisting his head all the way around, the *upanayaka* saw a group of men approach on horseback from the main road, where traffic had come to a standstill and onlookers had gathered in groups to watch the melee. Madhupura's guards made way for the horsemen, and as they drew closer, Swagata saw that the one in the lead was none other than Lavanyasurya, king of Madhupura.

"What unbelievable audacity is this?" Lavanyasurya remarked as the *nayaka* was hustled to the front and presented to him for inspection. "You are the ringleader of the troublemakers."

"He picked a fight because we refused entry to trade carts from Kosala that weren't shelling out the new tariffs, rajan," said the head of the guards.

"Tch-tch," Lavanyasurya shook his head regretfully. "We treat you well, give you a place to shelter, accord you respect and this is how you repay us."

The *nayaka* didn't reply.

"First, you won't pay our tariffs. Then, you cause a riot and make a nuisance of yourselves," Madhupura's raja went on, casting a cold glare over Kosala's soldiers before resting his gaze on Swagata. "Unmannered, uncultured swine, the lot of you."

*This is just a big misunderstanding. I must clear the air and resolve this.*

Lavanyasurya's attention had already shifted away from Swagata when the *upanayaka* licked his lips hurriedly and spoke. "The merchants didn't know the tariffs had been revised, rajan. They'd have paid had they had the money."

Lavanyasurya's eyes narrowed as they sought Swagata out in the crowd. "You, come here," he motioned with his fingers. The men holding Swagata prodded him forward to stand next to the *nayaka*.

"So, they'd have paid had they had the money," Lavanyasurya repeated, leaning forward to get a good look at the *upanayaka*. "And because they didn't, they chose to riot."

*I can resolve this. I know Madhupura. I know its king. He will understand.*

"The merchants didn't riot, rajan. They are innocent."

"Who then rioted, soldier?" the king asked in a singsong theatrical voice.

"We apologize, rajan." Swagata said, sensing the *nayaka* shoot him a sidelong glare.

"So, you and your friends are the ones who rioted," hissed Lavanyasurya.

"It was an exchange of words that got out of hand, rajan. We deeply apologize."

Lavanyasurya sat upright in his saddle to survey the surroundings. With a frown, he shook his head. "Apologies will not do. You live in the shade of Madhupura's goodwill and riot against its soldiers for performing their duty. You drag me away from important matters of state and expect me to be satisfied with an apology? No. Apologies will not do." He raised his voice to address a captain of Madhupura's guard. "Have the lot of them stripped and put under arrest in the city dungeon."

*No, wait—*

Swagata blinked, not believing this was happening; that less than half an hour ago, he had been basking in the warmth of his loving family, secure about his present and looking forward to his future with hope and confidence. There had been no dark of the dungeon on the horizon when he had left home and dropped the kids at their *patthshala*, he thought to himself, as someone took him roughly by the arm and started dragging him away…

*Wait—*

…away into the heart of the dungeon…

…away from the radiance of his beloved Vedika, Asmi and Nari…

---

About a mile to the west of Ayodhya, where the reeds grew in profusion along the Sarayu, was an old, abandoned mansion that had once been home to a royal line that had long since petered out. It was widely rumoured to be haunted, with the wind howling in its echoing shell during the monsoon, and bats sailing out of its gaping windows as night fell and fireflies rose to wink above the muddy pools that dotted the riverbank. No one approached the crumbling, moss-infested edifice, and the steps that swept down to the water's edge were empty except for a couple who sat side by side, very near the bottom step, watching the sun go down.

"What happens next?" asked Nandana, turning to face the sun so her skin glowed like bronze.

"I'm not sure," replied Dileepa. He wanted to caress the girl's face, feel her fire and her softness at his fingertips. "What do you mean?" he asked.

"Now that the guild master has been arrested… what next? Is your work done?"

"Yes and no. I mean we still have to prove his culpability in court, but we have the evidence."

"That means you go back to looking for the missing girl?"

"Umm…" the *dandapala* struggled with this for a moment.

"What?"

"Umm… nothing…" he said, still undecided.

"You don't want to tell me." The girl's face fell. "You don't trust me."

"It's not like that," Dileepa insisted.

"It is," Nandana turned away, the hurt showing in her eyes.

"I trust you, okay? But you must promise not to tell anyone." He stared deeply into the girl's face, seeking assurance.

"Whom will I tell? I hardly speak to anyone."

"Not even your aunt."

"Whom will *she* tell?"

"You say she is making friends with all the ladies of Ayodhya—"

"Okay, okay," Nandana placed her hand on Dileepa's forearm. "I won't tell her, fine?"

The woman's eyes were driving him to distraction, Dileepa realized. He wished he could sink into their depths and draw the night over both of them like a sheet—

"So, tell me."

"Right," the *dandapala* snapped out of his daydream. Dropping his voice, he said, "It's like this… The rajan thinks there might be others involved in the racket."

"In the court?"

Dileepa nodded.

"Who?" Nandana raised her eyebrows in childlike wonderment.

"We don't know. That's what he has asked me to investigate."

"How will you investigate if you don't know?"

"That's my job," he smiled casually, knowing he was showing off.

"You must be terribly clever," Nandana gave him an admiring look.

"Ah, nothing like that." Dileepa suddenly felt bashful in the face of the girl's praise.

They sat in silence for a while. The *dandapala* picked a pebble and tossed it idly into the river. It sank with a soft *plunk*. Four egrets skimmed over the water, returning home to roost. Away to their right, boats laden with goods and people crossed banks as the peal of temple bells rose into the darkening sky.

"Will your investigation take you away from Ayodhya again?" Nandana asked.

"I can't say," Dileepa said truthfully.

Nandana didn't say anything to that.

"Why do you ask?" the *dandapala* prodded. After a slight pause, he asked, "Is it because you'll miss me when I'm gone?"

The girl shook her head hard, but the sudden reddening of her cheeks gave her away.

Dileepa smiled and looked up and down the river. "I was thinking of going home to Kusinagara once this investigation has been wrapped up," he said.

"Why?" Nandana stared at the *dandapala* in mild apprehension.

"I should bring my parents and show them the city. Maybe they can meet you and your aunt."

"Oh…" Relief showed plain on Nandana's face. The subtext of what Dileepa had said was not lost on her either. "It will be nice for them to spend time with you," she remarked.

"I thought so too." A pause, then he pivoted the subject back to Nandana, "I think mother will like you."

The girl glanced at the *dandapala*. "You love your mother a lot."

"Very much." Dileepa's eyes acquired a faraway look. "She has done so much for me. Sometimes, I think I haven't done enough for her in return."

"I am sure you're doing your best and she is proud of you," Nandana said in encouragement.

"You know, ever since she got married and came to Kosala, my mother hasn't been to her place of birth. She has such fond memories of the hills of Pragjyotishpura and the majestic Lauhitya. She's always saying the Sarayu is a stream when compared to the Lauhitya. I know she misses the place a lot." He paused to draw breath. "I want to take her to Pragjyotishpura someday. To the village where she was born, nestled in the misty hills of her childhood... That'll make her truly happy."

"It will," Nandana agreed. "But Pragjyotishpura is very far away."

"It won't be easy," the *dandapala* sighed. "It'll cost money too. But I am saving what I can."

"Does she know about this?"

"Mother? No. I want it to be a surprise," he grinned.

"You really do love her a lot," the girl said again with a smile.

The sun had almost gone, and darkness was setting in swiftly. Mosquitoes hummed and looped over their heads.

"We should go," said Dileepa. "Ma will start worrying."

"She won't. She knows I am with you. But yes, I promised to help her with some dyes tonight."

They stood, climbed the steps and picked the rough trail through the grass back to the road that led to the city. Traffic was light and the twilight wrapped around them, drawing them closer so their shoulders brushed and their hands touched lightly. Dileepa extended his fingers and took the girl's hand into his. He heard a small sigh escape Nandana's lips.

"The rajan must be very pleased with you," she said after a while. There was pride in her voice.

"I think he is," Dileepa admitted.

"But you should be careful about the *adhipati*... the guild master's father-in-law."

"Sudhanva?" the *dandapala* asked.

Nandana nodded. "He will know you were behind the arrest of his son-in-law. He'll be angry, and he must want to take that anger out on *someone*."

# *nine*

SUDHANVA WAS FURIOUS.

He slouched on a high-backed seat on which generations of Sankasya's *adhipatis* had slouched and sat, his legs folded under him, arms crossed against his chest, eyes brooding and unfocused in the diminishing light of the day that was ending beyond the arches of the balcony where his son paced anxiously.

"He wouldn't have told the *dandapalas* anything," Yadudeva muttered almost to himself. "And there is no way they could make him talk," he paused before his father, seeking reassurance. "Everyone knows whose son-in-law he is. They wouldn't dare touch him..."

Sudhanva didn't reply. Taking this as a sign of defeat, Varnakavi, who sat on the white marble floor with her back to the wall, let out a wail of anguish. "That he is father's son-in-law didn't stop them from arresting him. Why would it stay their hand when it comes to torture?" She slumped against the wall and burst into tears. "Oh, nobody cares for my husband..."

A servant entered through a door at the far end of the chamber and flicked on a globule of light. Its glow had barely reached the three figures by the balcony when Sudhanva snapped his fingers to turn the globe off. A deeper darkness swamped the balcony, the three figures silhouettes in the gloom.

"We all care about Pushyanta, sister," Yadudeva's voice carried from the edge of the balcony. "Have some patience." As Varnakavi subsided into sobs, Yadudeva addressed his father, "Will they go ahead and present him in court tomorrow?"

"No idea," the *adhipati* growled.

"It'll all depend on whether the evidence they have against him is strong enough."

Neither father nor daughter had anything to say.

"We should find out who ratted on him," Yadudeva resumed pacing so that his voice moved with him.

"I curse whoever it was to rot to death," Varnakavi's distraught voice swelled with anger. "I hope their family rots to death… all seven generations rot to death—"

"Enough," Sudhanva admonished. "Stop being such a wreck." He looked at Yadudeva. "Please help your sister inside. She needs to lie down and rest a little."

"I don't feel like—" Varnakavi began.

"Now," the *adhipati* emphasized, making his annoyance clear to both his offspring.

"Come," Yadudeva walked over to assist Varnakavi to her feet, and they trooped out in silence.

Sudhanva heaved a sigh of relief. They had been getting on his nerves, she with her lamenting, he with his nervous prattle.

He had a very strong suspicion—which had since solidified into certainty—about the person who had ratted on Pushyanta. It was a doubt that had latched on to his mind in the morning, but the moment he'd learned that this person had been made the new guild master, doubt had given way to conviction. The guild master's position, granted as a reward for loyalty to the palace.

*Sheelabhadra, the worm.*

It wasn't a surprise, Sudhanva realized. The tension simmering between Sheelabhadra and him had come to a boil in court the other day, and he conceded that he had probably pushed too hard to alter the dynamic in his favour. The move had backfired, but not too badly, and it had looked as though parity had been restored. But the lord of Kusinagara had obviously felt threatened enough to come after Pushyanta, who, in his infinite foolishness, had been slack in running his little scam…

They'd told him that Sheelabhadra had happily accepted the guild master's office, content with whatever crumbs the palace threw at him, the fool that he was.

To think that he had once believed Sheelabhadra to be a worthy rival for the *kshatri's* post!

Now *that* was what really rankled him—the *kshatri's* post.

Sudhanva couldn't remember when the thought of becoming *kshatri* had first crossed his mind; it was a long time ago, that's all he knew. When they'd all been young and there was talk about Dashratha needing a *kshatri* to assist him. Everyone knew that the position was a rare privilege, given to the one closest to the king, the one the king trusted the most. There had been no doubt in the *adhipati's* mind that he was Dashratha's most trusted advisor, so he was certain he would be made *kshatri* whenever Dashratha thought it appropriate. Except that Dashratha first dallied, then turned down the idea of appointing a *kshatri* for himself; instead, he had chosen the collective counsel of mahamuni Vashishtha, and his friends, Sudhanva and Sheelabhadra. And Sudhanva's ambition of becoming *kshatri* had atrophied.

Strangely, the further the office of the *kshatri* receded, the stronger the fire, the *need*, to become *kshatri* burned in Sudhanva. He nursed this yearning quietly for years, hidden from the sunlight, until with the passing of Dashratha and Bharat's rise to power, the prospect of a *kshatri* being named resurfaced all over again. Yet, Bharat had also displayed a frustrating reluctance in making the appointment, happy to rely on the mahamuni's counsel like his father. But for the attack on the Sanctum and Vashishtha's stroke, things may never have changed, Sudhanva understood. Since then, he had missed no opportunity to remind the impressionable king that the position needed filling in the hope that the boy would take the hint.

At long last, this morning, Bharat had appointed his own father-in-law as his *kshatri*.

Kushadhwaja of Rajviraj.

On hearing the news, it had felt to Sudhanva as though someone had driven a fist into his stomach, doubling him up and leaving him reeling and gasping for air. He had always, *always*, dreamed of being the *kshatri*. A *kshatri* could influence opinion and policy. He had veto powers. He had full access to the king's coffers and the king's ears. Being *kshatri* was like being king. Thinking back upon it, Sudhanva realized that all his life he had wanted little else with as much passion.

But it was some outsider from Rajviraj who got to be *kshatri* instead of him. By virtue of being the king's father-in-law.

All these years of loyalty to Kosala's throne had meant nothing. *Nothing.*

Footsteps sounded by the door, and an assiduous servant flicked the globule back on. Sudhanva blinked at the sudden brightness, his brows knotting in anger.

"I *don't* want a light in here," he roared, snapping his fingers. The light went out and the footsteps scurried away in fright.

Darkness came down around the *adhipati*.

But this time, there were deeper shadows in the darkness. Heavier shadows. Black and slinking. Blind and cunning. All terror and malevolence. Shadows that had been birthed in darkness, that had never known light. Shadows that predated light and preyed on darkness.

Spawned from Varnakavi's anguish, starved for revenge, they leeched through the dark, rolling like smoke, smothering the *adhipati* and leaving goosebumps on his flesh. They burrowed into his mind—into his *soul*—seeking the shadows that brooded inside him and fusing with them. Growing, multiplying, filling out. Becoming more gluttonous, more rapacious, yearning to tear flesh from bone, thirsting for the blood that had been promised to them by their mother, Simhika.

Sudhanva gasped and reeled, afraid he would pass out, certain he would die.

The fear passed. So did its memory. Wiped clean. What remained were shadows of shadows, in the periphery of his vision.

He tried to remember what he had been thinking about—*Kushadhwaja, of course.*

Kushadhwaja. *Kshatri* and father-in-law. Favouritism. That was how the world functioned.

All these years of patience amounting to nothing, the *adhipati* thought to himself, the darkness growing around and inside him and slowly fusing into a tight ball of hatred against the palace…

…and against the man who had done him such a misdeed.

Amulya found his king out on the terrace next to his bedchamber, pacing and rubbing a hand over his sizeable stomach. Lavanyasurya wore a sour expression that took a turn for the worse every time he sipped from the jar he carried in the other hand.

"This acidity," the king grumbled, waving the revenue minister in. "The palace *vaidya* doesn't seem to have a permanent solution. Maybe I should get rid of him and find a better *vaidya*."

"All *vaidyas* prescribe the same medicines," said a weary voice from Amulya's right.

The guild master didn't have to look to know it was Rani Naika. He bowed to the dark figure on the stone bench, fanning herself with a spray of peacock feathers. "Greetings, rani. I didn't know you were here, pardon me."

The queen waved a hand to show it didn't matter or she didn't care, which was the same thing. The minister turned back to his king.

"What do you say to a new *vaidya*?" Lavanyasurya asked him, showing no sign of having heard the queen.

"We can look for a replacement," Amulya said, wondering where they could look next. Not in Madhupura, he was certain. The current one was the seventh *vaidya* in the palace in under three years, and word had spread within the city's community of healers that their king's afflictions were the result of acute hypochondria, which, as everyone knew, was incurable. Of course, no one had the courage to tell Lavanyasurya that, so the king vented his frustration by sacking *vaidyas* one after the other. He'd have to cast a wider net to catch some unsuspecting victim from some other town or principality, Amulya decided. "You wished to see me."

"Yes," Lavanyasurya grimaced and massaged the spot under his sternum. "What happened to the trade convoy from Kosala? Are they still outside the city's gates?"

Amulya winced inwardly at the diplomatic mess that he knew he would eventually have to deal with. The day he was not in town, the *one* day he and his wife had picked to pay her aged father a visit in the town of Agriha, across the Yamuna and twelve miles upstream, *that* was the day things had to boil over, ferment, go rancid, fester, become septic. Any other day, and he would have been around to keep tempers in check and manage the situation. But no, it had to be today, and things had gone hopelessly out of control…

"No, rajan. They have departed," he replied to the question.

"With all the goods they brought here to trade?" the king stared in surprise.

"Um… well, actually…" the minister paused before ploughing on, "…they sold whatever they had brought with them to merchants coming in from other places. Maybe not at market prices, but even at a small discount, they were able to clear their stocks—"

"Bloody cheats," Lavanyasurya cursed, knowing he had been outwitted. "Who purchased their wares? Have those merchants arrested for collaborating with Kosala's traders—"

"It is impossible to know whom they sold to, or who bought what from them, rajan," Amulya interjected.

The king let out a frustrated grunt, took another sip of the *kashayam* he'd been prescribed and flung the jar away in disgust. "It's not working," he roared. "Find me a new *vaidya*."

"Yes, rajan."

"I wanted to punish them," Lavanyasurya moaned, back on the topic of the traders from Kosala. "Showing up here and pretending they knew nothing about the scrapping of the concessions."

"It's possible they were telling the truth, rajan."

"Really?" the king cocked an eyebrow at the minister. "Educate me why."

"They were travelling by ox-cart, rajan. They arrived here this morning, which means they would have left Ayodhya at least five or six days ago. It's been only that long since our rider left with the note for Raja Bharat." Amulya paused. "Those traders would've already been on the road by the time your note was delivered. They couldn't have known about the change in concessions."

"Argh…" Frustrated by logic, Lavanyasurya waved his hand in anger. "Who cares! They were involved in rioting."

The guild master said nothing.

"To hell with them," the king said with feeling, his mind off the imaginary heartburn.

"What do we do about the soldiers, rajan?" Amulya asked.

"Kosala's? Let them be where they are. I mean to teach them a lesson."

"I think we should set them free, rajan."

Lavanyasurya planted his hands on his hips and stared at the minister in defiance. "Why?"

"We don't want to incur the displeasure of Kosala, rajan. You have made your point. Let them out before the situation takes a turn for the worse."

"Do you think I'm afraid of Kosala?" Lavanyasurya thrust his head forward in belligerence. "If Kosala dares to move against us, I will give them a war they won't forget."

"Yes," the rani's voice came from the darkened corner, startling Amulya. He realized he had forgotten she was also there. "If it's war, it's war. People shouldn't take Madhupura lightly." There was sudden and inexplicable vehemence in her tone.

The minister stared from his queen to his king in disbelief. It was a fact that Madhupura had a small, well-trained militia—trained by Kosala, ironically—but the force was no match for an army the size and strength of Kosala's. They would be slaughtered…

"—ruin Kosala… Ayodhya a city of the dead—"

Amulya blinked. What had Lavanyasurya just said while he had been occupied with visions of Kosala's army pulverizing Madhupura's militia?

*Ruin Kosala*? What was Lavanyasurya thinking? Where was he drawing so much bluster from? What was behind this exaggerated confidence—

"Are you even listening to what I am saying?" the king shouted. "Or should I search for a new revenue minister along with a new *vaidya*?"

"I am sorry," Amulya mumbled. "I… please go on."

"Leave Kosala to me. Just find me a new *vaidya*…" Lavanyasurya grunted, frowning at some imaginary pain. "Someone with real talent this time."

The guild master bowed and took his leave. As he retraced his steps through the palace, Lavanyasurya's words rang in his head… and he was overcome with a sense of disquiet that he couldn't quite put a finger on.

*I will give them a war they won't forget… ruin Kosala… Ayodhya a city of the dead…*

There were large tubs filled with dyes all around the well. Wooden tubs, tubs made of copper, tubs of clay. Some brimming to the top, dark with dye, silken yarn soaking in the colour, some with just a few inches of water, reams of fabric knotted in places and dunked in their shallows. A pot sat bubbling over a low fire, and Nandana stood stirring its contents with a stick. Beside her squatted Simhika, measuring dye into an empty pail.

"So, the *dandapala* has won the king's favour, has he?" Simhika squinted against the glare of the globe that burned over Nandana's head.

"I think he has… or at least has begun to."

"Good," Simhika grunted with satisfaction. "The closer he gets to the king, the better it is. One more lever in the palace for us to turn when the time is right."

"Totally unexpected," Nandana smiled. "I would never have thought this could be a way into the palace."

"Life is full of surprises," the older woman agreed. "I need more water in this tub."

Putting the stirring stick aside, Nandana tossed a pail into the well. The bucket sailed down and hit the water with a splash that sent the fish darting. The girl yanked the bucket to the top, black water raining back into the well. Nandana gave no sign of noticing the formless shadows that suddenly pitched and rolled in the depths of the water, darker than the dark of the well, and full of foreboding.

"When do you intend making your move on him?" she asked, emptying the water into the tub.

"The *dandapala*?" Simhika shrugged. "Not immediately. Let us see how deep he gets into the palace and to what extent we can use him." She looked at the girl. "Keep a close eye on him."

"Of course."

"He wants to bring his parents over and introduce you to them," Simhika eyed Nandana, and both of them burst out laughing. The women who worked the looms had left for the day, so the silent mansion shook as the laughter spiralled to where pigeons nestled for the night in the nooks and corners of the roof.

"He wants them to meet you too," said Nandana, grinning.

"Poor fellow, getting his hopes up," Simhika wiped her eyes. "If only he knew the truth."

"I feel a little bad for him," Nandana confessed. "He is so trusting."

"He'll learn not to be before this is over."

The girl nodded. They rinsed the yarn out of a tub and spread it to dry.

"Any ideas on how we might approach the rishis' wives?" Simhika asked.

Nandana shook her head. "I'm still thinking about it," was all she said.

"Think harder," the sorceress snapped. "We have to find a way to the Sanctum and the sacred fire. And find a way quickly, lest our lord lose patience with us… for we both know we don't want to face the consequences of that."

"Please… he is my son-in-law."

"I am not sure I can, yajmaan. There are clear instructions issued not to allow anyone—"

"If *I* don't tell anyone, and the four of *you* don't tell anyone, no one will know."

The *nayaka* shook his head and exchanged troubled glances with the three junior *nagarapalas*.

"Look, my daughter is beside herself with grief," Sudhanva locked his fingers in supplication. "She hasn't eaten a morsel since this morning and is inconsolable. I can't bear to see her in this condition. No father can. So please," the *adhipati* clasped the *nayaka's* hands in his own, "only for a minute or two… I want to see how he is, that's all… please."

The *nayaka* shot an uncertain glance all around. The *nagarapala* headquarters was very nearly deserted. Those who had been posted on patrols were already out, and the rest had left for the day. He could let the *adhipati* in, he realized. No one would be the wiser.

Knowing he was making headway, Sudhanva kept up the pressure. "What harm could an old man like me do?" he asked before stealing a glance over his shoulder and leaning closer. Lowering his voice so only the four militiamen could hear him, he added, "But this old man has influence in the court, which could come in handy. I could put in a word for the four of you as a token of my gratitude..." The *nagarapalas* were already nodding to themselves, and the *nayaka* was getting up... "I'll never forget your kindness..."

The *nayaka* led the way to the cell where Pushyanta was being held. The door was locked, but the bolts slid open in response to the imprint of the *nayaka's* hand. The door swung on its hinges.

"Give me a minute," Sudhanva said to the *nayaka*. "I shall knock when I am done." He crossed the threshold, pulling the door shut behind him.

"Finally," Pushyanta sighed with relief, swinging his legs off the bed he had been lounging on. "What took you so long—"

"Shh," Sudhanva said, patting the air. "Keep your voice down."

Pushyanta nodded. "What's happening?" he hissed. "I demanded to see you all morning—"

"All is well and under control," the *adhipati* smiled. "You are free to go."

"Oh, so they aren't presenting me in court tomorrow?" The younger man blinked in confusion. "The *dandapalas* kept saying they'll be pressing charges—"

"Nothing's going to happen. I've taken care of everything. You are free," the *adhipati* repeated. He pointed at Pushyanta's *angavastram* lying rumpled on the bed. "Get your things. Let's go."

The younger man bent to retrieve the *angavastram*. "They kept me here all day and treated me like a common criminal," he grumbled.

Sudhanva took two steps forward, narrowing the gap between himself and his son-in-law.

"We should lodge a protest with the palace for mistreating me like—" Pushyanta turned and stopped abruptly. "Oh…"

Sudhanva was standing so close to him—no more than inches away—that Pushyanta literally bumped into him. "What's happen—" Pushyanta began, but as Sudhanva's eyes bored into his, the question died on the former guild master's tongue.

His father-in-law's eyes were an impossible shade of black and horribly expressionless.

To Pushyanta, it felt like staring into a bottomless well, an abyss from where even echoes failed to escape.

He shivered. His mouth was dry. He darted a glance towards the door in the hope that someone would be there to stop what he already knew was going to happen. "Please," he croaked.

Sudhanva stared at the man in front of him, who was squirming like an animal caught in a trap, desperate for release. The shadows were already moving in from the periphery of his vision, and rising inside him at the same time. Hungry, ravenous for blood. He brought the curved *kshurika* to Pushyanta's throat, his senses revelling in the scent of fear, heart and spirit cavorting at the prospect of pain…

Staring at the beast that had moments ago been his father-in-law, Pushyanta felt he was in a nightmare. He wanted to scream, but the terror was so great that he couldn't find his voice. He wanted to run, but his feet felt clamped with irons. All he could do was stare into those dead black eyes and plead for a quick release.

"Please…" he wheezed as the *kshurika's* edge slid across his throat.

Opening the cell's door to Sudhanva's knock, the *nayaka* was jolted by the splatter of the blood on the *adhipati*'s face. The *nayaka's* gaze drifted to Pushyanta spreadeagled on his back on the bed, a bloodied dagger lying on the floor by his foot.

Sudhanva stepped close to the *nayaka*. "The guild master took his own life," he growled in the militiaman's ear.

"They will want to know how…" The *nayaka* turned pale at the sight of the *adhipati's* eyes.

"Just say you don't know," the *adhipati* shrugged. "Say you found him like this. And if *I* don't tell anyone, and the four of *you* don't tell anyone, who's there to dispute your word?" He took one more step forward so he and the *nayaka* were inches from one another. His voice turned even more menacing. "But should one of you tell someone… remember, *you* let me in. You broke the rules, you disobeyed orders, you helped me." Sudhanva paused to let that sink in. "Stay quiet. You know I have influence in court and I won't go back on my word…"

Using the *angavastram* draped over the *nayaka's* shoulders for a towel, the lord of Sankasya deliberately wiped his hands clean of his son-in-law's blood. Then, without another word, he stalked away from the cell, leaving Pushyanta's dead body staring at the ceiling.

Bharat padded into the room to see Mandavi folding clothes and stacking them in neat piles on the bed. She was facing away from him, humming softly to herself as she worked.

Bharat swept the room with his gaze as he approached the bed. "Where is Taksha?"

"God," Mandavi gasped, going rigid with fright. Letting her breath out slowly, she turned to stare at Bharat, one hand on her chest to slow the beating of her heart. "You always do this," she said. "Walking like a cat."

"I'm sorry," the king grinned, holding his wife's hand and gazing into her eyes. "It is never my intention to startle you, you know that."

Mandavi nodded as she disengaged her hand to return to her chore. "It's these disappearances. They're making me more nervy than usual." Bangles, brooches and rings were scattered on the bed, and an empty jewel box sat nearby. A large trunk made of seasoned *sala* and inlaid with ivory was on one side, open at its hinges to accommodate the clothes. "Nowadays, I fear for the kid all the time," she admitted.

"There's nothing to fear. This place is full of people. Someone is always around to keep an eye on him."

"I know, but fear is irrational."

Bharat gave an understanding nod. "Where is he?" he asked again, looking around.

"He has gone to listen to a story from his *nana*," Mandavi replied.

"This late?" Bharat's eyebrows rose. "He should be asleep by now."

"*You* tell him that when he is back," said Mandavi, moving a stack of folded clothes to one side before starting on a fresh pile. "He has refused to leave father's side ever since he learned we're leaving in the morning."

"He has become quite attached to father," Bharat agreed.

"They've both become attached to each other," Mandavi chuckled. "I think Taksha is the main reason father agreed to become the *kshatri*."

"So that he can be here, close to the boy?" the king laughed.

Mandavi nodded. "Here," she said, handing Bharat the corners of a sari. "Hold tight and don't let go." She walked backwards, holding the sari's other end, stretching its wrinkles and creases out. Bharat watched her, amazed that she would do this herself rather than getting a maid to do it for her. It was one of the things that had struck him about all four sisters; even Sita, the eldest of the lot and Seeradhwaja's pet, insisted on taking care of her own needs instead of relying on help.

Mandavi folded the sari back, slowly drawing closer to Bharat. "It's fine; you can let go now," she said, but her husband refused to release the corners of the sari. Instead, he tugged gently at the fabric, pulling Mandavi nearer.

"The boy will miss you," he said.

"Only the boy?" Mandavi studied her husband's face, her eyes dancing with mischief.

Bharat gave a lopsided grin. "Okay, not only he."

"I won't be gone long," Mandavi assured him, pulling at the sari. Bharat let go. "Spend time with Taksha. See that he doesn't miss me." She sighed heavily. "I am going to miss him as well."

"You could still take him with you."

Mandavi glanced at Bharat. He saw she found the idea tempting, but then she shook her head. "He's just started getting used to the idea of studies. I don't want him breaking the habit."

"He is a kid," the king countered. "He has his whole life to study."

But Mandavi stuck to her stand with another firm shake of her head.

"Fine," said Bharat. Going to a stand where a pitcher sat filled with water, he poured himself a glass. "Need any help with the packing?" he asked.

"No, I'm almost done." There was a slight pause before Mandavi looked at her husband. "I'm curious... What made you suddenly pick father as your *kshatri*? Even *he* was clearly surprised."

Bharat smiled at the memory of Kushadhwaja's face when he had made the announcement in court that morning. "Actually, it was Siripala who helped me decide on father."

"Siripala?" Mandavi stared, not comprehending.

Bharat nodded. "Siripala told me something interesting about father... *my* father," he clarified.

"Raja Dashratha."

"Yes. He said father believed that a person who didn't care about a post or its privileges was an ideal candidate for the post because that person's actions would be driven by the desire to do what is right, and not by the desire to stay in power."

"That's quite an insight," Mandavi acknowledged.

"Yes. And when I looked around me, I saw this one individual who had been offering me his counsel and guiding me with complete selflessness; his only desire was that I did right by this land and its people. That man was father… Raja Kushadhwaja," Bharat made the distinction again.

"Oh," Mandavi said. She wanted to add to that, but words were failing her.

"Father has been a source of great wisdom and foresight, particularly in this matter relating to Pushyanta," the king attested. "I realized I couldn't ask for a better *kshatri* than him."

Mandavi gave this a moment's thought. Then, dropping the *uttariya* she had been folding, she came over to Bharat and wrapped her arms around him. "Thank you," she said with a smile. "Father may not show this easily, but I can tell he is deeply honoured that you've picked him to be your *kshatri*."

"To say nothing of the fact that it allows him to be close to Taksha," Bharat grinned again.

Mandavi laughed and hugged Bharat tighter, but at that precise moment, they heard footsteps approach and turned to see Taksha waddle into view, accompanied by a maid. Mandavi let go of Bharat, and both parents smiled at the kid, who smiled right back as he sauntered into the room. The maid stopped at the door and withdrew with a bow.

"There you are," Bharat said, going up to the boy and dropping down to the child's eye level. "Shouldn't you be asleep so late into the night, young man?" he asked, staring kindly into the boy's face.

Taksha smiled at his father. "Ssleep," he lisped.

"Yes, sleep," said Bharat. He glanced down casually to find the boy holding something in his hands. "What's this?" he asked. Seeing it was a stylus, he pried the instrument carefully from the boy's fingers. "Did you take this from nana's room?"

"Nana room," the boy repeated, switching his gaze between the stylus and his father's face.

Bharat turned the ivory stylus over, his eyes widening, then narrowing abruptly as he recognized it from long back. Slowly, he got to his feet and turned to face Mandavi.

"This," he dangled the stylus between forefinger and thumb, "isn't something he picked from his nana's room. I know where this came from." His tone turned harsh and accusatory. "My question is, how did it end up in Taksha's hands?"

Mandavi gave Bharat a flat stare. "It was a gift to him from your mother."

Taksha was already hopping around his father's feet and stretching his hands, demanding the stylus back.

"And when were you going to tell me?" The king paused. "*If* you were going to tell me at all?"

"It's just a gift," Mandavi repeated.

The boy had begun whimpering and pulling at his father, a tantrum not far in the making.

"It's not just a gift," Bharat said in anger. "You know I don't want Taksha to have anything of his grandmother's." He looked at the kid and waggled a finger, "No, you can't have this."

As Taksha burst out howling, Mandavi threw her hands up in exasperation. "What is the big deal?" she yelled. "It doesn't even belong to your mother... It is Raja Ashwapati's stylus, so think of it as a gift from *him* to Taksha."

"No," Bharat was dogged in his opposition. "It ceased being nana's once he gave it to mother, so it is *hers*." He shook his head at the kid. "Not this. I'll get you a better one."

Taksha came bawling over to Mandavi, pointing towards the stylus. She scooped him into her arms. "You know something?" she snapped at her husband. "Your hatred for your mother is depriving this child of his grandmother's love."

A sneer appeared on the king's face. "Let me tell you that it is best if *no child* is ever exposed to his grandmother's idea of love."

Bharat turned away from mother and son and went to a table fitted with a concealed drawer. He pressed his fingers flat against a depression etched in the wood, and magic glimmered and fleeted over the table. The same instant, the drawer eased open without a sound.

"You have become a bitter man," Mandavi spoke to Bharat's back. Taksha still sobbed into his mother's shoulder, and she tried to console him by stroking his head.

"It's not of my choosing," the king replied. "I have been made into the man that I am."

Grim, hard-edged silence filled the room—and in it came the rush of footsteps in the gallery outside, swiftly drawing near.

Bharat turned to look towards the door. So did Mandavi. Both of them saw a pair of shadows fall across the threshold before they heard Chaitanya's voice.

"Rajan, there's a message for you."

"Yes?" said Bharat, facing the door.

The curtains parted for the soft-spoken marshal. A young *nagarapala* followed Chaitanya in, bowing anxiously to his king and queen. The arrival of the two men had distracted Taksha, who stared at them through his tears.

"What is it?" Bharat asked.

"Rajan..." the *nagarapala* cleared his throat nervously, "we... the old guild master is dead."

"Pushyanta?" the king gasped.

"Yes, rajan. He was found in his cell with his throat slit open, a *kshurika* by his side."

# *ten*

THE LATE AFTERNOON SKY WAS HARD AND UNFORGIVING, pressing down on the banks of the depleted Sarayu that flowed by, dull and lethargic. The river's south bank was vacant except for a crowd of a hundred, assembled around a pyre stacked high with logs. A majority of them were visitors from Sravasti, well-wishers and members of the dead man's extended family. In addition, there were some twenty people from Kosala's court, including Sheshagupta and Sheelabhadra. There would have been more, many more, had the circumstances leading to Pushyanta's death been different. In the event, there were plenty who had chosen to distance themselves from the man and his troubles. Curious children from the nearby village hung along the fringes, accompanied by dogs that panted and marked territories along the riverbank.

Towards the centre of the crowd, close to where the ex-guild master lay wrapped in white linen and waited to be cremated, his immediate family was gathered in a huddle: father, two brothers, two uncles. Yadudeva. Sudhanva. And Varnakavi, who clutched a girl of four close to her body and wept slow, bitter tears. Opposite them, on the other side of the pyre, stood Bharat, his head bare and bowed, his hands clasped under a faded *angavastram*.

As priests chanted from the scriptures, a lighted torch was handed to a boy who was a year shy of his teens. There were tear marks on the boy's cheeks, his expression one of incomprehension as he touched the torch to the pyre. The ghee-doused logs caught fire with a roar, and Varnakavi held her daughter tighter, her body racked with sobs as everyone stepped back from the heat of the fire. Smoke rose into the still air and drifted slowly towards the river, where boatmen offered quick prayers for the soul of the departed.

His eyes smarting from the smoke and the heat, Bharat came around the pyre to offer a *pranaam* to Pushyanta's next of kin. He bowed silently to each member of the family, acutely aware of the coldness that he was met with even though everyone took care to return the king's greetings. He stopped before Pushyanta's father. "I am sorry for your loss," he said.

"Kind of you to have come, rajan," the old man wheezed, all wrinkles and cataracts. He paused to draw breath and sharpen his tongue. "And brave of you to admit you're sorry."

Bharat stiffened at the breach of protocol. He was here to offer his condolences to the bereaved family, but rather than being gracious, they were baiting him with barbs…

*The old man has lost his son*, a voice reminded. *Be kind.*

Bharat let his breath out. With another bow, he moved on. Everyone either avoided his gaze or darted severe glares at him out of the corner of their eyes. He slowed before Varnakavi and the kids, but the widow shut him out, dropping her head and pulling the children to her, smothering them in her sari, cocooning them in her misery. The king drew away without a word.

Returning to his place across the pyre, he looked at the two children through the smoke and the flames as they held on to their mother and cried. He wished he had said something to them, but what? That it would all turn out fine, so they should not worry?

Their father had died in his cell, his throat cut with the knife. It would not turn out fine. Never. It didn't matter that their father had been cheating the kingdom and its people. He was dead now, and it wouldn't turn out fine for those two. He sighed, knowing what it felt like to be fatherless…

Bharat felt a presence next to him and looked to see Sudhanva standing by his side.

"The old man was overcome by sorrow," the *adhipati* said. "Thank you for having understood."

The king nodded. Smoke eddied as a hot breeze blew along the bank, kicking dust into spirals.

"It was murder."

Bharat glanced at the nobleman, who simply stared at the pyre.

"The *dandapalas* will get to the bottom of it," the king replied.

"*Dandapalas* paid by the palace investigating *dandapalas* paid by the palace," a sarcastic smile hovered on the *adhipati's* lips. "So much for impartiality and no conflict of interest."

Bharat's eyebrows went up. "Are you trying to say he was killed by the *dandapalas*?"

"They must've been trying to force a confession when something went wrong," Sudhanva went on. "They ended up killing him."

"The *vaidyas* conducted a detailed analysis," said Bharat. "In their assessment, no violence had been directed at Pushyanta. Except for the fatal wound."

"Somebody inflicted that," Sudhanva said flatly. "It was murder."

Bharat looked away. Around them, the ceremonial rites were drawing to a conclusion. People were disbanding into smaller groups, and those who weren't intimately known to the dead man had started making their way to the boats and chariots that were to take them back to Ayodhya, three miles to the northwest.

"Did it cross your mind that he might have taken his own life?" Bharat asked.

"If it was suicide, he was driven to it."

Sudhanva had spoken the words hotly, loud enough for people to hear and take notice. Glances were being directed at the two men from all sides.

"Perhaps he had something to hide," said Bharat, irked by the *adhipati's* tone.

"He had nothing to hide, but he was treated like a common criminal," Sudhanva countered, but he kept his voice in check. "He couldn't live with the shame, so he chose to take his life." The nobleman turned to Bharat. "You could have let me see him. I pleaded with you. But you were adamant."

"There was a case against him," the king insisted. "You know the rules—"

"And now you have nothing against him because he is no more," Sudhanva said. "Look at his wife there… look at his two kids…" he pointed. "What am I to tell the little one when she asks me when her father will come home?"

The king looked away. The sun had commenced its descent towards the horizon. The shadows were long on the sand.

"Things would never have turned out this way had your father been king," Sudhanva remarked. "Forget Dashratha… this would never have happened if Rama had been king. They would have listened. They would have considered the fallout of a false accusation. They would have shown restraint. They would have understood the value of good counsel. They would never have acted on impulse."

Bharat felt his lips go dry. A darkness appeared to fall over the bank, coming in from all sides to enclose him. Sudhanva was leaving his side, drawing away with a shake of his head.

"It wasn't on impulse," Bharat protested, giving in to the pressure to defend his actions. "It was a carefully considered decision, keeping the gravity of the charges against Pushyanta in mind."

The *adhipati* stopped and turned. "Is that true, rajan?" he asked in mock amusement. "Carefully considered? Did the possibility of my son-in-law ending up with his throat cut also come under consideration?" He looked all around, as though scanning the riverbank. "I wonder where our newly appointed *kshatri* could be when there's a murder waiting to be investigated? One would have expected a greater sense of responsibility under the circumstances."

The young king flinched.

"I should stay," Kushadhwaja had said to Bharat as soon as he'd learned about the disgraced guild master's death. "I can't go off to Rajviraj when there is a crisis building in Ayodhya."

But seeing the disappointment in Shrutakirti's face, Bharat had made them go. I will take care of everything, he had assured his father-in-law.

"He had to take Shrutakirti home. You know she is expecting, and it is a father's duty..."

"What about his duties as a *kshatri*? When one is a *kshatri*, one is *kshatri* first and everything else later. Nothing should be more pressing than the suspicious death of the kingdom's guild master, but..." Sudhanva threw up his hands as if in defeat.

*I will take care of everything*, Bharat remembered telling Kushadhwaja.

*This would never have happened if Rama had been king...*

*I can't go off to Rajviraj when there is a crisis building in Ayodhya...*

*They would have listened... They would have shown restraint...*

"He wished to stay but it was I who insisted that he go," Bharat asserted, reeling against the currents of disappointment slapping against him, threatening to knock his legs out and pull him under. He was making a mess of the situation and letting Kushadhwaja down by not standing up for him. "The *dandapalas* will ascertain what happened. There is nothing in this that demands a *kshatri's* presence." His lips were dry again. "Besides, the raja is yet to take the *kshatri's* oath of office."

Sudhanva nodded as he looked around the bank again. The place was emptying, the mourners heading back to the city.

"Pardon me, rajan," the *adhipati* of Sankasya said. "It is your father-in-law about whom we speak, so it is natural that you would defend him. But do understand that the man standing before you is also a father-in-law—the father-in-law of a dead man." He appraised Bharat carefully. "I am not going to rest until I find justice and retribution for my son-in-law."

"The talk in Kapisi is that Gandhara is mustering forces because of the brutal killing of its men by Kekeya."

"That is a lie," Yuddhajeet roared. "We didn't harm a single one of them."

"Traders who have come from Kapisi claim to have seen the bodies. Some of them shudder at the memory of what they saw."

"We did not kill anyone," Yuddhajeet repeated heavily. Then, seeing the men seated before him on the broad *sayyasana* weren't convinced, he said, "Let me ask, why would we bring the riders all the way to Rajagriha if the point was to kill them? It would have been easier to finish them off where we had caught them, right? Saved us the hassle of escorting them here, right…?"

Silence filled the chamber as the prince waited for the delegations from Madra and Trigartha to reply. Ashwapati sat cross-legged in his high seat, observing the visitors carefully. Sampada, the raja of Madra, short and scrawny, with a big, bald head that bobbed every time he spoke. And Parusha, the chief of Trigartha, short and chubby, with a nervous tic on the left side of his face. Both men had arrived with their retinues earlier that morning in the pelting rain, in a state of panic, demanding an audience with Ashwapati. The rain had since cleared, but the panic evidently still endured.

"We let them go," Yuddhajeet said finally in a tone that said he was ready to give up arguing.

"That's not what is being said in Gandhara," Sampada insisted. "Blood is up, and there is hatred brewing in Kapisi towards anyone from the River Kingdoms. Our traders are scared of making trips over the mountains."

"Maybe all we need to do is apologize to Gandhara." Parusha's voice had the quality of a goat's bleat. "Ask them not to attack us..."

"Apologize for what?" Yuddhajeet exclaimed in disbelief. "For something we did *not* do?"

Parusha, Sampada and the others from Madra and Trigartha exchanged glances.

"You don't believe us, do you?" Yuddhajeet stared incredulously at the faces in front of him.

"There is no evidence to show that you are telling the truth," Sampada said under his breath.

Yuddhajeet's face flushed with anger. "If there's anyone indulging in deceit, it is Madra, slyly paying tributes to Gandhara in breach of our agreement—"

"What agreement?" Sampada demanded.

"The one between the River Kingdoms where Kekeya would protect you—"

"Okay, so there was an agreement. But is it our fault that we don't feel secure any longer—"

"What has changed?" Yuddhajeet butted in. "We are still committed—"

"Please, please, everyone *please* calm down," Ashwapati's voice cut through the din, stamping its authority over the chamber. "If nothing else, let us at least converse like civilized men."

The raja's admonition brought the temperature down, and everyone quietened and watched as Ashwapati rose from his high seat. Propped on his staff, he shuffled over to the *sayyasana* and lowered himself down slowly next to the rajas of Madra and Trigartha. The message was clear. Kekeya was not talking down to its allies. The River Kingdoms were equal partners. In peace and in peril.

"There is no point in bickering among ourselves," he continued. "If Gandhara is coming, we will face them." He raised a hand to stay a protest from Madra. "We didn't harm the Gandharan soldiers, so if the belief in Kapisi is that we did, it is the outcome of a deliberate lie being spread to incite passions against Kekeya and the other River Kingdoms. The only purpose behind such an outright lie is the justification of war, so Nagnajit has clearly made up his mind about coming here."

A murmur broke out as the men from Madra and Trigartha shifted uncomfortably. Ashwapati again lifted a hand to seek silence. "Nagnajit is coming, and the only thing we can do is put our shields together and stop him."

"It is not just Gandhara," whined Sampada. "There are reliable reports of Kamboja horsemen gathering in Kapisi under their dreaded warlord Mahasa. Nagnajit helped Mahasa overthrow the old chief of Kamboja, and they say Mahasa is returning the favour by riding this way with Nagnajit."

"Let us seek Nagnajit's pardon, pay him tributes and plead for peace," said Parusha, looking sick with fear.

"Really?" Yuddhajeet interjected. "Where is the spine?"

"We are traders by calling," Sampada replied acidly. "All we want is peace."

"At what cost?"

"At any cost. We don't want to have our homes scorched to the ground by Kamboja horsemen."

"We are not warriors," said Parusha, addressing Ashwapati with joined hands. "Our militia can barely maintain order in Sakala and Trigartha. Do not expect us to be able to stand beside your men and fight Nagnajit and the Kamboja horsemen. There's no *us*. It will be *you* against them."

This time the silence was so deep, the sound of raindrops falling from the trees outside was loud in everyone's ears.

"We can get help."

All eyes spun slowly in Yuddhajeet's direction.

"We can counter the Kamboja horsemen with an equally fierce set of warriors."

"Meaning who?" Ashwapati voiced the question on everyone's lips.

"The Bahlikas."

Surprise, doubt and indecision flickered in the faces of the men. Some had started shaking their heads and voicing their reservations when the prince spoke again.

"Why not? They are fearsome warriors, and you have all seen evidence of that sometime or the other. They have protected our trade caravans and convoys and markets in exchange for money. There is no reason to believe they won't fight for us for a fee. That's their job. They are mercenaries, men for hire."

The visitors from Madra and Trigartha exchanged notes in low voices. Ashwapati looked at his son and nodded slowly. There was pride in his eyes. It was a plan and a good one. The Bahlikas were hell's own children when it came to bloodletting, and could be depended on—

"Can they be trusted?" someone asked.

"You have been trusting them with your caravans for years now."

"They won't come cheap," said Sampada. He was stating a fact, not putting up an opposition.

"True," Yuddhajeet admitted. "We will give them whatever amount you were willing to pay Gandhara as tribute. The same money, but here, you would be buying yourself freedom and dignity instead of the mercy of some warmongering invader from Gandhara."

"Strong words," Sampada said, even as his and Parusha's entourages warmed to the idea. He looked at Parusha, who inclined his head. "You have our backing if you can get the Bahlikas to fight on our side," Sampada went on. "But time is short. Nagnajit won't wait long to make his move. If you can't quickly convince the Bahlikas to fight for us, we will be left with only one option—yielding to Gandhara to save our kingdoms from ruin."

Yuddhajeet nodded. "I'm grateful for your support. The Bahlikas will come, it's my promise. I will bring them."

It was a ghost of a chance that dawned out of nowhere, when Nandana and Simhika were least expecting it.

Of course, they had heard about the consecration of the new *homagriha*, no questions about that. It was all that was being talked about in Ayodhya anyway, in the hope that once the *homa* fire was back inside the sanctorum, the troubles that were plaguing this city, this kingdom and the lives of its citizens would somehow miraculously evaporate.

So yes, Nandana and Simhika knew about the consecration ceremony that was due at the Sanctum in a fortnight's time. But it wasn't until a piece of information came their way that aunt and niece glimpsed an opportunity that had eluded them so far.

Simhika was chatting about the approaching consecration with two of the women who worked the looms when one mentioned that her nephew had been picked for the Sanctum garrison. She explained how only the best warriors were selected for the garrison, so it was an honour for the family and so forth. Simhika had almost tuned out when the woman remarked in passing that the army was still undecided about a uniform that would distinguish the Sanctum garrison from all other units of Kosala's army. Dropping the spool of thread she had been holding, Simhika had gazed into the distance, mouth open, eyes bright but unfocused…

Then, without sparing a second thought for the woman who was still prattling at her elbow, she had risen from her seat and rushed up the stairs, calling out to Nandana in excitement.

"What is it?" the girl asked, emerging from her room, looking concerned. "What's the matter?"

"I'll tell you. Come inside," Simhika grabbed Nandana by the hands, pulled her back into her room and slammed the door shut. She then came to the girl, took her hand again and smiled into her face. "I've seen a way."

"What way?"

"The only problem is we have very little time."

"What way are you talking about?" Nandana shook the older woman's hand to get her to listen. "A way to *where*?"

"Into the Sanctum… and a chance to get noticed by the rishis' wives."

"How?"

"Sit." Simhika led Nandana to the bed, and they sat down. "It's like this… You know there's a new garrison inside the Sanctum—"

"The Sanctum garrison," Nandana nodded. "Go on…"

"The garrison supposedly consists of Kosala's best warriors, so they want a distinctive look for it… something that will set it apart from the other Kosala garrisons."

"You mean… like a banner or a herald?"

"Like a *uniform*."

Nandana stopped breathing and stared as she finally saw what Simhika was getting at. "You mean…"

"Yes," Simhika nodded. "Imagine… not just the rishis' wives, here's a chance to bring even those who have been charged with protecting the rishis and the Sanctum under our control."

"How did you even find this out?" The girl's eyes were dreamy.

"The point is not everyone is convinced there's a need for a different uniform," said Simhika. "And those who think they should have one can't seem to agree on what this new uniform should look like."

"That's where we come in," Nandana grinned. "We convince everyone by showing them how a new uniform is such a great idea, and we dress the garrison up the way you want. Simple."

"Not simple. How are we going to talk to them, share our designs and convince them, when we don't even know where to start, or whom to talk to?"

"We'll find out."

"And to get all of this done before the consecration ceremony… *which is just two weeks away.*"

"Why the consecration ceremony?" asked Nandana. "What's the hurry?"

"Because no one will care about new uniforms after that. It's all about ceremony, dear."

The girl mulled this over. "It's too good an opportunity to miss," she muttered in agreement. "Assuming we make a contact within the army or wherever, will you have the fabrics and the designs ready in time?"

Simhika meant to look affronted by the question, but she changed her mind and nodded. "What are you thinking about?" she asked instead.

"Dileepa. He will make the introductions and open the doors for us."

"Can he?" Simhika cocked an eyebrow.

"I will get him to," Nandana replied. "This is where intimacy with a *dandapala* is going to come of use."

"Any breakthrough on Pushyanta's death?"

"No, rajan," said Dileepa. "The *nagarapalas* maintain they don't know what happened. No one came to see the guild master, and they heard nothing suspicious…"

"Either some of them are lying or Pushyanta had the knife with him all the time," said Bharat. "They were five of them, right?" Seeing the *dandapala* nod, he added, "We must keep an eye on them."

The *dandapala* looked out of the window where the sun had set, wondering if he could still go and see Nandana. Thoughts of her had occupied his mind all day, and he had been on the verge of leaving for the mansion when a message had arrived, telling him he was wanted in the palace. He should have been with Nandana now, holding the girl's hand while they stared into the well where the lotuses bloomed—

"The question is, could Pushyanta have been innocent? Did he kill himself because he couldn't live with the shame of being accused of a crime he hadn't committed?"

Dileepa blinked and looked at the king, who was considering him with grave eyes.

"It's possible he killed himself, rajan," Dileepa replied, weighing each word carefully, "but there's no question of his being innocent. You saw the evidence, rajan."

"I know," said Bharat. "I just want to be sure we considered every possibility before concluding he was culpable and having him arrested."

"He couldn't have been an unsuspecting victim of someone else's racket, rajan. He would have had to be monumentally stupid not to have known what was going on inside his storehouses. I was in one of them, rajan. I *saw*. There was no fear of anyone being caught as everyone was doing their master's bidding."

"That's true. Also, you used Pushyanta as your cover to gain entry into the granary at Banasi. That is *conclusive*." Bharat's face cleared with relief.

Dileepa let out a sigh. Now that the king's mind was at rest, maybe he could get to the mansion after all. It wasn't too late—

"He could still have taken his life out of guilt for what he had done," Bharat said.

"He didn't come across as the type to be overcome with remorse, rajan," Dileepa replied. "He was defiant right through the interrogation. Refused to answer any questions. He was certain nothing could happen to him. The arrogance of being an *adhipati's* son-in-law."

"His uncle is also an *adhipati*, in case you didn't know. Mihiradutta of Sravasti," the king said. "Power and privilege ran in Pushyanta's blood."

The *dandapala* drew his breath. The man he had arrested had not one but *two* powerful families behind him. Had he just made enemies out of two influential *adhipatis*? They could easily find out he had been behind the investigation, and if they wanted, they could destroy his career, ruin him—

"He wasn't harmed during the interrogation, was he?"

It took Dileepa a moment to get the king's question. "No, rajan. No one laid a finger on him."

"Good."

One of the light globules in the chamber flickered and lost a bit of radiance. The *dandapala* looked at it. It was happening inside the palace too. They were right in saying the magic was leeching out of Kosala, he thought idly, before bringing his mind back to more pressing and immediate problems...

What could they do to him? He was only carrying out his king's orders, nothing personal. But would that suffice as an explanation to *adhipatis* who were baying for blood, looking for means to quell their lust for vengeance, thirsting for payback? They could send hired killers after him; they could hound his family—

"If Pushyanta didn't kill himself, he was murdered," said Bharat. "But by whom?"

Dileepa scratched his cheek. "Someone who was afraid he would cave in and confess? Someone who wanted to prevent the guild master from spilling his name in court?" *Someone so powerful and well connected they had struck within the secure* nagarapala *headquarters without fear of being caught and exposed*, he thought with a shiver.

"Yes." Bharat's brows knitted in concentration. "Pushyanta couldn't have run this operation without help from other quarters." He looked at the *dandapala*. "Four storehouses full of foodgrains and other essentials *inside* Ayodhya... Now how did all that food get into the city without anyone knowing?"

The *dandapala's* eyebrows went up. He hadn't thought about that.

The king began pacing the chamber. "All that food would have reached the city either in carts or by river. Carts are more likely as boats would mean transferring the produce to carts on the waterfront, which increases the risk of being observed and caught. So, let's assume for now that it was by carts. Somebody must have cleared those carts at the city's gates. Wasn't the entry of the carts logged, and wasn't what they had brought in checked and filed? Didn't the storehouse officers see those reports... or did they see them and *not* file them to be sent to the revenue office? Or could the revenue office have known and suppressed the reports?" Bharat stopped to face Dileepa. "Or were they *all* in Pushyanta's pay? Could it be that Pushyanta too was only following orders and that the actual mastermind is someone else, someone roaming freely out there who decided it was too dangerous to let Pushyanta live...?"

Dileepa didn't know what to say. All the scenarios the king had put forward were possible.

"What else are you working on right now?" Bharat asked suddenly.

"The disappearances—"

The disappearances, of course, Bharat thought. What else...

"Let the other *dandapalas* handle the disappearances," he said. "I want you to concentrate on Pushyanta's death and this profiteering scam. I will speak to Mitraka."

"Yes, rajan."

"Get to the bottom of it. Who gains from the murder? Who wanted Pushyanta silenced? Who else was involved in the racket? How did they operate it? I want to know everything."

"Yes, rajan."

"I want results, but exercise discretion, at least until you have a bank of evidence ready."

"Yes, rajan."

"I want regular updates. If you face hurdles, let me know. But everything stays between us."

"Yes, rajan."

Dileepa walked out of the palace into a darkness that engulfed him from all sides, obscuring everything. He had no clue where to begin his investigation, where to search for answers.

He needed time to think, he realized.

Nandana would have to wait for another day.

*He was treated like a common criminal... He couldn't live with the shame, so he chose to take his life.*

*It's possible he killed himself, rajan, but there's no question of his being innocent.*

The problem wasn't whether or not Pushyanta had been innocent. The problem was that he was dead, killed by a knife drawn across his throat, thought Bharat, remembering the kids weeping by the pyre on the banks of the Sarayu. That was the picture he wasn't being able to get out of his head. The girl and the boy.

*What am I to tell the little one when she asks me when her father will come home?*

*Things would never have turned out this way had your father been king. Forget Dashratha... this would never have happened if Rama had been king.*

"Angara?"

Bharat glanced at the small figure of Taksha trotting by his side, the tiny hand wrapped around his little finger. It was too dark to make out the kid's face, but from the anticipation in his tone, Bharat could tell Taksha was excited about meeting his friend.

"Angara," Bharat smiled at his son, but in his mind's eye, he saw Pushyanta's daughter clinging to her mother.

*They would have listened*, Sudhanva had said of Dashratha and Rama. *They would have shown restraint. They would never have acted on impulse.*

It hurt to think that Pushyanta was dead only because *he* was king instead of his father or Rama. Would they have acted differently in light of all the evidence against Pushyanta? Was the former guild master's blood really on his hands? He knew that Sudhanva had been baiting and manipulating him by toying with his lack of experience, his shaky confidence, but the image of the two kids would not leave him…

"Angara," the tremor of eagerness ran through Taksha's voice as the path turned and the stable came into view. The boy had been waiting up for his father, refusing to go to bed so they could come to see the dog. The day had drained Bharat, but he didn't have the heart to refuse his son, so now they were plodding down the path that led to the rectangle of light that was the door to Siripala's quarters.

"Phooo," Taksha said, tugging hard at his father's hand to get him to whistle for the dog. "Phooo."

Bharat felt a rush of affection for the boy. "Okay," he laughed. Puckering his lips, he whistled.

A moment's silence, and the dog appeared from the direction of the buildings, slinking low, its tail wagging in delight. It looked to Bharat as if the animal was a little subdued—overwhelmed—and not its usual exuberant self. But the second it reached them, it leaped and pranced about, looping madly around them. Father and son petted the beast, which jumped on them in ecstasy and wrestled them to the ground. Taksha squealed with pleasure, and encouraged by it, Angara licked the boy's face and hands, its tail beating against Bharat's leg as he stood up to view the old ostler's dwelling.

"Siripala?" he called.

There was no reply from the direction of the lit door.

Bharat separated dog and child before helping Taksha to his feet. They headed for the buildings, Angara loping after them, trying to draw the kid back into play.

"Siripala," Bharat called as they neared the door. It was wide open.

"Stay here with Angara," he said to Taksha, who was more than happy to obey.

As dog and child turned their attention to one another, the king walked to the lighted door. He called to the bodyguard again, but when he got no reply, he put his foot inside the man's frugal dwelling. The mat that Siripala slept on was rolled and propped in one corner. In the other, the small hearth for the purpose of cooking was stacked with wood and charcoal, but it hadn't been lit for the evening's meal. Bharat looked to another corner where Angara's food bowl lay empty. He frowned. Despite the lateness of the hour, food hadn't been prepared, the dog hadn't been fed and there was no sign of the old man…

"Siripala… where are you?" Striding out, Bharat turned towards the stable, flicking on a globe of light as he went. "Siripala, can you hear me?" There was no response.

He cast a look at Taksha. "Come here," he ordered.

There was no one in the stable apart from the horses, but Bharat noticed that they had been fed. That usually happened around sundown, which meant Siripala had been around until then.

"Come," said Bharat, hoisting Taksha onto his shoulders, a leg dangling down each side. The boy was overjoyed. This was a rare treat. "Angara… come," Bharat called as he retraced his steps.

"Angara… come…" Taksha called, twisting around to see if the dog was following.

Nearing the palace, Bharat noticed a couple of sentries patrolling the far end of the stable ground. "Have you been here long?" he asked.

"Since sunset, rajan," one replied with a bow.

"Did you see Siripala?"

The sentries looked at one another and shook their heads. "No, rajan."

"Where are the stable boys?" There was an edge to the king's voice.

It took a couple of minutes for the sentries to fetch the four stable boys. They quailed in front of the king, not knowing why they had been summoned.

"Does any one of you know where Siripala is?" Bharat asked, keeping his voice soft.

They shook their heads, but one of them said, "I saw him when I took the grains for the horses."

"Was he alright?"

"Yes, rajan."

"Did he say anything about going anywhere?"

"No, rajan. He was cross with me for being late. He said he had to prepare his dinner and I had delayed him, and now he was going to be late eating his meal."

Siripala had been looking forward to having his dinner, so why hadn't he prepared it?

"Okay," Bharat said. "One of you… feed this dog and take care of it." He turned to the sentries. "I want a search party organized. Get ten or fifteen of you to comb the entire palace grounds. Look everywhere, in the grass, behind the trees, in the outhouses… See if you can find Siripala anywhere."

"Yes, rajan." A man turned and dashed off to do as told.

"Siripala," said Taksha, looking up at his father's drawn face.

"Oh, they will find him," the king forced a smile. "We will see him tomorrow. Come, it's time to go to bed now."

"Story," the boy said, doing everything to keep inevitable sleep at bay.

"Let us see."

As they turned to head into the palace, Bharat couldn't ignore the sense of something untoward having happened to the old bodyguard, a vague feeling of dread gnawing away at his innards...

# eleven

THE STREAM THAT YUDDHAJEET KNELT OVER, WATER dripping off his face and beard into his reflection, was one of the smaller tributaries of the Chandrabhaga.

He knelt in the shade of the trees, the water cooling his skin, the hum of tiny insects in his ears, and he felt a strange peace settle over him in this strange, far-off place. He wished time would slow to a stop, right here, right now, with only the water flowing and the insects humming in the clear morning light that burst through the foliage. He wished, irrationally, to inhabit this bubble of time forever.

The moment passed, and the prince's mind went back to the purpose that had brought him and his men to this spot of detached beauty.

They had left Rajagriha the previous evening after sundown and had ridden in the relative cool of the night, stopping to rest only on reaching the western bank of the Chandrabhaga. Waking at the crack of dawn, they had taken the ferry across the river and struck in a south-easterly direction. But the sun was on their faces, and in no time, their foreheads were beaded with sweat. The day was hot, the land dusty, and the sight of the stream with its leafy canopy was a welcome sight. So, they had reined in their horses to break for the day's first meal.

Dipping a hand into the stream and feeling the cold water rush between his fingers, Yuddhajeet wondered how much further they'd have to ride to get to where they were going. None of them had had occasion to come anywhere this way before, and though they'd been told the settlement was less than half a day's ride from the Chandrabhaga, along the northern fringes of the desert, that depended on whether they were holding a straight line. The prince hoped they could find the encampment before the sun climbed too high into the sky; being outdoors this close to the desert in midday heat would be punishing, if not life threatening.

Of course, deep in his heart, what he feared most was that they might unwittingly stray into the desert and—

"Don't move."

Distracted by his thoughts and hearing the voice without the words registering fully in his mind, Yuddhajeet began turning to look back over his shoulder—

"I said *don't* move."

Yuddhajeet froze. A woman's voice, he realized.

*The note of threat in it was unmistakable.*

Listening over the low gurgle of the stream, Yuddhajeet heard a footfall, followed by another. Whoever she was, the woman was approaching from his left, trying to stay as quiet as possible. She was roughly ten paces behind him, the prince calculated, silently slipping a *kshurika* out of its sheath, cleverly concealed in the strap of his sandal. He strained to catch the creak of a drawn bow, its string taut and pulled back to shoot, but he couldn't. The woman was armed with a sword or a spear, he guessed.

He prayed it was a sword. That would bring her within arm's reach. He listened to her footsteps, gripping the dagger tight and tensing his leg muscles, preparing to launch himself to his feet.

A pebbled dislodged and rolled away. She was really close, Yuddhajeet could tell.

Her shadow loomed over him, darkening the water.

*He sensed she was lifting her arm up, raising it high to strike.*

Rising and spinning on his heels, Yuddhajeet brought both hands up, the left one lifted to ward off the blow aimed at him, the right one arcing towards his assailant's throat, the *kshurika's* point searching for her jugular.

He had been too slow to react, he realized in horror.

The woman was already bringing her hands down, and even as the dagger drove at her exposed throat, Yuddhajeet felt something strike the ground hard, barely a few inches from his left foot.

The prince couldn't believe his luck. *The woman had missed completely.*

His hand shot out to grab the woman by her neck, his fingers squeezing, the dagger pressing against her windpipe. "Drop your weapon," he hissed, staring into her wild, black eyes.

The woman didn't move a muscle as she stared back in defiance.

"Drop it," he growled, pressing the *kshurika's* tip against her skin.

The woman gave no indication of doing as he had said, but she toggled her eyes downwards in rapid succession a couple of times. It took Yuddhajeet a moment to realize she was motioning for him to look down at something..

"Do you think I am stupid?" he sneered. Leaning into her, he said for the third time, "Drop it."

"Ma..." a small, scared voice whimpered just loud enough to catch Yuddhajeet's ear.

Surprised, his hands still at the woman's throat, the prince drew back just enough to survey the bank better. His eyes immediately fell on the girl standing by a clump of bushes, halfway between the top of the embankment and the water's edge. Not a day older than five, she wore her hair in two plaits that came down to her shoulders. Her hands over her mouth quivered in fright, and she stared at Yuddhajeet with tearful eyes that were the exact same as the woman's. A basket made of reeds lay by the girl's feet where she had dropped it in alarm.

Yuddhajeet relaxed the pressure on the woman's throat just a little bit, and she croaked, "My daughter." Then she nodded again, indicating that he should look down.

Keeping the *kshurika* pressed to her throat, the prince dropped his eyes, noticing that the weapon she was holding was in fact just the crude branch of a tree. He followed the curve of the branch all the way down until he stopped and stared, eyes widening in shock—

—at the snake that writhed *less than six inches from his foot*, its head pinned to the ground by the branch.

From its mottled pattern, he could tell it was a viper.

"It would have struck if you had moved," the woman rasped.

Yuddhajeet let go of her neck and stepped away gingerly. "You could've warned me it was a snake," he said.

"Had I said snake, you would have definitely moved. It's natural, but not a good idea with a viper." The woman rubbed her neck where the prince's fingers had left red welts.

She bent and caught the snake by its tail. Seeing her free the reptile's head, Yuddhajeet took several steps backward. The woman picked the creature up, and holding it at arm's length, carried it to a dense patch of reeds, where she released it. The reptile slipped among the reeds and slithered out of sight.

"You just let the thing go?"

"Yes."

Yuddhajeet stared. "Why? It is venomous. It could have killed me."

"This is its home," the woman stared back. "You are the intruder."

The sound of running feet was followed by the appearance of the prince's escorts at the top of the embankment. Both men had their *karapalas* drawn.

"Ma…" the girl called, suddenly afraid again.

Yuddhajeet shook his head at his men, sheathing his *kshurika* at the same time. Both men did likewise.

The woman knelt and stretched her arms towards the girl, who ran into the embrace, holding her mother tight, her eyes screwed shut. Yuddhajeet couldn't tell if it was out of fear or relief.

Getting to her feet, the woman took the child's hand, and together they went over to the fallen basket. The prince noticed that the basket held freshly picked herbs and deduced that that was what had brought mother and daughter here.

"I want… I must thank you for what you did," he said.

The woman straightened, basket in hand. She looked at him and inclined her head.

Yuddhajeet reached into the folds of his dhoti to extract a small pouch that jingled with coins. Extending the bag towards the woman, he continued, "I appreciate that you probably saved my life, while I was thinking of taking yours, so do accept—"

The woman shook her head in refusal. "Your thanks are enough."

Without another word, mother and daughter climbed to the lip of the embankment. Right at the top, just before they disappeared from view, the child turned to look at Yuddhajeet over her shoulder one last time, plaits tossing about her little head, her eyes wide and black, boring into the prince's, still full of apprehension, but also curious about him…

And then they were gone.

Later, as Yuddhajeet mounted his horse to resume the ride, he wondered why it hadn't struck him to ask the woman whether she knew the way to the Bahlika settlement, where he hoped to find Sailusha, chief of the mercenaries.

The gently flowing waters of the Ajiravati bore Pushyanta's ashes away in the silver *kalash* as the male members of the family waded back to the river's bank. Sudhanva watched the *kalash* bob and float in the currents, sunlight bouncing off its curved surface until the urn tipped over and went underwater in a sigh of bubbles.

The *adhipati* of Sankasya switched his attention to the people coming out of the river, taking in the bent and twisted form of Pushyanta's father Naresha, and Jayabhama, Pushyanta's older brother, who was assisting his father out of the water and up the bank's steps. These two would be critical to his plans, Sudhanva thought; these two, in addition to the heavy, bald-headed man standing on the steps, wringing water out of his dhoti. Mihiradutta, Pushyanta's maternal uncle and *adhipati* of Sravasti. Sure, there were many others in his son-in-law's extended family, but these three would be key to getting him the revenge that he thirsted for.

Unlike in Ayodhya, here on the banks of the Ajiravati in Sravasti, people had come to pay their last respects to the dead guild master in the hundreds. Men and women, the old and the young, commoners and members of the ruling class, everyone had turned up, and the banks were lined with mourners offering condolences to the grieving family. It was nearly an hour later that the convoy of chariots left the riverside and another quarter of an hour before they rolled to a halt in the wide portico of Mihiradutta's palace, built of wood and handed down from father to son for five generations.

Sudhanva, who had strategically hitched his ride back in Naresha's chariot, took the old man's hand and helped him dismount, then patiently guided him up the stairs to the verandah where reed mats had been spread for everyone to sit. Fresh buttermilk was served in earthenware jars as the fans began churning the air overhead to the occasional hum and crackle of magic. While the conversation was random, Sudhanva was pleased to sense an unspoken angst simmering at the base of everything that was said. All that was needed was a spark, a flame to dry kindling…

He turned to look at his daughter, who sat hugging her knees, her back to the far wall. Her hair was uncombed, her face drawn, but her eyes were dry. Catching Varnakavi's eye, the *adhipati* motioned with his hands to enquire about the two children. Varnakavi pointed with her head to say they were indoors… and Sudhanva made a sorrowful face and mimed the act of weeping to ask her if they were sad.

It was a gamble, an arrow in the dark, shot blindly with no real hope of hitting a target.

But the arrow found its mark. Sudhanva's little mime had its desired effect.

The thought of her children quietly crying for their father tore through Varnakavi's self-control, and tears welled in her eyes and ran down both cheeks as she dissolved into wails of self-pity. The women of the house rushed to console her, lamenting her lot, which only made Varnakavi feel even more miserable.

"My children…" she keened. "They have no father… They took him away, they made orphans out of my children…"

"Take her inside," said Mihiradutta in a gruff but not unkind voice, unable to watch the woman suffer like this.

"Yes, give her something to calm her down," Sudhanva added. She had served her purpose. He needed her gone now.

It wasn't until the women had escorted his daughter out of sight that the *adhipati* spoke again.

"The throne is unrepentant," he said, as if to himself, but loud enough to be heard by everyone.

Heads turned expectantly in his direction.

"It breaks my heart to see her like this," Sudhanva's voice inflected with emotion. He blinked, as if to hold back tears. "I can't help feeling bad for myself… but then, I stop when I think about what *you* are going through." He turned his eyes on Naresha, old and bent by his side. "I realize I still have my daughter, while you have lost a son. And then I realize we have *both* lost a son." He gave the old man's hand a slight squeeze. "But we both still have a daughter who weeps for her husband."

Everyone nodded and commiserated with the old man.

"But the throne is unrepentant about our loss," Sudhanva said again, looking at the faces around the verandah. "I spoke to the king… I told him I want justice for the boy's death at the hands of the *dandapalas* for trying to force a confession out of him. You know what the king said? He'll get the *dandapalas* to investigate the matter. It shows how much the palace cares." His mouth twisted in a smirk as dark looks were exchanged all around. "They're even trying to pass it off as a suicide. Suicide? Why would he commit suicide? It's plain murder. Committed by the only people who have easy access to the well-guarded *nagarapala* headquarters—the *dandapalas*."

"You are correct," Pushyanta's brother Jayabhama grunted in agreement. "We shouldn't spare the *dandapalas* who arrested and interrogated brother. We must make them pay with blood."

Sudhanva was happy to see the anger on the verandah rise several notches. "We will," he said, "but our first priority is someone else." Seeing he had everyone's attention, he went on, "I have asked myself this question: What is happening? We are being attacked by rakshasas. People are disappearing from Ayodhya without a trace. There's a drought in Kosala. None of this is being addressed. Instead, what we see is incompetence and apathy. The king indulges in games with his brother, games from Kekeya that no one here cares about. He goes horse riding. He spends half his time playing with that stupid dog of his. That's the level of incompetence we are talking about."

The afternoon had fallen so silent that not a leaf stirred. Those on the verandah latched onto every word being uttered.

"A year has passed, and the rakshasas have been forgotten. No one has a clue where those who are disappearing have gone… while more keep vanishing every second day. And the drought? Well, it's there and the people suffer. But the people aren't foolish, and the palace knows that. The king knows he is being judged. So, what does he do to look good in people's eyes? He gets an aristocrat arrested on trumped-up charges and persecutes him to show he is a man of action. Who doesn't like to see an aristocrat humiliated and cut to size? The people love it."

Restive murmurs ran around the verandah. Sudhanva waited, letting the mood sour even more.

"If I may ask, what sort of a future do you want for yourselves?" he asked. Of course, he didn't wait for answers. "One where our reputation and pride is ground to dust under the royal heel?"

"No," said Jayabhama. Emphatic. Categorical.

"Then you must think about Kosala's future."

"What do we do?" Jayabhama asked. He bore resemblance to his dead brother, but was heavier and a lot less pleasing to the eye.

"What *can* we do?" Sudhanva pretended to ponder. "We can't wait another ten to twelve years for Rama to return, that's for certain. Bharat would have destroyed Ayodhya in that time."

"Are you suggesting we get ourselves a new king?" Mihiradutta finally stepped in to parlay, pinning Sudhanva in his sights. "If so, who?"

"Shatrughna?" said Naresha from Sudhanva's side. "We could try."

"A kid with no experience in anything," rumbled Mihiradutta. "He's lived a sheltered life under his brothers, no sense of responsibility..." Sravasti's *adhipati* paused. "Still, he might work."

"Actually, his inexperience might be to our advantage as he'll be more pliable," said Sudhanva.

"That's all well, but will he go against Bharat?" asked Jayabhama.

Everyone looked at everyone. Then, everyone looked at Sudhanva.

"Even I don't have all the answers at the moment," the *adhipati* of Sankasya admitted. "We will have to see. We will have to explore all avenues, evaluate every option. Move fast, and still be watchful." He shot a look of warning at the faces around him. "We cannot afford even a single misstep."

Everyone looked at everyone and nodded.

"This is something I have been thinking a lot about," Sudhanva continued. "I took all of you into confidence as the moment seemed right. Let me work on this now. I shall refine the plan, figure out a way of putting it into action and come back. All I need from you," his gaze swept the verandah, "is the assurance that I can bank on Sravasti's support."

Stilted silence followed, the natural outcome of a call to commitment.

"Sankasya has been wronged, Sravasti has been wronged," Sudhanva appealed to the noblemen of Sravasti. "Can we work together to correct the wrongs that have been done to us?"

Mihiradutta eyed Naresha once before nodding at Sudhanva. "Pushyanta must be avenged. You can count on Sravasti, my friend."

He was alone in a hall hung with drapes and two old paintings of Raja Madhavraj and his queen at opposite ends, gazing at each other across a gulf of polished wooden flooring.

He had been waiting for close to an hour now, seated on a cushioned bench by a window that overlooked a small garden and the tiled roofs of some outhouses.

He had been told that King Lavanyasurya was not in town, but someone had been sent to inform the king of his arrival.

He knew they were lying.

From the gates of Madhupura to this hall in the palace, no one had mentioned Lavanyasurya's absence from the city. It was only later that everyone seemed to have discovered that their king was gone. It was Lavanyasurya's intention to make him wait, he understood. The idea was to toy with his patience, grate his nerves, wear him down. Show him who was the boss in these parts.

Shatrughna had encountered the trade caravan on the road the previous evening, returning from its disastrous excursion to Madhupura. Over dinner, the merchants had narrated the events that had led to the skirmish between Madhupura's troops and the men of the Kosala garrison. "From what we heard, our troops have been put into the dungeon on Raja Lavanyasurya's orders," the old merchant had said. "We were asked to leave Madhupura by sunset or risk being arrested."

All through the night—and through the morning's ride to the city's gates—he had wondered what his plan of action should be, how best to react to what had happened. Bharat had sent him to renegotiate trade terms and make sure the trade incentives to Kosala were reinstated, but the young yuvaraja knew that the situation had changed drastically, and pursuing that conversation was no longer a priority. If Kosala's men were in prison like the merchants had said, securing their release was his first responsibility.

With that in mind, Shatrughna had reached Madhupura, where the guards at the gate had been unsure how to welcome him. They obviously sensed that their city's relations with Kosala were souring, but they also saw their visitor was Kosala's king's own brother. They let him in finally and fetched someone to usher him to the palace, where he now waited for an audience with the king.

Stifling another yawn, Shatrughna wondered how much longer he would be made to wait. Apart from a palace hand who had brought him a jar of pressed sugarcane juice spiced with cinnamon, no one had come this way, and the only things that moved were the drapes and the shadows of the tree branches outside blowing in the breeze.

The duration of his wait would depend on how low-minded and vindictive Lavanyasurya was, Shatrughna realized. If the confinement of the soldiers was any indication, he'd be lucky to be granted a glimpse of the king before the day ended. At least he was pleased he had left the gifts that he had brought as part of diplomatic protocol with his men downstairs, instead of bringing them here to give to Lavanyasurya. No way did the man deserve Kosala's tokens of friendship—

Out of the corner of his eye, Shatrughna saw a shadow appear by the door and curtains swirled as someone entered the hall. He rose to his feet.

"What can I do for you?" a nasal voice whined, and Lavanyasurya waddled into the hall, short, broad-faced and turning grey with alarming rapidity. Remembering basic manners, he added, "I regret I couldn't come sooner. I had a sitting downstairs with artists for a statue of mine that they wish to make."

Shatrughna didn't miss the subtext in what had been said. The palace hands had told him their king was out. The king was telling him he had been in the palace. The king was making it clear to him that he had been lied to… because Madhupura didn't care about being truthful to Kosala. And of course, he was being told that a sitting with artists was of greater importance than seeing a visitor from Kosala.

"So, what brings you here?" Lavanyasurya made no move to sit down or to escort the prince to some other spot where they could both be seated. Clearly, he didn't expect to spend a lot of time with his guest.

"I heard there was trouble here," Shatrughna said.

"Yes, there was trouble. People don't follow rules, they refuse to pay the scheduled tariffs—"

"Our merchants didn't know the tariffs had been revised," Shatrughna interrupted. With a slight pause, he said, "Tariffs here are being revised with such frequency it's a wonder *anyone* knows what the latest rates are and how to keep track."

"You have a problem with our tariffs?" Lavanyasurya asked in a challenging tone.

"We have concerns regarding your tariffs," said the prince carefully. "The more direct problem is with our soldiers being held in custody here."

Lavanyasurya stared. "What are you going to do about that?"

"I would request you to let the men go."

"That's not possible. They led a riot against this city's soldiers and disturbed the public peace."

"They were only trying to mediate between your guards and our merchants."

"They started a riot," Lavanyasurya insisted. "One of your soldiers admitted to it."

Shatrughna frowned. This was problematic. The merchants hadn't told him that Kosala's troops had started the fight. "You're not going to keep them in prison forever."

"We'll keep them there as long as we deem fit."

They had reached a stalemate. Lavanyasurya wouldn't give way without extracting an apology, it was clear.

"If our troops have inconvenienced Madhupura in any way, I apologize for it," said Shatrughna.

"We could have started with the apology and saved our breaths," Lavanyasurya said pointedly.

Shatrughna nearly blurted out a stinging retort, but he bit his tongue at the right time and bowed. There was no point in spoiling a situation that was showing sure signs of repair. Besides, he needed Lavanyasurya to sit with him and negotiate tariffs. The sooner they put this affair behind them, the better…

"Thank you, rajan," he said. For good measure, he added, "Our troops will take care to see that whatever happened never occurs again."

"Oh, I intend to make sure there'll never *be* a repetition of that," said Lavanyasurya.

Something in the king's tone caught Shatrughna's ear. He looked more closely at the man. "I don't understand..."

"I want your men out of Madhupura."

"Out?" The young prince stared in incomprehension.

"I don't want your troops in my city anymore," said Lavanyasurya. Walking to the window, he looked out over the rooftops. "I see no reason for Kosala to maintain a garrison in this city any longer. What is the point of that garrison?" He turned to Shatrughna. "Fifteen to twenty men, sitting around and getting fat. Why are they here?"

Shatrughna thought about it. Why was the garrison here? "It has been a tradition, a symbol of the goodwill—"

"The goodwill has all gone, yuvaraja... *evaporated*," smirked Lavanyasurya. "Had there been goodwill, that riot wouldn't have happened. Your soldiers tried to bully my soldiers into letting the trade carts in. Where is the goodwill in that?" The raja shook his head, eyes narrowed in anger. "That's it... no more Kosala garrison. Your men leave, and with them goes the possibility of a repeat of what happened here two days ago."

Shatrughna stared at Lavanyasurya. Engorged with spite and arrogance, the man was uprooting a tradition that went back to the time of their fathers. He was snapping ties with Kosala. Clearly, there was no point in bringing up the matter of the tariffs now; Lavanyasurya was not going to alter his mind about that either, Shatrughna could tell. He felt the sting of Lavanyasurya's insult to Kosala like a slap on his face. Blood rushed to his head. *Scores will be settled*, he thought to himself. *I will come back and break your neck one day...*

"I will be departing for Ayodhya before the day ends," he said in a formal, jagged-edged voice. "Please pass the order to have my men released so that they can ride home with me."

The baby monkey on the young Bahlika's lap clung to its master's *angavastram* with tiny hands and observed Yuddhajeet with large, curious eyes. The Bahlika sat stroking the monkey's back with long fingers, his own piercing eyes on Yuddhajeet as he drank in every word being said.

"So here I am at your doorstep, bearing the hopes of the River Kingdoms," the prince of Kekeya concluded, spreading his hands in appeal as he switched his gaze from the man with the monkey to the much older tribesman sitting directly opposite him. "My appeal to you, lord," Yuddhajeet addressed the older of the two, "is to ride out in aid of the River Kingdoms in return of rewards that the River Kingdoms promise you and your tribe."

The prince leaned back to show he was done talking, and the two Bahlikas did likewise as they exchanged glances. The older one was the Bahlika chief Sailusha, a giant of a man with large, calloused hands, a heavily tanned face and a curling white moustache. The other was also large in build, with a dense mop of black hair and a black beard. If anything, he was even taller than Sailusha, and the baby monkey looked hopelessly fragile in his big, capable hands. It was this man who had met Yuddhajeet and his escort at the gate of the settlement and brought the prince to the chamber they were now in, but he hadn't given Yuddhajeet his name.

"Hmm," said Sailusha as he plucked a pair of black *drakshas* from a bunch that lay on a basket in front of him. He pushed the basket in Yuddhajeet's direction, offering the berries to his guest, the lines on his brow deepening as he considered the proposal that had just been made. Accepting a berry out of courtesy, the prince of Kekeya took the opportunity to study the chamber, which was bare for the most part, furnished with just the reed mats on which they sat. The walls were paved with mud and lime, the windows small and set high to allow ventilation, but also designed to keep the rays of the desert sun from flooding the room. The settlement comprised two dozen houses, a few shops that sold essentials, a blacksmith's foundry, a stable with thirty horses, and a communal sheep's pen. The whole was surrounded by a wooden stockade mounted with wicked spikes. It was like any of the other Bahlika settlements that dotted the region south of the Chandrabhaga, which the nomadic tribe of sheepherders had gradually made their home over the last generation.

"Why me?"

Yuddhajeet looked at Sailusha in confusion.

"Why me?" the chief repeated. "I mean I am not the only Bahlika chieftain hereabouts. There are others. So, why come to me?"

The prince hadn't anticipated this question. "We were told if anyone could help us, it would be you. You are respected by your clansmen, and your call can rally the tribe quicker than anyone else can."

Sailusha seemed satisfied with the answer. "We have no enmity with Gandhara," he shrugged.

"You have none with the bandits either," Yuddhajeet pointed out.

"Gandhara and the bandits are not the same."

"Pardon me, but there's little to tell between Gandhara and the bandits. Both take what isn't theirs by force, both deprive others of the fruits of their labour. Both resort to violence to get others to comply with their demands. What the bandits don't have is a kingdom and a flag to lend license and respectability to their greed and plunder."

Again, Sailusha nodded. "You mentioned rewards," he said, twirling his hand to encourage the prince to expand on the topic.

"The River Kingdoms agree to pay you the exact quantity of goods and money that Gandhara was extorting from Madra and Trigartha," said Yuddhajeet. "Four horse loads, but as the tribute has already been paid to Gandhara twice, that makes it *eight* horse loads of tributes to you."

The Bahlikas looked at each other. Sailusha shook his head. "Too much trouble for eight horse loads of tributes. Eight horse loads of anything won't suffice to go around all our settlements."

"That is all I am allowed to offer," said Yuddhajeet.

"Please wait for the sun to lose some of its heat before departing," the chief said as he prepared to rise. "The afternoon sun is the worst in these parts."

"Five percent of all trade profits," Yuddhajeet blurted. He was not authorized to make that kind of offer, but he was beyond caring. He hadn't come all this way to return empty-handed.

"Five percent," he repeated. "It's the best I can do."

Sailusha sat down on the mat. Plucking another juicy *draksha*, he popped it in his mouth and chewed slowly. "Five percent *plus* the eight horses with tributes."

"Deal," said Yuddhajeet.

"Deal," the chief smiled for the first time to show big teeth.

"I shall get my men to draw up the contract," Yuddhajeet nodded in relief.

"I have a question," said the younger man. His eyes were still sharp and the smile was missing. "There have been rumours..." he said ominously, "...that the Gandharan convoy you intercepted was slaughtered in cold blood and that you had the bodies tied to their horses and dragged all the way—"

"Lies," Yuddhajeet said heatedly. "All lies concocted by Nagnajit to inflame passions in Kapisi."

The man raised one dubious eyebrow. "Really?"

"Really. We did not harm even one of the soldiers. We let them go. Look, I am willing to swear on anything... I would not lie to you."

"Why not? You need our help."

Yuddhajeet glanced around the room, his shoulders slumped. "You can believe me, or you can choose not to," he said at last. "If you don't believe me, I shall leave, and you needn't come to our assistance. But know this. One day you will learn the truth, and that day, the blood of those who die in the Gandharan invasion will be on your head because you chose not to believe in the truth. That's all I have to say. The rest I leave to you."

The man and his monkey looked at Yuddhajeet for a long time. Then, as though in unison, man and monkey looked at one another. The man nodded at the prince. "I will take your word."

"My dear nephew believes you," Sailusha grinned and clapped his hands. "That is good enough for me. Come, let us share a meal while your men work on the contract."

"Does your nephew have a name?" Yuddhajeet asked. With a smile meant to take the edge off his words, he looked at the younger man. "I like knowing the names of those I am dining with."

"Ambareesha," the man said, a smile kindling in his eyes.

"And his name?" the prince pointed to the monkey.

"She," Ambareesha corrected, his face brightening. "She doesn't have a name. She is monkey."

The sun was making the last quarter of its journey to the western horizon when Yuddhajeet and his men left the shade of the hall and walked to where their horses were tethered, Ambareesha by the prince's side. The contract had been ratified with seals, and Sailusha had endorsed his commitment with gifts of the finest sheepskin and colourful woollen shawls for the heads of the three River Kingdoms. The chief had wanted Yuddhajeet to stay back for a feast in his honour, but the prince had talked Sailusha out of it on the grounds that all of them needed to start preparing themselves against the coming Gandhara invasion. Sailusha had let Yuddhajeet leave, promising to have a few thousand of his horsemen deployed on the banks of the Vitasta in under a week.

Yuddhajeet squinted against the sun at the monkey on Ambareesha's shoulder. The two were almost inseparable. "Can I ask you something stupid?" he said with a grin. "I get the impression that the two of you talk to each other." He pointed at the animal and laughed. "Do you?"

Ambareesha chuckled. "No, but we definitely understand each other."

"How old is she?"

The mercenary shrugged. "I found her in the forest a couple of months ago. She was tiny, and her mother was dead. She just crawled up to me and caught my leg. That's it. From that moment, we've been friends for life."

Yuddhajeet smiled. "Something like the dog that adopted my nephew a few years ago."

"Your nephew?"

"Yes. Bharat."

Ambareesha thought about it. "Of course, Bharat of Ayodhya. I've heard about him."

"What have you heard?"

"Not much. His brother was exiled from the kingdom, so he became king. That's all I know."

"Right." Yuddhajeet was making up his mind about telling the Bahlika more about Bharat, so he almost missed noticing the woman coming from the opposite direction. It was only when Ambareesha slowed to wave a greeting that Yuddhajeet spotted her, his eyes growing wide as he recognized her and the little girl in tow.

"All well?" Ambareesha enquired.

"Yes," the woman nodded and stopped to look at Yuddhajeet. "What are *you* doing here?"

Ambareesha eyed her and Yuddhajeet in surprise. "Do you know each other?"

"We met this morning," the woman said.

"He is Yuvaraja Yuddhajeet from Kekeya," Ambareesha made an introduction. "He is here to see the chief."

Yuddhajeet bobbed his head politely. The woman did likewise. The prince smiled at the girl, but instead of returning the smile, the girl looked at him with scared eyes and ducked behind her mother. With a nod at Ambareesha, the woman resumed walking, the girl hiding carefully behind her so Yuddhajeet wouldn't see her. They passed the men, who continued towards the stable where their horses awaited them.

"Where did you meet?" Ambareesha asked Yuddhajeet, motioning with his head at the woman.

"An hour's ride away," the prince answered. "We had stopped by a stream for water. She saved me from being bitten by a snake."

The Bahlika chuckled. "Saving people is her particular skill." Seeing Yuddhajeet's puzzled expression, he added, "She's a medicine woman. She would have saved you even if the snake had bitten you." He laughed.

"Who is she?" Yuddhajeet asked.

"My cousin Abhisarika, chief Sailusha's daughter."

Yuddhajeet turned to look back at the departing figure to find the little girl scrutinizing him over her shoulder. Their eyes met, and the girl immediately averted her gaze, looking in front as she trotted by her mother's side.

"And the child?" he asked the mercenary.

"That's her daughter, Smara."

"Are you angry with me?"

Nandana didn't offer a reply. Instead, she continued to sit by the edge of the well, hands wedged under her thighs, shoulders rigid and standoffish, her eyes on the lotuses blooming in the water.

"Look at me, at least," Dileepa pleaded in a small voice.

The girl turned her face to the *dandapala*. "Okay," she said, both voice and face expressionless.

"What's wrong?" Dileepa asked, staring into those large, lovely eyes that were cold to him.

Nandana shrugged and turned away. "Nothing's wrong."

"Why are you behaving like this then?"

The girl took a while to answer that. "Why are you here?"

"What do you—I… I'm here to see you."

"Why? Because *you* felt like it? You'll drop by only when *you* feel the need to see me?"

The *dandapala* blinked. "I don't understand—"

"Exactly," Nandana snapped and turned away.

"Listen, tell me what wrong I have—" Dileepa stopped on seeing the girl's head whirl in his direction.

"I was waiting for you all of yesterday."

"Look, I had every intention of coming, but the king called me—"

"Of course, the king is more important…"

"I can't refuse to obey the king's orders," Dileepa reasoned.

"Fine. Okay. But not a word from you all morning—"

"I had planned to come in the evening, so I thought… See, I'm here now. Let's not fight, okay," the *dandapala* reached a tentative hand out towards the girl.

"You only care about yourself," Nandana sulked.

"That is not true at all," Dileepa said earnestly. "All the while I was in the palace, I was thinking about you, I swear. All of yesterday, actually. Had I known you were waiting—"

"I was."

"I am sorry."

"If only there was some way of getting in touch with you," Nandana said softly, looking down at her nails.

"Well, I am here."

"But what if I wanted to meet you?"

"Okay, I will come over every day, alright?" Dileepa bent his head to peer into the girl's face. "Alright?"

Nandana turned to bestow a smile upon the *dandapala*. His shoulders sagged in relief, and his own face was illuminated with a smile.

"Whew," he blew his cheeks out and shook his head. "God, you almost had me dead there."

"You had me sad and angry all of last evening and all of today," the girl pouted playfully.

"I am really sorry. It won't happen again."

"An apology… that's all?" Nandana looked at the *dandapala* sideways.

"Tell me how I can make amends," Dileepa said eagerly. "Tell me what you want."

"Mmm…" the girl put on a thoughtful face and tapped her chin, thinking, as she looked up at the mansion's domed ceiling. She was being theatrical, and both of them knew it. "There is nothing I need that I can think of…" She stopped, and her face brightened as she remembered something. "But there is a thing you can do for Ma," she said, turning to Dileepa.

"What is it?"

She turned so she sat facing the *dandapala*. "You know how Ma is working hard to grow her business here… She is so good, so she needs all the support she can get."

"Absolutely," Dileepa agreed.

"Ma has got to know that there is some talk about getting the soldiers of the Sanctum garrison new uniforms. Something to do with the consecration ceremony that's coming up."

"I see…"

"Yes, so she wants to get in touch with someone who can give her an opportunity to design the uniform. She is so good there's no doubt she will manage getting the deal, but she hasn't a clue how to go about this, whom to approach…" Nandana looked at Dileepa with pleading eyes. "Help her, please. I know you can do this."

"Hmm," the *dandapala* rubbed his chin thoughtfully. "The Sanctum garrison is under the direct command of Gajakarna, who is also the *mahanayaka* of Kosala's army."

"Excellent," Nandana trilled with excitement. "Will you put Ma in touch with him?"

"I?" Dileepa looked incredulous. "How can… I don't even know him, and I'm just a common *dandapala* while he's a *mahanayaka*. I won't—"

"You're no common *dandapala*," the girl corrected. "You're the *dandapala* who works for the king, the *dandapala* whom the king trusts, whom he personally entrusts assignments to. There's nothing common about you, Dileepa." The words that left her lips were fervid and intoxicating. "Nothing common at all."

It wasn't often she addressed him by name. Dileepa felt a ripple of delight course through him. It was as though his name had become sweeter by passing through those fragrant lips.

"Well… if you put it that way…" he gave a self-conscious grin.

"So, will you help Ma?" Nandana asked. "Just this once… *please*?"

"I… let me see what I can do," Dileepa said, his mind already working out ways of getting the woman to meet Gajakarna or whoever it was who took these decisions.

"Thank you," Nandana reached for his hand and gave it a grateful squeeze. "Do this, and you're forgiven all your mistakes," she added with a laugh. "And please hurry. There isn't much time."

The *dandapala* smiled and caught her hand before she could withdraw it, pleased to hear that tinkle of laughter, glad that she was no longer angry with him.

Introducing Parnalata to Gajakarna was a small price to pay to keep the girl happy, he decided.

# twelve

SIRIPALA WAS GONE. JUST LIKE THE OTHERS.

Gone. Just like that. Without leaving a hint about his whereabouts. Here one moment, gone the next.

The search for the old bodyguard had gone on late into the night before recommencing at the crack of dawn. Every room in the palace was examined, every inch of its grounds was combed. Stables, cowsheds, kitchens and outhouses were turned inside out, and searchers rooted through storerooms, pulled aside hedges and peered down wells. *Nagarapalas* went around Ayodhya's localities, enquiring if anyone had seen the missing man, while boatmen were called in to scour the Sarayu's banks and its waters for clues.

Still, despite all of this, nobody had found anything that could help trace Siripala.

By the afternoon, word of the ostler's disappearance had spread through the city, giving rise to a panic that wasn't easily quelled. A disappearance from the palace meant no place in Ayodhya was entirely safe, so as the evening drew near, people retreated into their houses in fear, pulling doors and windows shut, while citizens in every neighbourhood formed watches. Commercial establishments shut before sundown, and the streets emptied even before the first stars flickered in the sky.

Standing by the royal stable, Bharat stared at these stars as they brightened in a darkening sky, wondering where Siripala was and whether he would ever see the old man again. His heart felt heavy with a dull ache that wasn't exactly sorrow, nor nostalgic longing, nor the deep emptiness that comes from a crushing certainty of loss. He had an urge to weep, but he couldn't find reason enough to let the tears flow. Siripala had disappeared; he wasn't dead. At least they didn't know if he was or wasn't.

The young king tried to recollect the last conversation he had shared with the bodyguard and realized that he couldn't. Strange how we squander our thoughts and words, he thought, not realizing which ones we would later wish we had treasured.

*You ride well, kumara.*

Bharat had turned to look up at the man in surprise. He had been brushing his horse's coat after the ride, something his mama Yuddhajeet had taught him to do in Kekeya, insisting that it built trust between horse and rider. He had not heard the man come up behind him, so he was startled when the deep voice addressed him.

"Thank you," he had lisped through the gap caused by the falling of the last of his milk teeth. He knew the man had been his father's bodyguard until not long ago, and of late, he had seen him around the royal stable quite a bit.

"My name is Siripala, and I am the new caretaker of the stable."

"My name is Bharat," nine-year-old Bharat had replied.

"Why are you brushing the horse, kumara?" the man asked in his rough, gravelly voice. "Leave that to the stable boys."

"My mama says it creates a bond between the horse and me."

"Your mama is a wise man. Did he teach you to ride?"

"Yes. Yuddhajeet mama sat me on a horse when I was two years old."

The man made a face to show he was impressed. "Your mama is also a good teacher then."

"He taught Shatrughna too."

"Then you are a good learner, kumara." The man bent and dropped his voice so he couldn't be overheard. "Of my rajan's four sons, you ride the best. Better than the others."

*You ride the best. Better than the others.*

That had probably been the moment Bharat had decided in his heart that he liked the bodyguard. Before this, no one had ever told him that he was better than his brothers—*better than Rama*—at anything. He had even come to accept that he couldn't be better... until Siripala had limped up to him and told him otherwise.

The memory of that conversation from so many years ago and the mention of Shatrughna helped Bharat remember his last conversation with Siripala on the evening of the day before. Taksha and Angara had been gambolling in the grass as usual when Bharat had heard Siripala's uneven step at his side. The ostler had been lugging water to the troughs where the horses drank, and he put the pail down and cracked his back as he watched the kid and the dog with a smile.

"I can't wait for the day when the boy will sit astride a horse," Bharat had remarked.

"Patience, kumara," Siripala replied.

"I know. I just hope he develops into a good rider."

"He will. I think he takes after you."

A moment's silence, then the bodyguard had looked at the king. "That contest between you and yuvaraja Shatrughna the other day…" Seeing Bharat lift an eyebrow, Siripala continued, "I'm not sure you lost that final round and the yuvaraja won."

"But he did," said Bharat.

The bodyguard eyed the king keenly. "Did he? I saw you draw away from the target at the very last moment."

The king didn't reply.

"Yuvaraja Shatrughna said the game was a test of swordsmanship and the better swordsman won. But this game is a test of *horsemanship*, so the better rider should have won."

Bharat still kept quiet.

"He had beaten you fairly twice," Siripala had persisted, showing excellent perception. "You needn't have let him win."

"He was going to Madhupura on a critical mission," the king said finally. "I could be wrong, but I believed winning the contest would be good for his confidence and self-esteem. And as you said, he had beaten me twice, so he could have beaten me a third time as well."

Siripala had thought about this for a while before nodding. "I believe you did right, kumara."

"Siripala?"

Bharat blinked, and a lone tear spilled down one cheek. Surprised, he brushed his cheek with his shoulder and looked at Taksha, who stood looking up at him. The dog was behind the kid, tail wagging slowly as it too gazed up at Bharat, as if waiting for an answer to the question. The bodyguard had literally brought Angara up, and it was easy to tell the dog was missing him.

"Siripala will come soon," the king said, crouching before the kid. "He has gone somewhere, but he'll come."

But would he? Bharat wondered, suddenly feeling all alone in this world. Siripala, who had told him he was better than the others…

He made up his mind.

There was a way of turning this tide of misfortune. It was just a matter of convincing Surochi.

*There is a heavy price attached to the creation of magic.*

"Siripala come," Taksha said brightly.

Bharat drew the kid into his embrace, and Angara nosed its way in, resting its head on Bharat's shoulder. The king put one arm around the dog.

*Let it be, rajan. The price is not worth the effort.*

The decision was his, not theirs, and he was their king. The rishis of the Sanctum were obliged to listen to him. He would bend them to his will, he would make them listen…

They were led out of the dungeon at nightfall, hustled by guards in the uneven torchlight. Thirteen soldiers, two cooks, four stable boys. They emerged into an open yard, blinking, stumbling and falling, then staring up at the stars and breathing in fresh, clean air for the first time since their arrest two days earlier.

Swagata glanced around the walled-in courtyard hopefully, a small smile on his lips. It did look as though they were being set free. The rumour had been doing the rounds since afternoon; two guards had been overheard talking about it between shifts. The inmates from Kosala had waited on tenterhooks, wondering if there was any truth in what the guards had been heard discussing, but as afternoon turned to evening, hope diminished. They had reconciled to another evening's fare of hard rotis, insipid gruel and base insults when the guards had appeared and hauled them out into the open.

"You're heading home," barked the dungeon master, tossing old dhotis at the soldiers so they could cover themselves. Their own clothes were gone, discarded somewhere. Maybe someone else will get to wear them when they are released from custody, Swagata thought idly as he wrapped the dhoti he'd been given around himself and tucked its pleats at the waist. The javelins and swords they had carried were also gone, though he doubted those had been discarded… or would be returned. They were probably housed in Madhupura's armoury for later use. He didn't care.

*You're heading home.* That's what mattered. At last, after—how many days was it? two? three? he couldn't seem to remember—after *a long time*, he would be seeing Vedika, Asmi and little Nari. He had tried to get a message out to them, letting them know he was well and asking them not to worry, but both the guards he had approached had flatly refused any help. Anger against Kosala's troops was running high, and despite everything the *upanayaka* did to demonstrate his love for Madhupura, the guards had remained unimpressed.

It didn't matter now. He was going home. In an hour or less, he would be united with the three people he loved and cared the most about. They would be back together as a cosy, happy family. They'd put the last few days behind them, an unforeseen nightmare that had blessedly come to a swift and painless end. Life would go on, he and Vedika would buy that plot of land to grow mangoes in...

"Fall in line," the dungeon master roared. "Hurry up, you maggots."

The men of the Kosala garrison were led out of the courtyard to an open ground in front of the building that housed the dungeon. The place was swarming with guards, while onlookers ringed the edges of the ground, staring in curiosity and anticipation. Swagata's eyes were drawn to the left, where a group of horses stood around a tall peepal, saddled and waiting to be ridden. The whole place was lit with torches, the magic over Madhupura still not abundant enough for the city to be able to illuminate public places with magic-powered lights.

"Go on," a guard shouted, pushing Kosala's men towards the waiting horses. "That way. *Go.*"

Bewildered, Swagata let himself be herded by the guards, wondering why so many people were gathered to see them, that too at such a late hour. And what were all these horses here for?

"What's going on?" a colleague from the garrison hissed, sidling up to his elbow.

"No idea," said Swagata, mystified.

As he drew closer, the *upanayaka* realized that the horses were from the Kosala garrison. Not all of them, though. The garrison had only thirteen horses, one each for the thirteen soldiers posted there. The cooks and the stable boys had no horses, but here, in front of the dungeon, there were nineteen horses in all.

"Look for your mounts and get on," a guard called out, urging them to make haste. "Quick, quick."

Swagata found his horse, a placid mare that recognized him and nuzzled his hand for sugar. Stroking the beast's neck, the *upanayaka* looked around for a guard. Seeing one close by, he walked his horse over to the man's side.

"Sir, if I may ask, where are we being taken?"

"You'll find out," the man snapped and moved away, nixing the conversation.

Once all nineteen of them were in their saddles, the guards led them into the streets of Madhupura, where its citizens had lined up to jeer and shout out insults as the men from Kosala rode past. Animosity came off the crowds in waves, and a low roar of disapproval accompanied the riders as they threaded in and out of streets. Some of those in the crowd started pelting the cavalcade with projectiles, and Swagata saw the garrison's *nayaka*, who was up in front, being hit by one of the thrown objects. It wasn't anything dangerous, luckily, and Madhupura's guards stepped in to control the rowdier elements in the crowd. But the booing and the insults continued, and people took to spitting to show their disgust and hatred. Swagata felt giddy and nauseous at the bile being directed at them, and the crowd—

*Father.*

—became a blur of angry, taunting faces in the torchlight—

*Father.*

—sweaty and oily in the heat of the evening—

"Father."

It took the *upanayaka* a moment to realize someone was calling out to someone as 'father'.

"Father."

"Father."

Two voices. High-pitched and far away, one almost an echo of the other. Barely audible in the tumult of noises around him.

"Father."

Familiar voices.

*Asmi. Nari.*

Sitting up, Swagata twisted in his saddle to scan the crowd, eyes roving this way and that.

"Father... here."

He saw them. Asmi and Nari, pushing through the uncaring crowd, waving their hands to attract his attention. And a little behind them, Vedika. Striving to stay with the kids, her beautiful eyes on him.

"Asmi. Nari." The *upanayaka* reined in his horse, turning it to one side. "Vedika," he called.

"Father," Nari screamed. "Where are you going?"

"Hey," yelled one of the guards. "You there... *get back in line.*"

"My darlings," Swagata called, unable to focus his vision. To look at Vedika, he had to tear his eyes off the kids. To look at the kids, he had to take his eyes off Vedika. *Why weren't they all together... where were they taking him...* "Children, I will be with you..."

"You... *fool...* what are you doing...?"

A thunder of hooves and suddenly Madhupura's guards were all around Swagata. "Keep going."

"Father..."

Hands grabbed his horse by the bridle. Swagata looked at Asmi, tears streaming down her face. Figuring the kids were the problem, a pair of guards had dismounted to close in on them, cutting them off from the street…

"Don't do anything to them," Swagata screamed. "*They're harmless.*"

He felt his horse being yanked around, then the beast abruptly began moving under him, pulled forward by the guards who had their hands on the bridle. Swagata meant to resist, but his fingers were suddenly powerless to hold the reins. He shot a glance over his shoulder to see the guards restraining the kids, both looking at him in despair. Behind them and the guards, Vedika stood staring after him, eyes wide with fear and uncertainty. Swagata saw her lips move as she uttered something, but the only sound to reach his ears was the volatile cry of the crowd and the hard beat of the hooves.

"They are my family," he said, appealing to the guards.

There was no reply. The guards rode by his side, dragging him along, away from his family.

"Where are you taking me?" he asked.

"Shut up," one of the men snarled. "You'll see."

Swagata felt the world shutting in around him, and after a moment, all he was conscious of was the movement of the horse and the wind on his face. He had no idea where he was being taken, but he knew it was away, *far away* from his beloved family. The pain lulled him as he soaked into it, and he drooped in the saddle in surrender, resigned to his fate, not putting up resistance, accepting what came…

Sensing the horses drop speed, the *upanayaka* stirred and looked around. He was surprised to find that they were passing under the city's eastern gate, out past it, onto the road going east, past the exact spot where trouble had erupted—was it two days ago? three? yesterday? why couldn't he remember clearly?—*a few* days ago. Trouble that had now brought him back here—

"Hold," came a command from up ahead, and the whole cavalcade drew to a stuttering halt.

Swagata saw people gathered here too, but in fewer numbers, and they seemed less threatening. They stood on both sides of the road, their eyes switching between the soldiers of the garrison and a small knot of riders who stood waiting further down the road. This group of riders caught the *upanayaka's* attention and he strained to see better, but he couldn't make out any details at this distance.

"Come," the lead guardsman motioned, walking his horse towards the group of riders. The men from Kosala followed slowly, caught between curiosity and caution.

Madhupura's guardsman drew to a halt a dozen yards short of the waiting riders. "Your men, yuvaraja," he called. "As promised by my king."

The riders came forward into the torchlight. Swagata's eyes widened in surprise on seeing the man in front.

Shatrughna, the youngest son of old Raja Dashratha.

He had not seen the yuvaraja on more than three occasions in his life, but the last time had been five years ago, when he had gone to Kosala for his mother's funeral. He had dropped in on a cousin who worked at the palace as a keeper of the grounds, and it was sheer chance that the strapping yuvaraja had been out riding on the grounds that morning. Swagata had been struck by the charisma that the prince exuded, and five years later, outside Madhupura's east gate, the *upanayaka* recognized the yuvaraja by that same charisma and demeanour.

"Thank you," the yuvaraja said to the guardsman. "I hope none of them have come to any harm."

"You have my word," the guardsman replied. Seeing Shatrughna nod, he bowed quickly and withdrew, flicking the reins and thundering back towards the gate. The rest of Madhupura's guards also turned their horses around to return to their city.

The *nayaka* of the Kosala garrison dismounted, and everyone else followed. Swagata pushed himself forward, and *nayaka* and *upanayaka* presented themselves to the prince.

"We are at your command, yuvaraja," the *nayaka* said. Both he and Swagata bowed.

"Are all the men here?" Shatrughna asked gently. "Is every one of you well?"

"Yes, yuvaraja," the *nayaka* replied to both questions.

Shatrughna nodded. "Soldiers and men of Kosala," he raised his voice so he could be heard by everyone. "What occurred here two days ago at this very spot is unfortunate, but what happened subsequently to you and to the garrison is even more unfortunate." He paused; when he spoke next, his voice rang with resolve. "A time will come in the not distant future when we will call for a settlement of accounts, when debts that have been incurred will be paid. Today is not that time. Now is the time to heal, to let wounds turn to scars that will help us remember old debts. Now is the time to renew. Now is the time to go home. I am here to take you back to Ayodhya."

"We thank you for coming for us, yuvaraja," the *nayaka* said with another bow. "We will ride home with you, and we will consider it an honour to ride with you when it is time to settle all accounts."

At a signal from Shatrughna, everyone got back on their horses, but Swagata was slow to mount his steed. *A time will come when we will call for a settlement of accounts.* The prince's words played on the *upanayaka's* mind, and a chill went through him as he understood their significance. Once Kosala decided to settle accounts with Madhupura, Madhupura would be brought to its knees. War would devastate Madhupura and its people. His Vedika, his Asmi and his Nari would have to deal with untold suffering.

"Come, let us ride," Shatrughna called, and the cavalcade set off for Kosala.

Empty and hollow with fear inside, Swagata turned to look back at Madhupura retreating into the dark. He watched the east gate shut with a resounding thud, cutting him away from those who meant everything to him.

*I can't do this.*

The water was dark, pressing around him, and almost impenetrably black except where the light from the two torches illuminating the pool melted in, allowing him to see shadows in the water, slipping from darkness to darkness. Fish, he presumed.

*I can't do this, brother.*

*Why not?*

*I am not trained to be king.*

*You have a good heart.*

*How does that matter?*

*That's all that matters, Bharat. Goodness of heart is the only qualification needed to be king.*

He rose to the surface, the water sluicing off him as he released his breath and joined his hands in a *pranaam*. The night was warm and his skin broke into gooseflesh. He closed his eyes.

They had been sitting side by side on the banks of the Mandakini. It had rained in the morning, so the land was wet and vibrant, Mount Chitrakuta behind them still cloaked in cloud and mist. Kingfishers dove into the river in search of food while women from nearby villages filled their pots on the opposite bank. Rama looked entirely at peace as he surveyed the rustic scenery, with the tiny hamlet of eight houses and a hermitage in the distance. Bharat could tell that Rama had accepted his exile, had made his peace with it.

"That's it? Goodness of heart?" Bharat asked, idly twirling a stalk of grass between thumb and forefinger. "What about statecraft… I thought *that* was important."

"That can be learned," Rama had replied. "Everything else can be learned. But not goodness. That has to come naturally. That is why it is such an important qualification."

They had sat in silence pondering the future, each indirectly responsible for the other's destiny.

"I still don't think I can do it," Bharat shook his head. "Not for fourteen years."

"You can." Rama put an arm around his brother's shoulders. "Like I said, you are already kind and considerate. All you have to do is be fair and just, and act to alleviate the people's concerns and problems. Your role as king is to protect the people from harm. Anything you do to achieve that end will be worth the time and effort."

Bharat waded out of the water and climbed the steps leading up from the pool, leaving large, wet footprints on the stones. The torches cast their flickering light over him, standing wet and dripping on the top stair, faced by Surochi and two other rishis of the Sanctum. All the three rishis looked unhappy, their eyes clouded with apprehension and disapproval. Surochi took a couple of steps towards Bharat, but the king spoke first.

"I am ready, munivar."

Surochi, who had spent the better part of an hour trying to dissuade Bharat before finally giving in, gave a nod of great reluctance.

"What you are intending to put yourself through…" he searched for the word, "…is *daunting*. By performing the *agnimanasa*, you are putting yourself at the service of magic… *at the altar of magic.* You are becoming the *homa* flame to strengthen magic in the atmosphere." He paused to consider Bharat. He was repeating everything he had said in the hope that he would somehow prevail upon the king to change his mind. But Bharat only nodded to show he understood. "This isn't something we recommend, given the consequences, rajan. Are you certain you want to go ahead with this?"

*Your role as king is to protect the people from harm. Anything you do to achieve that end will be worth the time and effort.*

"The people are in fear and are clearly suffering, munivar," Bharat replied. "Kosala hasn't seen a good rain in two years, the magic is failing us, and almost every day, more people are disappearing."

"The rain will come and the magic will grow strong again once the sacred fire has been reinstated in the *homagriha*, rajan. I told you the other day." Surochi considered the king with imploring eyes. "Let us wait until the fire has been reinstated. You will find that this wasn't necessary."

"What of the vanishings?" Bharat insisted. "How many more people will we lose while we wait for the consecration?" The king shook his head. "The consecration of the *homagriha* is still far away, and we cannot wait that long, munivar. The people of Ayodhya and Kosala are wrestling with all sorts of problems, and I owe them a solution." He took a step forward. "We know this is a solution… perhaps the only one."

The rishis were circumspect as they tilted their heads uncertainly and shrugged.

"Come then," Surochi said with a sigh.

The king and the rishis made their way to a raised platform where firestones had been laid for a *homa*. They were in a secluded segment of the Sanctum, away from the centre of activity—though there was hardly any activity to speak of this late in the night. The three rishis took their places around the firestones while Bharat crossed into the pit where the *homa* was meant to be lit. As he lowered himself between the firestones and crossed his legs, Surochi addressed him.

"Just to be absolutely clear, you understand that when you offer yourself up for magic, there is a trade-off… a sacrifice. You are bound to lose something precious. That is how the magic invigorates itself. What, when, where, no one can say, but losing something dear is inevitable when you use yourself as a source for magic. You understand this."

"I understand, munivar," said Bharat. "As long as Kosala gets a reprieve, I am prepared to bear the consequences. But…" he paused, "I have a request to make of you." Feeling the rishis' gaze settle on him, he continued, "Given the character of the *agnimanasa* and its toll, I would prefer to keep what we are doing here a secret, particularly from the palace. It is not my desire to keep anyone in the dark, but I don't want Mandavi or Shatrughna or the queen mothers to worry on my behalf. This is *my* decision, so let its burden be solely mine."

The rishis exchanged glances. "It is a heavy burden you choose to bear, rajan," said Surochi, kindness reflecting in his voice. "But it shall be as you wish. No one will learn of this *agnimanasa* without your sanction," he promised.

Bharat bowed his thanks. "Let us begin then, munivar."

With another little sigh of resignation, Surochi gave a signal for the rites to begin.

The rishis sat around the *homa* and started chanting mantras. Taking a deep breath, the young king spoke a mantra and a thin filigree of magic enveloped him.

The light drizzle created dimples in the Mandakini as he and Rama had walked by the water's edge in silence. He had done his best to convince his brother to return to Ayodhya, but Rama had resolved to complete the full term of his exile and was unshakeable in his determination. It had slowly come to dawn on Bharat that he would have to lead Kosala in Rama's absence.

"I shall wait for your return, brother, and in the meanwhile, I will do my best to keep our people safe from harm."

"I trust you will," Rama had smiled and clapped him on the back affectionately.

Bharat closed his eyes, and as the chants gained strength, an ellipse of fire erupted around the king. The fire roared, golden in colour, reaching over the king's head, and soon all that was visible of Bharat was an outline, a penumbra.

Then, through the fire, Bharat began to glow. *Shine.*

Orange. Gold. *Incandescent.* Shedding light.

The chants grew in pitch and intensity. The fire slowly parted at the top, and tiny particles of light detached from Bharat's body to ascend into the night sky. Soft. Light. Airy. Dreamlike.

Millions and millions of light particles, streaming into Ayodhya's atmosphere and winking out of sight…

# *thirteen*

THE FOOD WAS TERRIBLE," THE *NAYAKA* RECOUNTED, "WE weren't provided water to clean ourselves and Madhupura's guards never missed a single opportunity to ridicule Kosala and us."

It was absolutely still, and except for the hum of magic in the fans overhead, not a sound was audible in the large hall despite it being filled with Ayodhya's courtiers and palace officials all the way to the back.

"The fact is," Shatrughna added, "I have no idea how long Raja Lavanyasurya meant to keep the men imprisoned. He was definitely in no hurry to let them go, so if I hadn't reached when I did…" he shrugged expansively, leaving the rest unsaid.

"The audacity of it," Gajakarna exclaimed in an outburst of fury. "How dare he keep my men in a dungeon!" His use of the term 'my men' instead of '*our* men' showed how personally the *mahanayaka* of Kosala's army was taking the affront.

"It's a clear breach of protocol," a courtier shouted from the back.

"It's more than just that. It's an insult to Kosala," someone else called out.

Reports of the fracas between Kosala and Madhupura's troops had been trickling into Ayodhya since the afternoon of the previous day, borne in bits and pieces by traders who had heard about it from other traders in *chhatras* and market squares. With all kinds of wild stories being shared, tempers in Ayodhya were on the rise, even as it was getting harder to tell the truth from fiction. In order to quell the flood of rumours, Bharat had summoned court and decreed that while Shatrughna was already in Madhupura, Kosala would send a force of another hundred men along with a diplomat to ascertain the facts and to assist Shatrughna in whatever way necessary. Calling for restraint, Bharat had urged everyone not to fall prey to speculation, and instead wait for official word on what had happened.

The diplomatic mission had left around sundown, but barely three hours into its ride, it had encountered Shatrughna and his escort returning with the soldiers rescued from Madhupura. It was past midnight when Shatrughna got back to the palace and briefed his brother, and the king had called a council the next morning, where Shatrughna, the *nayaka* and the *upanayaka* of the Kosala garrison narrated the events leading to the arrest, imprisonment and freeing of Kosala's soldiers.

"The men were doing their job by coming to the aid of our merchants," Sheelabhadra chipped in, slipping into the role of the guild master. "Their offer to host the merchants in the garrison was an act of nobility and kindness. Why should Madhupura take exception to that? They had nothing to lose..."

Exactly. So true. Everyone expressed solidarity with the soldiers.

"And how dare he ask us to leave *our* garrison!" Gajakarna bristled.

"We should have refused to leave," a young courtier said without thinking. "We should have defended the garrison."

"The men had all been imprisoned. The garrison was already in Madhupura's control. Where does the question of defending it arise?" Shatrughna asked, giving the courtier a stare for his stupidity.

"And thirteen men were not going to be enough to take on Madhupura's entire force," Vijaya reminded.

"To think we taught them to fight," another courtier complained.

"What is important to note," Bharat said, speaking for the first time, "is the vindictiveness that Lavanyasurya has displayed in this whole affair. There are thirteen soldiers," he glanced at the *nayaka* for confirmation, "and Lavanyasurya is convinced all thirteen are somehow responsible for the fight. Let us believe that, for argument's sake. So, he had those thirteen arrested. That makes sense. But that's not all. He also had both the cooks and the garrison's stable boys arrested and dumped in the dungeon, even though they had nothing to do with the fight." The king looked around the room. "Lavanyasurya was clearly taking his anger against Kosala out on the poor men."

Heads nodded at the king's analysis.

"We mustn't rest until we've taken the garrison back, rajan," Gajakarna made an impassioned appeal to Bharat.

The young king nodded, struck by a simple fact that everyone seemed to be missing. Something had emboldened Lavanyasurya to take on Kosala's might. Something had changed in the equation between the two states, a fundamental shift that gave Lavanyasurya the confidence to challenge Ayodhya. Until a couple of years ago, Lavanyasurya had barely shown his presence as a leader of any consequence, but now, all of a sudden, he had become assertive—*combative*—in his interactions with Kosala. What had brought about this change? Madhupura was still a fraction of Kosala in size and strength. Yes, the city had a stranglehold on trade, but that wasn't enough of a military deterrent; Kosala could override Madhupura in two days if not less. And Madhupura's magic wasn't a patch on Kosala's. Yet, far from being circumspect, Lavanyasurya was actively provoking Kosala, drawing it into a conflict where, realistically speaking, no good could come to Madhupura. What was Lavanyasurya playing at then—

"I am with the *mahanayaka* on this."

Seeing Sudhanva rise from his place, Bharat turned to the *adhipati*, who continued speaking. "It's not just the garrison and the imprisonment of our men. We've been seeing Madhupura's growing insolence in the way they have been raising tariffs and generally behaving with us. It is my opinion that Lavanyasurya needs to be taught a lesson for testing Kosala's patience." Glancing at Gajakarna, Sudhanva added, "I extend my full support for military action against Madhupura before this court."

Voices instantly clamoured in agreement with the proposal. Someone clapped, and fists were raised at the back in support.

"What about the two of you?" Sudhanva asked Sheelabhadra and Sheshagupta.

"The court has my support," Sheelabhadra said to an outburst of more cheering.

Eyes turned to the revenue minister.

"I think we should give Lavanyasurya an indication of our displeasure," Sheshagupta said at last. "A warning—"

"No warning," a voice interrupted from the crowd. "They didn't give us any warning before putting our men in the dungeon." There was no logic in this argument, but the mood was such that the words drew shouts of approval.

"They'll get their warning when our army shows up at their gates," someone else remarked. Laughter bubbled as an endorsement of the view.

"Is it so difficult for the members of this court to let the respected minister speak?" Bharat's voice rose, gritty with irritation. He stared around the hall. "Has this court chosen not to listen anymore?"

Eyes dropped. The temperature dropped. Voices quickly muted into silence.

"Please continue," the king said to Sheshagupta.

"Nothing," the revenue minister ceded. "I realize that if Lavanyasurya was to heed a warning, he would never have acted the way he has in the first place."

Precisely, thought Bharat. So, what was making him act in such an irrational manner?

"The court has spoken its mind," said Sudhanva, nodding at everyone in gratitude. "Kosala's honour and standing in Jambudvipa are at stake. A puny man like Lavanyasurya imagines he can insult this kingdom built by the Ikshvaku kings. He must be shown the error of his ways. This court backs military action against Madhupura." He turned to face Bharat. "Rajan, it is now up to you to decide the course of action."

The king's gaze drifted over the gathered courtiers, who had already voiced their unequivocal support for punitive action. Everyone wanted Kosala to stand up to Lavanyasurya's bullying, and in all fairness, whatever his agenda, Lavanyasurya had done plenty to needle a reaction out of Kosala.

"We have been wronged," Bharat said. "The imprisonment of our soldiers is not acceptable, especially when there is evidence that they were provoked into violence while mediating on behalf of our merchants. The mistreatment of our soldiers constitutes a breach of goodwill. It is an act of aggression against Kosala, to say nothing of the disrespectful welcome that was accorded to yuvaraja Shatrughna. We have been wronged, and it is on us to right the wrongs. I give my consent to military action against Madhupura."

Voices rose in excitement around the hall. The king had granted permission for war. Fighting would soon commence, leading to the siege of Madhupura. The thought of the conflict being overwhelmingly one-sided in Kosala's favour made it even more pleasing in the minds of the courtiers. Who didn't like a war in which the outcome could only be victory?

"There is still one individual's support this court needs," Sudhanva eyed Bharat deliberately. "The palace recently appointed a *kshatri*, but as he isn't in Ayodhya, we don't know what his position is on this matter." The *adhipati* paused and addressed Bharat. "Rajan, do we wait for his return…?"

"Thank you for reminding us about the need for the *kshatri's* endorsement," the king said, seeing how Sudhanva was trying to draw everyone's attention to Kushadhwaja's absence at a crucial moment in Kosala's history. "It is unfortunate that Raja Kushadhwaja is not with us, but I am certain this court can expect his full backing in our move against Madhupura."

"It is well," said Sudhanva. "We shall accept your guarantee on behalf of the *kshatri.*"

A rousing chatter swept through the hall as anticipation swelled at the prospect of payback. Madhupura would be taught a lesson, Lavanyasurya would be put in his place and everything would go back to being the way it had been.

In a season full of despair, the war had appeared as a bright spot for everyone to look forward to.

Bharat turned to Gajakarna. "When can we expect to see our military plan of action?"

"In a couple of days, rajan," the *mahanayaka* answered, twirling his grey moustache.

The king nodded. "We should aim to march against Madhupura as soon as the consecration of the new *homagriha* is complete."

Dazzling sunlight blinded Swagata as he emerged from the darkened interiors of the palace and walked down the pathway leading to the palace gates, but neither the light nor the growing heat of the day seemed to affect him. Hurrying along streets where shops hadn't opened for the day and pedestrian traffic was mainly the devout coming from temples, the *upanayaka* bumped into passersby, drawing angry stares and a few curses. He walked fast but without purpose, crossing the same street twice and going past the tank beside the guild the same number of times without realizing it.

*Father.*

His eyes did not see where he was going.

*Father... Where are you going?*

His eyes looked inward, seeing Asmi and Nari's faces—scared, scarred, tear-stained—watching him from the edge of the crowd, seeing him being taken away from them. His eyes saw Vedika looking at him, drinking him in, as she drew away from him to the insane clatter of hoof beats.

Hoof beats.

And a clatter of wheels on sandstone. Loud. Close.

*"Hey!"*

"Watch out..."

A hand grabbed him by the elbow, yanking him to one side.

Two horses, identical in their shiny black coats, thundered past on the street, drawing a chariot.

"Are you blind, fool?" the charioteer shouted. A nobleman on the chariot glared at Swagata.

His heart beating wildly, the *upanayaka* stared after the departing chariot before turning to the person who had saved him from being run over. A boy of seventeen, selling crushed sugarcane juice out of an earthen pot.

"Watch where you are going," the boy said, not leaving Swagata's elbow. "Are you okay?"

Swagata nodded.

"Why don't you try some of my cane juice then?" the boy instantly jumped at the chance to strike up some business. "Only two *karshapana*s..."

The *upanayaka* shook his head and freed his arm. "Thanks," he said, walking away.

"Alright, for you just one karshapana, yajmaan," the boy called after him, but Swagata was already not listening.

His mind was on the king's words, uttered less than half an hour ago in court, where Swagata had gone with the *nayaka* to tell the courtiers what had happened that morning in Madhupura four… *five?*… he still had trouble remembering how many days ago it had been. Why was it so hard to remember clearly?

*I extend my full support for military action against Madhupura before this court.*

That wasn't the king. That had been the *adhipati* who had the look of a warrior, the one with a white beard, the one who wanted to fight the most…

*We have been wronged.* That's what the king had said. *And it is on us to right the wrongs.*

That was the moment Swagata had felt a shiver run up his spine. Until then, the talk of war had still been only in the realm of speculation. But when the king had spoken of righting the wrongs, the *upanayaka* had realized with certainty that war was inevitable.

*It is on us to right the wrongs. I give my consent to military action against Madhupura.*

Listening to the king, Swagata had felt a rush of panic. Everyone in court seemed to favour war, but didn't anyone see how innocent lives were being put at risk to feed the greed for war and vengeance? War meant the loss of life and property, but when the belligerents were as poorly matched as Kosala and Madhupura, the consequences for the losing side were invariably far worse for having dared to stand up to the winner. And Madhupura was a city and nothing else besides, so it would be the battlefield as well as the target for post-war pillage and plunder, a terrible plight to envisage…

The thought of his family coming under the shadow of war was unbearable to Swagata. What if something were to happen to Vedika or Asmi or Nari? What if something were to happen to all three—

No, a voice screamed in his head. *No.*

He couldn't allow this. He *wouldn't* allow this.

*We should aim to march against Madhupura as soon as the consecration of the new* homagriha *is complete.*

A week. He had one week to stop this war. To stop Madhupura from being reduced to rubble, to save its people from being slaughtered. One week to get Lavanyasurya to see his mistake and seek Kosala's pardon. He knew a man who worked in Madhupura's treasury. *He* would know how to access the king. And Vedika had this acquaintance whose uncle had once been assistant to the head cook in the palace. *He* would know…

Swagata's feet turned in the direction of the market. He had to find transport to Madhupura.

One week. That's all he had.

In under a week, thirteen more people had vanished.

While eight of these disappearances were in Ayodhya, five were from other parts of Kosala, a new and worrying phenomenon. Until now, the problem, whatever it was, had been localized. Now, it appeared to be expanding.

The count was now in excess of thirty.

The fear that had gripped Ayodhya escalated into something approaching terror, and everyone was literally jumping at every tiny sound, every movement of a shadow. If earlier people wouldn't step out of homes alone, now they'd given up coming into crowds unless it was unavoidable. The neighbourhood watches had swelled to groups of fifteen and twenty people, all bunched together and holding torches and staffs and clubs and still looking scared while they waited for day to break so they could retire to their homes. Even the *nagarapala* patrols were larger, eight men in every beat. The riverside emptied at sunset, and only dogs roamed between the beached boats until the next day dawned.

Thirteen vanishings in under a week was nearly as many as all the vanishings of the preceding weeks put together. Thirteen vanishings had scared the city witless.

But inexplicably, two of those who had gone had come back yesterday.

The basket-maker's daughter and the moneylender's son. No one else. Just these two. Just like that.

The basket-maker's daughter had been found standing beside the well where she had been sent to draw water. And the moneylender's son had simply walked in on the family as they had been sitting down for lunch.

Expectedly, there was surprise, wonder, disbelief as well as lots of relief and happiness in both households. Neither the girl nor the boy seemed to have suffered any trauma, and both appeared in perfect health. But neither was aware they had been missing for considerable periods of time, and both were under the impression they were simply finishing the errands that had taken them from their homes the day they had disappeared. The passage of such a lot of time between their departure and their return was something they didn't comprehend, and neither had the faintest clue where they had been all the while they had not been in Ayodhya.

Ironically, the news of the return of these two spread more unease than relief among Ayodhya's citizens. The fact that someone had simply disappeared was somehow less scary than someone reappearing… and having no idea where they had been all the while. All sorts of conjectures were made, each one more fanciful than the other. They had been kidnapped by the rakshasas, who were still hiding somewhere in Ayodhya, and had been subjected to hypnosis before being released. An *aghori* who was picking victims for ritual sacrifice had returned these two because they were somehow unfit for the sacrament. Vengeful ghosts of those who had drowned in the Sarayu were claiming payment from the city but had rejected these two for some reason… and now, the city would feel the anger of the ghosts. Stories were spun to add to people's fears, and an already scared city shrunk into itself in growing terror…

The palace, of course, was greatly frustrated by the disappearances—and angry with the *dandapalas* for their inability to explain, solve or prevent even a single one of them. The fact that two of those who had gone were back in their homes reinforced the palace's belief that the *dandapalas* were not putting enough effort into finding those who were missing.

"The girl and the moneylender's son are in front of your eyes," Bharat was haranguing the five *dandapalas*. "They are not dead, so where have they been? Find that out, and you will know where to look for the others. The people of the city are scared. And the fear is moving to the hinterland.

We can't let terror seize the kingdom. Get to the bottom of this and put a stop to what is happening. I won't tolerate any more slacking off on this case, is that clear?"

Overhearing the admonitions, Dileepa felt relieved he was no longer part of the investigation into the disappearances. He felt sorry for his colleagues. He had it easier looking into the hoarding scam and the death of Pushyanta, he knew. He had leads—people he could track, places he could visit, records he could check. The men examining the vanishings had nothing but two people who didn't even know they had vanished. So, he gave the five *dandapalas* a sympathetic smile as they trooped past him on their way out. What he got in return were cold stares, five in number, that said he had earned the aversion of his colleagues for being left out of their investigation.

Not my fault, Dileepa defended himself to himself. I wanted to be a part of the enquiry, but the king ordered me off it...

"Dileepa... come."

"Yes, rajan."

The *dandapala* stepped inside the chamber to find Bharat seated on a *manchika*. Opposite him, sitting cross-legged on a reed mat, was Shatrughna. Between the brothers was a table on which lay four or five maps embroidered on silk. Dileepa didn't need to look at the rectangles of cloth to know the maps were of Madhupura and its environs.

"What have you got?" Bharat asked a tad impatiently. Dileepa could tell the king was in a hurry to get back to the maps.

"Traces of things rather suspicious, rajan."

"Tell me."

"Taking your suggestion, I began investigating Ayodhya's gates, through which everything passes to come into the city," said Dileepa. He hadn't expected to see the king's brother, and he had no idea if Shatrughna was familiar with the case. "I examined the records of foodgrain entries into the city, cross-checking each entry against the logs at the storekeeper's office and the revenue office. The records tally perfectly, rajan."

"You're saying the revenue department's records match the records entered at the city gates," the king repeated. Seeing the *dandapala* nod, he said, "That means whatever was brought to be stored in Pushyanta's storehouses was never entered into the records maintained at the city gates."

"That is correct, rajan." Seeing the brothers exchange glances, Dileepa reckoned Shatrughna was up to date on the case.

"Okay, even I could have guessed that much," the king said. "Any progress beyond that?"

"Yes, rajan. Next, I studied guard duty appointments over the last three months in the hope of discovering a pattern. I focused on appointments at the city's gates," Dileepa gave a dramatic pause, "and I found something interesting. As a matter of routine, all guards are deployed to discharge their duties at random, but every four to five days, one set of guards keeps showing up at one particular gate. It's always the same five guards, always together, always posted at the city's east gate."

"Excellent," Bharat sat up. "They are being deployed every time a consignment is scheduled to enter the city. They've been instructed to let the cargo in without making entries."

"What is also revealing is that the five have not been appointed for duty in twelve days… and it has been about that long since Pushyanta was arrested and the storehouses were sealed."

"That is so telling." Again, the brothers looked at each other. "Those five are your targets."

"Yes, rajan."

"Well done. Take the five into custody."

"Not immediately, rajan," said Dileepa. "Whoever is scheduling them is the next link in the chain and I don't want to alert that person. If I bring any one of the five guards in, the news will travel up the chain and doors will start closing. Let us not shake this tree yet, rajan. Let us stalk our prey carefully rather than scare it away."

The king considered this before nodding. "You are right. Keep me updated."

The *dandapala* was nearing the palace gates when a chariot rolled into view, hooves and wheels churning the gravel as the charioteer fought to control the horses. Dileepa stepped aside, letting the chariot sweep by as it headed for the main entrance. He looked up at the man on the vehicle and remembered seeing him with the king the night they had arrested Pushyanta.

Yes, this was the king's father-in-law. Kushadhwaja. He had heard someone mention that the king had made him the *kshatri*.

Judging by the speed with which the chariot was being driven, the *dandapala* guessed the new *kshatri* was in quite a rush to see the king.

The clacking of *padukas* on the cool marble floor made Bharat and Shatrughna look up from the maps.

"You are back," the king's face brightened on seeing Kushadhwaja. Shatrughna smiled as he got up to greet their father-in-law.

Kushadhwaja nodded as he strode over and looked at the maps scattered around the brothers. "Put those away."

"What?"

"You can't be serious about attacking Madhupura," the older man stared at Bharat. "Put those away."

It was Bharat's turn to stare—in dismay and disbelief.

Had he just been discouraged from going to war against Madhupura? Had he heard right?

He rose from the *manchika*. "You are aware of what Lavanyasurya did, don't you?" he spoke searchingly. "He had our men arrested—"

"I know," said Kushadhwaja. "I heard. He put Kosala's soldiers into a dungeon."

Bharat darted a glance at Shatrughna. "He also threw our men out of Madhupura. *Dismissed* them. *Drove them out*." The king's tone hardened with every word. "Luckily, Shatrughna was around to bring them home."

"I heard that too."

"Yet you say we shouldn't go to war…" Bharat scrutinized the other man's face.

"I do," Kushadhwaja replied. "Because Lavanyasurya has technically done nothing wrong."

"Nothing wrong?" Bharat stopped, his hands in mid-air. "*Nothing wrong?*"

"Okay then, what has he done?"

The king's hands dropped in vexation. "Didn't I just *tell* you? He disbanded the garrison and asked the men to leave."

The older man drew a deep breath, filling his lungs with air.

"According to the agreement between your father and Madhavraj, Kosala had permission to use the garrison, but the garrison was *always* Madhupura's property. Madhupura belongs to Lavanyasurya, so the garrison also belongs to him. Telling our soldiers to leave Madhupura reeks of boorishness and shows the utter ungraciousness of Lavanyasurya's character, but his demand is legitimate. Lavanyasurya is within his rights to want our soldiers out and take his garrison back." Kushadhwaja paused for an instant, then added, "Also, though he asked the men to leave, no one was harmed, and each of the soldiers was returned safely."

Bharat gritted his teeth. "But before that, he put our soldiers in a dungeon."

"For instigating a riot."

"That is a *lie*," Bharat cried. "Our men were mediating between Madhupura's guards and our merchants."

Shatrughna fidgeted, unhappy with the way this row was building but unsure of how to stop it.

"I've heard that one of our *upanayakas* admitted that we started the fight," Kushadhwaja said evenly. "It seems something insulting was said that wounded Madhupura's pride."

"You will believe *one* man over so many others." It was less a question and more an accusation.

"If he is telling the truth, yes," Kushadhwaja said. He took a step towards his son-in-law. "Ask yourself what this *upanayaka* stands to gain by sticking to what he said.

Nothing. He is disliked by his colleagues; he is disliked by his countrymen. Why, even his king doesn't like him much. And it is not as though this will win him Lavanyasurya's approval. Still he doesn't change his stance."

Bharat said nothing.

The resentful silence was broken by Kushadhwaja. "Okay, let me ask... what if Madhupura's soldiers had rioted in Ayodhya? What would *you* have done?"

"The *upanayaka* also said that our *nayaka* was pushed around," Bharat dodged the question. "Our men were provoked into retaliating."

"Madhupura's guards probably assumed our men could be bullied because they were hugely outnumbered," the older man said. "The stronger side should always show restraint and keep the peace." Seeing Bharat nod vigorously in agreement, he added, "That is why we shouldn't march against a much smaller Madhupura. Let us not escalate this by provoking Madhupura."

"Why are you taking Lavanyasurya's side?" the king's voice rose.

"I am not, Bharat. I am firmly on Kosala's side." Kushadhwaja walked up and placed a hand on the king's shoulder. "That is why I don't want you to attack Madhupura. Because if you do, Kosala will be seen as the aggressor. Remember, Lavanyasurya is not technically in the wrong, so you will lose moral ground. Also, though small, Madhupura sits behind a fortified wall that's going to be hard to breach. You will have to lay siege to the city, *lay siege to a trading centre*. Trade is bound to suffer during the conflict, and Jambudvipa's traders don't take kindly to any side that starts a war unless that war is entirely justifiable. March against Madhupura now, and you won't be easily forgiven."

Bharat shook his head in defeat and looked down at the embroidered maps. The markings made by Gajakarna to show troop movements and battle tactics were clearly visible on two of them.

"Father would never let an affront such as this one pass unnoticed," he said in a final gamble to turn the argument in favour of war. "He would see it as a slap on Kosala's face and would extract a penalty for it."

"If that is what you think, you've never really understood your father, Bharat," Kushadhwaja asserted. "Dashratha would never go to war without justifiable reason, and only when he was absolutely certain he was in the right. He had immense love and pride in his heart for Kosala, but he never let that fact alone influence his decision-making. In all the years I knew him, Dashratha never made a threatening move against a neighbouring kingdom. The only wars he launched were those to protect Kosala from rakshasa invasions."

"Father was fortunate to have had contemporaries like Raja Madhavraj while I'm stuck with his son," Bharat smirked.

"True," Kushadhwaja agreed. "Nevertheless, we must remain steadfast in our principles."

The king considered his father-in-law. "Lavanyasurya has been toying with our patience for quite a while now, you know that. He needs to be taught a lesson."

"Then you must find a better reason to go after him. Not this."

Bharat walked back to the *manchika* and sat down. He looked weary as he studied his palms.

*We don't know what the* kshatri's *position is on this matter... Do we wait for his return...?*

Sudhanva's bearded, hawk-like face swam in front of Bharat's eyes, followed by an image of the courtiers waiting for his answer.

*It is unfortunate that Raja Kushadhwaja is not with us, but I am certain this court can expect his full backing in our move against Madhupura.*

"You must be regretting your decision of making me your *kshatri*," Kushadhwaja remarked. Noticing a ghost of a smile on his father-in-law's lips, Bharat wondered if the man could read minds.

"I just don't know how everyone will take this," he said. "All of Ayodhya, all of Kosala, is in preparation for war. Ask Shatrughna. People are really looking forward to Madhupura being humbled, and everyone is eager to see that justice is done to our soldiers. If we back away at this stage, it will feel like a severe loss of face, and it is bound to hurt." He gave his head a mournful shake. "And once word of this reaches Madhupura, Lavanyasurya will spin this as a climbdown and turn this whole affair into a victory parade for himself. The people of Kosala are going to be very disappointed, I can tell you."

"Then find some other way of getting back at Lavanyasurya so that the people get their fill of revenge."

The king appraised his father-in-law with a blank stare. "How?"

Kushadhwaja came around and cleared space on a reed mat. Sitting down, he crossed his legs, placed his elbows on his knees and steepled his fingers under his chin in thought. The chamber was so quiet that the sounds of the *nagarapalas* doing their drills carried all the way from the training compound.

"The merchants may have shown us a way," Shatrughna said, his eyes twinkling as he looked from Bharat to Kushadhwaja.

"Which merchants?" Bharat stared, puzzled.

"Those who were stopped from entering Madhupura, for whose sake our soldiers fought with Lavanyasurya's guards."

There was no change in Bharat and Kushadhwaja's blank expressions.

"It's like this," Shatrughna squatted in front of the others to get to eye level. "The merchants didn't set foot in Madhupura, but they still managed to sell everything they had brought with them. All they did was sell their goods to traders who had come to trade in Madhupura from other parts of Jambudvipa."

"I still don't understand," the king confessed.

"What Shatrughna is saying is that with or without Madhupura, there is plenty of demand for goods produced in Kosala," Kushadhwaja said, slowly catching on.

"Indigo and sugar, definitely," Bharat agreed. He eyed Shatrughna. "But what are you getting at?"

"I am saying we dispense with Madhupura. Let us build another market—*our market*—in the vicinity of Madhupura, somewhere along the banks of the Yamuna." Shatrughna shifted from one foot to another in excitement. "We build a garrison and a market where those who want to trade with us are welcome. The merchants have shown us this is possible."

"We bypass Madhupura completely," Bharat exclaimed, finally getting in. "We sell and buy whatever we want, without having to deal with Madhupura's tariffs."

"I love this idea." Kushadhwaja squeezed Shatrughna's shoulder. "We hit Madhupura by not giving them any of our business."

"If the idea is to hit Madhupura, let us hit even harder and make Madhupura bleed," Bharat's eyes blazed as he warmed to the idea. "We will levy lighter taxes to attract traders from other places to trade in *our* market. Unlike Madhupura, our market needn't depend on trade for its survival, so we can afford easier tariffs. Let us cripple Madhupura by diverting as much trade away from it as possible."

"And the beauty of it is Lavanyasurya can do nothing to stop us," Kushadhwaja pointed out. "We are not invading his city. We are building an independent market because we oppose the tariffs that Madhupura charges. And anyone can build a market anywhere in Jambudvipa."

"If we do this smartly, we could shake Madhupura by its foundations," Shatrughna chuckled.

Heaving a sigh of approval, Kushadhwaja nodded. "There are so many ways of hurting those standing against us, see? War isn't the only means of bringing the enemy to his knees."

"A market and a garrison to rival Madhupura," Bharat smiled with satisfaction, savouring the idea. "Lavanyasurya won't like this one bit."

"Too bad," replied Kushadhwaja. "If he tries to fiddle around, *he* will be the aggressor."

"Exactly." The king's eyes were hard, staring into a future in which Lavanyasurya would get his comeuppance. "And when that happens, we will take him down."

# *fourteen*

THERE WAS MORE THAN AN HOUR OF DAYLIGHT LEFT, BUT Ayodhya's streets were emptying quickly as people hurried to get back home before dark. There was no logic in this; most of those who had disappeared had gone in broad daylight. But night has always kindled a nameless, atavistic fear in people, passed down over generations like a legacy, fear that stalks where the eyes can't see but the mind with its fecund imagination can. So, shops closed and the streets cleared, allowing Dileepa to surreptitiously slip Nandana's hand into his as they strolled the aimless, meandering stroll of those helplessly in love.

"I'm amazed by your aunt," the *dandapala* said, looking down at Nandana. "I honestly didn't think she would be able to convince everyone to let her design the new uniforms."

The girl laughed. "You'll be surprised to know all that she can do."

"Really," Dileepa marvelled. "Convincing the officials is itself quite a challenge. Convincing Gajakarna is a feat. I had been warned the man is old-fashioned and adamant, stuck up about doing things the traditional way. Getting him to consent to the change is remarkable."

"I think he saw what Ma had designed and realized they had to do it."

"It's that good? I can't wait to see it."

"You'll see it at the ceremony in a few days."

The *dandapala* nodded. "I wonder what gave them the confidence that the uniforms would be ready in such a short time."

"You doubt Ma's word?" asked Nandana, looking just a little offended.

"Please *no*, that is not what I meant," Dileepa stressed, hastening to placate the girl. "Not at all. I was only saying the garrison has three hundred men, so weaving three hundred uniforms in such a short time sounds impossible to do. That Ma was able to assure them she would do it is… *brilliant*."

"The women have been working the looms nearly non-stop to meet the deadline," Nandana said.

"I heard them when I came to fetch you," Dileepa winced at the thought and smiled. "It was quite a racket!"

The girl laughed again. "I have had cotton plugged in my ears all morning. I couldn't escape anywhere because I had to help out."

"Considering you are all so busy, it is a wonder Ma allowed you out with me. Perhaps she took pity on you."

"I think *you* are the one she took pity on," Nandana chuckled. "She saw you had come all the way to take me out and she didn't want to disappoint you."

Dileepa laughed. Then, as a thought struck him, he sobered down. "You said you couldn't go anywhere in the morning…" his expression became grave. "Be careful. Don't go out alone. If there is one thing common between all these disappearances, it is the fact that all those who went were alone, all by themselves, when it happened. In not even one instance has someone disappeared when in the company of others. So, stick with other people. No going out alone, okay? Promise me."

"I promise." Then, looking up with a frown, the girl asked, "You are going to be alone once you drop me home. What about *you* until you get home… or doesn't the rule apply to you?"

"Nothing will happen to me."

"Why? Are *dandapalas* immune to what's happening?"

"Nothing will happen—"

"How can you tell?" Suddenly, Nandana was anxious and insistent. "And how would *I* know all is well with you? You will drop me and go, but I won't have any way of knowing whether you have reached safely. You will go away on some assignment the king gives you, and I will keep worrying if you are fine—"

"Shhh…" Dileepa hushed the girl, squeezing her hand and gently drawing her close. "Quiet."

"Easy for you to say that," Nandana pouted in reply.

"Shhh…" the *dandapala* said again. Then, with a mysterious smile, he reached into the bag hanging from his shoulder. "I have got something for you, actually," he said. "I had meant to give it to you later, but now is also a good time." He extracted something wrapped in red silk. "Here."

"What is it?" the girl asked, taking the bundle.

"Open it," he prompted.

Nandana peeled back the silken folds and gasped when she saw what was concealed inside. A pair of mated listening bells, three bells per set, crafted out of copper and wood.

"This is lovely," the girl said, carefully lifting one set up.

"That one is for you," Dileepa smiled, "and this one is for me. Use these whenever you want to reach me. No more worrying about where I am, whether I am well, when I will drop by…" He peered into Nandana's face. "Happy?"

"Yes," the girl's eyes were shining. "How do they work?"

"To send me a message, just hold the bells up to the wind and speak your thoughts."

"That's it?" Nandana stared. "And how would I know when you have sent me a message?"

"The magic makes the bells glow, as if they've been lit by moonlight. Then, you do the same thing. Hold them up to the wind and listen."

The girl stroked the bells in amazement.

"Keep your messages short," the *dandapala* said. "These aren't powered with high magic, so they can't send long messages over a great distance. But we can easily send short messages to each other within Ayodhya." He looked rueful. "I had wanted to get better ones, but listening bells aren't cheap."

"You needn't have got these," Nandana said.

"But I wanted to." Dileepa returned one set of bells to his bag. "Remember, the other day you were wishing there was a way of staying in touch… I decided to get these that same day. For your peace of mind."

The girl shook her head. "I've heard the magic in these things is expensive. Where did you get the money from?"

"I had some saved."

Nandana looked into Dileepa's face. "That was money you'd been saving to take your mother to Pragjyotishpura," she whispered, disbelief swimming in her eyes.

"I *will* take her, don't worry," the *dandapala* assured her. "I shall start saving straightaway."

The girl studied the bells in her hand.

*For your peace of mind.*

He had bought her listening bells so *she* wouldn't worry about him. From money that he had been setting aside for someone else who was dear to him. Something stirred in her.

"Night is approaching," Dileepa noted. "We should turn back."

"Right," said Nandana, wrapping her bells back into the folds of silk. "You have to get home too."

"Today, you will know when I reach home. Look out for my message. Remember… the bells will glow."

Gripping the bells tighter, the girl leaned lightly into the *dandapala*. "I shall wait," she sighed in a voice that sounded as if she was speaking to herself.

The stupa of the *homagriha* dominated the Sanctum complex, its arched marble dome drawing the eye and setting it apart from the older wood and red sandstone buildings scattered around it. The sanctorum had also been relocated onto higher ground so it was unmissable, even from across the Sarayu, the flagpole at its apex glinting in the sunlight. The scaffolding still remained though, with masons and artisans perched on it, applying finishing touches to their labour of love. Down below, rubble and construction materials were being carted away, and the entire complex was being spruced up in preparation for the consecration of the *homagriha*. The deep chanting of mantras issued from the shrine where the sacred fire had been burning while the *homagriha* was being rebuilt, and rishis were performing ablutions and cleansing rituals in anticipation of the consecration.

Away from the comings and goings, far to the back, in the shadow of the sanctorum, two figures walked with their heads down and shoulders hunched, deep in consultation. One was Sudhanva, the other was *mahanayaka* Gajakarna. The latter seemed to be nursing a particularly foul mood, a storm brewing on his brow, its fury barely on leash.

"So, we are going to build a market," Sankasya's *adhipati* snorted. "We should be readying to march out and humble Lavanyasurya, but instead, we are making plans to build a market. That is how low Kosala's pride has plummeted."

Gajakarna said nothing.

"I would hate to trade places with you, to be honest," Sudhanva said, not letting up. "What will you tell your men, who are preparing to go to war with so much enthusiasm, who can't wait to avenge the treatment meted out to their brothers in Madhupura? How will you defend your king's unwillingness to seek redressal for the insults Kosala's army has had to bear?" The lord of Sankasya shook his head. "You have my sympathies, my friend."

The *mahanayaka* gave his head a disgusted shake but stayed silent, holding his anger in.

"This shouldn't come as a surprise though," Sudhanva said, continuing to stoke the fire. "One thing was amply clear to me even on the day Shatrughna returned from Madhupura with our soldiers. Our king has no stomach for a fight." He turned to the commander. "I remember how you kept insisting that we should take the garrison back, literally *pleading* for action against Madhupura. Everyone in court wanted to see our men avenged, but Bharat..." the *adhipati* made a face, "...he showed no inclination towards taking a decisive step. It wasn't until I declared my support for military action and got Sheelabhadra and Sheshagupta to back the army that Bharat made some noise about waging war against Madhupura."

"I remember that," Gajakarna grunted. "It was a relief to see someone showing guts."

"I wasn't left with a choice," Sudhanva said passionately. "If the throne wouldn't stand up for our men, somebody had to." He paused as some workers bearing gravel passed them. It wasn't until they were safely out of earshot that the *adhipati* spoke again. "I knew I had pushed Bharat into committing himself, but I was happy for Kosala's sake. Little did I guess that all he needed was an excuse to backtrack and call off the war."

"He assured us that the *kshatri* would back the war," Gajakarna glowered. "But the opposite of that has happened."

"That *kshatri*..." the *adhipati* stole a glance around to ensure they were alone. "He is a terrible influence... He is emasculating the king, turning him into a wimp."

"What can you do?" the commander grumbled. "You can't ask for his removal. He's the king's father-in-law."

"Exactly," Sudhanva leaped on this before the topic could shift away. "*Exactly*, my friend. Do you see what is happening here? He's got Bharat under his influence. It is a plan to take control of Kosala. Think about it. The *kshatri* of Kosala has always been someone from Kosala. Never in this kingdom's glorious history have we had an outsider as *kshatri*. Now we do. For the first time, so much power is within the reach of an outsider. What a slap on our faces! As if we don't have people of competence here. But this has nothing to do with competence. This is a plan to take Kosala. If today, an outsider has been appointed as a *kshatri*, the day isn't far when an outsider will be named *mahanayaka* of Kosala's army." The *adhipati* paused for effect. "You should be very careful, my friend."

Gajakarna was silent for a long while, lost in thought. This time, Sudhanva didn't hustle him.

"Whose plan is this?" the *mahanayaka* asked suspiciously.

"Videha, Rajviraj… I don't know," Sudhanva shrugged. "All I know is Kosala is ripe enough to be picked by anyone who cares. Look at it. Dashratha is dead. Rama is in exile. And we have this man who doesn't have the mettle to take on a small kingdom like Madhupura. Just imagine if Dashratha or Rama had been king now. Madhupura would have been finished. See what I mean?"

They had reached the far end of the Sanctum, where a dozen ashoka trees towered over a pond that had dried up in the heat, the earth caked and cracked, yellow moss growing where the water had left its mark on the mud. From where they stood, the men could see a portion of the Sanctum garrison's roof abutting the Sanctum's wall.

Sudhanva heaved a disconsolate sigh. "If mahamuni Vashishtha were to recover, we could easily arrest Kosala's free fall. But short of a miracle, I don't see his condition improving, so it would be foolish to pin our hopes on the mahamuni coming to Kosala's rescue."

An extended silence, loud with the buzzing of insects in the undergrowth.

"What do you want from me?" the *mahanayaka* asked slowly.

The *adhipati* breathed in deep. "Everything is going downhill in Kosala," he said. "The drought is bad. The economy is in a sad state… I have seen the treasury numbers. People are disappearing like it is an epidemic, and there's no solution to any of this in sight. The reason behind this…" he pointed at the *homagriha*, "…the rakshasa attack, has been forgotten. Likewise, Madhupura's insult will soon be forgotten. As someone who has seen and lived the glory of Kosala, can you stand by and watch everything disappear? No, never. *You* cannot and *I* cannot. So, we must act. We must remove Bharat from the throne."

"You are calling for a rebellion," Gajakarna pinched the ends of his moustache. His words were both a question and a statement.

"To save Kosala, yes."

The *mahanayaka* was quiet for a long time. Sudhanva waited, knowing the old warrior was not one to be rushed into anything. Impatience and eagerness could swing the whole thing the other way, he realized.

"If Bharat is overthrown, who will replace him?" the commander asked.

"I don't know," Sudhanva admitted. "Shatrughna is an option, but ever since I learned that the market idea was his, I'm no longer sure he'd be a good replacement."

"He's a kid," Gajakarna remarked. "He might have been going with the flow, that's all."

"It's possible. Anyway, what is important is that if I have your support, I can start planning."

"Who else have you spoken to about this?"

The *mahanayaka* was shrewd. "No one here in Ayodhya, not yet," Sudhanva replied. "But I have the support of the *adhipati* of Sravasti."

"Mihiradutta? Pushyanta's uncle?"

"Yes. He wields substantial clout. He can win the support of other *adhipatis*. As can Jayabhama, Pushyanta's older brother. It's a powerful family."

"And they are backing you?"

"Absolutely."

"Okay. As long as it's not just the army rebelling against the throne, I'm fine with it. There has to be civilian support. Otherwise, I am not doing it."

"There is, there is," Sudhanva insisted, barely able to contain his excitement.

*There has to be civilian support. Otherwise, I am not doing it.* What Gajakarna meant was he needed the complicity of Kosala's *adhipatis* and ministers so that the army wasn't singled out for censure later, Sudhanva understood. What it also meant was that the *mahanayaka* had just committed himself to rebelling against Bharat.

"I need to know the detailed plan," said Gajakarna. "And I must have the support of *adhipatis* in Ayodhya."

"If I have your support, Mihiradutta and I can open conversations with the other *adhipatis*."

The commander nodded. "But be careful you don't disclose me by name. Just tell people they can count on Kosala's army when it is time."

"I will," Sudhanva replied. With a grim look of determination, he added, "Let us do this for Kosala, and for our old king and friend, Raja Dashratha."

The trail by the side of the Vitasta was narrow and hemmed in by tall grass, so the riders had to go in single file. There were seven of them, Yuddhajeet in front, followed by Ambareesha, then a young rishi. The four riders at the back were Bahlika warriors, looking nearly identical in their shawls, lengthy beards and the long *kuntas* they bore.

The mercenaries had started arriving in Kekeya in bands of fifty to hundred men, each faction owing allegiance to an independent chieftain, but bound by bonds of brotherhood that made them respond to Sailusha's call to rally behind the River Kingdoms. Ambareesha came early to take charge of all the Bahlika units, binding them under his command until Sailusha could join the mighty force in defence of Kekeya and its allies.

The horses walked at a leisurely pace and the riders were relaxed in their saddles, but their eyes stayed sharp as they continually scanned the landscape on the other side of the glistening river, looking for signs of Gandharan troop movement. The air shimmered in the rising heat, creating deceptive illusions of movement along the far horizon. The small party had left Rajagriha early, bound for the river market of Mithuna, which lay another hour's ride north. The town was one of the strategic locations along the Vitasta where the Gandharan army could attempt a crossing, so efforts were being directed at fortifying it. Mithuna would also double as a command centre for the adjoining region.

"If you were to lay a wager, where do you think they'll cross?" asked Ambareesha.

Yuddhajeet glanced over his shoulder, then looked in front again. "My money would be on the south of Mithuna."

"We might be making a mistake by not paying enough attention upstream of Manglapuri," said the Bahlika.

"In the hills?" Yuddhajeet sounded unsure.

"It is a densely wooded area, so they will have better concealment. And the river there is a lot narrower, so a quick crossing is possible."

"Narrow, yes, but the water is also swift and treacherous. Plus, the same wooded banks would make landing more complicated. And you forget that they'd have to carry the boats they'll need for the crossing through those hills and forests. All in all, way too risky and cumbersome."

"That is true," Ambareesha admitted. After a moment's pause, he said, "I would try crossing at two or three different points."

"If they did that, the Gandharans would be spreading themselves thin," Yuddhajeet argued.

"But they'd have succeeded in spreading our defence thin as well," the Bahlika pointed out. "Now imagine they started crossing at one spot, but not at the others. How are we supposed to react to that? If we pulled our troops from everywhere to support the men fighting the breach, we would be leaving the other crossings vulnerable. But if we didn't pull back, their opening thrust could be enough to break us." The giant paused to let the enormity of what he had said sink in. The track had opened up, and he drew alongside Yuddhajeet. "A move like that could leave us guessing and totally paralyzed."

Yuddhajeet looked troubled as he gazed westward. "It's impossible to predict their strategy without knowing something about their troop movements and deployments. The sooner we know, the more time we'd get to counter their plans."

"How many scouts do you have deployed between here and the Sindhu?" Ambareesha asked.

"About twenty." The prince glanced at the baby monkey riding on the Bahlika's shoulder. "I hope you're not planning on bringing that animal into battle with you," he said, only half in jest.

"Not at all. I will leave her behind in someone's care," Ambareesha replied in all seriousness. Then, switching back to the topic of the scouts, he asked, "Are twenty enough to cover such a lot of ground?"

Yuddhajeet smiled drily. "No number of scouts or spies is ever enough. We are also keeping our ears on gossip among traders coming from the west. But we must be careful in deciding what to believe as some of that gossip might easily be planted to misdirect us."

"We could double the number of scouts," the Bahlika said. "I can spare my men."

"It's not the number of men that's the issue. It's the number of listening bells we can afford."

Ambareesha's eyes went to the cluster of bells that hung from the belt at Yuddhajeet's waist. The bells were small, made from silver and copper. He had heard about these things but had never seen them at such close quarters. "I don't understand," he said.

"Having more scouts is of no use if they can't send us their reports fast enough. It is the bells that allow the scouts to communicate with us swiftly, but the magic that makes all these bells work needs to be cast into the atmosphere and maintained… which is an extremely difficult thing to do." He gestured towards the rishi. "In Kekeya, we have no more than six rishis who can weave magic, and he is one of them."

Ambareesha looked back at the rishi, who appeared lost in his own thoughts.

"The bells are usually mated in pairs, so messages can be relayed between two sets of bells," Yuddhajeet explained. "What complicates matters for us is that all the scouts' bells are mated with this one," he patted the bells at his waist and they jangled twice, "so that this can receive messages from every scout. This level of magic is so much harder to achieve and sustain."

"Phew," said the Bahlika. He still didn't entirely comprehend what the prince had said, but he realized that the concept was complicated. "What happens if the magic fails?"

"The messages get lost and don't get delivered."

"That's not good."

"No."

They lapsed into silence.

"This same magic helps you fight better, doesn't it?" the Bahlika asked after a while. "I heard it makes weapons stronger…"

"The magic doesn't do anything by itself. You have to channel it," said Yuddhajeet.

"Oh," Ambareesha's face fell.

"It's only a question of knowing how. Then there's no stopping you," Yuddhajeet added.

"Oh," the giant brightened.

"The stronger the magic, the better you can fight and the better you can use your strength and your weapons. And the better the warrior you are, the better you can channel the magic."

"Wait, wait, wait," Ambareesha blinked. Everything was so complex. "Say that again?"

"It's really simple. The better the magic and the better the warrior, the greater are the chances of victory," the prince said. "And wherever rishis are more powerful, magic will be stronger."

"So, powerful rishis create strong magic, which good warriors channel for victory?"

"Correct. And all this is achieved with the help of the sacred fire." The prince's eyes became wistful. "You should see the magic in Ayodhya. What it allows you to do, how it manifests. It has to be seen to be believed."

Ambareesha nodded. "And you can do this? Channel the magic?"

"Yes, to some extent."

"Can we also…?" Ambareesha asked haltingly. He meant the Bahlika fighters. "Is it easy?"

"Channelling magic? You will have to learn." Yuddhajeet tilted his head to indicate the rishi. "His job is to make the atmosphere over Mithuna richer and more conducive to magic… and to teach all of you how to tap into it."

"He will teach us how?" Ambareesha's eyes widened in anticipation. The monkey, which had climbed down to his lap, looked up at her master in curiosity.

"Learning all the stuff takes years," Yuddhajeet hurried to temper the giant's excitement and expectations. "He will impart basic skills, which will give you an edge in a crunch."

The Bahlika turned to glance at the rishi with new respect. He had understood that one of the reasons for this trip was to escort the rishi, but he hadn't fully grasped the importance of the rishi's need in Mithuna until now.

Turning back to Yuddhajeet, he asked, "How will he know who is a better warrior to train?"

"He won't," the prince answered. "He will only teach you what he can in the little time there is. Like always, it is the battle that will throw up the better warriors."

"That is quite an achievement."

Observing the horse cart draw away from the mansion bearing the uniforms for the Sanctum garrison, Simhika heaved a sigh and looked at the women standing around her. They were all in her employ, and all of them seemed short of sleep but pleased with themselves.

"Quite an achievement," Simhika repeated with satisfaction, stressing each word for impact.

The women beamed at her in response.

"Three hundred and fifty dhotis, three hundred and fifty silken sashes, and three hundred and fifty lengths of cloth for their turbans. All on such a tight deadline, dispatched well in time for the *homagriha* ceremony. Well done, all of you. Without your hard work, I would never have managed honouring my word given to the *mahanayaka*. *You* kept Ma Parnalata's promise." Extracting the drawstring pouch where she kept small change, she fished inside it. "Money isn't the best way to show one's gratitude, but accept this as my thanks." Simhika pressed a couple of small silver *rupa*s into each hand. "Your work will be the central attraction at the ceremony," she promised.

The women positively glowed with pride… and the unexpected bonus to their earnings.

Once the women had gone home, all having earned a well-deserved rest, Simhika walked into the inner courtyard and sat down heavily on the couch in its centre. Drawing a *tambulam* chest to her, she opened it, extracted a betel leaf and applied some lime to it. A sprinkling of diced areca nuts followed, after which she tucked the preparation into the inside of her cheek. Savouring the explosion of flavours, she rocked gently back and forth, enjoying the quiet that had returned to the mansion after so many days of non-stop activity.

"The silence almost feels strange," remarked Nandana, coming down the stairs.

"It does," the sorceress agreed, patting the couch, inviting the girl to sit with her. "We did it," she smiled.

"Yes," Nandana smiled back.

"All thanks to your *dandapala*."

"Yes."

"Useful fellow," Simhika looked at the girl. "He's gaining the king's confidence, you said."

For a fraction of a second, Nandana hesitated. Then, she gave a nod.

"Very good," Simhika said, already thinking up ways she could use this to their advantage.

"I doubt he'll be able to influence the king, though," the girl said slowly. "The *mahanayaka* is one thing… the king is quite another."

"You have such little faith in the man, sweet child," Simhika laughed. "Once you earn someone's trust, you can bend them to your will." She stretched to pat the girl's arm. "See for yourself. Look how you earned the *dandapala's* love and trust and got him to introduce us to Gajakarna."

Nandana nodded.

"It's the same with everyone. If the king starts trusting him, he will listen to the *dandapala*, and that can only be good for us."

Nandana nodded again.

"Where is he, by the way?" Simhika looked towards the door as if expecting to find Dileepa there. "Not come to take you out today?"

The girl shook her head. "He's had to go out of town."

The sorceress looked up. "Really? How did *you* know? Did he send a message?"

Nandana caught her breath. "No… I mean, he told me *yesterday* he wouldn't come today."

"Oh, but you didn't tell me yesterday when I asked," Simhika looked mildly peeved.

"I must have forgotten in the middle of all this confusion of getting the uniforms ready."

"Hmm," Simhika nodded.

Nandana studied the sorceress out of the corner of her eye, hoping her answers had sounded credible. She had to be more careful in what she said, she realized.

She thought back to Dileepa's message, received on the listening bells just over an hour ago, telling her he couldn't come that evening as he had to chase an important lead. The bells were such a marvel, the magic in them allowing people to converse over great distances. Sure, they had similar magic in Lanka too; powerful magic that she had often used to send messages to their lord. But rakshasa magic was more tedious, not simple like what the humans had here in Ayodhya.

"What are you thinking about?" Simhika asked.

"Nothing." She was thinking of the lustrous light of the bells when a message came through.

"You look tired," said the sorceress.

"Maybe it's the stress of the last few days. And the noise of the looms. The silence is sleep inducing." The girl smiled.

"Get some sleep then," Simhika gave her an affectionate smile.

Returning to her room, Nandana pulled the door firmly shut. Going to her bed, she rummaged under her pillow for the silk bundle Dileepa had given her the previous evening. She opened it and looked at the bells inside. Copper and wood. No moonlit luminosity. No message from Dileepa.

She wrapped the bells back, then without even realizing it, she stroked them through the silk, letting her fingers slip over their curves and contours.

She had given plenty of thought to telling Simhika about the *dandapala's* gift. The bells had consumed her thoughts all her way home the previous evening, and she understood it was her responsibility to tell Simhika the truth, her duty to their lord in Lanka. Still she had hesitated. And on getting home, when Simhika had asked about her outing, Nandana hadn't said a word about the bells. She had felt informing Simhika would be a violation, a betrayal of something that had awoken inside her. Something new and alien and nice, a lightness she couldn't quite describe or understand…

And that was it. The bells were now a secret she had to guard for all time.

Oddly, Nandana didn't feel any guilt in keeping the truth from Simhika. The bells were hers. They had been given to her by Dileepa. Simhika had no reason to know about their existence.

*...the other day you were wishing there was a way of staying in touch... I decided to get these that same day. For your peace of mind.*

Removing the bells from the bundle, she went to the window and leaned out with a smile. To the west, the sun was going down across the Sarayu. Four kites on strings braced and whirled in the sky, tethered to the wind.

She held the bells up so the gold of the setting sun shone on dull copper. It looked as though the bells were sunlit now. Sunlit for messages sent, moonlit for messages received.

She faced the wind, seeing Dileepa's face in her mind's eye.

For *our* peace of mind, she whispered into the bells. Mine and yours.

# *fifteen*

IT WAS AS A NINE-YEAR-OLD BOY THAT NAGNAJIT HAD first set foot inside the great hall of Kapisi. His father, a cousin of the newly crowned king Ukshma, had had to prove his loyalty to his brother by journeying to Kapisi and washing Ukshma's feet with his blood in accordance with Gandharan tradition. For reasons best known only to his long-dead father, Nagnajit had been hauled along on that trip to the capital, an adventure that had filled the little boy with wonder. Brought up in a crude homestead nestled in the harsh mountains to the north, Nagnajit drank in the landscaped beauty of Kapisi, marvelling at the sights and sounds of the throbbing, decadent city. The palace was the biggest feat of human architecture he had ever laid eyes on, and the echoing great hall had overwhelmed him.

Standing next to his father and gaping at the raya's seat, and later, observing a line of lords who had sworn their allegiance to Ukshma bathe the raya's feet in a basin of water mixed with their blood, the boy had come to vaguely understand the significance of what it meant to wield power over other men.

That trip to Kapisi ended in a couple of days, and life quickly went back to surviving in the wilderness. It was a full thirteen years before Nagnajit was once again reminded of the great hall at Kapisi—this time in a way that left a permanent impression. He had been out trapping hare in the hills when he chanced upon a strip of snakeskin lying on his path. Gandharan oracles could divine the finder's future in snakeskins, so Nagnajit took the skin to an oracle to see what his future held. Studying the weaves and patterns on the flaky skin, the old man had raised the lamp high so he could see Nagnajit's features better. Then he had spoken the words that had changed the young man's life forever.

"It is ordained that the one who finds this skin will rule from the great hall of Kapisi."

Nagnajit rose from the raya's seat—the same one he had set eyes on as a boy—to the roll of half-a-dozen small, handheld drums. The court nobles bowed and offered him *pranaams* as he walked down the steps, down the great hall and out onto a covered portico, where hundreds of men, painted in oils and dyes, danced with *sambrani*-filled clay braziers. The air was heavy with smoke and incense, the smoke parting like a curtain to let Nagnajit through to the mountain goat tethered to a stake in the middle of the portico.

Not for the first time, blood spilled across the portico's tiles, and stepping away from the animal he had just slaughtered, Nagnajit was reminded of the day two years ago when, standing at this very spot, he had killed the last of Ukshma's seven sons, leaving him the sole contender to Gandhara's throne. That day, twenty-five years after an old oracle had foretold that he would rule from the great hall, he had finally barged into the great hall and staked his claim over Gandhara, and the nobles and courtiers had bowed and scraped so he would spare their lives. And the people had rejoiced—because with all except one of the squabbling heirs to the throne dead, peace finally had a chance of returning to their land and to their lives.

The people of Kapisi had feted him, poems had been composed about his valour, artists queued up to paint and sculpt him, and in his honour, mothers took to naming their newborn sons after him. The rough boy from the mountains, who had been an outlier in the scramble for power, had been accepted by the cultured people of Kapisi as one of their own.

Perhaps because he had experienced the struggle from up close and watched so many favourites for the throne fall that Nagnajit understood that power and adulation were never to be taken for granted. Power could be gained or squandered overnight on the back of one decision, while the mood of the people was even more fickle; whether a courtier, commander or cart-maker, people were easily dissatisfied, easily bored and easily swayed. So, to impress his people and bind their loyalty to himself, he had chosen to squeeze tributes out of the River Kingdoms of Madra and Trigartha. No raya before him had ever considered expanding Gandharan influence beyond its borders, and the move straightaway cast him in the image of a visionary leader. The tributes also helped pay off Gandharan troops, and as a consequence, he didn't have to raise taxes, which pleased the nobles no end. Win-win for everyone.

But then, Kekeya had interfered, cutting off the tributes and challenging his supremacy, leaving him with no other option but to retaliate or fall in the eyes of the court and the people of Kapisi.

The moment the goat's throat was cut, a roar went up around Nagnajit that rolled and cascaded down the palace and into the streets of Kapisi, where the air was already alive and festive with the sounds of flute and drum. Listening to the cheer echoing around Kapisi, Nagnajit raised his hands in salutation to the mountain gods of his youth, and those dancing around him came to a standstill. All but two drums fell silent, their beats softening and taking the shape of a rhythmic lullaby.

Turning around to face his courtiers and nobles, the raya spoke: "The blood of our soldiers was shed across the mountains in the same manner as the blood of this goat. This goat was innocent. Our men were innocent. The only way the blood of the innocent can be avenged is by shedding the blood of the sinners who rule the River Kingdoms," he thundered. "We will avenge blood with blood."

*Blood with blood... Blood with blood...*

The chant rose up around Nagnajit as he led the cavalcade through Kapisi's streets. There were people everywhere, hanging out of windows and terraces, thronging the thoroughfares, waving Gandhara's red-and-yellow flaming-torch flags as the pipes played, cheering him and his men along, joining in the cry for revenge, showing their love for him...

In return for the love they had showered on him, he would give the big-hearted people of this city the River Kingdoms as a gift of gratitude, he decided.

*Blood with blood... Blood with blood...*

The chant followed the raya and his army out of the city to where Mahasa sat with his riders, waiting.

*Blood with blood... Blood with blood...*

The chant came after the combined armies of Gandhara and Kamboja like an obstinate echo as they took the road leading east over the mountains.

"What is this soldier's name?"

"Swagata, rajan."

"Hmm… and he was one of Kosala's soldiers posted here?"

"Yes, rajan. He was an *upanayaka* at the Kosala garrison."

Lavanyasurya turned an acidic gaze on the captain who stood before him. "Don't ever refer to it again as the Kosala garrison," the king hissed. "*It is Madhupura's garrison.*"

"Yes, rajan."

"Whose garrison?" Lavanyasurya insisted.

"Madhupura's garrison, rajan," the captain dropped his eyes, cowed and penitent.

Satisfied, the king returned his attention to the gooey *kashayam* that he was drinking out of a jar. He sat alone on a terrace, watching the sun set over the trees. "This soldier claims that the court of Ayodhya has taken a decision to march against us."

"Yes, rajan. He says the intention is to start troop movements as soon as some ceremony in Ayodhya gets over one of these days."

Lavanyasurya stirred the contents of the jar and scooped a mouthful. He made a face, taking his time swallowing the sludgy preparation. Finally, he looked at the captain. "Why would a soldier of Kosala take the trouble of coming all the way here to inform us that *his* kingdom is preparing to attack us? What is in it for him?"

"He says he came to warn us because he fears for Madhupura's safety, rajan."

"Why would he care for Madhupura's safety?"

There was a pause as the captain gathered the courage to tender an opinion. "Maybe because he has a family living here in Madhupura."

"Family?"

"A wife and two children, rajan."

"Really?" The raja's eyebrows rose in interest. "You mean he's married locally?"

"Yes, rajan."

It was starting to make sense. "He fears for his family's safety," said Lavanyasurya. "That is his motivation." An *upanayaka* from Kosala with a loving family in Madhupura. Nice, nice. This was a situation that he might be able to bend to his advantage sometime, he realized. He looked at the captain. "Take very good care of this soldier," he said. "Make sure his family is also well looked after."

"Yes, rajan."

He raised a cautioning finger. "But see that the family never leaves Madhupura. The soldier mustn't take them away with him to Kosala or wherever. If he tries to, they must be stopped. Am I clear?"

"Yes, rajan." The captain hesitated. "What do we do about the attack from Kosala, rajan?"

"Leave that to me," the raja waved a hand to terminate the discussion. The captain bowed and left the terrace.

Lavanyasurya rose and walked to the end of the terrace. He leaned on the parapet and looked from right to left, taking in the Yamuna as it curved in the distance.

Kosala was going to move against him, if the soldier was to be believed. Kosala had reason to feel miffed after he had shut the garrison down and ordered its men out, and the *upanayaka* had sufficient cause to warn Madhupura. But the question remained whether the *upanayaka* was telling the truth at all. Knowing he had a family here, Ayodhya could have sent him over for the purpose of spreading misinformation, though what Kosala could gain by leaking plans of an upcoming attack wasn't clear to him. But Lavanyasurya knew he couldn't blindly trust the *upanayaka* without verifying his claims. He had to know if Kosala was indeed thinking of marching against Madhupura.

The problem was that time wasn't on his side. The *upanayaka* had said Kosala had decided to start moving once some ceremony got over, and the ceremony was due anytime now. If that was how it panned out, Kosala's troops could be outside Madhupura in less than a week. In which case, should he, in a preemptive move, go ahead…

Lavanyasurya killed the idea even before it took full shape in his head. He wasn't adequately prepared to pull off what he had in mind, on the scale that he had envisaged. He needed more time.

The sun had disappeared under the horizon and night came swiftly. The raja walked back into the palace, into the dark of his unlit chamber. He would wait to see if Kosala made a move against Madhupura. If it did, his hand would be forced, and he would do what he could to even the score. If it didn't, wonderful. He would strike at a more opportune moment when the effect on Kosala would be crippling.

Either way, he needed to move faster with his plans, Lavanyasurya decided, wincing as a stab of pain went through his abdomen.

He had to hurry up, build towards critical mass and set the pieces in place before opening the gates to chaos…

Sitting in the gathering darkness, Simhika could tell rain was coming.

Of course, there wasn't a cloud to be seen in the sky; there hadn't been one all day, all week. It didn't matter. The clouds were gathering, she could tell.

She smelled the rain's undercurrent in the stillness of Ayodhya's air, felt its cadence thrum in her sinews and saw its electric joy in the frolicking of the fish and eels that populated the old well.

The prospect of rain surprised the sorceress because she didn't think there was enough magic in the atmosphere over Kosala to attract rain clouds. Magic had been thinning here for the last couple of years despite the rishis at the Sanctum doing their best to replenish the stock, and she didn't know what had changed for the rain to put in a sudden appearance. Maybe it had to do with the consecration of the new *homagriha*, which was due in a couple of days. It didn't seem likely, but no one had fully made sense of the moods and mysteries of the elements, so…

Whatever the reason, rain was coming, and it reminded her that the reinstitution of the sacred fire in the *homagriha* would give magic a boost. More rain would come, bringing relief to the land. Magic would flow unhindered and Ayodhya would gain strength and become harder to break down.

She couldn't let that happen. Her purpose in Ayodhya was to make sure that didn't happen.

Leaning over the lip of the well, the sorceress extended one hand towards its gloomy depths, speaking words that weren't words but sensations and emotions. The evening darkened, and the mansion narrowed and expanded around Simhika, falling into itself and outwards and up until suddenly there was no mansion, no neighbourhood, no Ayodhya around the sorceress.

Only she, the well… and infinite shadow all around.

Shapes—*forms*—emerged from the well, oozing, leaping, wriggling, pulling themselves up by Simhika's hand. Sinuous, ghostly and formless, the shadows writhed against the sorceress, slipping through her loving grasp, sliding over her shoulders, coiling around her body, joyous about the attention being lavished on them. Simhika played with the shapes, allowing them to shower their love back on her, running her hand over their formlessness, caressing them…

They were her pets, these shadows. They were also her weapons.

*Tell me about the adhipati*, she smiled at the forms falling into her embrace. The well literally boiled with shadows, all wanting to get out, all craving for her attention.

The shadows cackled soundlessly at the sorceress's appeal for information.

*hekilledhekilledhekilled*

*I know he killed his son-in-law.*

*wekilledwekilledwekilled*

The laughter was starting to feel delirious.

*Yes, yes.* You *killed the son-in-law*, Simhika gave an indulgent smile. *What else is he up to?*

*angryangryangryangry*

*That's good.*

*makeangrymakeangrymakeangry*

The shadows were all suddenly hostile around Simhika. Sullen anger spreading outwards in waves. Infinite shadow, infinite anger. The sorceress understood. Sudhanva's resentment was growing and touching others.

*Very good*, she smiled in delight.

*angryangryangryangry*

Her praise drove the shadows back into frenzied ecstasy. They laughed, whooped, cavorted in paroxysms of rapture.

*angryangryangryangry*

For all their playful prancing, Simhika detected a fretfulness in the forms, an impatience that mirrored her own. Growing, gnawing at the restraints…

Patience, she whispered, though it wasn't clear whom she was speaking to: the shadows or to herself. The consecration of the *homagriha* was nearly upon them. She had placed her bet on the rishis' wives being impressed with the uniforms. If they were impressed, she would have taken a major step towards unleashing her shadows into the lives of the unsuspecting rishis.

*nownownownow makeangrymakeangrymakeangry*

The forms spun around the sorceress, a hideous swirl, hysterical, overwrought and screaming in pleasure and pain, tormented and pleading to be set free so they could spread their rot and ruin.

Bharat half expected to come upon Siripala limping around the stable yard, ensuring the horses were fed and had enough water to last them the night.

He wasn't wrong in thinking it was possible, the king said to himself. They were coming back. In ones and twos.

First, the moneylender's son and the basket-maker's daughter had returned. Then, the boatman's wife and the *nagarapala*. Yesterday, a fortune teller had reappeared at his shop, seven days after leaving home and vanishing. And two hours ago, a young cowherd had been found sleeping under the tree where he had last been seen by some other cowherds thirteen days earlier. Six returns in all.

*Six people, who had all come back after the* agnimanasa, Bharat reminded himself.

Six was a small number in comparison to the three dozen or more people who had disappeared. In fact, over the past four days, six fresh disappearances had been reported from around Kosala. Still, people *were* returning, it was important to bear in mind, returning *safely* from wherever they had gone. So, Bharat's eyes searched the darkness in hope as he and Taksha followed the path to the stable.

Angara shot out of the dark to greet his friends, black movement against black stillness, leaping and dancing while Taksha squealed with excitement. The boy's visits had become daily affairs, and Bharat could tell the dog looked forward to the routine as much as Taksha did. They chased each other for some time in the grass before tiring and walking around the yard, inspecting the horses. No one had been appointed to replace Siripala as head of the royal stable, and the stable boys had been given the additional charge of tending to the royal horses and feeding Angara. They were generally done by this time though, and the place was most often vacant, so even Bharat had begun craving these outings. The quiet of the night and the dog's unconditional love were like a balm after the frictions and anxieties of the day.

"Give that to me," said Bharat, demanding the ivory stylus that Kaikeyi had gifted the boy. He didn't want the dog to injure itself accidentally on the writing point of the instrument.

Taksha handed the stylus to his father. Bharat had been quite adamant about not letting the boy have the stylus, but he hadn't bargained for Taksha's own adamancy. The kid had whined and pestered relentlessly, until out of sheer exasperation, Bharat had turned the instrument over to get him to shut up. The surrender had worked like a charm, and the boy and his stylus were almost inseparable. Taksha seemed to understand that his father's submission in this matter was final, which was why he never thought twice about giving the stylus to Bharat for safekeeping.

As Angara and the boy pushed and rolled against one another, Bharat turned the stylus over in his hands, his mind going back to Rajagriha, where Ashwapati had probably used the stylus for the first time to enter agricultural records. He thought about the days he had run through wheat and sugarcane fields in pursuit of flying kites that had been cut and had spiralled to earth. Then, his mind went to the horses in the enclosure behind the palace, grand beasts that came in wild before they were tamed by men like his mama Yuddhajeet, who had taught him how to nurture a bond of trust and love with his mount. As the memories unfolded, a recurring stab of nostalgia went through the king, and he wished he was back in Kekeya. He hadn't met his nana ever since he had been escorted to Ayodhya two years ago to be made king, and he regretted not being able to go to Rajagriha despite having received the news that his grandfather had suffered a seizure. There was just so much work to be done as king that he didn't know when he would find the time for a visit.

All because of her, the thought crossed his mind. Because *she* had wanted him to become king. Not caring about what he wanted, what *he* had hankered after. A word of praise, a touch of love.

*The idea behind praising Rama was to set him as an example so you'd push yourself harder.* That had been her explanation. *I didn't praise you because I didn't want you becoming complacent and settling for second best.*

Suddenly, the memory of him aiming at that fifth red-painted bird returned. The tension in his shoulders as he pulled the bowstring back. The feel of the ridged arrow under his thumb, and the strain of the bow on his forearm. And his father watching him, watching the target.

Red-painted bird. Made of clay so it would shatter on impact.

He had shot four of those birds in succession. One more to equal Rama's score.

He had shot, and he had missed.

Missed that final shot and shattered like clay on seeing the delight on Dashratha's face.

Once again, second best to Rama.

Bharat ran his thumb against the nib of the stylus. Sharp and pointed. Kaikeyi's gift to his son. And what had been her gift to him? A kingdom that he didn't want, and a kingdom that didn't want him. Sharp and pointed.

A low growl escaped Angara's throat, drawing Bharat out of his rumination. He realized a wind had begun to blow, and lightning flickered in the sky. His heart leaped at the hope of rain. The *agnimanasa* had worked...

He looked at the dog. It stood braced on all fours, chest and ears up, staring into the trees behind the stable. Even Taksha seemed intrigued, standing beside the dog...

"What is it, Angara?" Bharat asked. He walked towards the kid and the dog.

The wind blew harder, rustling through the undergrowth and setting the trees swaying. With another growl, Angara launched into a fit of frenzied barking. It clearly sensed an underlying threat.

It was probably sixth sense. Or a primitive reflex. The king flung out a hand while uttering a mantra.

A shimmering mesh of energy formed in the air between the trees and where he stood with Taksha and Angara. And not a moment too soon, for a stubby arrow zipped into the glow of the curtain from the direction of the trees.

It had been aimed at the dog. It collided with the mesh and atomized.

"Taksha, Angara... here," Bharat shouted. "Come to me."

Triggered by the edginess in Bharat's voice, Angara started yapping harder. Then, observing something in the trees, the dog charged, crossing the energy curtain into the open.

"No, Angara!" Bharat called, frantic. "Get back here!"

"Angara," Taksha called.

Without warning, the kid ran after the dog.

"Wait," Bharat's voice quavered as the boy slipped outside the curtain's protection. "Taksha, *wait*."

The dog was halfway to the trees, discernable more by its bark than by sight. Taksha was also fading as he bounded after Angara, barely an outline in the pale light cast by the mesh. If he had heard his father's orders, he wasn't paying the least bit of heed.

The wind was now sweeping across the ground, tugging at the mesh and bending the trees. Bharat made out a vague shape in the trees. At this distance, it could have been anything.

"Angara," Taksha called. "Angara."

The dog was barking its head off.

The shape moved, stepping out of the trees.

Bharat—his throat dry, his legs shaking, his heart hammering in his chest—mouthed a mantra and drew his hand back. With all the strength he could gather, he hurled the stylus at what he imagined was the head of the shape in the trees. The stylus left his hand and sped through the energy curtain, catching fire as it passed the curtain's filaments. It blazed like a firecracker, sizzling over Taksha's head, over Angara…

…and in its white light, Bharat saw the figure clearly.

A man wielding a *vajramushti*, his face concealed under swathes of dark cloth.

*An assassin.*

Baring its teeth, Angara approached the man, but the stylus beat the dog, striking the attacker on the head. Bharat's magic triggered an explosion, and the man's head imploded and caught fire. Dropping his hand, the assassin blundered back into the trees with a high-pitched wail of terror.

Bharat had yet to release his breath when lightning dazzled overhead, illuminating the stable and the trees. The king went rigid with fright at the sight of *a second assassin* emerging from hiding, lining up his *vajramushti*…

Angara readied to spring on the second assassin, who was distracted by his partner's screams.

"Taksha…" Bharat cried, seeing the boy run behind the dog. "*No*…"

The first assailant swerved left, then right, flailing his arms and screaming, his head engulfed in white flames. Sensing the threat from Angara, the second assassin swung his arm around to shoot, but Angara was already into the leap, chomping its teeth into the assassin's hand. The man yelled in agony while the dog swung in the air, dragging the hand down with its weight, tearing lacerations in his flesh…

"Taksha," the king screamed as he sped past the curtain, yanking the shimmering energy after him like an *angavastram* made of light. "Angara…"

The man grappling with Angara heaved with the full weight of his body and flung the dog to the side, wrenching himself free and screaming as the animal's teeth shredded his hand. The other attacker had fallen among the trees, where he lay shrieking and burning to death.

More lightning flashed. Less than two yards separated Taksha and the second assassin, whose arm was mangled to the bone, eyes crazed with pain and fear. Seeing the kid come towards him, the man raised his bloodied arm again, bringing the *vajramushti* up and around…

"*Taksha*…" Bharat screamed.

For no reason, the man screamed back.

The air around the stable was just one scream after another.

Taksha stopped and stared as the man lined up his weapon. Bharat, six or seven metres away, tossed the curtain at the kid with all his might, powerless to do much else, desperately hoping it would fall over his son and cover him…

The mesh sailed through the air in a slow, lazy spin.

Lighting flashed again. Close. The wind had died completely.

The man took aim, preparing to shoot.

Sensing danger, Taksha turned to flee as the mesh sank towards him.

Thunder crashed nearby, shaking the ground.

Angara lunged at the assassin with a feral roar, the force of the leap knocking the man's hand aside and sending him sprawling. But the thick arrow had already left its groove.

It came flying at Taksha.

Bharat watched the bolt, a blur in the light of the falling curtain as it settled over the boy.

The boy ran two steps… before being hurled forward. He came down hard, flat on his face.

"Taksha," Bharat screamed again. He couldn't believe the kid had been struck by the bolt.

The skies opened up, and the first hot, fat drops of the monsoon came down on Ayodhya.

Rushing over, the king whipped a bubble of energy around himself and the kid as he dropped beside the boy and drew back the mesh with trembling hands. From somewhere behind them came Angara's snarls and snaps as the assailant crashed through the undergrowth. Raindrops bounced off the bubble, and as the rain intensified, all sounds were washed away. Bharat bent over Taksha. Weighed down with dread, barely able to breathe, he examined the boy's back for a wound from the bolt. Nothing. Very carefully, he turned the kid around on his back. He couldn't find any injuries.

"Taksha," he called softly, patting the boy's cheeks. "Taksha, my son…"

Nothing. Not even the flutter of an eyelid. The boy was hardly breathing.

*There is a heavy price attached to the creation of magic…*

Fear swooped down on Bharat at the memory of rishi Surochi's words.

*When you offer yourself up for magic, there is a trade-off… You are bound to lose something precious.*

The boy wasn't responding. His son wasn't responding. His son… Bharat fought to hold on to that so he wouldn't be swamped by the rising tides of panic.

Bharat scooped Taksha up in his arms. Lurching to his feet and cradling his son, the love of his life, to his chest, he sprinted towards the palace. The rain came down hard around Bharat as he ran, and he felt his feet go leaden, the tears running down his cheeks, hot and full of the anguish of the universe.

*The loss is inevitable. It is a sacrifice that the magic demands and exacts.*

Bharat screamed at the rain as he ran. Again and again. Angry. Defiant. Broken.

The boy flopped in his arms, head lolling to one side, one arm trailing down. Limp.

End of Book One